Not Quite by the Book

Not Quite by the Book

A Novel

JULIE HATCHER

LAKE UNION
PUBLISHING

Text copyright © 2025 by Julie Anne Hatcher
All rights reserved.

Published by Lake Union Publishing, Seattle

www.apub.com

Amazon, the Amazon logo, and Lake Union Publishing are trademarks of Amazon.com, Inc., or its affiliates.

ISBN-13: 9781662523465 (paperback)
ISBN-13: 9781662523458 (digital)

Cover design and illustration by Elizabeth Turner Stokes

Printed in the United States of America

This book is dedicated to Taylor Swift, Cecily Mullins, and Karma, who, in equal measure, returned me to the light.

Chapter One

My relationship with Emily Dickinson began at my family's bookstore when I was ten. My mother, busy with customers, had interrupted my anguished tale of the school's meagerly stocked library by shoving a tome of the poet's works into my hands, and I fell instantly, irrevocably in love. When my mom was diagnosed with cancer a short time later, I spent long hours with her at the hospital, reading those same poems. When she beat the odds, I'd wondered if Emily's words saved her.

Mom, on the other hand, concluded that her time spent planning an extravagant vow-renewal ceremony led to her full recovery. She declared hope a miraculous thing and me her bridesmaid. The event became an annual joy-filled affair, and I'd become the world's youngest wedding coordinator.

Twenty years later, my feet, head, and heart ached after the most recent vow-renewal celebration. Happy as I was for my parents, decades of long-suppressed misery had risen unbidden to the surface mid-Macarena. A tipsy gray-haired guest ambushed me on the dance floor, bottom lip protruding, and jeered, "Poor Emma Rini, always a bridesmaid, never a bride."

I'd heard those words before, but something about being in a vast sea of smiling couples, and the deep inner knowledge that she was right, sent pain reverberating through me. I'd never wear the big white dress, share the first dance, or leave a church hand in hand with my soulmate. In the moment, I'd briefly, shamefully, imagined tripping her. But instead, I left the dance floor in search of water and tried not to dwell on the fact that, year after year, I remained solo. I'd tried everything to skew the odds of finding love in my favor, including intermittent fasting, Pilates, and prayer. Sadly, nothing had worked.

I'd returned home around midnight, sans heels, SPANX, and any hope of finding true love.

This morning, the opening line from one of Emily's most famous poems formed a loop in my head.

> If I can stop one heart from breaking, I shall not
> live in vain.

The words hit differently because the heart in question was mine, and I was determined to stop it from breaking. I just wasn't sure how.

The shop's front door opened, knocking the little brass bell into a tizzy and pulling me back to the moment.

I refreshed my smile and redirected my thoughts. "Welcome to Rini Reads!"

My family's store had been around for thirty-one years. Opened the year I was born, the store was originally named Rini's Romance Reads, but it had expanded its inventory, slightly, over the decades. The clientele was loyal but aging, and I itched to make updates to engage a wider crowd. My family didn't share my enthusiasm, which was unfortunate, because the store's prime location and longevity gave it great potential as a community hub.

The hours raced by as I made recommendations for customers' next reads and shared news of upcoming store events, then sent my parents a quick text after the morning rush. They typically spent a night or two at a B&B following their vow renewal, and this year wasn't any different. When my sister, Annie, and I were young, they'd work at the shop during the days and get us a sitter at night, but by the time I'd graduated from high school, I managed the shop alone and kept an eye on Annie. The last few years I saw more of our parents via photos on their social media accounts during their getaways than in person. And it only bothered me a little that they'd generously shared details of this year's trip planning with Annie and her husband, Jeffrey, but sparsely with me.

I nearly rolled my eyes at the childish thought. This was exactly why I needed to make big changes in my life. I was on my way to becoming a cranky old lady.

I wished my parents happy travels, then put the phone back into my pocket.

My new delivery guy arrived a few minutes later. "Hey, Emma."

"Hey, Caden," I said.

Caden was a senior at the local college, fit and fine but too young to hold my interest. He passed me his clipboard with a smile. "I just need your signature."

"Here you go." I signed and passed the paper back to him, and his gaze traveled curiously over me.

"I like this look on you," he said. "You've got a whole geek-chic vibe going."

I stilled, suddenly remembering my ensemble and glasses. I'd worn my softest jeans with an ivory camisole and a ten-year-old cardigan. I'd decided that from now on, I'd dress as comfortably as I wanted because I was no longer concerned that it might be the day I experienced a real-life meet-cute that led to true love. I'd even skipped wearing my contacts as a small rebellion.

No more brokenhearted Emma. I was a bookstore manager in transformation.

"Looks good," he said with a wink and a weird two-finger salute. Then he saw himself out.

I sighed and went to change the window display.

Rini Reads was deep and narrow, with floor-to-ceiling shelves along the walls and a generous window facing the sidewalk. Armchairs were tucked into quiet corners at the back, and the apartment where I'd lived since college was right upstairs.

I removed the books from their pedestals and replaced them with a selection of Penguin's Clothbound Classics. The gorgeously repackaged tomes were proven fan favorites and sure to catch the eyes of passersby. I arranged silk leaves in autumn colors around each book, then spread the rest of my supply on the ground and strung card-stock cutout letters above to spell *Fall in Love with a Book*. Typically, I waited a bit longer to set up the fall displays—it was only the first of September—but apparently I was jonesing for change all around.

The bell above the door rang again as I reshelved the other volumes, and Jeffrey appeared, holding the door for Annie to stride inside.

I straightened and worked up a bright smile for my little sister and her handler.

She wore an adorable floral sundress with a matching headband and sandals. She'd curled her long brown hair into ringlets that fell over her shoulders.

Envy hit at the sight of her beautiful curls. I could only pull the sides of my recently cut locks into a messy little knot while the rest continuously reached in vain for my shoulders.

Jeffrey moved dutifully behind her, dressed in business casual and carrying her purse.

"Out for your weekly date?" I asked rhetorically as I stepped forward to give her a hug. Annie only bothered showing up at the shop once a week since her baby bump had appeared. In truth, Annie had pulled back on her hours the moment she'd gotten married. Our parents had supported her choice, claiming new marriages needed time and attention to thrive. And who could complain about a pregnant lady not working more? "You look beautiful."

"Thanks." She set her hands on her swollen abdomen when I released her. "We can't stay long. We have a prenatal appointment, then lunch plans, and we're going to take a walk in the park if the weather holds up."

"That sounds really nice," I said, meaning it to my core.

Jeffrey stood behind her, gently rubbing his big hands up and down her arms. He'd joined the family, unofficially, during Annie's freshman year in college, when they'd met by absolute happenchance and fallen head over heels in love. It was a story they shared almost as often as our parents told of their bolt-of-lightning, kismet first encounter. Both true love stories had begun on the University of Massachusetts campus. Personally, I'd spent four years on that campus without any marital prospects, but that was my life. Commuting forty-five minutes to classes and back so I could help with Annie and the bookstore had made my college experience very different from the rest of my family's.

Jeffrey had become an official Rini following a spring wedding two years back.

I'd been Annie's bridesmaid too.

"Can we bring you anything for lunch?" he offered. "We're eating at the Bistro. It wouldn't be any trouble. Our treat."

My gaze flickered to the fancy restaurant on the corner across the street. "No, thank you." I appreciated the offer, but they had a baby on the way and only one real income. The expression on Annie's face said Jeffrey was working off the cuff—i.e., he'd offered without her preapproved consent, and I imagined she wasn't keen on visiting the bookstore, or me, twice in one day. I didn't want to start trouble in paradise, so I refreshed my smile. "I packed my lunch."

"Well," Annie said, glancing around. "Everything looks great here, as always. You've got it all under control."

I frowned. Something seemed off about Annie lately. I couldn't put my finger on the exact change or properly explain my intuition, but I hated the new distance between us. Despite vast personality differences and a seven-year age gap, for many years I was her favorite person. She was still mine.

Before I could ask if there was something more she wanted to say, Annie turned to her husband. "We should go. I don't want to be late for the doctor."

Jeffrey nodded and opened the door again. "Good seeing you, Emma. Take care."

"You too," I said. "Bye, Annie."

She wiggled her fingers and moved back into the day.

Not one of her longer visits, but I had to take what I could get. If I didn't see her on their weekly dates or Saturday-night dinners with our folks, I wasn't sure when I'd see her at all.

Time rushed ahead from there as I impersonated a spinning top, greeting and ringing up customers, stocking inventory, and placing orders. All while firming up my internal resolve for personal change.

The words of Emily's poem played again in my mind, and I acknowledged my quietly broken heart. I, Emma Rini, wanted what everyone else seemed to have already. I wanted the happily ever after. The deep, abiding love I saw in my parents, in movies, in books. I wanted it, but it didn't want me. On a slightly brighter note, I realized, I was at least in good company.

Emily Dickinson had never married or had children, and she'd been brilliant. She'd found peace and beauty all around her. Why couldn't I do the same?

I didn't need someone to love me the way my dad loved my mom. I could embrace my inner Emily and learn to find peace and beauty in my life. I could learn to love myself instead.

That's exactly what I'd do. I lifted my chin in audacious resolve.

Where to begin? I made a quick mental list of ways to emulate Emily's life. She'd liked to bake and had been an avid gardener. I could do those things. She'd also liked to read and journal, write poetry, and correspond with friends. I could easily add those activities to my routine as well. Soon I'd be so busy learning new things and finding new passions, I wouldn't have time to date or worry about love.

When shoppers disappeared after lunchtime, I settled behind the counter, feeling optimistic, and opened my prepackaged salad. I used to go pick up my lunch when Annie shared the workload, but without her to cover my breaks, I couldn't even run upstairs to grab something from my fridge. Instead, I had to plan ahead, pack a thermal lunch tote, and eat around one o'clock, when business generally slowed.

My apartment was technically rent-free, but it definitely came at a price. Most notably, it made me the one to open and close the shop every day, and I was forever on standby to sign for deliveries before and after hours.

I dragged the box of books Caden had delivered a little closer, then opened it as I ate. The packing list on top was correct, so I breathed a little easier. Unfortunately, the stack of books beneath was wrong.

"You've got to be kidding me." I slouched onto the stool and stuck another forkful of lettuce into my mouth.

I'd ordered several copies of Nicholas Sparks's latest novel but received a stack of works by Nicholas Evans instead. "Un-freaking-believable."

Nothing against *The Horse Whisperer*, but I'd been hoping to receive what I'd asked for this time. I made a note to contact the distributor and file a complaint. It had taken too long and too much hassle to return the last shipment they'd sent in error, and I was fast becoming a one-woman show.

The lonely thought sent a pang of grief through me, and I squared my shoulders.

Being alone was fine. I was fine.

My phone rang, and Mom's number appeared on-screen.

I set my salad aside and answered.

"Good afternoon, sweetheart," she cooed. "I got your text. How are you? How's the shop?"

"Everything is great," I said, smiling a little at her pep. "How are you and Dad?"

"We're wonderful. Heading out for a late lunch before leaving town, and I can't wait. It's so nice to get away once in a while. You know?"

Her quip caused me to blink. Did I know? I wasn't sure when I'd last had any sort of getaway. I scraped the back of my mind for details as Mom continued to talk. I had one guaranteed day off per week when the store was closed, and a second on the day my parents worked—though that was less regular lately—and I often spent most of that day off catching them up on the business. Reviewing our book-keeping or brainstorming the next quarter's events.

I'd made several road trips to other indie shops recently, searching for books to put on reception tables for the wedding-vow-renewal cele-bration. Did that count as getting away? I wasn't working for the store at the time, but I'd been acting as my parents' volunteer wedding planner. If those trips didn't count as getaways, then when was my last—

"Oh, wow." The words popped out when the realization hit. Had I not taken time off since I'd had my appendix removed? That was—I performed the mental math—seven years ago. Seriously?

"We don't have to get it all sorted right now," Mom said, the earlier pep gone from her tone.

"What?" I jerked back to the moment, confused and a little dis-gruntled. "Sorry. I was trying to remember something."

Mom chuckled nervously. "That's supposed to be my line. It's exactly what I was saying. Once you're over sixty, like your father and me, the memory starts to go. Along with everything else. Which is why we want to talk to you about this."

"About what?" I asked, still daunted by the possibility I hadn't had a day off since I was hospitalized and literally, physically unable to work.

"Retiring," Mom said. "We aren't getting any younger, and we want to spend our time enjoying one another, spoiling our grandbaby."

Somewhere in the back of my mind, a record needle screeched. "You want to retire?" That couldn't be right. "You're only sixty-one. And you rarely work more than one day a week. Who will take your places?"

The line went quiet for a long beat, and realization smacked my head like a toppling bookshelf. Of course, I already knew the answer. "Me."

"Well," Mom said. "That's the point, isn't it? You don't need us. You've got it all under control."

You've got it all under control. That was exactly what Annie had said earlier. Intuition flared. "Did you already talk to Annie about this?"

Silence stretched anew.

"Mom?"

"We didn't want to upset her by offering the store to you without telling her first. We have two children, after all, but you're the one who loves Rini Reads, and Annie . . ." She let the sentence drift.

I pressed a hand to my forehead, then began to pace. She'd already spoken with Annie about my future. Was I even a part of this family anymore? "Annie has a husband and a baby on the way," I filled in. "Of course she doesn't want the store. It's hard work. It's long hours, and too much responsibility."

I had no idea how she'd handle a baby. Then again, she wasn't alone. She had Jeffrey—and our parents—to help.

"We didn't think she'd mind," Mom said. "And she didn't. She has other priorities, and Jeffrey does well financially."

And I was a spinster. Married to the store I'd been groomed to take over.

"She wants you to have it as much as we do," Mom continued. "Once you take over, you can make all the changes you want. I know you have big ideas, and your father and I are only holding you back."

I released a shaky breath. "Welcome to Rini Reads," I called out to the empty store. My traitorous voice cracked on each word. "Mom, I've got to go. A customer just walked in, but we'll talk soon. Enjoy your trip."

I disconnected and fought a round of frustration tears.

How had this become my life? How could I start my journey to peace while being given more work? How could I stop my heart from breaking?

Chapter Two

The home screen on my phone lit up, and the line from my Daily Dickinson app appeared on-screen.

"Hope" is the thing with feathers.

I pushed the words to the back of my mind as images of my future morphed grotesquely in my head. All hope of embracing my inner Emily by reading beneath shade trees, writing, and harvesting vegetables from my garden were replaced by images of me and my sixteen cats running the bookstore while village children tossed stones at the windows and dared one another to go inside.

I refocused on the errant book order. Before I finished typing a heated message about the second shipping error, a notification from my favorite online group, the Independent Bookstore Owners of Massachusetts, or IBOOM for short, appeared on-screen.

I smiled despite my mood.

I'd found incredible camaraderie with the other indie bookshop owners and managers over the years. We often watched the University of Massachusetts football games together online, bantering in IBOOM via comments and silly GIFs. I'd missed a great game last night, according to the posts and highlights.

There were fewer than fifty members in the group and fewer than twenty independent stores left in our state. I appreciated the friendship of other booksellers who single-handedly kept shops like ours alive. Because paying the bills was one thing. Affording enough staff was another. And we all knew what it meant to hustle. I liked everyone in the group, but Historically_Bookish was definitely my favorite. Her real name was Grace Forsythe, and she was the solitary proprietor of Village Books in Amherst, home of UMass and the Minutemen, as well as my nineteenth-century BFF, Emily Dickinson. Grace didn't post often, but when she did, it always made me smile. Despite a significant age difference, we had a ridiculous amount in common, from our shared love of dad jokes and our tendencies to overwork to our taste in hot wings. I'd been genuinely shocked when I ventured to her shop in search of books for the reception tables and realized Grace was nearly a decade older than my mom. Mom didn't get half my jokes or any of my references. She rarely worked and hated hot wings. I loved that Grace and I clicked so well despite our difference in age.

My interest piqued when a missed post from Grace appeared beneath chatter about the game.

Historically_Bookish: As some of you know, I rent the historic manor on my bookstore's property. I've reluctantly conceded to a complete remodel, so this will be the last season it's available in its current, mostly original, state. If you know anyone who might be interested in stepping back in time for a night or two, please let me know.

My inner Emily Dickinson sat up straight and smoothed her skirts. Grace had never mentioned a rentable historic property, but the timing was cosmic. This could be the perfect place to embrace my inner Emily.

I followed the shared link to a website featuring a beautiful stone structure, backlit by a setting sun. A wreath of wildflowers hung on the red wooden door. A bicycle stood on the gravel lane out front, its basket filled with books.

My focus dropped quickly to the words below. "Welcome to Hearthstone Manor," I read aloud. "Spend your days falling back in time. Located on a quiet lane, behind a carriage house turned bookstore, you'll find plenty of time and space to immerse yourself in eras gone by. Enjoy a fire in one of the original fireplaces, lose yourself in a classic read, or attend The Lost Art of Letter-Writing classes at the bookstore. Peace and tranquility await."

Inner Emily began to vibrate.

I scrolled to check the price.

The cost per night wasn't unreasonable, and a side note added, *Interested in staying longer? Contact the owner for a quote.*

I clicked to respond before I could change my mind. Annie was well into her last trimester, and my parents wanted to retire. If I was going to take control of my life, even for a little while, it was now or never.

I dashed my thumbs across the screen with haste, filling in my email address and message on the website's contact form.

Hello! I'm ED_Fan from IBOOM. I'd love to come for an extended visit! How much to rent the manor for six weeks?

I sent the request for information, then returned the phone to my pocket with a panicked squeak. *Six weeks?*

I couldn't leave town for that long. What had even possessed me to ask?

I walked outside for fresh air and released an embarrassed chuckle. My brain was clearly low on oxygen.

The warm breeze was an instant balm to my nerves, and my heart rate immediately began to settle. The neighborhood surrounding Rini Reads was quaint, with narrow redbrick buildings and logoed awnings over big shop windows and glass front doors. Absolutely postcard worthy. Black lampposts and wrought iron benches lined the streets of our small downtown, the blocks bookended with small grassy nooks, including a spectacular dog park, and outdoor cafés. I loved the outdoors and envied people who had time to sit in the sun and take walks.

I switched to the camera app on my phone and leaned against the streetlamp at the curb, angling for the best possible photo of my new window display. Might as well make myself useful while I had an internal breakdown. "Two birds, one stone" and all that.

Besides, requesting a quote didn't obligate me to move to Amherst.

"It's fine," I whispered, reassuring myself gently. I snapped a few photos, then checked them on the little screen. "Not bad, Rini."

A woman I recognized from her daily trips to the dog park waved from across the street.

I smiled and returned the gesture.

She was petite by any standard, and her dog was contrastingly massive. The woman wore jogging gear. Her dog, wearing a pink collar with silver studs, kept its eyes on the prize: a beautiful leash-free experience just a half block away.

This was my favorite time of day to people watch—when a parade of pups in every shape and size, guided by happy humans, made their way to the park.

I'd always been an animal lover, but my family had never had pets. If I had a bigger place and more time, I'd adopt a former racing greyhound. I was obsessed with the breed and a financial supporter of our local rescue.

My phone buzzed, drawing my eyes back to the screen. A message notification appeared.

I released a shuddering breath and clicked.

Historically_Bookish: Hi ED_Fan! No one's ever asked to rent the place for so long, but I know you'll appreciate the time here. I'm willing to negotiate on price, and I'd love to work this out.

A thrill shot through me. The number she'd suggested was steep, but it could be my new beginning and I had the money. I lived rent-free and worked around the clock. Plus, I'd been saving for years—since the days I'd first gotten lost in bridal magazines beside my sick mother, and then as I watched the planning and execution of her vow renewal carry her back to health. I had been saving to help my parents afford my dream wedding, but now that I'd decided to give up that dream, it seemed incredibly poetic to spend the money this way instead.

Assuming my parents didn't use it to cover my funeral after they killed me for asking to take six weeks off.

A familiar laugh disturbed my reverie, and I turned to watch a group of people emerge from the Bistro across the street. Dad kissed Annie's cheek, then shook Jeffrey's hand. Mom smiled at Dad's side. They'd coupled up and left me to eat prepackaged salad while they shared a nice meal thirty yards away.

Emotion returned with a brutal smack and immediate resolve.

I was no longer asking their permission.

✺

Cecily, my lifelong best friend, arrived a few minutes before the store closed, a pair of disposable cups from the hospital's coffee kiosk in her hands. She wore blue scrubs, and her ponytail was slightly askew. Cecily worked long, erratic shifts as a trauma nurse at the local ER, and I couldn't imagine life without her. I needed her input and her blessing before I made this leap. "I got your text and came straight from work. What's going on?"

I flipped the sign in the window from **OPEN** to **CLOSED**, then locked the door. "I had an epiphany, and I did something big. Now I'm kind of freaking out."

Her gaze roamed over me, and her brows furrowed. "Does this have anything to do with the Emily Dickinson line you texted me earlier?"

"Yep." My traitorous heart filled with grief reluctantly saying goodbye to the hope I'd one day meet my soulmate. The man who'd sweep me off my feet with his handsome face and charming smile, then smother me in adoration and beg me to be his wife. "I've decided to give up on love."

"You're kidding."

I shook my head. "I'm tired of feeling like I'm missing out on something because I haven't met the right man or fallen in love. Not everyone is meant for a partner in life. Maybe I'm one of those."

"Marriage isn't for everyone," she agreed. "But you want the big, epic love story."

"Do I?"

"Yes."

"Do I?" I repeated.

She tented her brows and passed me a cup.

"What if I've only assumed that was what I wanted because I grew up with the kissiest parents in all the land, in a bookstore dedicated to romance novels. I mean, did I ever really have a chance to want anything else?"

"You've always wanted a dog," she said, smiling softly. "You never got one of those, but you will when the time is right."

I sighed, saddened by yet another truth. "My life isn't conducive to canine joy. I live in a small apartment and work twelve hours a day." Even when I wasn't at the bookstore, I was thinking about, or working peripherally on, the shop's success, planning social media projects, scheduling speakers and events, or any number of other things no one else saw me doing.

Cecily sank back on her heels, either considering my need for change or the possibility an impostor had taken over my body. I wasn't sure which.

I clasped my hands, eager and a little desperate. "I'm letting go of my need to find a significant other, and I'm just going to be happy by myself."

"I support your quest for happiness. So, what's the plan?"

"I've decided to get in touch with my inner Emily Dickinson."

Cecily smiled. "That sounds about right."

"Exactly. She never married. Never had kids or a big, loud life, and her words have always spoken straight to my heart. We're a century apart, but we share a wavelength. If I can tune into that and be more like her, then maybe next year I won't spend my parents' entire ceremony daydreaming of running away."

A small sad smile formed on Cecily's lips. "Is that what you were doing?"

I forced myself to meet her gaze. "I want love too badly, and it's starting to make me miserable. I'm obsessing, and I don't want to feel this way anymore."

"Aw, sweetie." She straightened and wrapped me in her arms. "I'd love to find true love, too, but I don't think becoming more like Jane Austen would fix anything. You know she's my favorite, and she never married either. But the point is that you have to be happy where you are. I know it's hard to want something you can't control, but changing yourself won't bring you joy. The best thing you can do right now, even if you're hurting, is to accept that you want a big, epic love and to remind yourself that it's exactly what you deserve. Just get comfortable and have fun doing other things. Don't put your life on hold, waiting for the right guy to come along."

"Or." I wet my lips and stepped back. "I could spend my wedding fund on something remarkable enough to alter my outlook on life and change my entire future."

Cecily hiked a brow, then moved around the counter and took a seat on my stool. "I'm going to need a minute to finish this coffee. The ER was nonstop today, and I feel like I've fallen down the rabbit hole." She took several sips from her cup, one finger lifted, indicating I should wait.

I shifted foot to foot.

Cecily set the cup beside the register a moment later and rolled her shoulders. "You've been saving that money since middle school. You have a highly organized three-inch binder filled with details for your dream wedding, reception, rehearsal, and bachelorette weekend. Why are you spending your wedding fund?"

"Because I found this." I pulled the phone from my pocket and held it out to her, the Hearthstone Manor website already on the screen. "It's fate."

Cecily took another long drink before accepting the phone. "Become a part of history inside the walls of this delightfully inviting manor. Embrace the past in Amherst, Massachusetts."

"I'm giving myself a do-over," I said. "Six weeks in Emily Dickinson's hometown, living in a place that existed when she actually walked those streets. She could've been in a carriage on that lane, rolled right by the house where I'll stay, or even known the family who lived there. And now it's available to rent at the exact time I need to get away. For an amount of money I can afford."

This was the day my stars aligned.

My date with destiny.

"Six weeks?" Cecily gasped, clearly stuck on the wrong detail.

I nodded.

"Your parents are going to flip out," she said. "And Annie's going to straight-up bare-handed murder you."

She wasn't wrong, and I'd had similar concerns, but I was sure I could make it work. "I'll come home if Annie goes into labor before the end of my stay."

She arched a brow. "Like that will matter. What about your folks?"

"Cecily," I whispered, raising my hands to my chest in prayer pose. "I already planned to embrace my inner Emily Dickinson. Now I can do it in her hometown." I dropped my jaw dramatically for effect. "I can finally stop pining over a man who doesn't exist, stop going on an endless barrage of terrible dates, and stop giving my heart to the occasional decent, but undeserving, guy who doesn't want a future with me. I can focus on myself and be happy again."

Cecily frowned. "Come here." She reached for my wrists to pull me closer, then leveled me with a caring, but firm expression.

I chewed my lip, unable to hide my disappointment.

"Are you okay?" she asked. "Because this isn't like you. I know you've been unhappy lately, but this feels as if you're running away."

"I have to do something for myself while I still can," I said, throat tightening with desperation. "Annie won't come back to work after the baby's born, and my parents want to retire. They're all leaving me to do this alone. This is my last chance for an adventure."

Cecily's brows knitted; a flash of heat blazed across her hazel eyes as she released me. "All right. Let's talk this out." She folded her arms. "You're the busiest, most people-loving person I know. What if you get bored or lonely? The website says there's a fireplace. Can you even build a fire? What if you're unhappy and I can't bring you coffee? I can't go with you. I'd have to call in dead to miss that much work. Even then, it's no guarantee my boss would allow it."

I smiled and took a sip of my drink, thankful beyond measure for her presence in my life. "Amherst is less than forty miles away. You can see me whenever you want. But I need time to rearrange my priorities. Forget about finding love and focus on finding myself."

"What will you do all alone in a creaky old house?"

I shrugged. "Read. Journal. Maybe I'll bake something."

"Bake something," Cecily repeated, features bunched, as if I'd suggested fire eating or tiger training.

"Emily Dickinson was an excellent baker."

"For the record, I don't think living like some eighteen-hundreds recluse is going to solve anything. You should stay here and be you. Everything else will sort itself out."

"I need this," I said, fixing her with my most pleading expression. "And I need you to have my back or I'll chicken out, and I'll always wonder if this trip was the thing that could've made life better."

Her shoulders drooped. "First you have to admit this is a wacky idea."

"I'm soul-searching."

"You're cosplaying a dead poet for six weeks. I think that's the actual definition of wacky."

"Cecily."

She sighed. "Are you sure you want to do this?"

I nodded, and she opened her arms to wrap me in another hug.

Now I just had to tell my family.

Chapter Three

I dragged my feet leaving the apartment the following Saturday evening, dreading the conversation that was to come. Even as I'd packed my things for Amherst, I'd promised myself I could cancel if the night went poorly. I desperately needed the fresh start but wasn't sure I could take it at the cost of hurting my family. Which was exactly what I feared would happen.

My phone buzzed with an incoming message as I climbed into my car and willed myself to be brave. I smiled when I saw the message was from Grace.

Historically_Bookish: Watching the game today?

ED_Fan: Of course. Plus Saturday-night dinner with the family. You?

Historically_Bookish: Yep at the pub for drinks and wings

ED_Fan: Pregame rituals are delicious

Rini family dinners were always low key, but during football season, Saturdays were casual in the extreme. A UMass game often played on the big screen. We ate homemade wings and pizzas, cheered the Minutemen, and talked smack about the opposing players. With a little luck, an early points lead today would put everyone in a good mood before I broke my news.

I drove to my folks' house feeling a little lighter, then climbed out and rang the bell.

Annie answered the door with a frown.

Now that I'd arrived, I wasn't sure what to do. Charge ahead or turn back before it was too late? I'd asked myself a thousand times if I really needed to go to Amherst, or if maybe just knowing I could go was enough to catapult me into change. Unfortunately, there was really only one way to find out.

"Well?" Annie asked, one hand on the open door as if prepared to shut it in my face. She wore her hair in smooth waves over her shoulders and was dressed casually in flats, jeans, and her old UMass Cheerleading sweatshirt. "Are you going to come inside, or just look at me like I smell bad?"

I stepped into the foyer. "Sorry. You smell lovely. I was lost in thought, but I brought wine." I lifted the bottle in my hand before remembering she couldn't have any.

"I wish." She turned for the kitchen and left me to close the door.

"Sorry." I cringed. "I wasn't thinking. I've got a ton on my mind. I should've brought something for you. I can run out for a milkshake!"

She kept walking. "I'm fine."

I followed her down the hall of the old Tudor-style home where we'd grown up.

"How was your appointment?" I asked Annie's back, hoping to lighten the mood before I dropped a bomb.

"Great."

I frowned and hurried to catch up. "Is everything okay?"

"I can't see my feet. I'm gaining weight every time I inhale, and I have two months before I can try to lose it."

"But you'll also have a baby," I said, working some big-sister enthusiasm into my tone.

She didn't respond.

My parents and Jeffrey were in the kitchen, chatting and snacking around the island. They looked cozy and inviting in their game-day ensembles, UMass alumni shirts and warm smiles. The tangy scent of hot wings in the slow cooker seasoned the air.

Annie drifted to her husband's side, drawn by the invisible force I craved.

Mom's eyes caught mine, and she rushed to wrap me in a hug. "Emma! We're so glad you're here. How are things at the shop?"

I stifled a grimace. I wanted to complain and say I had other things going on that she could ask me about, but that was historically inaccurate, and she had no reason to think otherwise.

"Things are great," I said, stepping away from her to hug Dad. "I worked late this week setting up the deliveries during my absence and arranging autopayment for invoices. I scheduled email reminders on the mailing list for our upcoming events and laminated copies of the daily and weekly tasks as quick-reference guides."

Dad chuckled as he set me free. "You're a natural," he said proudly. "No one runs a ship as tight as yours."

Jeffrey raised a hand in greeting. "Good to see you again, Emma," he said. "Sorry we won't make it into the shop this week. Annie has an early-morning appointment, and our usual date day is out the window."

"No problem," I said. If things went well, I wouldn't be at work for a while anyway. "I brought wine."

"Set it there," Mom said. "We just opened a bottle. Annie has juice."

Dad filled an empty glass with a robust nine-ounce pour. "We're celebrating again today," he said. "Not every family gets to spend time with their grown daughters every week, like we do."

"And their spouse," Mom said, raising a glass to Jeffrey. "And their grandbaby on the way."

Annie folded her arms.

"How about a toast to the Rini ladies?" Jeffrey suggested, passing a glass of apple juice into his wife's hand.

"Great," she said.

"Great," I echoed.

Great was the default word Annie and I used when things were, in fact, the opposite. And oftentimes, especially in the presence of our parents, it sometimes meant *fuck off.*

In retrospect, Annie had answered the same way when I'd asked how her latest prenatal appointment had gone. My brow furrowed, and she looked at her feet as she leaned against her husband's side. Intuition scratched at the back of my mind.

"Are the notes you wrote up for when you hire help for the shop?" Dad asked.

I bit my lip. "I'm sure any new hires will find the notes useful, but that wasn't the only reason I made them."

"Well, cheers," Mom said.

Dad and Jeffrey echoed the statement.

I looked more closely at my sister while we toasted, wondering when we'd become so distant and hating it more than ever. I opened my mouth to ask if something was wrong and if I could help somehow.

"So, Emma," Mom interrupted, flashing a smile briefly at Dad. "We're speaking with our attorney and financial adviser this week. We'll get things sorted, then bring you in for the paperwork."

Wow. They were just diving right into things.

I wasn't sure if my parents planned to legally transfer their business to me as an early inheritance, if they hoped I'd buy them out, or if they wanted to create some kind of co-ownership, but I couldn't bring myself to ask. Not yet. Not now.

Panic burbled in my gut as I looked into their eager faces. It was time to tell them.

Tell them. Tell them. Tell them.

"What do you think?" Dad smiled hopefully. "We can ask your aunt Stacia to cover the shop while you meet with us to go over the details. She never minds putting in a shift or two."

I always appreciated when my aunts or cousins popped in to help during our busy times, but we rarely left them alone in the store for long. What if they ran into trouble or had a question? I pushed the thought aside. My moment was passing, and I could feel my inner chicken urging me to go home and email them instead.

Emily seemed to speak to me then, bringing her precious words to my mind. Life was composed of a million tiny moments, of a million little *nows*—and my *now* was happening.

"Actually, I have news," I said. I cleared my throat, then swallowed a gulp of wine.

The stares of eight expectant eyes locked onto me.

Mom's brows rose. "News?" She glanced at Dad, then Annie and Jeffrey, excitement illuminating her face. "You met someone?"

I slouched. "No." Jeez. Why was that always their first thought? And why did it feel like a slap every single time?

"Is this about taking over the shop?" Mom asked, drawing my attention back to her. "I know we kind of sprang it on you, but it's been on our minds a long while."

Dad smiled. "What are your thoughts so far?"

I released a slow, steadying breath. "I'd like some time off before you retire."

"Of course," Mom said. "Completely understandable. Your dad and I have things we want to do before we step down anyway. We'll take care of those while you get away."

Dad, the least oblivious of the Rini clan, stiffened slightly, and I got the feeling he was the only one picking up on my tension.

"Thank you," I said. "I'm glad you're on board. I've already made plans for this month."

"When this month?" Mom asked. "Our calendar is wide open now that the vow renewal is over and we're on standby for our first grandbaby."

"The rest of it," I said. "And about half of next month as well."

Annie scoffed. "You're taking off work for the rest of September?"

"And fourteen days in October," I clarified.

Jeffrey murmured something against her hair.

Our parents exchanged a look.

"But I'm having a baby in eight weeks," Annie said.

"I know, but I'll only be away for six."

Her eyes narrowed to slits, and Jeffrey slipped his other arm around her, presumably to prevent the bare-handed murdering Cecily had predicted.

Dad rubbed a finger across his bottom lip. "I don't understand. You want to take all that time off work?"

"Yes."

Mom drained her glass of wine.

"Why?" he asked.

That answer was complicated, and not something I wanted to share with the group. So I focused on the facts I thought they'd understand. "I rented the manor behind Village Books, the indie bookshop in Amherst. I know the owner through our online group, and she's a very nice lady. I'll be safe."

I scanned their pinched faces, seeking support. When I didn't find any, my gut demanded I take the words back immediately.

Inner Emily rooted her feet in place.

If I didn't do this now, I'd wind up working a hundred hours a week until I died restocking the shelves and some unfortunate patron discovered my miserably single skeleton, probably surrounded by cats.

Annie set small, outraged hands on newly rounded hips. "You're leaving town for the entire rest of my pregnancy. Why are you always so dramatic?"

"I'm taking an overdue break from work," I snapped. "That's not being dramatic. Besides, like you said, you aren't due for eight weeks."

"First babies can come early."

"Or they can be late," I said. "Just like every baby. This isn't about you, Annie. It's about me. And if I don't go now, when can I?"

Her jaw locked. "So, you're just going on vacation and leaving Mom, Dad, and me to handle everything at the store?"

I blinked, wondering why she was so angry.

I looked to Jeffrey for help, but he kept his eyes on his wife, his lips whispering softly in her ear.

Mom climbed onto a chair at the island, looking ill. "I don't understand. You're leaving?" She set a hand on her middle, apparently processing the worst news of her life. "Why didn't you talk to us about this? This is big. Something you know we'd want to hear as soon as possible."

"The decision is new," I said, my earlier guilt slipping away. "I just made the deposit last week, and I planned to tell you the next time I saw you or talked to you. But I haven't seen or heard from any of you in six days." Not since I'd seen them leaving the Bistro together on Monday. When they'd pointedly left me out.

I hadn't bothered trying to reach them, either, but that was the point. If I didn't call or text, I'd never hear from them.

Dad raised his palms in an attempt to de-escalate the situation. "Let's take a minute to process this before we get too far ahead of ourselves." He looked to Mom. "Mary?"

She nodded, eyes fixed on me. "Is this why you did all that extra work?" Mom asked. "For us? Not because you plan to hire new help?"

I nodded, though I absolutely planned to find a way to hire help as soon as possible. "A lot of things have changed since you've done the bookkeeping and ordering. I've streamlined and updated processes everywhere I can because I'm usually on my own. I thought the lists would help."

I'd expected to back down if my family became upset, but now that the moment had arrived, indignation stiffened my spine. "All you have to do is show up and handle customers. I've taken care of everything else."

"Ed?" Mom looked to Dad for help.

"It's fine," he said, forcing a patient smile. "We can handle it. Take the break you need, Emma."

"Dad!" Annie yelled. "Are you serious?"

Jeffrey held her, while Mom and Dad tried to make everything sound better. Their agitated and disappointed voices clashed and collided around me.

Annie's words eventually cut through the noise, and I raised my eyes to meet her angry gaze. "Anyone else would take a weekend off, or maybe a week. But a month and a half with zero notice?" Annie's expression turned miserable and defeated. She sank back against her husband's chest. "This is selfish, Emma," she muttered. "Even for you."

My jaw dropped, and I snapped it shut, locking it in place.

Inner Emily rolled her shoulders and cracked her knuckles. "I'm truly sorry for the short notice, but I've needed a break for a while, and no one noticed. This opportunity is too good to pass up. I need this, and I won't apologize for it."

I moved forward on wooden legs, kissing Mom and Dad on their cheeks. I hated confrontation, and I never stood up to my family. I was the giver, the helper, not the one who left others in a pinch. Especially not my parents and sister, who I cared for most in the world. I hated the shock and confusion on their sweet faces, but I wouldn't recant; I'd already made it that far. "I have to finish packing. If you want to see me off tomorrow morning, or want to review those notes about the shop, I'm leaving at ten."

❧

The next evening, I followed my GPS's instructions past miles of rolling farmland toward Amherst. I checked my messages when I stopped for gas and laughed at the supremely dorky post made by Historically_ Bookish in IBOOM.

Beneath a photo of her new *Outlander* display, she'd written *Diana Gabaldon, master of time travel, always thinking outside the clocks.*

Several group members had already responded with eye roll GIFs. I selected something with Michael Scott from *The Office* shaking his head regretfully.

Historically_Bookish responded to me almost immediately.

Historically_Bookish: I knew you'd love it

I snorted. Then responded because I couldn't help myself.

ED_Fan: I do! I was obsessed with time travel once, but that's all in the past now

Responses of thrown tomatoes in GIF format piled into the comments, and I put my phone away feeling satisfied.

Grace had told me, in her last email with specifics for accessing the manor, that she and her friends had tickets to see a local show, so she couldn't meet me at the manor but looked forward to seeing me soon at the bookstore.

My family had shown up to say goodbye at nine in the morning. They'd stayed all day, reviewing my notes about the shop and when to water the plants in my apartment. Then my parents took us out to eat before finally saying goodbye.

Mom and Dad spent our mealtime trying to convince me to stay, and Annie barely spoke. She wished me well on the sidewalk outside the restaurant and hugged me tightly before I climbed into my car, but she appeared miles away the entire time. We didn't eat at the Bistro, and I never asked why they'd left me out last week. But I'd missed three exits so far, winning a long-overdue argument against Annie in my head.

My phone buzzed as I got back behind the wheel. A new message had arrived.

Historically_Bookish: See you tonight

My smile returned. Apparently her plans had changed, and that sounded absolutely perfect.

I pulled out of the gas station and merged into traffic, feeling immeasurably thankful for Grace and her rentable manor.

Soon, large historic homes appeared along the roadside, sparsely at first, then more abundantly as downtown drew nearer. I took in the quaint details and sidewalks dotted with students wearing cross-body bags, backpacks, or shirts with their school logo. Nostalgia hit like a punch.

Annie and I had been close until I started college and she'd started middle school. After that, the doting little sister I'd always known began growing and changing, becoming a strong, independent woman. I hadn't chased her when she pulled away. I'd never imagined I wouldn't get her back.

I cast the weight in my chest aside and refocused. This trip was about me. I'd already made a list of sights to see and places to visit, including the Homestead, Emily Dickinson's childhood home, now a museum in her honor. Her brother's home, the Evergreens, still stood next door. After five years of driving past during my college years, perpetually late for class or in a hurry to return to work, I would finally go inside.

A thrill rocked through me as I slowed outside my destination. The historic carriage house turned bookstore stood at the corner of Pleasant Street and a long tree-hugged lane. I stared into the slowly bruising sky for long moments, then eased down the gravel drive toward Hearthstone Manor, my new, if temporary, home.

Waning shafts of sunlight stretched through the canopy of reaching oaks above, dappling the road in a haze of fiery hues. I adored this time of year, when change was afoot and the world aglow. By the time I left, the lane would be an explosion of fall colors, a fall-foliage lover's dream.

Slowly, the two-story stone manor came into view through the shadows, looking exactly as it had on-screen. The same regal face and cheery welcome mat. The same floral wreath and window boxes filled with blooms. Even the inviting old rocking chair on the wide cement porch looked familiar, and I couldn't wait to test it out.

This was the place where my life would irrevocably change. Where I would finally find peace and new joy.

I parked and took a picture, attaching it to a message for Cecily, but my cell signal had disappeared. No available Wi-Fi either. Thankfully, I was here to become Emily Dickinson, so I had no need for those things. Besides, I could walk back up the lane, or to the bookstore, anytime I wanted to use the internet, or text and call Cecily and my family.

Meanwhile, from my position before the manor, on a rocky lane surrounded by trees, it truly seemed as if I'd stepped back in time. Sounds of frogs and crickets, a light breeze, and chasing squirrels played the evening score around me. I felt like the only person in the world.

I found the manor's key hidden in the potted flowers as promised, and I slipped it into the front-door lock with anticipation. Grace had left a light on in the foyer, and a welcome basket on a round mahogany table beside a vase of wildflowers.

A passage across the grand foyer led to the kitchen, and an open archway on the right led to a sitting room. Stairs curved up before me. Everything looked clean, peaceful, and inviting.

I took a spin around the room, admiring the attention to historic detail in the decor and taking my time as I perused the collection of black-and-white photographs hung on one wall. Frowning couples and stoic babies, thoroughly overdressed, stared back. I returned to the table and smiled at the collection of handmade soaps, fresh fruits, baked goods, and stationery. The packaging on each item declared it grown, produced, and sold locally. Then I lifted the sheet of thick ivory card stock with my name scripted beneath the fold at its center.

Emma,
Welcome to Hearthstone Manor. I hope your stay is everything you want it to be. If you need anything, just call.
    Best regards,
    Grace

She'd written her personal phone number and the number of her nephew, Davis, across the bottom. Beneath the latter were six words. *Davis is good with a toolbox.*

I returned the note to the table and took a deep breath.

This was where my new story began.

Chapter Four

It took three trips to carry my bags from the SUV.

Once I had all my possessions safely inside and the door locked securely behind me, I went to explore the entirety of my new home. The air smelled of potpourri and flowers. I flipped on the lights as I moved room to room, adoring the dedication to the overall preservation of detail. Emily Dickinson would've loved the small study at the back of the home. Built-in bookcases stretched to the ceiling, and there was an honest-to-goodness rolling ladder attached to a metal rod along the tops. I wanted to curl on the padded window seat and read until dawn.

The staircase had a switchback three-quarters of the way up, with a hand-carved railing and spindles. I paused on the small landing, trapped in a patch of rising moonlight streaming through a decorative stained-glass window, like a cat caught in a sunbeam. The glass featured a single iris in full bloom, bathed in golden light. "Stunning," I whispered, continuing my climb.

Every room had high ceilings, at least nine feet, maybe more. The home must have been remarkable in its day, and I was honored to be a part of its history.

There were three bedrooms on the second floor. I chose the one nearest the only bath, then drifted down a narrow enclosed staircase to the kitchen.

A rear door overlooked a brick patio, and I knew exactly where I'd spend my mornings, sipping tea and overseeing my future garden.

Forget falling back in time—I'd landed in my best dream.

I fetched my list of personal goals from my purse and attached it to the refrigerator with the single available magnet, an ad for Village Books.

1. Journal
2. Read
3. Write poetry
4. Connect with myself
5. Bake
6. Garden
7. Embrace the solitude
8. Become my best Emily
9. Be happy
10. Give up on love

My heart grew heavy as I read the last line. It wouldn't be easy to let go of something I'd wanted so badly for so long, but it was the reason I was here.

Thirty minutes later, I'd completely unpacked and returned to the kitchen for tea. I set a kettle on the stove, then retired to the sitting room, where I folded myself into an armchair before the massive fireplace, waiting for the water to boil. The chill of an early-fall night dragged goose bumps down my spine. I tucked my legs beneath me, curling my shoulders forward over a book on Emily Dickinson's life.

By the time my kettle boiled, I'd read the opening page a dozen times without retaining a single word. Too distracted by the gonging silence and unnerving cold.

I fixed my tea and returned to the fireplace, giving it a careful exam. It was the first one I'd seen without a control switch on the wall. At my parents' home, the logs were fake. The pokers, stage props. A gas flame waited to ignite.

I pulled my phone from my pocket to ask Siri how to build a fire, then remembered the manor didn't have Wi-Fi. I considered looking for the thermostat but resolved to try it Emily's way first.

A box of long-stemmed matches caught my eye, and I sighed. "Here we go." I struck a match and threw it onto the logs, where it immediately died. I lit another and set it gently upon the logs. Where it also died.

I struck a third match and placed it under the small iron stand, letting the little flame lick upward against the logs, but it wasn't enough to ignite the wood. Memories of Dad making campfires in the backyard returned to me, and I closed my eyes to clutch onto them.

He'd used crumpled papers and small twigs as kindling.

I hurried through the manor in search of something I could burn and returned with the gifted stationery from my welcome basket. I felt a little guilty about setting it on fire but resolved to buy more later, as I was currently on a mission. The papers lit easily and blazed against the underside of the logs, creating smoke. I crouched and puffed softly, hoping to stoke the flames.

A moment later, I stilled as featherlight ashes lifted and hovered several inches from my nose. For the space of one heartbeat, they were suspended like magic. Then a whoosh of cold air whistled down the chimney and blew a pound of ancient soot into my face.

"Fuck!" I rocked back on my haunches, coughing and tasting dirt and ash on my tongue. The pale-gray flecks became black smears as I tried and failed to brush them off my skin and clothing.

I stormed through the house, swearing, searching for more kindling, and wondering if Emily Dickinson ever said unladylike words, or if that was one more thing I needed to address.

I returned with the last of the stationery and Grace's welcome letter, then tossed it all beneath the logs and struck another match. The fireplace had picked a fight I planned to win. I was sure both Grace and

Emily would approve. Grace had called me tenacious more than once when I'd shared bookstore frustrations with her; then she'd celebrated my victories when I'd refused to give up. Emily had famously written that she dwelled in possibility. At the moment, I dwelled in the determination to make a damn fire.

Slowly, the logs began to smoke again.

"Come on." I willed the flame to catch before the paper turned to ash. If I could start my journey on the right foot, building a fire with nothing but a match and kindling, just like Emily had, it would set the tone for everything that followed.

I lowered to my knees and chanted desperately encouraging words. Wind whistled, and I cringed. Knowing what would come next.

"Damn it!" I closed my eyes and jumped back as another gust of air blew down the chimney, extinguishing the fire.

I jerked onto my feet and fiddled with the metal thing I assumed controlled the flue. Too much air was getting in, and I'd run out of matches if I kept this up. I couldn't even call Grace or her nephew for help. I'd burned their numbers.

I struck another match, and it went out before I got to my knees.

I fell onto my backside, hands covering my face, and a decade of pent-up emotion unleashed. The ugly sobs caught me off guard, but I went with them, needing the immense release and glad no one would ever know. My family, who I loved dearly, had absolutely drained me, for years, and they hadn't even noticed. I'd had to move to another town just to find the time to cry.

I collapsed backward several minutes later, cries turning to hysterics at the ridiculousness of it all. Arms and legs splayed, I stared at the ceiling. Defeated by a two-hundred-year-old fireplace.

"Time to find the thermostat," I groaned, levering myself off the floor.

A thin haze of smoke hung in the air as I rose. I fought the urge to cough and considered opening a window.

The doorbell rang, and I paused to puzzle. Who on earth would be at this door after dark? I grimaced at my filthy hands and blinked stinging eyes as I shuffled into the foyer, hoping axe murderers didn't ring the bell.

Maybe Grace had finally arrived? Surely she could help with the fire.

I peeked through the curtain. A white pickup truck sat in the driveway. A shadowy figure fidgeted on my porch.

I flipped the switch, bathing my visitor in a cone of light, and nearly swallowed my tongue.

The best-looking man I'd ever seen stood just outside my door.

I made an unintelligible sound as I opened the heavy wooden barrier, silently cursing karma. My perfect meet-cute, ruined.

The man raised curious gray eyes to mine and frowned as he took me in. "I'm Davis Sommers," he said. The smooth tenor of his voice sent a delicious shiver down my spine. "I'm looking for Ed Rini."

I frowned, wholly confused and hating every speck of ash and dust on my face, hands, and clothing. "That's my dad," I said. "I'm Emma."

His strong, straight jawline flexed, and he extended his hand. "Your dad?"

"Yep." I gave his hand a quick shake, then leaned against the doorjamb for support. Everything about his presence, from his dark tousled hair to his brown work boots and blue jeans made me feel slightly intoxicated and a little giddy. He'd even rolled up the sleeves of his button-down shirt to expose his forearms. I loved that. But I'd come here specifically not to think about men.

The wind blew a wayward curl into my eye, and I chased it off my forehead with soot-smeared fingers. Then I died a little inside, thinking of what I must look like.

"Trouble with the fireplace?" he guessed.

"A little."

His attention rose over my shoulder, and he stepped forward, causing me to step back. "Is that smoke?"

I followed his gaze and gasped as he pushed his way inside. The haze from the sitting room had spread into the foyer behind me.

"Did you open the flue?"

I closed the door and followed as he strode toward the sitting room and fireplace. "It was open when I started, but the air kept blowing out my matches." So I'd made an adjustment that hadn't helped.

"This is why we only rent the place on the weekends," he muttered, barely loud enough to hear over my pounding heart.

"You rent this place?" I asked, confused by his words. "I thought this was Grace's house."

"It's a family home," he said, immediately reaching for the flue handle. "I help her manage the property."

I scooted to a stop in front of the smoldering wood. Suddenly registering his name. "You're Grace's nephew?" The one who's good with a toolbox? I'd expected a middle-aged man with a comb-over and six kids, or maybe a nice adolescent who was actually her great-nephew. It hadn't occurred to me Davis could be my age. Or gorgeous. "How old are you?"

"What?" He waved his arms to circulate the smoky air. "Thirty-four. Why?"

Completely age appropriate. I'd clearly done something to upset the gods.

The blast of a belated smoke alarm nearly launched me through the ceiling.

Davis began to cuss, and I pointed at the flashing red light high above our heads.

"That doesn't seem very historically accurate," I said flatly, annoyed by his annoyance. I obviously hadn't intended for this to happen.

"Smoke detectors are legally required in all rental properties," he said. "And clearly necessary if I don't want my tenant to burn the place down." He swiped the poker from the fireplace and spun it in his hand, then stretched onto his toes and pressed the handle against the reset button on the alarm.

I didn't imagine climbing him.

The home fell silent.

Davis returned the poker to the hearth, then went to the kitchen and washed his hands. "I've got to tell you," he said over his shoulder as he lathered and rinsed, "there are a lot of more modern, comfortable, inns where you could stay long term. A weekend at Hearthstone is an experience. Six weeks will be rough. There's no Wi-Fi, and cell service cuts out about halfway up the lane. The televisions have terrible reception, and the DVD library is stocked with scratched discs from when we were in middle school. The fireplace in the large room across from the bathroom has a history of bats in the chimney, so you can't use it. And those are just a few of the reasons this place needs a complete overhaul."

"You help Grace with this place?" I asked, circling back to the detail I was still processing, while forcefully ignoring the bat comment. I had planned to sleep in that room tonight. He didn't seem thrilled to have me here, but she had been overjoyed. I wanted to stay, but I didn't want to cause a problem between them, so I needed more information.

"Something like that." He turned to rest his backside against the sink as he dried his hands on a small white linen towel. "I can help you find a place better suited to a lengthy stay. I know everyone around here."

I wrinkled my nose. "I'm doing something that makes this place kind of perfect. I'm not ready to give up over a little smoke. Plus I told Grace I'd stay."

He frowned. "Grace isn't the one who has to come out here and fix everything that fails, breaks, or doesn't go right for you over the next six weeks."

I felt my mouth open in shock, and I snapped it shut.

I should've known anyone with a face like his would have the personality of a curmudgeon. I supposed it helped my cause. I didn't want to be attracted to him, so the reveal of his true colors worked in my favor. If Cecily were here, I'd say, "He's a ten with the personality of those old-man balcony hecklers from the Muppets." And she'd say, "He's a two."

"Old homes can be quirky," Davis said, moving back toward the sitting-room fireplace, "and a cold snap is supposed move in this week. I'll get a fire going before I leave."

I turned on my heels and followed him.

He crouched before the hearth, and I watched closely as he prepared, then lit the fire. Part of me hoped it would go out.

My traitorous gaze traveled to his backside, and a sudden, mischievous thought registered. If the house needed as much work as he implied, I could be seeing a lot of Davis in the weeks to come.

"Emma?" he asked, pulling my eyes to his.

"Hmm?"

"I asked if you wanted to clean up while I make my rounds and get everything running for you. I'll take a look at the furnace and stove while I'm here. Check the pilot lights and your water pressure."

I bit my lip, eager to change clothes and remove the ash from my face. "I'll be right back."

I hustled up the steps and flipped on the bathroom light, regretting it immediately. My eyes were red from the smoke and a crying jag. My cheeks were covered in soot, minus the faint tear tracks.

I cranked the metal cross knobs on the sink, their porcelain inlays declaring *H* and *C*, for hot and cold. Then gasped when I splashed the icy water on my face. Hopefully it would warm as it ran. I pumped soap onto my palms and scrubbed it over my skin, effectively soaking the front of my dirty shirt in the process.

"Everything okay?" Davis called from the bottom of the steps. "I thought I heard you scream."

"Cold water," I said, projecting my voice toward the stairs. "I'm fine. Almost done."

I rinsed my face with another splash of icy water, then darted into my room and swapped the wet sweatshirt for the first dry top I saw and beetled back to the first floor.

Davis was in the kitchen. He turned with a jolt, hands stuffed into his pockets.

"Earlier," I said, stuck on something from the previous conversation, "you said you know everyone around here. You can't mean in all of Amherst." Could he? The town had five colleges and dozens of small businesses, not to mention all the year-round residents.

He shrugged, lips downturned. "My dad is deeply involved in the community. You'll find his fingerprints everywhere if you stick around."

I matched his sour expression. I was absolutely staying.

His eyes dropped to my shirt. "Prose before bros." Dark brows crowded above his eyes.

I looked down at the text and familiar female silhouette on my torso. "It's Emily Dickinson. I'm a big fan."

Davis's mouth opened, and a small dry laugh escaped. A complement to his defeated expression.

"*ED* is for Emily Dickinson," he said.

I narrowed my eyes. "Yeah. So?"

"You don't own Rini Reads."

"No. Well, not yet. My parents do now, but I'm not sure what's happening when I get home." I bit the insides of my cheeks to keep from saying more.

Davis rubbed a giant hand over his face and moved toward the front door. "I've got to go."

My eyes landed on the refrigerator and my to-do list, trapped beneath a magnet. Was that what he'd been reading when I'd returned?

1. Journal
2. Read
3. Write poetry
4. Connect with myself
5. Bake
6. Garden
7. Embrace the solitude
8. Become my best Emily
9. Be happy
10. Give up on love

I let my head fall forward, silently cursing my life; then I rushed after him. "Where are you going?"

"Home." He was already on the porch when I caught up.

Why did he keep walking away like that?

Why did I keep chasing him?

"Well, thank you," I said. "I feel as if I should give you something for your help. I would've frozen tonight without it. Are you sure I can't at least make you a cup of tea or coffee?" Maybe clear up how he knew my dad and why he seemed so irritated and baffled.

He turned, and I deflated as a realization came to mind.

"I actually don't have coffee." I hadn't been to the market, but there was tea in the kitchen. "But there's plenty of cold water," I joked.

Davis lifted a hand, then climbed into the cab of his truck.

I stared as he performed a three-point turn and drove away.

Chapter Five

I woke to the sensation of warm morning sun on my cheek and smiled. I had nowhere to be, no one expecting me to do anything, and no cell service to interrupt my peace.

I was a character in a storybook. A woman of leisure.

I dressed in a short-sleeved peasant top and faded capri jeans, then wrapped a cardigan around my shoulders and carried a cup of tea and a book to the back patio. The brick pavers felt cool beneath my fuzzy socks, and I pulled my feet onto the chair with me. Dew clung to the grass, shielded by shade trees, and fog hovered over the distant fields like an apparition. Fall was shoving away the remnants of summer inch by inch, making nights colder and shortening the days. It was my favorite time of year.

I closed my eyes to absorb the precious moment.

This was the official beginning of my new, happier future.

The words of one of Emily's poems danced and twirled in my thoughts.

> There is no Frigate like a Book
> To take us Lands away

I opened my eyes, took a few more sips of tea, then relocated to the study. I sat at the little desk with a biography about Emily's life I'd brought with me, and began to read. When I'd finished my tea and felt properly inspired, I made my first entry in my journal.

I jotted the date at the top of the page, then made a list of things I could do today.

1. Explore the grounds
2. Read
3. Try my hand at poetry
4. Start a garden
5. Walk to the bookshop and thank Grace for her kind note and care basket
6. Do not mention burning the gifted stationery
7. Do not ask for details about her nephew or his relationship status

I wouldn't stick this list on the refrigerator.

I pressed the memories of Davis's clear gray eyes from my mind, along with the strange, crackling tension I'd felt in his presence. A result of the old Emma's lifelong focus on finding love, no doubt.

"Out with the old," I said, giving a dramatic swing of one hand. "In with the new." I studied my list. "Now. What will I do first?"

It was barely 9:00 a.m., and I was restless. Itching to get busy somehow. I returned to the book at my side, eager to check reading off my list when I finished.

I skimmed the opening pages about Emily's family. I'd always struggled with the fact Emily wasn't especially close to either of her parents. She cared deeply about so many things. I wished that she'd been close with her mom or her dad. Sadder still, she lived in the family home until she died of a stroke at age fifty-five. I cringed. That was six years younger than my parents, which was far too young.

Emily had a younger sister named Lavinia, whom she often called Vinnie. Their personalities were drastically different, much like Annie's and mine.

Maybe all sisters had some points of contention.

I turned the page, moving on to the attachment Emily had to her older brother, Austin, and her deep and abiding friendship with Austin's wife, Sue, to whom Emily had written more than two hundred fifty letters.

My thoughts moved easily to Cecily, and I reached for my phone. Then I remembered I'd have to walk down the lane if I wanted to text her.

I pursed my lips and carried on. A moment later, I grinned at the mention of Emily's favorite book, Charlotte Brontë's *Jane Eyre*. "Just one more thing we have in common," I told the pages.

I closed the book when I reached the end of the chapter.

The manor was far too quiet.

The silence a weight on my chest and shoulders. Grace hadn't put that in the brochure.

I let my thoughts drift to Annie, hating the way life had come between us somehow and wishing I knew how to fix it. I'd stepped in to care for her when she was a toddler. When Mom had been too sick and exhausted from chemo treatments herself, and Dad had been forced by medical bills and a mortgage to go back to the bookstore and work. Distracting Annie, dressing her, feeding her, and combing her hair, along with a dozen other chores, had become my responsibility. Even at ten years old, I'd known I couldn't cure Mom's cancer. But I could keep my little sister happy so Mom had one less thing to worry about. And that was what I'd done.

Jeffrey's mention of Annie's upcoming early-morning doctor's appointment returned to mind, along with her overreaction about my absence. I had no way of knowing if those things added up to something, or if I was just a nervous auntie. Not that it mattered. I'd have to wait and see what happened, because Annie wasn't big on sharing with me these days.

I turned back to the list in my journal and suddenly knew exactly what I needed to do next. Like with Annie's pregnancy, the clock counted down my time here, and that meant I had to move quickly if I wanted a garden. Thankfully, I'd seen a small nursery on my way into town.

I stuffed my feet into comfy sneakers, then grabbed my sunglasses, purse, cell phone, and keys.

My first official Emily-themed Amherst adventure was underway.

꧁❦꧂

The Seeds of Love nursery was only two miles away, situated on a property speckled with goats, chickens, and sheep. I parked in the small lot and walked around a sprawling white farmhouse toward a series of greenhouses in back. Other shoppers pulled wagons with flats of flowers, mulch, and topsoil. Some carried baskets with bags of birdseed or succulents. All seemed delighted to be there.

I ventured into the first greenhouse and scanned the rows of leafy plants and fully bloomed flowers, unsure where to start. The cactus I'd had in college eventually turned brown and died. So when Annie gifted me a small succulent for my desk at home, I'd watered it dutifully for two months before she caught me and told me it was plastic. I wasn't a plant lady. At least, not yet.

An older woman in denim overalls and red rubber boots smiled in my direction.

"Good morning," I said, probably looking as lost as I felt.

She swung an empty basket onto the crook of one arm and headed my way. "Good morning. Can I help you find anything?" Her voice was soft and kind. Her heavily freckled skin tan from the sun. Defiant tendrils of long silver hair curled down from beneath the hat. "I'm Olivia Love. This is my nursery."

I smiled, the name of her business sounding infinitely sweeter. "Emma," I said. "I'd like to plant a small garden, but I'm only in town for six weeks. I'm not sure where to begin, or if it's too late in the season."

Olivia tipped her head over one shoulder, a pleasant expression on her rosy cheeks. "Absolutely not. In fact, September is prime planting time for a number of herbs, veggies, and flower bulbs. You won't get the benefit of the bulbs until next spring, but planting them now would be like leaving a surprise, or a little gift, for whoever comes after you."

I imagined a flower garden rising in the spring, where none had existed before, and what Grace would think of the blooms. Would she realize I'd planted them? Or see them as a sign of hope and love from the universe? Both possibilities warmed my heart. The idea of paying her back for the lifeline she'd unknowingly offered widened my smile. "I want to do that."

"Let's see what I've got." Olivia led me to the next greenhouse, waving to shoppers and seeming to evaluate every plant we passed. "So, tell me, Emma. Why are you leaving so soon? Just changing residences in town, or is Amherst not for you?"

"I'm vacationing," I said. "Hoping to reboot my life. Embrace the solitude and history while I'm here."

She nodded. "Then you've come to the right place. But I have to warn you, life here can be addictive. We've got everything from farms to nightlife."

"You do," I agreed, loving the tone she used when speaking of her town. "I attended UMass as a commuter about twelve years ago," I said. "I live and work in Willow Bend." In some ways, being back in Amherst felt comfortable and familiar. Mostly, however, being in town as an adult, and at my leisure, was like seeing the place for the first time. Or at least through a different lens.

I dragged my fingertips over the fuzzy green leaves of a stout plant, admiring Olivia's peaceful ease. I was on edge when I worked at the bookstore. Too many things to do and too little time to accomplish it all. Managing a busy store was exciting, but the burdens had erased my joy from the work. And though I was surrounded by people all day, I still felt lonely.

The clarity in those thoughts shook me a little. I'd never given myself time to think of how I really felt about my work. I enjoyed the busyness and satisfaction of a job well done, but I hadn't actually enjoyed running the shop in a long time. I loved the customers, but they came for the books, not me. Not for the first time, I thought how nice it would be to have a dog to keep me company and greet customers. A big lug to lay around and make guests smile.

"I love plants," Olivia said, returning me to the moment as we lingered in an aisle of small green sprouts. "I'm a third-generation farmer. My family has worked this land for a hundred and eighteen years. I think there might be fertilizer in my soul."

I laughed and she winked. "I grew up surrounded by romance novels," I said. "I was raised on Brontë and Austen instead of Dr. Seuss and Judy Blume. Though I got to those eventually. My parents can be snobs about literature."

"They wanted to share their favorites with you. That's how people are. We share what we love with the people we love." She led me to a row of small potted plants. "I've got radishes, turnips, beets, and carrots already growing, which are perfect since you're short on time. You can transfer these to your garden with some quality topsoil and keep your eyes on them. You'll see produce in a few weeks, as long as you protect them from insects and animals." She set a few pots into her basket. "Flowers like chrysanthemums, asters, and zinnias will be your friends right about now too. Just transfer them, same as the veggies. And we'll grab a few bags of bulbs from the rack near the register."

I followed her up and down the aisles. She made gardening sound simple and beautiful. A magical experience anyone could have.

I couldn't wait to get started.

"Oh. I forgot to ask about your budget." She turned to me with tented brows. "I get carried away."

"It's okay." I waved a hand between us. "I budgeted for this." And I'd kept an eye on everything she picked up. So far, nothing came close to breaking the bank.

Her shoulders drooped in relief.

"I appreciate the thought," I said. "Plus, I feel as if I'm getting a free degree in horticulture just listening to you."

She blushed slightly as she headed toward a cash register. "If you have any questions when you get home, just let me know. My contact information is on our website, so you won't have to drive all the way back here."

"I appreciate that, but I'm only a couple of miles away, and the place I'm renting doesn't have Wi-Fi, so you might wind up seeing a lot of me."

Olivia finished the transaction with a curious look in her eyes. "You're not the guest at Hearthstone Manor, are you?"

"I am."

She looked delighted. "Grace Forsythe is one of my oldest and dearest friends. She mentioned meeting you a few months ago when you picked up some books for a wedding."

"My parents' vow renewal," I said. "I wish I could've spoken with her a little longer that day, but there was a line at her register, and I had to hurry home to relieve my folks at our store. I hope she didn't think I was rude for racing away."

"Quite the opposite." Olivia's eyes twinkled. "She told everyone how lovely you were."

"I feel the same about her. That was the first I'd met her in person, but she's always been one of my favorites in our group. We have a lot in common."

Olivia pursed her lips, and the apples of her cheeks grew pink, as if holding back a smile. "Is that right?"

"It really is. Especially our love of Sam."

A mass of clouds skated over the sun, cooling my skin and the air.

Olivia passed the basket to me with a frown. "Who?"

"The UMass mascot. Sam the Minuteman. We've been making jokes at the poor guy's expense for at least three years, but we love him,"

I explained. "It's fun finding other ladies who love football. My mom, sister, and I are diehards."

"I do my best to root for the home teams and turn up at homecoming events, but . . ." She shrugged.

"You prefer plants," I said.

Ten minutes later, she waved when I climbed behind the wheel as if we were old friends. "You can leave the plants outside when you get home. No need to rush getting them planted. Looks like rain."

I smiled, buckled up, and turned on my phone, daring a peek at my missed messages.

My phone came alive with a string of chirps and dings, notifications populating like popcorn in the fifteen hours or so since I'd shut the device off at the manor.

I greedily devoured everything I'd missed. Notes, memes, and anecdotes from online friends and communities. Likes, hearts, and comments on my personal social media accounts and the bookstore's page. Everyone loved the new window display, including Historically_ Bookish, and my chest puffed with pride.

A dozen texts from Cecily waited.

My smile grew as I scrolled through the messages, reading her questions about the drive to Amherst and the manor. But it was her intense frustration with *Relatable Romance*, an obviously scripted television show billed as reality, that brought tears to my eyes. As a former theater nerd, I enjoyed the terrible acting posed as improv. But as a devout history buff, Cecily became frequently unhinged over errors in cultural context or wardrobe. The show continually changed locations, and sometimes eras, attempting to stand out among its competitors—i.e., *The Bachelor* and *Big Brother*—but they often failed.

The phone rang before I could finish wiping my eyes.

Cecily's name and number appeared on the screen.

"Hello, you nut," I said. "I was just reading all your texts."

"It's coming to Massachusetts," she said, breathless, and skipping all manner of greeting. "And that fan site, *Relatable Romance* Reporter, says next season will be a special Regency-era production." A wild and youthful squeal pealed through the speaker, and I cracked up all over again.

I listened as she caught her breath. "I'm okay," she said. "I'm pulling myself together now."

"Oh yeah?"

"Mm-hmm, and I want to hear everything about your major life change and recent relocation before we talk about a silly television show. I just had to get that little fangirl moment out of my system."

"I like your fangirl moments," I said. "Besides, that show usually makes you homicidal. I'm glad they're finally doing something right." Hopefully they'd get the details correct for the Massachusetts episodes. Cecily loved the Regency era. If they messed it up, she'd probably drive to the set, and I'd need to come up with bail money to get her out of whatever trouble she caused.

She made a deep, throaty noise. "First tell me about your trip."

I grinned, watching folks walk to and from the nursery, holding hands or babies and towing their wagons full of plants. "Well, my parents are stressed about taking over full time at the shop again, but they're trying. Annie came to see me off, and she didn't stick gum in my hair when she hugged me goodbye, so that was another win. The drive was long and boring. The house is great. My handyman is a hunk. Obviously sent by fate to distract me from my mission, but I shall persevere. Oh! And I just bought a bunch of plants to start a garden. Now. Back to you. *Relatable Romance* is coming to Massachusetts?"

"Yes!" Cecily was quiet for a long beat. "We're circling back to the handyman."

"Okay."

"I think I'm going to apply to the show as an adviser. They want locals with significant familiarity in various categories including local history and the community. I set up notifications so I can jump when they make the official announcement for *Relatable Romance: Regency Era*. I'll play up my lifelong residency in Massachusetts, plus the fact I nearly graduated with a history degree before I realized I wanted to go into nursing."

It'd taken Cecily nearly two extra years to finish her nursing degree, but she'd come alive in those classes, and I'd loved watching the change. These days, anyone listening to her talk about her job could understand why she wasn't worried about finding her soulmate. She was already in love. With her work.

"Also," she continued, "I'm the perfect candidate after working at four different local museums and volunteering at dozens of reenactments. Plus, who wouldn't want a registered trauma nurse on set, with all those intoxicated twentysomethings drinking twelve hours a day?"

All excellent points. "You're overqualified," I said.

The soft tapping of her fingers on a nearby keyboard echoed over the line. "Noted. I wonder if I should ask one of my old professors for a reference, or maybe someone from one of the museums?"

"Both," I said. "This is a once-in-a-lifetime opportunity. Go all in. Sounds like you might get to live like Jane Austen after all," I teased. She'd said she'd never want that, when I'd mentioned my plan to become Emily, but perhaps the right opportunity just hadn't revealed itself.

"That's not why I want to do this," she said. "I just want to work behind the scenes on a show I've watched for years. I want to know how the pudding's made. And speaking of snacks, tell me more about this hunky handyman."

I grinned. "It's completely cliché. I came here to start fresh, but my brain wants to keep up old patterns that don't work for me. Then, boom. A six-foot temptation. I can practically hear the voice-over asking how I will possibly resist."

"First, wanting to fall in love and find a life partner isn't just an old pattern. It's been your dream for as long as I've known you. And second, how will you resist?"

I snorted a short laugh. She was right about my previous long-standing dream, but that was the problem. Most of my relationships that lasted more than a month should've ended inside a week. I'd made excuses and accommodations for bad behaviors, all in the name of remaining open minded. I was patient when they were moody and short tempered, accepting when they were habitually late, and I'd dutifully provided the princess treatment to every single frog. Thankfully I'd since learned there was a difference between staying open minded and being a willing doormat. "Regardless. When an unfulfilled desire starts to hurt, it's time to reevaluate," I said. "Otherwise, the whole thing is unhealthy. Which is why I came here, to recharge and redirect my path. In fact, I plan to spend the rest of my day knuckle-deep in mulch, dirt, and topsoil. And I just learned dirt and topsoil aren't the same. Look at me growing."

Cecily was quiet again, and this time I could almost see her frown. "What?" she asked.

"Plants won't thrive in dirt, but topsoil has natural organic matter that's good for vegetation." When she didn't reply, I added, "I'm gardening."

"Why?"

"I told you. Emily Dickinson was a fantastic gardener, and pursuing this hobby is a great way for me to stay busy at the manor. By myself. After all the plants are in the ground and I'm cleaned up, I plan to journal about my experiences."

"Right," she said slowly, drawing the word out for several syllables. "For the record, I still think this is a bad idea. I mean, I get what you think you're doing, but you're not a recluse. You're not even shy. You'll lose your mind gardening and writing in journals for entertainment. At least have a little fun while you're there. Enjoy the time off. Refuel. Whatever you need, but please kiss the hot handyman and send me details."

I barked an unexpected laugh. "Definitely not going to do that last thing, but I plan to have lots of fun refueling and learning to be happy as an eternally single spinster. I might even find a few cats to adopt."

"No," she said flatly. Then, "Next topics. When can I come visit? And why didn't you respond to my messages sooner? I've been waiting on pins and needles to tell you about the show."

"You'll never believe it." I filled her in on the lack of cell signal and internet at the manor; then we agreed she'd visit as soon as she got two consecutive days off work. Until then, we'd exchange letters, like Emily and Sue. I'd keep her posted about life as an 1850s poet, and she'd fill me in on her application progress with *Relatable Romance: Regency Era*.

The moment we said our goodbyes and disconnected, my phone rang.

"Hey, Mom," I answered brightly. "I was just going to call you."

I activated the phone's speaker option, then eased away from my parking spot and veered onto the road, eager to drop off the plants and make a trip to the grocery store. My stomach was beginning to growl, and the breakfast bar in my glove box wasn't going to sustain me.

"Hon," she said, a note of relief and reprimand in the single syllable. "Why is it so hard to reach you? I worried last night when you didn't let us know you'd arrived safely."

"I'm fine. The manor doesn't have internet or cell signal," I said. I hadn't even noticed a landline anywhere for emergencies. "How are you and Dad? Did everything go okay when you opened the shop this morning?"

"We're on our way there now," she said. "We stopped to see Annie for breakfast, then visited that little coffee shop I love near the park. Your dad is buying some flowers for the counter."

I checked my watch as Village Books appeared up ahead; then I slowed to make the turn. "It's nearly ten. You haven't been to the store yet? Did one of the aunts open for you?"

"We didn't think it was necessary," Mom said. "We'll be there any minute."

I blinked. Stunned. People stopped at the store on their way to work. Moms, who'd probably been up since dawn, brought kids in strollers, and people who met for breakfast came inside afterward to browse. Surely my parents knew this. Surely they cared.

"We've got it covered," she said. "Don't worry. What's important is that you're enjoying yourself. Are you enjoying yourself?"

I cringed, pulling onto the gravel lane. I'd felt better before we started the conversation.

The SUV rocked gently toward the manor while I fumed at my mom's apparent disinterest in the success of her own business.

When had I swapped roles with her without noticing? When had I become the store owner and she the employee?

Why did my parents asking me to take over so they could retire suddenly feel like a betrayal instead of an honor?

"You know," Mom said, her voice beginning to break up, "you didn't have to move out of town to get some time off. We would've stepped in more often, if we'd known you needed us. But you never said a word."

I jammed the brake pedal, stopping the SUV before I lost signal, and flinched at her implication. As if my feelings of professional abandonment were of my own making. "I was trying to do a good job," I said. "I didn't want you to worry."

"And you're doing a terrific job. You're always amazing at everything you do. We never worry when you're in charge, and we appreciate you so much. I feel as if you don't know that, and I can't for the life of me understand why."

An unexpected pinch of emotion drew tears to my eyes. "Sorry. Thank you." Then another thought occurred. "Hey—do you or Dad know a man named Davis Sommers?"

"I don't think so," she said, then repeated my question to Dad. "No. Doesn't ring a bell to us. Why do you ask?"

I flipped mentally through my bizarre and frustrating conversation with Davis the night before. "I met him last night and got the impression he knew Dad." Hadn't he said as much?

What had he said exactly?

"Emma," Mom cooed. "Why don't you come back? Talk to us about whatever you're going through. Let us help. We want to be here for you."

Part of me longed to accept the offer, admit everyone was right, and go home. But then I'd end up right back where I was before I left. Miserable and aching for something that wasn't meant for me. And I couldn't spend another minute like that. I wouldn't. So the dramatic part of me, the one Annie had called out, lifted her chin and doubled down on her mission.

The beautiful manor beckoned to me from the end of the lane. Its floral wreath and cobblestone walkway begged me to run inside and shut the door, locking out my every care. I imagined staying forever, basking in warm sunlight on lush green lawns and raising flowers to make fresh bouquets for the vase in the foyer. In those images, I was content, unhurried, and happy. Alone.

I inhaled deeply and straightened in my seat. "Thank you for saying all that, Mom, but I have to go. I love you. Tell Dad I love him too. I'll write you a letter soon."

"But—"

"Take care of yourselves," I interrupted. "And keep me posted about Annie and the baby. If you need anything, or if there's an emergency, you can reach me through Grace at Village Books. The number is on the website, or reach out to her on IBOOM."

Mom blurted a hasty goodbye, sending her love in a flourish before I disconnected the call.

I watched the bars of service disappear as I drove the rest of the way down the lane; then I slipped the device into my pocket and got out. I unloaded the cumbersome bags of mulch and topsoil from my hatch, hating that they were wet and heavy, not to mention incredibly awkward to haul. But at least the effort kept my mind off my mom's words, begging me to come home. It was too soon for me to give up. I hadn't been gone a full twenty-four hours, and she hadn't even made it to the shop.

My previously ivory peasant top was streaked with mulch and top-soil by the time I reached for the final bag, and I forced my thoughts away.

"Today is the first day of my new forever," I reminded myself. I'd had a couple of setbacks last night, but that was then, and this was now.

A clap of distant thunder drew my eyes skyward as I recalled Olivia's warning. I squared my shoulders, steadfast and unbothered by a little rain. I had plenty to do inside, and weeks to plant my garden. This was my time to shine.

A fat drop of rain promptly plunked my forehead, interrupting my moment of self-empowerment.

Then the heavy bag ripped, pouring black mulch down the front of me and onto my shoes.

"Great."

Chapter Six

Rain threatened to keep me indoors the rest of the day, but I persevered, walking the grounds, then went into town during a break between showers. I enjoyed a leisurely lunch under the protection of a maroon-and-white-striped café awning. The street-facing patio tables provided a lovely view of Amherst while I sat, unconcerned with the time.

The weather had slowed traffic, but it hadn't stopped people from enjoying the afternoon. Everyone seemed so young and carefree.

I thought of Emily's poetry, too, as I sat alone at the table, her words dancing in my mind. Emily loved life, but she knew loneliness despite a vibrant family and the many connections all around her.

It was believed that Emily spoke of her own loneliness in her writing, and that she, like me, wondered if she'd only feel worse if she gave up the only life she knew. I'd traveled to another town, hoping to give up on the epic love I'd always wanted. But part of me wondered if resigning myself to eternal singledom by choice would leave me in a worse condition than when I'd started.

"I hear you, Emily," I whispered into the rain as I headed back home.

I popped into Village Books before going to the manor, immediately overcome by the enticing scents of warm cinnamon and apple cider. A display table just inside the door held a little sign beside a hot drink dispenser, cups, and napkins, saying, PLEASE HELP YOURSELF. I cheerfully obeyed. "Don't mind if I do."

The shop's interior was gorgeous, open, and inviting, with a front wall of windows and wide whitewashed floorboards. Reclaimed-wood slats hung from the walls, working through their retirement as decorative shelves, displaying framed black-and-white images of Amherst over the years. Aisles of books filled the shop's center.

I passed several shoppers enjoying their free drink and a good book. Some lingered by the shelves. Others sat in comfy armchairs near the wall.

Two long tables were positioned near a stack of wooden cubbies at the back of the store, where I imagined demonstrations and classes took place.

"Pardon," I said, slipping past a pair of young women huddled around a display of classic literature. I couldn't help overhearing them as I slid into the next aisle.

"Is this the poet who lived in Amherst?" one asked.

"I don't know," the other responded.

I looked over my shoulder at the book in question, then turned back to stick my nose where it didn't belong.

"Hi," I said, using my most pleasant tone and smile. "Sorry. I'm not trying to interfere, but I heard your question, and I think I know the answer."

They stilled and stared.

"This poet wasn't from Amherst," I said, pushing ahead. "I think you're looking for Robert Frost. He and Emily Dickinson both lived in town. This is Walt Whitman." I pointed a finger toward the book they'd been inspecting. "*Leaves of Grass* is a fantastic collection, but this guy lived in New York and New Jersey."

The girls smiled, and I breathed easier. "Thank you!" they said, returning the book to the shelf. "Do you have any Robert Frost collections here?"

"Uh." I glanced around, nonplussed by their assumption and not wanting to accidentally step on an actual employee's toes. "I don't know. This is only my second time in the store. I just know a lot about poetry."

"Oh." The duo looked me over more carefully. "Do you write?" one asked.

I grimaced. "Not well."

"Hello there." Grace appeared. "I work here," she said. "We have a number of Frost's collections over there." She pointed, and the young women took their leave. "If we don't have what you're looking for, we can order it," she called after them. "Just let me know."

Next, she turned her bright eyes on me. "Emma," she said. "I'm so glad you're here."

"I'm glad to be here," I said, smiling as if I'd just won the lottery. In a way, I supposed I had. One of my favorite online friends stood right in front of me, and I could finally thank her in person for all the times she'd made me laugh when I wanted to scream or cry. Or all the times she'd saved me from telling a book distributor where to stick their outrageous return policies.

Her expression lit up, and wrinkles gathered on her cheeks and forehead as she pulled me into a hug. "We didn't get to chat long enough last time. Today I'm not in any hurry."

I nearly melted at her touch. I missed hugs, and it had only been a day since my last.

"I'm sorry I wasn't here to greet you last night," she said. "I considered popping by this morning on my way to open the store, but I thought you might want to sleep in. Then I spoke with Davis, and he said you wanted privacy, so I was hesitant to come knocking at lunch."

I frowned. "I'd love for you to stop by anytime." *Please, please do,* I thought. Even recluses had visitors. And what made Davis think I wouldn't want to see anyone?

"I hear it was a good thing he called on you. Trouble with the fireplace." She smiled apologetically. "I'm sorry about that. But it was lucky timing. He's the one you'll need if anything goes awry."

My cheeks heated at the recollection of my encounter with her nephew, when I'd accidentally filled their beautiful historic family home with smoke. "I loved the welcome basket," I said instead, steering the conversation into more upbeat territory.

"I'm glad," she said. "A few of the local shop owners and I put it together for you. If you need more of anything, I left a list of where the items originated with the stationery."

I pressed my lips, unable to admit I'd burned all the paper. "Would you mind giving me your number, and Davis's, again?"

"Of course!" She tipped her head toward the counter and moved in that direction. "Here's my business card." She plucked one from a holder near the register and scribbled their numbers on the back. "Call anytime you need anything."

"I really appreciate it," I said, placing the card securely into my wallet.

It was odd to hear her speak in person. She never said things like *popping by* or *going awry* online. She sounded more formal in person.

"The property and the home are exactly as the website described." I smiled. "All we need is a hot-wing buffet on game day, and it'll be total perfection."

Her silver brows furrowed. "We have a number of popular places for wings in town. Have you had a chance to get out and explore?"

"A little. I met Olivia during my trip to Seeds of Love."

"Olivia's a dear heart," she said. "One of my favorite humans. But don't let me stop you from shopping. Take your time and let me know if you need anything."

"I will, thank you."

I moved into the aisles and selected several novels I'd been meaning to read for some time. With a little luck, I could lose myself in the stories to pass the long, silent hours of my days.

I carefully curated the stories that would evermore be tied to this adventure and the weeks in Amherst that changed my life.

Some people's lives were marked by songs. An opening chord or favorite lyric took them to another time or place. For me it had always been books.

Eventually, I hefted my load onto the counter, and a young man in a logoed shirt dragged the pile closer and began to ring up my sale. The name on his badge was Michael. "You're staying at Hearthstone?" he asked, catching my eye and smiling.

"I am."

"It's nice, right? We had a holiday party there once for the book-store staff, and it was like a trip to another century."

"It's beautiful," I agreed. "I'm Emma."

"Michael." His smile widened.

I leaned against the counter, curiosity getting the best of me. "What do you know about Grace's nephew? We met last night, and you could say we did not hit it off."

Michael chuckled. "Really? What happened?"

I frowned, recalling our exchange. "I'm not sure. I kind of hoped he's a natural grump—that it wasn't something I did."

Michael said, "As far as I can tell, he likes everyone. Almost every-one," he amended.

"Who are we talking about?" Grace asked, appearing from thin air. She set a small box of inventory on the counter.

Michael went silent, suddenly absorbed by my purchase.

"Davis," I said, attempting to sound innocent and light. Instead of like the prying gossip that I was. "Your note said he's good with a toolbox. Is he a contractor?"

"He's an architect," Michael said, setting the full bag before me. "Like his dad."

My lips parted, but words didn't come.

"And that's not where the similarities end," Grace added. "They're both incredibly smart, driven, and good at what they do. Davis prefers to work with old homes and restorations. His father deals with new builds and commercial properties, along with anything and everything business related in this town."

"They're kind of a thing around here," Michael said.

Grace tipped her head over one shoulder then the other, as if in reluctant agreement.

I tried to fit the semigrouchy man I'd met last night into my idea of a professional and well-known architect.

He did say he knew everyone.

"Oh!" Grace perked. "One more thing." She hurried to a small community board and pulled a flyer from a clip. "This is for our letter-writing class. In case you need a little human interaction." She winked. "Going from running a bookstore to six weeks of solitude must be quite a change."

"You have no idea."

"I think you'll really enjoy it," she said. "We break for the summer, but every September you'll find me with a few regulars and a handful of newcomers right back there." She pointed to the tables in the back. "We're a cross section of folks from all around town. Students, shop owners, café workers, retirees. It's a good mix, and they're great company. We meet several days a week, if you're interested, and class starts this week."

I took the flyer with a smile. "Bless you."

She grinned. "The class has become quite popular. More of a club, really." Pride tinted her tone. "We're very informal. We talk about written communication as a lost art and share famous letters from history. Then we write a few ourselves. You can pop your messages in the mail after class or leave them for one of your classmates. Everyone gets a cubby with their name on it for collecting letters." She pointed to the small wooden cubes I'd noticed earlier. "And there are always cookies."

Guaranteed weekly human interaction sounded like heaven. I'd already planned to write to Cecily and my mom. Plus, inner Emily would surely appreciate the effort. Historians used Emily's letters to learn about her life, especially her reclusive years.

"Count me in," I said.

"Excellent." Grace produced a stack of crisp unlined paper, envelopes, and a pen from beneath the counter and added them to my booty. "These supplies are for class, but you can get started whenever the mood strikes."

"Thank you," I said, accepting the materials. Maybe letter-writing would be my new favorite thing.

Chapter Seven

I went to bed reflecting on my first full day back in Amherst. I'd succeeded at six of my seven list items. I'd read about Emily, explored the grounds, tried poetry, visited Village Books, and avoided mentioning the burned stationery and asking about Davis's relationship status. I hadn't been able to start my garden as planned, but all the plants I'd purchased received a healthy drink, thanks to the rain. As a bonus, my day had been introspective. I'd discovered, for example, that Amherst was a far more vibrant place than I'd thought. In the past I was too distracted by other things, like getting to class on time or watching Annie cheer, to notice much. I'd seen everything through a pinpoint lens. But today I'd learned a little about gardening from Olivia and made a new friend. I'd also realized I was more of a people person than I'd previously imagined, definitely more so than Emily Dickinson, which could poke a hole in my plan to become a recluse. But Grace's letter-writing classes would provide social interaction. Hopefully time and practice would improve my poetry, because I'd also learned I was not a natural poet.

Every attempt I'd made at penning something profound and beautiful, or even rudimentarily observant, had failed. In the end I'd resorted to dirty limericks and the most basic haiku to get something on paper so I could check writing poetry off my list. Emulating Emily Dickinson was proving harder than anticipated in every possible way. But I had to start somewhere, and I was nothing if not tenacious.

Tomorrow I'd work on the tougher items, like number seven, *Embrace the solitude*, number nine, *Be happy*, and ten, *Give up on love*.

✦

I woke early the next morning, teeth chattering and every muscle in my body clenched against the cold. The old stone home seemed to insulate against the warm afternoon sunlight and leak any heat provided by the furnace. I took the blankets with me when I rose and went hunting for the thermostat. I found it set to fifty-eight degrees.

"For the love of—" I cranked the wheel on the ancient device, only stopping when the little arrow pointed to seventy.

A primal, exhausted moan rumbled through the old house. Vents rattled inside the walls. Slowly delivering and circulating the distinctly dry scent of an aging system.

I scrunched my nose and glanced around. "Just keep it warm for forty more days, and we'll get along fine."

I made some coffee and contemplated how to spend my day. Thankfully the rain had stopped, and Grace's first letter-writing class was this morning. I just had to pass a few hours before going to the bookstore. After that, I'd tackle the garden, or visit Emily Dickinson's house. I couldn't wait to walk the halls where she'd lived. The thought sent goose bumps down my arms.

First I'd journal about my feelings, dump the chaos from my brain onto the page. Had leaving Willow Bend been the right thing to do? Was it selfish? Would I adjust to the silence in the manor, or would I start talking to a volleyball before my time was up here?

I selected a piece of thick paper from the materials Grace had given me, then loaded an ink cartridge into the pen she'd provided and immediately discovered I had no idea how to make it write. And I couldn't google it. No internet. I sighed to recenter myself, enjoyed a little more coffee, and tried again.

Finding the correct angle for the metal tip against the page was an ordeal, but eventually a thick line of ink appeared as I pulled the instrument down. A win! When I swept upward, however, attempting to form the rest of the single letter I'd started—no ink. I shook the pen and tried again. No ink. I pushed harder and scratched the paper.

"Nope." I rose from my chair. "Not today, Satan," I said, walking away, chin held high. I would not begin my day being defeated by a pen.

I dressed in jeans, sneakers, and a light sweater, then parted my hair down the center and twisted my curls into braids. By the time I'd applied a little mascara and lip gloss, I was sure it had to be time for class. But only about forty-five minutes had passed.

I returned to the desk in the study and willed myself to feel peaceful and happy.

In reality, I felt frustrated and bored. My thoughts moved quickly, unintentionally, to my family. Everything was changing at home. Everyone was moving into their next stage of life and happiness, while I remained stuck at the same place I'd dwelled for nearly a decade. I'd been living in a personalized episode of *Groundhog Day* since college graduation. And every year, my world became smaller, more hyperfocused on the store. My friends had fallen away over time, pairing off and getting married, like Annie. Starting families. Relocating for jobs. My entire reality centered on a single building where I worked and lived. Where I'd spent the better part of my entire life. I'd lost more than one perfectly good boyfriend over the years by prioritizing the store or my family over him. Amir Devi came instantly to mind. If I could've built a life with any of my exes, it was Amir. He had been open and ready for a partnership. I'd been distrusting after a particularly bad breakup several months before. When he'd invited me on a trip over the holidays, I'd declined, because I had to work. Christmas was Rini Reads' busiest season, and I didn't want to let my family down. When he'd encouraged me to push back after a fight with Annie, I'd turned on him and taken her side. When he'd begged me to choose him, or to at least choose myself once in a while, and see where the relationship between us might go, I'd thought him overbearing, then cried as he walked away.

The possibility that my very full and busy life was actually as lonely as Emily's reclusive one shook me. I searched my mental archives of her work to find a soothing verse or line, then opened my notebook.

Success is counted sweetest
By those who ne'er succeed.

When I thought of spending six weeks alone in the manor, isolated and freezing, only to return home unchanged and still searching for love, I wanted to scream.

I had to succeed.

I faced off with the blue lines on the page, with a normal, modern pen in hand, determined to win this battle. My muscles tensed and brow crunched, but no words appeared.

I rolled my shoulders, then shook my hands out hard at the wrists. Maybe I was making this too difficult. Overthinking. I'd start with another haiku. It'd been my default style in writing courses when poetry was assigned. Three lines. Five syllables, then seven, then five. I had to start somewhere, then hope to grow.

I am no poet, I began. Then counted syllables: one, two, three, four, five. *Though I hope to be,* I wrote, then counted. One, two, three, four, five. Not enough. I ran a line through the words and started again. *I long to be like Emily,* I tried. Eight syllables: too long. I tapped my pen against the page and checked the wall clock, which I suspected was broken. An eternity later, I finished my poem, exhausted.

I am no poet
Hopefully I'll someday find
My talents elsewhere

I dropped my head onto the desk.

Maybe morning exercise was the answer. I stood and stretched, practiced mindful breathing and a few yoga poses, then went outside to get some sun. All healthy, solitary activities. None took more than a few minutes.

Suddenly I understood why the average person died so young in Emily's days. Time passed differently when there wasn't anything to do. Someone who reached my age had probably already endured eighty-five years' worth of time.

I went back inside and returned to my book on Emily's life, determined to understand her, to truly connect. The book made her life seem dull and grim, a popular take on the subject. History regularly painted her as averse to people, obsessed with death, and more than a bit sad. Not the image I held of her, or the one I wanted. Emily saw beauty in the world. Her writing proved as much. She valued love, family, and friendship. Her heart was pure and open, the way I wanted mine to be.

My bag of novels from Village Books caught my eye, and I switched gears. I needed something light to improve my mood before class, so I closed my eyes, reached in, and pulled out my next read. A story of lifelong best friends fulfilling a childhood promise to open a historic bed-and-breakfast together in Cape May. Two dozen chapters, a lot of laughs, and a round of tears later, the grandfather clock in the foyer announced it was time to go.

I filled my favorite canvas tote with the supplies Grace had given me and a pair of ballpoint pens and hurried to Village Books. Shoppers lingered in aisles and lined up at the checkout. Others had gathered near the wooden cubbies and the long rectangular tables in the back.

Michael waved to me from the register. "You made it!"

"I did," I agreed, thankful for the friendly face. "Fancy seeing you here again."

"You'll find me here nearly as often as you find Grace," he said. "Are you ready for class?"

I looked at the gathering letter writers and bit my lip. "I hope so."

A customer approached the register, setting me free to join the others, and I lifted a hand to Michael in goodbye.

A man carrying a cup of coffee paused when he noticed me. His shy smile put me instantly at ease. "Are you here for the letter-writing class?" he asked.

I smiled and nodded. "I'm new."

"I'm Paul," he said, offering me his hand. He was tall and lean, probably only a few years older than me. His grip was nice, warm, and gentle.

"Emma."

"Emma," he repeated. "Are you new to the area? Or just new to the class?"

"Both, I guess. I'm in town for an extended vacation," I explained.

"In that case," he said, swinging an open palm toward the refreshments, "let's get you a cup of coffee and introduce you to everyone. It's always good to have a few friends in a new land."

I followed Paul to the refreshments table and watched while he poured me a cup of coffee. His congenial disposition was a welcomed change from the grumpy handyman who'd helped me build a fire.

"Where are you from?" he asked, as we settled in with a cluster of men and women around our age.

"Willow Bend." I smiled when a few of the people nodded in recognition. "I run my family's bookstore."

"I think it's safe to say you've found your people." Paul adjusted the glasses on his nose. "We're all a little bookish here."

❧

Grace approached the group a moment later with an affectionate grin, trading hugs and air-kisses with the folks I'd just met.

Slowly, everyone settled into their seats.

"Welcome, class," Grace said sweetly, moving to the head of the table. "I'm glad, as always, to see so many familiar faces, and I'm delighted to see a few new ones as well. This is my Lost Art of Letter-Writing class, where we get back to the pretexting, preinternet, and pre-instant-messaging times of ole and actually write our thoughts on paper to communicate with others." She clasped her hands before her and widened her eyes, as if to say "Imagine that!"

"In a time when messages are everywhere," she continued, "posted on social media for all the world to see, or thrown into a tweet, this class will help you focus on writing what's important and what it is you truly long to say. You can't backspace or even erase, so you should think carefully about what you intend to convey, then say exactly that. If you make a mistake that can't be overlooked or eliminated satisfactorily by drawing a single line through it, you'll have to get a new piece of paper and start over. A letter full of scribbles and black marks is a no-no. The message won't be received in the same way as a letter that was clearly written after careful thought. Keep that in mind before you begin. Now, for today's inspiration."

She lifted a sheet of paper in one hand and positioned glasses on her nose with the other. "I'm going to give you some food for thought from author John Steinbeck, often called a giant of American letters. He wrote this letter to his son, Thom, in response to Thom's letter from boarding school announcing he'd fallen in love."

Grace offered a warm smile to the class. "Love is something we can all understand, whether romantic, platonic, or the sort we have for family. Love is the little silver thread connecting all of humanity, around the globe, century to century, forevermore."

My heart sank and stomach tightened. Whatever I'd expected from letter-writing class, it hadn't been to discuss love, the exact thing I was in Amherst to denounce.

"Steinbeck begins with a greeting, of course, and then jumps right into the good stuff. He tells his son that being in love is a good thing, maybe the best thing, and he tells him not to let anyone ever make light of that. Then, he issues a warning about the sorts of people who wield love like a weapon, who are unkind and use the attachment to control their partners or break them down. But the right kind of love, that sort that comes from all that is good in oneself and based on true respect for their partner, will lift you to new heights of confidence, strength, and wisdom."

Grace paused to let us process the words. A classmate or two jotted something down. I waited, invested and eager. She raised the paper, and my breath caught in anticipation. The immortal romantic in me danced, giddy for more. "He goes on to say love should be reveled in. Rejoiced in and deeply, truly appreciated."

Grace dragged her hand down the page, letting the top portion of the printed work droop backward as she skimmed.

I found myself thinking of Steinbeck as more than a Nobel Prize–winning author. He'd been a regular person with a life and a family. A father giving advice on love.

"Here we are," she continued. "Another fatherly bit of advice. Sometimes people find themselves in love with someone who doesn't return their affections, but that does not invalidate the feeling, because it is always beautiful to love. And as a final note, Steinbeck reminds his son that his words come from a place of understanding, because he, too, is in love, and he's quite happy that his son has found this great joy."

She set the paper down and searched our expressions. "Steinbeck loved. His son loved. They loved romantically. They loved one another. Love is powerful, crippling, and motivating. But always universal. So"—she set the paper aside and clasped her hands—"let love be your inspiration this week. Write to someone you love. Write about someone you love. Write with love. Your choice. Take a deep breath. Think. Then write."

Several classmates went to work immediately.

I stared, unsure how I could muster anything good enough to follow Steinbeck.

Eventually Annie came to mind, and I began to write. The words were casual at first, like a diary entry, then too formal. I crumbled the sheets and started again, this time writing to my parents. It didn't take long before my hostility over a million small offenses stopped me mid-sentence. I balled that page up as well.

The woman on my right sighed. "Why is this so much harder than it should be?"

"Right?" I rolled my eyes, then lowered my forehead to the table briefly.

"Is this your first class?" she asked.

I puffed my cheeks as I straightened. "Yep."

She smiled. "Me too. I'm Daisy."

We fell into an easy rhythm, writing for a few minutes, then taking breaks to complain, refresh our drinks, or get to know one another a little more. Daisy was Annie's age and a graduate student at UMass working on her MFA. Her big blue eyes, golden curls, fair skin, and dusting of freckles reminded me of the china dolls my grandmother had collected.

"Did I hear you mention Emily Dickinson?" Daisy asked. "I'm writing my dissertation on her vivid portrayal of nature in prose."

"That's amazing," I said, loving Daisy all the more. "I've been in love with Dickinson's poetry since I was ten. I'm here on a quest, and she's my muse."

Daisy chewed her powder-pink lip. "I love a good quest. How much do you know about Emily?"

"Quite a bit," I admitted. "I've been obsessed with her poetry since I was a kid. I plan to visit her home while I'm in town. Maybe even today."

"Excellent idea. Society tends to romanticize her, but in truth, she was a bit of a weirdo."

An unexpected bark of laughter broke on my lips. I was on the side of society.

Daisy wrinkled her nose. "Sorry. An eccentric?" she tried.

"You're the expert," I said, still smiling. And by most accounts, my life in Willow Bend made me a bit of a weirdo too. Thirty-one and single, spending all my time alone at the bookstore, wishing for something big to happen and hating every day that it didn't.

"So far, the most relatable thing about Emily Dickinson for me is her love of ice cream," Daisy said. "Do you know the story?"

I did, and I searched my memories for the details.

"She rarely left home, but she went to Washington with her father and sister when she was around my age," Daisy said. "He was a member of the Whig Party."

A little zing of electricity carried up my spine. I'd never met anyone else invested in Emily's life. "That's right."

"She had her first taste of ice cream in Washington," Daisy said. "She loved it, which wasn't surprising. She loved all sorts of sweets. Cakes. Doughnuts—"

"And she loved to bake," I said.

Daisy's smile grew. "She went back for more ice cream every day in Washington. I've never related to anyone more."

We laughed, and I lifted my coffee cup in a toast. *To new friends,* I thought. *Thanks, Emily!*

"Who are your letters for?" Daisy asked.

I looked at the growing pile of paper carnage. "Family, but I think it's going to take more than this class period to write anything worth reading."

"I feel that." Daisy checked her watch. "Oops. I have to go—I have class in twenty minutes. But I'll see you back here this week?"

"Absolutely." I waved, then opted to pack up. I needed to give my letters more thought. Anything I said to Annie she would surely use against me, and I didn't know what to say to my parents. Maybe I'd start with a letter to Cecily.

Paul made his way in our direction, stopping at the seat Daisy had vacated. "What'd you think?" he asked. "Is this going to be your new favorite hour of the week?"

"Maybe," I said. "I didn't make any progress today, so I'll be back again soon." According to the schedule, the class met three days a week. I would likely attend them all.

Paul crossed his arms, and his fair brows tented. "Are you a writer?"

"What if I say I love the idea of writing?"

He smiled. "Bookstore manager loves reading and writing. Makes perfect sense to me."

"How about you?" I asked. "What do you do when you aren't here?"

He adjusted round Harry Potter glasses on his narrow nose. "I teach creative nonfiction to bored upperclassmen at the college. The rest of the week I try to recuperate and keep my creative juices flowing."

"Ah," I said. "That makes perfect sense." No one had ever looked more like a professor than Paul.

"It's easy to get stagnant delivering the same material for years." He rocked on his heels, looking slightly embarrassed. "And I'm an oversharer."

I grinned.

Paul dug in his satchel and removed an envelope. "I hope it's not weird, but I wrote a letter for you. It's supposed to be welcoming and maybe a little encouraging." He cringed. "Now that I'm giving it to you, this feels a little weird and creepy."

I laughed. "Grace said we could leave letters for one another. I think it's nice you thought of me. Thank you." I accepted the offering with a sincere smile.

Then I let Paul walk me out.

Chapter Eight

The Emily Dickinson Museum was a masterpiece. With every step I took on the grounds and through the homes, I wondered repeatedly why I'd never come before. The Homestead, a brilliant yellow structure with green shutters and a small conservatory lined with windows, made me feel as if I'd gone back in time. The interior decor had been painstakingly returned to that of Emily's time, and standing in the foyer, I could easily imagine Emily appearing on the staircase, headed to the kitchen for a little baking, or on her way outside for a walk.

I felt her presence everywhere.

I moved slowly, room to room, poring over every displayed photo, note, and commentary. And smiled at a plaque outside the library with words from one of Emily's letters, regarding her father. *He buys me many Books—but begs me not to read them—because he fears they joggle the Mind.*

My father bought me many books as well.

I listened as the guide mentioned Emily being odd. Her poems being occasionally dark. Her life marked by loss. And I appreciated all the more that Daisy's dissertation was about the poet's love of nature.

The type of gardening she preferred was slightly different than I'd expected, but interesting nonetheless. Unlike the vegetable plants I'd bought from Seeds of Love, Emily had focused on flowers. Her family somehow managed to raise grapes and corn in the rough New England weather, but her beds were filled with annuals, perennials, and bulbs.

Which reminded me of the work I had waiting for me at the manor.

⚜

An hour later, I poured a mug of herbal tea and took a seat at the kitchen table, then opened Paul's letter.

> Emma,
> Your unexpected presence was a bright spot in my day.
> It was lovely to meet you, and I hope to repeat the pleasure soon.
>> Sincerely,
>> Paul

I read the words a dozen more times and planned to use the gift as inspiration to get my letter mojo flowing. I found a comfortable seat, a pen and paper; then I began to write.

First, I knocked out a simple update to Cecily and another to my parents—none would fault me for my terrible letter-writing skills—and I expected they'd humor me and write back. My hands were cramped into claws from using a pen for so long, and frankly, I'd had enough. It was beyond time to switch gears.

My energy level had depleted by half since returning home. Time alone was definitely draining my battery instead of refilling it, but I'd come to Amherst on a mission. I had to learn to be happy on my own.

"How did you do it, Emily?" I wondered aloud. The isolation didn't feel as relaxing as I'd imagined. More like being punished or put in a weekslong time-out.

Images of her bedroom, where I'd stood only a short time ago, flashed into mind. She'd written the majority of her poems, more than 1,800 of them, there. Surrounded by floral print wallpaper, before a window draped in green, on a little desk facing the glass. She'd thrived in solitude.

I was sure I'd perish.

Perhaps the key was staying busy. Wasn't that the key to everything? Don't want to think about a nasty breakup? Find something to do. Trying to avoid the other half of the cupcake you're saving for later? Find something to do. Embracing spinsterhood with dignity?

Find something to do.

I changed into a pair of old jeans and a T-shirt, then went to survey the yard. According to Olivia, all the plants I'd purchased needed full sun, and thanks to yesterday's rain, they'd all had plenty of water. I walked the area contemplatively, and I found the perfect spot, free from the crawling fingers of shade, about fifteen yards from the patio. The grass looked slightly different there, and I wondered if someone had once had the same idea. The possibility another garden had grown where I planned to plant mine brightened my mood, and I clung to the thought.

Maybe that was another reason Emily hadn't minded the years she'd spent alone. Maybe she'd found ways to connect to the people who'd come before her, and those who would follow, by reading, writing, and growing beautiful flowers.

My desire to emulate the poet in all her quiet, nature-loving glory filled my heart in a burst. If I could tap into the peace she found while gardening and roll that into contentment elsewhere as well, I'd be happy with my long single life.

The sun brightened, and I lifted my chin to absorb its warmth. Emily's words floated through my thoughts. And a smile formed. Yesterday's clouds were gone. I would embrace this day. "Superior glory be."

I started by rooting through the little toolshed I spotted beneath an oak at the side of the manor. I found a shovel and old floral-printed gardening kit with gloves that fit my hands. I couldn't imagine Grace caring if I used them. I'd asked about possibly planting a garden on the night I'd made my reservation, and she'd thought the idea was lovely. I remembered specifically because she'd used the word *lovely*. It'd struck me as almost a bit odd and rather proper. Then again, she'd taken on a more formal air altogether when it came to our correspondence about the manor, which had made perfect sense. I certainly didn't email customers or vendors in the same tone I used when posting in IBOOM. Her spoken language matched her email correspondence, making her persona on IBOOM the anomaly. Something I never would've known had I not come to town.

I got busy pulling weeds around the patio's edge and removing the grass covering the site of my future garden with the shovel. My back, shoulders, and arms ached from the effort. Carrying the heavy bags of mulch and topsoil from the front yard to the back only added to my discomfort. But I persevered.

I scooped mulch from the broken bag into a pail, then lined the sacks of topsoil on my newly degrassed patch of land and split them open with the shovel. Each whack felt deeply satisfying.

Hours later, when the prep work and my aching body were finished, I considered dying on the spot. At least it would be easy to bury me. I was already covered in dirt. I rolled onto my back in the grass and remained motionless for an undetermined amount of time, willing my noodle arms and legs to firm up.

"I don't know how you did it, Emily," I said, pushing myself into a sit. "I'm dehydrated. Exhausted. And filthy. Not my idea of a good time."

Clouds raced over the sun, and I forced myself upright. I hadn't come this far to quit, and I refused to be defeated again. Plant by plant, I kept going until my energy fully depleted and my arms had pinkened from the sun. I transferred veggies into the garden, small shrubs and flowers into a narrow mulch bed around the back patio. Then I carried all the trash to the bins out front and flew a mental flag of victory.

I couldn't feel my legs as I wobbled into the manor. My clothes were black with dirt and mulch, and my unruly curls stuck to the drying sweat on my neck and cheeks. I'd need two baths to feel clean again.

The climb to the second-floor bathroom nearly finished me. I sank dramatically to my knees, hanging both arms over the edge of the claw-foot tub.

I turned the knobs and tested the water, wincing at the cold and waiting for it to warm. I rested my cheek on the cool porcelain, but the water didn't heat up.

I groaned, wrenched upright, then grimaced at my reflection in the mirror above the sink. I couldn't take a cold bath, and I couldn't call Davis for help. If he found me looking like this again, he'd think I was the human incarnate of that *Peanuts* character, followed perpetually by a cloud of rolling dirt.

Not that I cared what he thought.

I turned off the water and went back downstairs to reconsider dying in the garden.

❧

Twenty minutes later, I'd washed my face and hands in the sink and put my letters, destined for Willow Bend, in the mailbox at the end of the lane. I turned the flag up to let the postal worker know they were inside; then I spread a blanket beneath a tree and took a seat. I unpacked my bag, a pen and paper, cheese and crackers, apple slices, and bottled water. I needed sustenance and rest before dealing with a cold bath.

I chose a purple gel pen and gave the fountain pen a dirty look. I needed to unload my troubles, not compile them. Gentle wind fluttered the page as I began to write.

> Cecily,
> It's been a long while since I've written proper letters.
> Probably since we had pen pals for third grade English
> class, and mine never responded. Please respond.

> Life in 1855 is lonelier than I expected. I'm not
> sure how Emily found inspiration in solitude, but
> maybe I need to be patient and let myself adjust.

I paused to stack sliced cheese on a cracker and munch. All around me, the slowly changing leaves on ancient oaks danced on the breeze. Hearthstone Manor stood in the distance, the sun shining beautifully overhead. Why was being here so difficult for me? Everything was exactly as I thought it would be. I just hadn't anticipated how much I wouldn't like it. Hopefully I'd find my rhythm soon.

I sighed and stuffed an apple slice into my mouth, then began to write again.

> I have to call Davis, the handyman, soon,
> because there's no hot water today, and there's some-
> thing wrong with the furnace as well. I get the feel-
> ing he doesn't want me here, though it doesn't make
> any sense. Why would he care who rents the place?
> Anyway, I'll keep you posted on that. Hopefully every-
> thing will be working when you come to visit. Until
> then I'll be counting the days.
>
> Do you think the real reason I'm unhappy lies
> within me?

I stared at the words, hating them and questioning their truth.

Would I be sad wherever I went because I was the problem? Not my family, my job, or my singleness? I shoved the thought aside. All that mattered was that I made big changes in the next few weeks and went home happy. Besides, it'd only been a couple of days, and I was a work in progress.

I finished my letter, and then I closed my eyes and thought of all the times Emily mentioned home in her poetry. This town was important to her, and it was important to me too. This was where my life would change.

Nearly an hour later, when my meal was gone and my spirit was revived, I carried the letter to the mailbox. Then I walked home to fight my next battle.

I dropped my lunch container in the sink and peered through the kitchen window at all my hard work outside. The process had been laborious and new to me, but I'd seen it through, and the results were worth the trouble. "I did that," I whispered, letting pride swell in my chest.

The ring of black mulch around the patio was dotted with colorful mums and rosebushes. Leafy green plants stood like soldiers in tidy little rows several yards away. Maybe I could talk to them sometime—to help them grow.

Maybe I was lonelier than I'd thought.

I rolled my eyes as I contemplated my new plant babies and my unreasonable feelings toward them. Then something dark caught my eye at the corner of the patio. A brown-and-white cat pressed its body into the shadows beneath the eaves.

I strained my eyes to search for a collar. If the cat was a stray, maybe we could be friends. I made a mental note to put out a bowl of cream after I cleaned up. I'd always thought of myself as a dog person, but maybe that could change too.

The feline stilled, and its backside rose, twitching slightly as if preparing to pounce.

Across the lawn, a little rabbit hopped into my garden.

I watched in horror as the adorable fuzzball stopped near my newly planted turnips and nibbled.

"Hey!" I said, fumbling to unlock the door.

The bunny, unaffected, reared its head, stretching and ripping a leaf off its stem.

"Stop!" I called, rushing out and waving my arms. "Knock it off!"

The bunny stilled midchew. Its long white ears turned like satellites, as if trying to make sense of my appearance in its dining room.

It took another bite.

I launched toward it, fueled by adrenaline and despair. Two frantic steps later, I wobbled on tired spaghetti legs, tripped over my feet, and crashed to my hands and knees. Then I thumped onto my chest. A sound like "oof" blew across my lips as the air left my lungs.

Birds lifted from the treetops in a wave of complaints. The bunny darted away. And I rocked upright, noting the rip in my pant leg and sting in my skinned palms.

Living like Emily Dickinson stunk.

It took an hour and eleven trips up the steps to heat enough water on the stovetop to fill the bathtub. I pulled twigs and bits of mulch from my hair. After I'd dried off and redressed in sweatpants and a hoodie, I crawled onto the bed for a short rest.

Hours later, a full-body shiver opened my eyes to moonlight and darkness. The temperature inside the manor was frigid.

I craned upright, cussing a little as I gripped and kneaded the tender muscles along my neck and shoulders. I still didn't know how to make a fire, and I didn't want to fill the house with smoke again.

I took a moment to visualize the tantrum I was too tired to perform, then pulled on a pair of sweatpants and a hoodie and crawled back beneath the covers.

Chapter Nine

I watched the sunrise the next morning, unaccustomed to sleeping more than a few hours at a time. In Willow Bend I typically had too much on my mind, and too many things on my plate. But a day of labor in the fresh air and sunshine, followed by carrying gallons of water, had knocked me out cold. Minus my midnight trip to the thermostat.

I shivered around the first floor, starting a pot of coffee, then checking the temperature in the house. "Fifty-eight," I read. "Ridiculous." I had to contact Davis. The nights would only get colder as October drew near.

I wound the dial to seventy and waited for the latent lament of an ancient furnace struggling back to life.

Sunlight streamed through the window above the sink, bathing the white cabinetry and appliances in a warm golden glow. Woven baskets and antique kitchen gadgets decorated a baker's rack on one wall. Eyelet curtains hung over the small rectangular glass in the back door.

I took my steaming mug of coffee onto the patio, then into the grass for a better look at my garden and flowers. Many were missing buds and leaves.

"Damn bunny."

I set a bowl of cream on the pavers for the cat, eager to lure it back and maybe keep the rabbit away. Then I made a hearty breakfast and carried it to the study.

I started the new day with another book about Emily's life, determined to see her as the warm, hopeful woman I wanted her to be. I searched my soul for a connection to her in the process. I needed to strengthen that tether if I planned to stay my course. Unfortunately, the more I read, the more evident it became that Emily had preferred the company of plants to people. And hours of contemplation over conversation.

I could not relate.

For the first time, I wondered how Emily and I could be so painfully different when her poems spoke the words of my soul.

Time dragged on as I struggled to write and reflect. My hand cramped and ached from the fruitless attempts at more letters to my family. Meanwhile, I started a third for Cecily. I missed my wireless keyboard. I missed talking to people.

The grandfather clock in the foyer chimed, and I jerked to my feet. I'd write more before bed. Until then I wanted to go exploring.

I collected my phone, purse, and keys as I headed to the door.

I thought I might visit the local library and research ways to keep a rabbit from eating my garden, or how to fix a pilot light. Davis had mentioned checking the water heater's pilot light on the night we'd met. If I was staying put, I should probably know how to fix it. Especially since I wanted to avoid the handyman as much as possible.

After lunch, I'd visit the grocery store for baking supplies. Maybe baking would be the thread that tied me closer to Emily. My little failures so far were starting to add up, and I needed a win. I had a pile of authentic recipes, fresh ingredients on my list, and a modern-ish oven at my disposal. As an added bonus, the idea of making my own breakfast breads and muffins made me feel incredibly self-sufficient. And, in true Emily fashion, I could share them by delivering extras to the shops and ladies who'd donated to my welcome basket. Another excellent and reasonable excuse to get out and meet more people.

A smile bloomed. An errand list like this one could easily keep me busy all day. My feet hit the lane with a little kick in my step, and I fought the urge to twirl.

I'd text Davis about the furnace before returning to the manor, and he could come over to take a look at the problem later.

I made it halfway up the lane before my phone rang, and I startled. Apparently I'd reached the signal zone. I knew I should stick to letters while I was on my mission, yet—

"Hey, Mom," I said, hoping to sound at ease and delighted instead of desperate for conversation.

"Hello, hon," she said. "How are you doing? Still enjoying Amherst?"

My chest constricted at the sound of her voice, and suddenly, I felt homesick. I missed my warm apartment and the busy store beneath. I missed seeing the people I loved in person and all the familiar things I'd taken for granted. Why had I thought leaving town to live alone and do hard things would solve my problems? I couldn't even take a hot shower. I had to settle for a lukewarm bath.

"Emma?" Mom asked gently. "Are you okay?"

"Mm-hmm," I said, silently giving in to my dismal thoughts of failure.

"What is it, sweetie? Is there anything your dad or I can do?"

I shook my head, though she couldn't see me. Her mention of Dad pulled me back to the moment, and I checked my watch. It was after nine. "I'll be okay," I said. "Are you at the store?"

The distinct sounds of traffic told me they weren't.

"Not yet," she said. "We're meeting Annie and Jeffrey for breakfast first. I thought I'd give you a call on the way and make sure you know we're all thinking of you and missing you every day."

I ignored the irrational jab of jealousy on multiple counts. "Is Annie still mad at me for leaving?"

"She's very pregnant," Mom said. "She has a lot on her mind, and a heavy load of hormones affecting her thoughts. She'll be fine in a few weeks."

"She called me selfish." The words popped out of my mouth before I'd thought better of them. I hated how much I'd let Annie's outburst bother me, but I didn't mean to drag Mom into our rift. We weren't children, and Mom didn't need the added drama.

"I'm sure she's worried about her upcoming delivery and all the major changes she's facing. She doesn't want you to miss it. That's all."

"I wish she'd just say that," I complained. "Then we could talk it through. It's not as if I moved across the country. I can be home in less than an hour. All she has to do is let me know when she goes into labor. It's no big deal."

Mom was quiet.

"The drive, not the labor," I corrected. "Of course the labor is a big deal." I pressed a hand over my eyes, feeling unintentionally rude and ridiculous. "I'm glad you and Dad are visiting her in the mornings. But you should probably change the store hours if you aren't going to be there at nine." Otherwise, we'd lose our batch of regular morning shoppers. There were only so many times a person would visit a store and find it locked before they stopped dropping by.

"Already done," Mom said. "I put a sign in the window last night letting folks know we'll open at lunchtime this month. Now your dad and I won't have to worry about rushing around to get there."

I clamped my mouth shut, processing the news. I hadn't slept in— or had breakfast out—in years, because I felt obligated to open the store at nine. But as soon as I took a few weeks off, Mom just taped a sign to the window, and poof! The hours were now more convenient?

Did she even care about sales? Was her store wholly my problem now?

"You know," Mom said. "It's not too late for you to come home if you're bored or lonely. I can't tell you how much you're missed. By us. By Annie. By the store and customers. They ask about you every day."

My eyelids fell shut, and I swiped a frustrated tear from the corner of one eye. The possibility she only wanted me home to run the store replaced sentimentality with anger. "I can't," I said, forcing the words through a tightening throat. "I'm not done here yet."

If I gave up, all the trouble I'd caused by leaving and all the little obstacles I'd already faced would have been for nothing. "I have to go, Mom," I said. "I hope you have a good day. Tell Dad and Annie I love them."

I disconnected and tucked the phone back into my pocket with a soft growl. I had work to do in Amherst before I could worry any more about the state of affairs in Willow Bend. Even if my parents were messing things up.

It was afternoon when I dragged myself and my shopping bags through the manor's front door and into the kitchen. I'd taken my time browsing the shops and created haiku as I went.

> Alone, not lonely
> Enjoying a pretty day
> Learning to be fine

The best part of going about my day was seeing several familiar faces from my letter-writing class, and each of them had recognized me too. We traded smiles and waves, then a few casual words that made me feel like part of the town.

I'd forced myself to text Davis on my walk home. He'd responded to say he'd visit after he finished at work. I wasn't sure how I felt about seeing him again when I was lonely at the manor and he was unfairly attractive. So I concentrated on the moment at hand.

I heaved my bounty onto the countertop and unpacked the newly purchased baking supplies into orderly rows on the counter.

"Black cake, coconut bread, or gingerbread?" I asked the empty kitchen. I'd found three recipes from the 1850s, and all sounded delicious. Gingerbread felt a little too Christmassy, however, so I set that one aside. I loved coconut, but the black cake involved cognac and hazelnut liqueur. "Black cake it is."

I made a cup of coffee and checked the clock. Not that time had any meaning in a world where I had zero responsibilities. I dosed the coffee with liquor, then hummed and sipped as I prepped the pan.

The oven made a number of questionable sounds as it preheated, but the appliance appeared to be about my age, so I assumed it was doing the best it could.

"All right. What's next?" I asked, examining the recipe I'd propped against the backsplash. "Raisins and a bunch of dried fruits chopped into raisin size. No problem." I grabbed a knife. "Currants, apricots, prunes, pears, dates. Yeesh." I finished my coffee and sampled the brandy as I worked.

The process was a lot more labor-intensive than all those cupcakes and brownies I'd made from boxes. Being required to do all the extra steps felt a little like being held hostage.

I hated tedious tasks.

I sagged in relief when I'd finished the chopping, then checked the clock.

When Davis had stopped by after work on the night of my arrival, it'd been dark. Based on that, I reasoned I probably had time to finish the cake and my minigarden project. As long as I kept moving.

I took another look at the recipe. "Flour, baking soda, baking powder, salt, cinnamon, cloves, mace. Good grief." I was going to need a larger bowl.

"Nutmeg, cardamon, ginger, butter, sugar, eggs, vanilla." I groaned miserably.

I tested the cognac again, which helped.

Maybe Emily only thought she enjoyed baking because she was drunk.

Eventually I had the batter mixed and ready for the oven. Understandably, the pan weighed about fifty pounds. I hadn't packed enough stretchy pants to eat this on my own.

I set the timer on my phone because the ancient oven didn't seem to have one; then I gave myself a short break and read Paul's letter once more. I never imagined how much I'd enjoy receiving notes from friends and classmates. I hoped my letters made Cecily and my parents smile too.

Next, I moved on to Project Protect the Garden. I set the letter on the table, then collected my supplies before heading outside with stakes, twine, scissors, and aluminum pie plates in hand.

I gritted my teeth at the condition of my garden. Several plants had been completely ruined; leaves were shredded on some, missing on others; and two carrot buds had been fully removed from the ground. I silently cursed the bunny.

"I hope you enjoyed yourself," I said, projecting my words to the nearby trees. "'Cause this restaurant is closed."

Something moved in the shadows, and I grinned when the bunny came into view, nose twitching as it watched from the tree line.

"Not. Going. To. Happen," I whispered.

Across the lawn, the brown-and-white cat strolled onto my patio and took a seat. It licked its paw as its attention moved from me to the bunny and back.

"That's right," I said. "I'm taking over now."

I wondered, briefly, if either animal had a name. Then smiled as the words to one of Emily's poems whispered in my mind. *I'm nobody! Who are you?*

Strangely, I'd thought I'd known exactly who I was when I made plans to come to Amherst, but in my few days I'd learned things I hadn't expected. And none of it so far had anything to do with my dreams of love. In a family of extroverts, I'd considered myself quiet and shy. But I wasn't. I'd thought I craved solitude, but now I was positive I hated that. I'd even considered talking to the plants for company.

I couldn't do that if they were all dead, and I couldn't save them if they were all dismembered.

According to advice I'd found online, stringing aluminum pie plates around the perimeter would keep wildlife away without harming the plants or the animals. The movement of the plates in the breeze would frighten animals somehow, as would the reflection of sunlight as the silver discs bobbed in the wind. The job seemed relatively simple, so I was willing to give it a try.

I hammered dowel rods into the four corners of my garden, then punched holes in the pie plates and strung them with twine. After that, I crawled around the little square, securing the string to the dowel rods.

My hands and knees were sore when I finished. Dirt packed into the scrapes from my fall the day before. I dusted together my palms, then stretched upright to knock the dirt off my jeans.

Fiery hues of waning daylight reflected on the plates, and pride drew a smile over my lips.

A moment later, I tensed. The sun shouldn't be setting already! How long had I been outside? I still needed to clean up before Davis arrived, and what had happened to the timer on my phone? I patted my pockets and looked around. But the device wasn't anywhere to be found.

A new horror rushed into mind. "The cake!"

"Oh, no, no, no." I gathered my remaining supplies from the grass and hustled across the lawn and patio toward the manor.

Chapter Ten

The scent of burning cake hit like a brick as I wrenched open the back door. A dark haze filled the kitchen. My phone lay silently on the counter where I'd set it while trying to carry everything outside with two full hands. A notification on the screen indicated that I'd missed my alarm twenty-seven minutes ago.

I said a few choice words as I opened the oven and fanned away plumes of smoke.

True to its name, my cake was in fact, very black.

The smoke detector went off, and my heart rate doubled. A red light flashed, and shrill beeping pierced the air.

"Shit!"

I hefted the pan with pot holders and kicked the oven door closed. I dropped the cake into the sink and turned on the water to stop the dessert from smoldering. Then I used the back door like a fan, swinging it enthusiastically to circulate the air and pull the smoke outside. When the alarm continued to screech, I grabbed the broom.

Frustration and anger mixed with a heaping helping of self-pity as I climbed onto a chair and raised the long wooden handle toward the tiny reset button on the wailing alarm.

I aimed carefully at the little target, and the alarm silenced. I pumped a fist for the victory, but the joy passed quickly. My eyes landed on the soaking-wet brickette of a cake in the sink. Partially cloaked by the room's smoky haze.

Another failure in my quest to be like Emily.

I dropped my celebratory fist and stepped backward, ready to dispose of the fruited corpse. Then I screamed, momentarily airborne as the chair scraped over tile and clattered to the floor. In the space of that half heartbeat, my brain cued in on my predicament, and my body braced for impact. It seemed a fitting end.

Before I hit the floor, a pair of strong arms curved around my middle, saving me from becoming a heap of clumsy regret. The arms pulled me against a broad chest.

My broom bounced and slid away with a whoosh.

Davis looked down at me, sincere concern swimming in his stormy gray eyes.

I heaved several rattled breaths before I could speak, thankful for his perfect timing, and confused by how he'd seemed to manifest from the smoke. The same electric charge that had filled the air between us on the night we'd met zinged to life once more. I could've broken my neck, but he'd caught me. It was a meet-cute for a bestseller. A story to tell at parties for the rest of our lives.

Except we'd already met. And like before, nothing about me or this scene was cute.

Why did he keep showing up when I was a complete mess?

My silly, swooning heart performed a little kitten purr.

Inner Emily really needed to get up and kick my ass.

Instead, she whispered the words of "That It Will Never Come Again," a poem I'd always treasured. She believed only having one life to live, one chance to exist to the fullest, was what made living so sweet. A strong reminder to absorb and cherish the moments at hand, because time wasn't something any of us could get back.

Did I want to hold on to this particular memory? Filthy and embarrassed—but in Davis's arms?

"You okay?" he asked, loosening his grip by a fraction.

I planted my hands against his chest, leaving dirt marks. "Yeah. Oh. Sorry." I attempted to rub the stains away, but scents of his shampoo, cedar, and mint befuddled my brain.

I jerked back, suddenly sure I smelled like sweat, burned cake, and topsoil.

"Still trying to burn the place down?" He cast a pointed look around the hazy kitchen.

I pointed to the sink. "This was an accident."

"You have a lot of accidents."

"Two is not a lot." I bristled, stepping away to cross my arms.

Davis tucked his hands into his pockets, gaze sweeping to my ruined dessert. "What is that?"

"Black cake," I said pitifully. "I was outside trying to protect my garden, and I lost track of time. Then I fell off a chair."

I glanced at the open back door. I'd forgotten to close it after using it as a giant fan.

"Good thing I came when I did. I tried the bell, but you probably didn't hear it over the blaring smoke alarm and all your cussing."

I nearly rolled my eyes. There was the curmudgeon I'd met before.

"When I didn't see you through the window, I came around to check the kitchen."

"Thank you." I took another step away from him and leaned against the sink, still too buzzed from his nearness to think clearly. "I wasn't expecting you until later. Last time you came after work, it was already dark."

He bent to right the toppled chair; then he lifted the broom from the floor and returned it to the corner. "I wrapped things up early to have dinner with my buddy Clayton, at his bar."

I frowned, trying to imagine Davis with friends. Strange that one of his friends owned a bar. Grace's friend Olivia owned a farm, and on IBOOM she'd often mentioned visiting another friend's pub on game days. Maybe local business owners had their own little community.

The possibility made me wonder about Davis and his dad. According to Michael at the bookstore, both Sommers men were well known, and the elder was deeply involved in local affairs. What would Davis's dad be like? Probably a middle-aged grouch. If not from genetics, then from dealing with his frown-faced son for thirty-four years.

Davis moved his hands to his hips, clearly impatient to get going. "Your text said the hot-water heater and furnace are giving you trouble?"

The words pulled me back to the moment. "I had to heat water on the stovetop and haul it upstairs in pots for a bath," I blurted.

My traitorous bottom lip wobbled at the remembered trauma. I bit the insides of my cheeks to maintain emotional control.

Davis shifted, and I knew he saw my unshed tears.

"I've had a very frustrating couple of days," I said, apologetically wiping the corners of my eyes. "And a very cold couple of nights. I'm tired, sore, and I hate asking for help, but can you please—" I cleared my throat and swallowed before forcing the final words from my lips in a whisper. "Please help me."

His expression softened, and he shoved one big hand through his perfectly tousled hair. "I'll look at the hot-water heater first," he muttered. "Then you can clean up, if you want, while I move on to the furnace. And I'll show you how to make a fire."

Emotion pushed against my eyes. I straightened my spine and nodded. "Thank you."

Thirty minutes later, I was waist deep in a hot, but not steamy, bubble bath. Not exactly the luxurious, relaxed soak I'd fantasized about before my arrival, but I was trying to appreciate the small wins. Even if Davis was somewhere in the manor, fully dressed, banging on vents and pipes. I nonsensically wished for one of those curtains on a rod around the bath, then scrubbed a little faster. The next time I filled the tub, I vowed to light a candle and bring a book. Maybe I'd even use the new loofah I'd brought to pamper my long-ignored skin. Maybe I'd buy a cedar plank and set it across the porcelain to hold my things.

For now, however, I hurried. I toweled off quickly, squeezing the water from my hair. Then I paired soft black yoga pants with a comfy tank top and a cropped zip-up hoodie. The muted ivory color detracted slightly from my sunburn, which was more pronounced without the added dirt. I drove a wand with sheer gloss around my lips and coated my lashes in fresh mascara, then beetled down the rear steps to the kitchen, a pair of fuzzy socks in hand.

Davis turned from the window when I hit a squeaky stair. He'd put on a kettle for tea.

"Are you finished already?" I asked, unsure if the house was getting warmer or if it was just his effect on me.

"Pilot light was out," he said. "Easy fix."

I gave myself a mental pat on the back for looking into pilot lights earlier. Next time the water didn't warm, I could fix it myself. I took a seat on the nearest chair to pull on my socks. "Did you clean my kitchen?"

All evidence of my failed black cake was gone. The counter was wiped, and the ingredients were put away.

He glanced around at his efforts. "It was the least I could do, since you've had so much trouble here."

"Well, you also saved me from a nasty fall," I said. "I think we're even."

A muscle in Davis's jaw clenched, and I wondered if he was thinking of the moment when he'd held me. I certainly was. "Fair enough." He turned to the stove, hiding his face, and poured two cups from the kettle. "Tea?"

"Please."

"Milk or sugar?"

"Both. Thanks for doing all this," I said. "Fixing the furnace and water heater was plenty. Cleaning the kitchen and making tea is officially above and beyond."

He ferried two cups my way. "I'm just sorry you were cold last night. And that you had to haul water for a bath."

I accepted a steaming mug, and Davis took the seat across from mine.

"My offer to help you find another place stands," he said. "No hard feelings. I suspect things like this will continue to go wrong, so getting out now, while you can still enjoy your time in town, might be best."

I sipped the tea and gave my head a small shake. "I'm not interested in leaving. Not unless you know someone else with a historic place like this. Off the beaten path so I'd be alone. And somewhere the owner would let me make a little garden."

He stared, the wheels of his mind almost visibly turning. "That's very specific."

I shrugged. "This place is exactly what I was looking for. As long as I don't freeze to death or have to carry any more water for baths, I'll be okay." I smiled when he made eye contact, hoping he'd know I was teasing.

He didn't smile back. "Is it that you can't go without gardening? Or because you don't like people?"

"I love people," I said. "It's nothing like that. I'm just—doing something."

"What?"

I set the cup aside. "It's—personal. So, I'd rather not say, but I can deal with the temporary inconveniences."

Davis didn't respond, but his presence put me at ease.

I thought again of him catching me when I fell, and how the air seemed to thicken around us. I liked the way our energies flowed together. How comfortable he made me feel, even when he was scowling for no good reason.

"I came here looking for new perspective," I said, breaking the awkward silence. "I wasn't happy with how my life was going, and I thought getting away from my usual routine was exactly what I needed. So, here I am, and I'd like to stick it out, if at all possible."

Davis rested his forearms on the table, looking unreasonably interested. "You're here to find happiness?" His gaze roamed to the open letter between us.

I folded the note and set it aside. "My little sister thinks I just want attention, and my parents would prefer I give up and come home, but this is something I need to do."

He scanned my face, curious eyes probing mine. "Why weren't you happy before?"

I released a long breath. Where to start? "I run the family bookstore while my parents and sister enjoy their lives. They used to work as much as I did, but over time, things changed. Annie got married. Now she's pregnant. My folks got older and more interested in retiring than working. They spend a lot of time with Annie and her husband, doing couples things or talking about their first grandbaby. It's all very sweet, and I'm glad for them, but one day I looked up and I was alone. I'm not sure they've even noticed."

"Ah." He kicked back in his seat, stretching his long legs beneath the table until they bumped mine.

"What's that mean?" I asked. "'Ah'?"

He raised his cup and sipped. "You're a people pleaser. You miss the attention."

I made a cuckoo face. "Obviously. Especially when it comes to my family." I laughed. "I can't help it. I love them all so much, and I want them to be happy. If I can help with that, it makes me happy too."

Davis cocked his head. "You sure about that?"

I wanted to say "Of course!" But I wasn't convinced anymore. "What matters is that I'm trying to make some overdue changes."

"And these changes require a historic property where you can be alone and garden," he said.

"Yep. Though I need to add more flowers. And I'm battling a bunny over the produce."

He bobbed his head in faux understanding, then admitted, "I don't get it."

I laughed again. "You'll just have to trust me."

"Does this have anything to do with the list that was on the refrigerator the last time I was here?"

I cringed inwardly. Suspicion confirmed. He'd seen the list, and I was glad for the jarring reminder of my goals here. I was supposed to be breaking old habits, not forming new, one-sided crushes.

Davis raised his palms. "Sorry. I probably shouldn't have read that."

"Definitely not," I agreed.

"One of the goals was to become your best Emily." He squinted. "Does that mean Emily Dickinson?"

"Never mind that," I said.

"What about the last item? Give up on love. I'm guessing there's a story behind that one?"

I clenched my teeth and gripped my mug until I thought it might crack. "Not one for today."

He stared another long moment before speaking. "Grace says you're making quite an impression at Village Books. She said a few of the male classmates took an immediate interest." He grinned. "She even saw one man hand you a letter."

My mouth fell open, then snapped shut.

"Grace is a bit of a busybody," he said. "I mean that with love. She only wants the best for everyone, but if you're going to be around awhile, you should be aware. She has a special interest in you."

"We've been friends for years," I said, finding my tongue. "I think it's nice that she's looking out for me."

"She'll try to marry you off, if you aren't careful," he warned. "And based on that list, it's not what you want."

My traitorous heart split down the center, simultaneously longing for love and wanting to reach my new goal of happiness on my own.

"Who's Paul?" Davis asked, tone casual, expression curious. He flicked smart gray eyes in the direction of my letter once more.

"A friend I met in Grace's letter-writing class." Also, none of Davis's business.

He cupped his big hands around the teacup. "What's he like?"

"He's nice," I said, unsure where this conversation could possibly be going and why I felt compelled to answer.

"The class works well with your Emily Dickinson related goals?" he guessed.

I nodded.

"What about Paul? How does he fit into giving up on love?"

I balked. "Don't tell Grace, but her nephew is kind of a busybody," I said.

Davis smirked. "Touché." He stood and carried his cup to the sink. "I need to meet Clayton for dinner. Do you want me to show you how to build a fire before I leave?"

The urge to kick him out warred with my need for heat, so I nodded.

Chapter Eleven

We moved into the sitting room, and Davis walked me through the process of using the old fireplace. I split my attention between listening to his instructions and thinking about ways to get him to stay a little longer.

"Have you lived in Amherst all your life?" I asked, taking a seat on the couch.

He turned when he had the fire going strong. "I lived right here, actually, for my first ten years."

"*Here* here?" I asked. "You mean in this house?"

He nodded. "With my parents." His tone and expression softened slightly. "Dad never liked it here, but Mom insisted. She loved this place and ran the bookstore with Grace."

"Grace is her sister?"

"Yeah. Older by eleven years. Dad moved us into one of the more sought-after communities on the edge of town as soon as he could. He's still there. Technically," Davis corrected. "Though it's probably more accurate to say he lives at the office."

I put that detail, and the way his voice hardened when he said it, into a little mental box to look at later.

"Did you like the new place?" I asked.

"It's okay."

The idea of Davis as a kid was intriguing, and questions piled on my tongue at the thought. What had his life been like before? Before he'd become an architect, landlord, and object of my unfortunate fascination.

"There's a pool," he said. "I thought that was nice."

I smiled. "I've never lived anywhere with a pool. How'd your dad talk your mom into leaving this place?" Was that when they turned the manor into a rental property?

"She died." Davis folded his hands and averted his eyes for a long beat. "Ovarian cancer," he said, answering the question I'd yet to formulate. "She caught it early, but the disease was aggressive. She tried everything to defy her odds, and it was a long, exhausting fight to the very bitter end. Which was barely more than a year from diagnosis to loss."

Tears gathered in my eyes as memories of my mother's fight with cancer flooded through me. I'd been the same age as Davis when we'd gotten the news. Knowing his mom had lost her battle a year later, when my mom was in remission, crushed my chest like an empty soda can. "I'm so sorry."

"Thanks," he said, lifting his eyes to mine. The vulnerability I saw there gutted me, and I fought the urge to cover his hands with mine.

"What was her name?"

"Iris." His cheeks darkened and his voice deepened when he spoke her name.

I nodded, understanding some of the pain there. "My mom had breast cancer when I was ten." I coughed lightly to clear the lump in my throat. "She recovered."

He looked briefly away. "Good. It's nice to be reminded cancer doesn't always win. I hope to see a day when it loses far more often."

In that instant, I felt both connected to and a million miles away from the hurting man before me. Because we'd both suffered too much, too young. But my mom had lived.

"Do you have any brothers or sisters?" I asked, hoping he'd at least had someone to help carry his grief. No one could understand the loss of a parent like a sibling.

Emily had written a number of poems about death. I'd skipped over them when I was a kid, then grew obsessed with them as a young adult. These days, the topic of death was something too sad for me to enjoy. Nonetheless, her words seemed especially poignant as I sat with Davis. She believed that those we love never truly die. They live on in us and in our hearts. In that way, our love gave them immortality.

I was sure his love kept Iris alive.

He shook his head. "None. You have a sister?"

I smiled through the pain clenching my heart. "Annie. She's seven years younger."

"Are you close?"

"Not as much as I'd like. She can be a pill."

He grinned. "I hear that's the job description for younger siblings."

"Yeah, well, she could lead the union."

Davis checked his watch and moved toward the foyer.

"You're close to your aunt?" I asked, knowing he was. I saw it in his eyes and hers, anytime one mentioned the other.

"Grace is like a second mother," he said. "She raised me after my mom passed. My grandparents, Mom and Grace's parents, were in Florida. Dad's a workaholic, and I was a grieving kid. Grace became everything I needed. Comforter, cook, chauffeur, confidant. I owe her a lot more than I can ever repay. I help with the shop whenever I can, but she mostly asks me to deal with tech related things, especially her websites and social media. When she needs me, everything else waits."

That information didn't dampen my crush at all.

"Do you like helping with the bookstore?" I asked. Selling books was a far cry from restoring historic homes, even if he loved the shop's owner.

He looked almost wistful as he nodded. "I might be happiest surrounded by books."

I set a hand on my collarbone, melting a little at his perfect words. "Me too."

"The store's social media, on the other hand, is going to be the death of me," he said with a chuckle. Probably trying to lighten the mood. "It's something Grace has no interest in doing, but it's necessary, so I've been trying to build a following."

"I met Grace online," I said. "I've been talking to her for years without realizing she's my parents' age. Older, actually. She's one of my favorite people."

Davis watched me intently, seeming as if he had something to say.

When my cheeks began to heat under his stare, I started talking again. "Social media campaigns for the store are tough. I work at it all the time. Do you have to handle those things for your job too?" I asked. "Grace told me you're an architect."

"Did she?" His brows rose. "What else did she say?"

I shrugged, hoping to look more casual and less eager than I felt. Also wishing he'd skip dinner with his friend and stay. "She seemed quite proud. She told me you prefer to work with historic properties." Now that I knew how much his mom had loved Hearthstone Manor, and his unimaginable loss, it was easy to understand his passion for homes like this one. "Are you any good at it?"

Davis gave a small, suppressed laugh. "I try."

"And you're the one renovating this place?"

He appeared conflicted for a long beat before nodding. "As soon as possible. There's a national historic restoration competition going on right now. The winner gets their work on the cover of *Architectural Digest* and a feature story inside. The recognition would be monumental to my career. It might even remind my dad there's value in what I do."

Davis had followed his dad's career path, yet his dad somehow faulted him for his restoration work? That didn't seem fair. Shouldn't a child's only remaining parent work double time to foster the relationship? "Is there prize money too?" I asked instead, hoping to change the direction my thoughts had taken.

"Some," Davis said.

"What will you do with it?" I asked, hoping to find out even more about him. In my experience, the way people treated money reflected their character, or at least their personality. Was Davis a saver? A spender? Would he travel? Buy a new truck? Maybe a new property investment? Or pay off his student loans?

"I'd donate it to the Ovarian Cancer Research Alliance."

Davis was a giver.

My mission was doomed. How could I possibly resist a kind, handsome, successful man who loved his aunt and mourned his mom? Who followed his passion and made a difference in his community, who gave to charity and loved books?

I imagined dropping my head dramatically forward in defeat.

He pulled his phone from his pocket and tapped the screen. "Looks like Clayton is canceling. Someone didn't show up for their shift, and that puts him on duty." He glanced toward the kitchen. "Feel like sharing your cognac?"

"Absolutely." I hurried into the other room and returned a moment later with the brandy bottle and our teacups; then I poured a little of the amber liquid into each.

"You buy the good stuff," he said, tapping his cup to mine.

"It's for baking."

He gave the bottle, significantly depleted from my sampling, a long look, then fixed me with a wry smile.

"I did some taste testing."

He snorted, then took a sip.

"How's your list coming along?" he asked.

"Not bad. I've been journaling and reading about Emily Dickinson. I visited the Homestead and planted a garden. My poetry sucks, but I'm working on it."

"You also baked," he said, lips quirking on one side.

"I baked," I agreed, fighting a smile of my own.

"And the other things?"

The other things on my list. I bit my lip. *Embrace the solitude. Become my best Emily. Be happy. Give up on love.* "It's a work in progress." And that would have to be good enough for now. At least I was finally trying to change, instead of doing the same things every day and complaining that nothing ever changed.

"Why Emily Dickinson?" he asked. "There are plenty of great poets out there. Why choose to emulate her when you seem nothing alike?"

I frowned. Emily spent her time observing and contemplating things I regularly buzzed past without noticing. Always on my way to the next set of goalposts. "I feel like I know her," I confessed. "Like I've always known her. And sometimes it feels as if she knows me. I love the way she saw the world. She wrote heartfelt poems about the smallest things, like birds, bees, and dandelions. If not for her words, I'd rarely think of those things at all."

To my surprise and delight, Davis didn't laugh or mock me, so I made another unexpected confession. "When my mom was sick, we'd lie together in her bed and read from a book of Emily's poetry. Mom gave me the collection before finding out she had cancer. When she was at her weakest, I'd rest my head on her shoulder and read to her. The words seemed to soothe her. In a lot of ways, Emily's been with me through all the most crucial moments of my life. Good and bad." I shifted to look more closely at him, searching for the right description of what Emily's poems meant to me. "If my life was depicted on a massive tapestry, showing all the most important parts in order, beginning to end, her words would be a golden thread running through it all."

My thoughts jumped to something similar Grace had said during class. *Love is the little silver thread connecting all of humanity, around the globe, century to century, forevermore.* How sweet to know there were things in life that touched us all.

I looked to Davis. Had he ever been in love? If so, what had she been like?

Approval flashed in his eyes. "You appreciate her."

It took a moment for me to understand what he meant. My thoughts had fixed on the imaginary, gorgeous, intelligent supermodel who once held his heart. I nodded. "I do." I doubted anyone other than Emily could've motivated me to leave my life in search of something more, and I was deeply thankful for that.

I was also immensely thankful for Davis's company. "What will you do to this place?" I asked. "It's so beautiful already."

"I'm going to gut it."

"What?" I asked, a little too loudly. "Why would you do that?"

Davis grinned at my response. "The plan is for a complete overhaul and update. I'll stay true to the era and preserve the integrity of the original craftsmanship as much as possible. But it's time for major changes."

I gaped at him. "I'm no architect, but the words *gut it* sound like destruction to me."

"Sometimes it's necessary," he said. "My goal here is to honor the past while serving the present. Old and outdated plumbing, wiring, heating, and AC, for example." He hooked a thumb over one shoulder. "That's all on the way out. No one sees those systems, but everyone will appreciate it when they're updated. I'll also put in premium Wi-Fi and all new appliances. Because it's not the nineteenth century anymore. I think we can love and appreciate history without suffering for it."

"What about all this gorgeous woodwork?" I asked, mesmerized by the idea of giving the beautiful home a complete overhaul as he described. And already regretting that I wouldn't be around to see the finished product.

"I'll take the wood out before the demolition. I plan to repair and refinish it myself, then return it when everything else is in order."

The look on my face must've said I still had questions, because he kept going.

"First the paint has to go." He pointed to a tall piece of baseboard with a chip in the top layer of paint, revealing pale green and yellow below. "I'll use a solvent to do most of the work for me. Then I'll sand the pieces by hand and stain them in a natural tone. I'll use the same process on the floors. Once the hardwoods are resurfaced, I'll bring in era-authentic area rugs. The biggest and most incongruous changes will be on this floor, to make everything ADA compliant. I'm widening doorways for wheelchair accessibility and adding a bathroom with a roll-in shower. Not everyone can or should manage the stairs. Soon, they won't have to, and this place can be enjoyed by far more guests. The space I'm currently using for storage will become a primary bedroom with access to the new bath. The bedroom with the fireplace upstairs will get an en suite bath as well. I've already consulted a number of designers who specialize in this era to talk about fresh decor. I'll proba- bly add a busy wallpaper in the study. Something with ridiculous birds, or giant flowers. What?" he asked, stopping abruptly.

I schooled my smile. "You're very passionate about this. I like it, and I'm a little jealous."

He frowned. "You don't have a passion?" he asked, sounding a little saddened by the notion. "What about the things you're doing here?"

I lifted and dropped a shoulder. "I've always thought of books as my passion. Or Emily Dickinson, if a poet can be a passion."

"And now?"

"Now, I'm not so sure." I'd struggled in the short time since my arrival, and I wanted to go home more than I let myself believe. "Sometimes I wish I could revamp the bookstore. Get a dog. Emily Dickinson loved dogs. Mine could be a Rini Reads mascot. Or maybe all pets would be welcome on leashes while their humans browsed or read from a favorite book." I waved the thoughts away with one dismis- sive hand. "I don't know. It'd be a complete overhaul, like this house." And I hadn't come all this way to think about the place I'd left.

"Sounds like an excellent project," Davis said.

"And a lot of work and money."

"If anyone can do it, you can. So, what's the problem?"

I bristled at the challenge in his tone. "Of course I can do it. I'm just not sure how." At the moment, I was in the midst of a complete overhaul on myself. My eyes narrowed. "How do you know I can do it?"

"What?" he asked, smile faltering.

"You said if anyone could do it, I could. How do you know?"

Davis's expression sobered. "You said you run the store already. You're obviously unflappable and tenacious, coming here alone for six weeks, determined to live in a home that really isn't worthy of a long-term occupant."

"Six weeks is hardly long term."

"It is when the house is two hundred years old," he countered. "Which is why I need to get in here and start the overhaul."

I considered his words. I was long suffering and exhausted, but was I unflappable and tenacious? I used to be. Could I be again?

More importantly, was it awful of me to want to finish my time here? Grace didn't seem to think so, but she wasn't the one burdened with managing the property while I bumbled around, fighting the buggy furnace, stove, and water heater. And I wasn't standing in the way of her career's full potential.

Davis rose and carried his cup to the sink. "I should get going," he called from the kitchen.

The sudden announcement rattled my thoughts. Why was he leaving?

"You have things to do," he said, as if reading my mind. "Baking. Writing. Embracing your inner Emily." He turned for the foyer and held me in his gaze a moment longer than polite or necessary.

I frowned briefly at the reminder he'd read my list, but the wave of heat rising through me pressed the breath from my lungs. Did he feel that too?

"Thanks for the nightcap." He offered a sad smile. "Emma—I want you to get everything you came here for."

The words felt pointed and hard as they entered my heart. "Thank you. I appreciate your help today, and the company. I'm trying to be happy on my own, but it gets lonely."

"I hope you won't become a recluse like Dickinson." He looked me over. "I don't think her life is one to aspire to, but maybe that's me. There's a big world out there to explore, and you strike me as someone who'd thrive on adventure."

I followed him into the night, stopping when we reached his truck. His words circled my heart, tightening like a vise. "I think I'd like adventuring."

His cool gray eyes met mine, and the air charged between us. "Do it. Be fearless," he dared. "You've come this far in search of happiness. Don't be afraid to find it."

I thought of my list. I wasn't becoming a very successful Emily Dickinson for more reasons than one. For starters, I hadn't yet given up on love.

Davis raised a gentle hand to my cheek, brushing away a strand of hair caught on the night breeze. His fingers slid onto my neck, curling beneath my hair, and tilting my face to his. The invitation open. I only needed to respond.

We stood frozen and on the verge of a kiss until my heart thundered in my ears, and I couldn't think of a single reason to walk away from this man. I stepped forward, closing the space between us, and rose onto tiptoes.

His lips were soft and yielding when I pressed my mouth to his. His protective arms, a refuge against all that pained me.

My body melted against him.

Maybe it was the historic manor at our side, the starry sky above, or magic in the air, but our kiss felt otherworldly. As if we'd done exactly this a thousand times.

I stepped back a moment later, before I was fully ready, when my breaths came short, my nerves undone.

Davis blinked, eyes belatedly finding focus. He scraped a hand through his dark hair, looking both stunned and miserable. "I'm so sorry, I—"

He was sorry?

I took another step away, accepting the gut punch I totally deserved. "No." I shook my head and lifted my palms. "My fault."

"Emma." My name broke on his lips, carved through with audible regret.

"Good night, Davis." I waved and hurried inside.

Chapter Twelve

I tossed and turned through the night, unable to get Davis's kiss out of my head. I felt the weight of his strong hands on my waist until dawn and would savor the delicious scrape of his calloused fingers along my neck, cheek, and jawline until I died. Our embrace had been a moment of sweet perfection for me.

For him, it was a mistake.

How could I have misinterpreted something so severely?

The memory played on a loop in my mind. He should've flung me over one shoulder, fireman style, and carried me back inside. We should've ended the night giddy with the knowledge that something new and intimate existed between us.

Instead, he'd expressed his instant regret, thoroughly crushing my hope and joy while nearly embarrassing me to death in the process.

I spent the next several days hiding from Davis, and my feelings, while establishing new routines. Mornings at the manor afforded me the time I needed to work on my baking. I'd gotten marginally better as a result. And I read a variety of books on Emily Dickinson's life while I waited for my sweets to cool. I found a rhythm of journaling in the evenings, then writing poetry at night. Which meant I consistently checked off numbers one through five on my list of goals. Happiness came and went as I worked on finding peace in the solitude.

I filled my notebook with thoughts about my personal growth and penned an excessive number of haiku. Most were about Davis.

A grouchy-faced man
Nearly upended my plan
Ignore him, I can

Best of all, I received letters from Cecily and my mom. I wrote them back immediately and anticipated more responses soon.

Cecily's first letter was short, a brief response to my request for a pen pal.

Dearest Emma,

I'm writing to accept your proposal. Pen pals for six weeks. But I will also be texting, because I live in the modern world, and some news is far too important to wait on, unnecessarily, for days. Example: I need more information about this handyman. Does he have dreamy eyes and enough hair to run your fingers through? Does his voice give you goosebumps? Have you seen him without a shirt? Please describe. The moment you kiss him, I want details.

Your deeply invested friend,
Cecily

As it turned out, a lot could happen in the space between one letter and the next. I wrote Cecily immediately and a number of outraged texts arrived two days later. The digital messages populated when I took my daily walk into town. Each contained multiple swear words and exclamation points. I chose to respond with another letter, and she followed suit.

Dearest Emma,

You kissed him! That was so brave! It doesn't matter if you went there looking for romance or not. Romance found you, and you went for it. It's his fault for being so particularly stupid that he left without carrying you away to ravish you. I think his apology was about your list. I'm sure it wasn't you. I'll bet he didn't want to ruin your quest to become a crazy cat lady. Unlike me. I think you're already perfect, and you should consider this a fabulous vacation instead of time to improve yourself, because like I said. Perfect.

    Your cheering friend,

    Cecily

I set her letter aside and dressed in jeans and a tunic after my tepid bath. I made a mental plan for the day while my minimuffins baked.

I peeked outside on my way past the back door but didn't see the bunny. I'd borrowed a book on rabbits from the library during my last outing and learned the animals were crepuscular, meaning they were apparently busiest at dusk and dawn, then slept most of the day. The description tracked with my experiences, typically seeing it munching on my flowers or plants while I enjoyed my morning coffee or the evening sunset. I'd added a few pansies, violas, and asters to the ring of mulch around the patio yesterday. They were already missing most of their petals and leaves.

I returned my attention to the oven, donned a mitt, then moved the pans onto the stovetop, where they could cool.

"Please don't be disgusting," I whispered, pinching off a bite to taste. Then I smiled. "Not bad, Rini. Maybe you're becoming a little like Emily after all."

I loaded my finished products into the welcome basket Grace had left me, then carried it to town. Amherst was a kaleidoscope of fall colors, cheery voices, and laughter. Shops had set up pumpkin and gourd displays in their windows and at their doors. Scarecrows and hay bales adorned every flower bed along the main drag. October was coming, and this town was ready.

I adored slipping in and out of the familiar shops and making small talk with new friends. I ran into Daisy shopping at an adorable boutique, and she invited me out after our next letter-writing class. I didn't see Paul, but he'd given me a letter at the end of each class.

I nibbled on apple pie biscotti and enjoyed my coffee all the way home. I was putting myself out there, and the effort was paying off in fantastically social ways.

Emily Dickinson once wrote that fortune came to those bold enough to go after it. And as usual, she was right. I liked that Cecily had called me brave. I was taking steps in the right direction.

When I reached the lane to Hearthstone Manor, I collected the letters from my mailbox, then climbed the steps to Village Books and took a seat on the rocking chair outside the door. I loved this end-of-day ritual. I pulled my phone from my pocket and dialed my mom, who insisted on a proof-of-life call daily.

All the time spent at Rini Reads during my absence had helped my parents see how much had changed since I'd taken over. And it'd given them a realistic perspective on how badly we needed to hire some part-time help. Yesterday Mom even admitted to understanding why I'd wanted the time off.

Neither of us broached the subject of their retirement. But at least she'd stopped asking me to come home.

I tucked one foot beneath me on the rocker. Village Books would close soon, but I'd learned from previous evenings spent this way that Grace never left at closing time. She stayed late to prep for the next day. A practice I embraced as well.

The setting sun backdropped the distant downtown and the leafy trees, lighting them on fire as I waited for my call to connect. Curlicues of smoke rose from nearby chimneys, and the faint beat of the UMass marching band made me smile. I'd miss tonight's game because I didn't have a ticket or the internet, but I didn't mind. In moments like these, though I was technically alone, I didn't feel lonely at all. I certainly didn't feel as if I were missing out on anything.

I felt like one little piece of something much bigger. I was some-one who delivered appreciation muffins to members of the community, many of whom were beginning to recognize and greet me by name. It was both strange and wonderful to think I could belong to a new place in barely more than a week. And it inspired me to get out of the book-store back home and make more connections there too.

"Hello, Emma." Mom's chipper voice sprang through the line, bringing my thoughts back to her. "I've been looking forward to your call. I love hearing about your adventures. I only hate that we never talked this much when you were here."

My spine stiffened at her words, which sounded like a complaint. Part of me wanted to point out how little time I'd had in Willow Bend to make calls or do anything outside of work. But I kept those thoughts to myself because another part of me wondered if it wasn't just about my long hours.

I hadn't called or reached out to her or Dad very often before leaving town. I'd shown up for Saturday-night dinners, but otherwise waited for my family to come to me at the bookstore. Whenever they hadn't, I'd added it to my list of reasons to be upset with them.

The realization was a little startling. So instead of trying to defend my behavior by complaining about hers, I simply said, "Me too. I look forward to calling."

She sighed, and the amount of evident relief and love in that breath pinched my heart. "I love you, sweet girl. Are you having fun?"

"I am." I told her about my day and all the things on my mind. Then we laughed over the ridiculous but infuriating bunny who'd hit the jackpot when I arrived.

Mom told me about her day too. She and Dad were catching on to my new, streamlined systems at the store. She liked some, and hated others, but they saw that the revised processes worked.

When I asked about Annie, Mom told me to call her.

After saying goodbye, I sent Annie a text. Like the nightly messages I'd sent before, this one was quickly marked as delivered, then read.

Then ignored. This time, I sent a follow-up, making sure she knew I loved and missed her.

Next, I got comfy and opened my newest letter from Cecily.

> Dearest Emma,
> Amherst sounds adorable. I can't wait to get some time off so I can visit. The ER was infuriatingly slow today, which is nice for everyone who isn't in need of emergency medical attention, but it's been a bummer for me, personally. I can't help people if they insist on being safe and healthy.

I laughed. "How completely ridiculous of them."

I'd filled Cecily in on the details of my daily routines in my last letter, emphasizing how I'd doubled down on my stance against finding love. Then I'd complained a little about Annie.

Some days I'm completely brokenhearted by her, I'd written. *And other days I wake up thinking I should drive back to Willow Bend and pull her hair.*

Her response and reference to my complaint about Annie surprised me.

I miss your contagious energy, she'd written. *There are only ever two options with you. And both are extreme.*

I stared at the words a long moment before reading on. Cecily thought I was being dramatic.

Just like Annie.

My sister's words returned like a slap in the face.

I moaned. Was Annie right?

An older man with a mini sausage dog crossed the street in my direction. "Hey, Emma."

"Hi, Frank. Hey, Archie."

The foot traffic increased as folks headed to and from dinner.

My heart grew heavy when Cecily's letter ended, and I briefly considered calling her. The nights were long and lonely, but I had something extra to process tonight. Apparently I should've been a theater major.

I peeked through the bookstore's window as I rose, contemplating popping inside for a few minutes with Grace, when a soft bark turned me toward the street.

A golden retriever flounced in my direction, its long blond hair lifting in the breeze.

"Hey, you," I called, reaching for the friendly dog on instinct.

The incredibly attractive man on the other end of the leash arrived a heartbeat later. It took an extended moment for my brain to realize the man was Davis.

Dressed in sneakers, a UMass T-shirt and gray joggers, he looked youthful and fun. Like a college kid on his way to the game with friends, instead of a successful thirtysomething architect.

My body straightened, and I contemplated a fast escape. My brain, however, wanted to stay and get to know his dog and learn what Davis's life was like when he was off the clock. But that was the problem. The sparks I felt in his presence would burn down my entire mission if I let them. And he'd already apologized for kissing me. Before he ran away.

"Hey," he said, brows furrowed as he glanced from my face to the shop behind me.

"Hi." I moved off the bookstore's porch and onto the sidewalk. "What are you doing here?"

"I worked late and missed kickoff, so I decided to spend the evening with my favorite girl instead of at the game."

My mouth fell open.

Davis adjusted the dog's leash, and I chastised myself internally.

The dog was his favorite girl. Not me. Obviously.

Get it together, Rini.

I squatted to hone my focus. "Introduce us?"

"This is Violet," he said. "Violet, Emma."

"That's a very ladylike name," I told her, digging my fingertips into the doggy's soft fur.

"I found her on a jobsite a few years ago. The vet suspected she'd been abused and ran away. She was starving and freezing, so I took her home and nursed her. At the time I thought it would be a foster situation, but the minute she raised those big brown eyes to meet mine, finally feeling safe and no longer afraid, I was a goner."

I gave up on squatting and sat on the ground, pulling Violet onto my lap for a full-body cuddle.

"I was reading a book with an awesome orphaned heroine at the time, so I gave the name to this girl."

I raised a brow in question. "Give me another hint."

"About the book?"

I nodded, and he wrinkled his nose.

"*The Bad Beginning.*"

I laughed. That wasn't much of a hint. It was the title. "Lemony Snicket?"

He shrugged. "I saw an ad for the series on Netflix, and it made me want to reread the books. Violet was always my favorite, and she was an orphan. Not quite the same thing, but—"

"It fit." I bobbed my head, understanding. "I reread the Harry Potter series every time a new movie hit theaters. There were times I'd barely finished and another movie was on the way."

Violet licked my face and lowered her head to my lap, tail flopping.

"She loves people," Davis said. "But it usually takes her a few introductions before she climbs into someone's lap."

"Clearly she has fabulous judgment. Plus, I have an effect on people. Keep running into me like this, and you'll be next."

Davis snorted, and my cheeks flamed.

"You know what I mean."

He crossed his arms, a pleased smirk on his handsome face.

"'Dogs are better than human beings because they know but do not tell,'" I said, lost in a sea of fluffy golden fur.

"Are you quoting Emily Dickinson?"

I guffawed. "You knew that?"

"I grew up in a bookstore. In Amherst," he said. "Plus, our local school system is obsessed with her and Frost."

I bit my lip, hating how much I liked knowing those things about him.

The lights inside the bookstore went out, and I sucked in a breath.

The door opened, and Grace stepped into view.

Violet jumped up to greet her.

Grace looked from me to Davis, then smiled. "Hello, young people."

Davis bent to press a kiss to her cheek. "Hello, Auntie."

Something fluttered in my chest at the sweet show of affection.

"Enjoying the night?" she asked.

"Yes," we answered in near unison, and her smile grew.

"Well, don't look so guilty about it. Life is supposed to be fun. I'm going to the farm to split a bottle of wine with Olivia and talk about the men in our pickleball league. Let me know if you ever want to join us, Emma. For pickleball or boy talk." She rubbed Violet's head, then winked.

"I will," I said. "Thank you for the offer. Tell Olivia I'm fighting a bunny to keep her plants alive. I'm losing shamefully."

Grace snickered as she headed for a yellow convertible Volkswagen at the corner. "We'll have to come by sometime and take a look," she said. "Olivia can fix it. I'll bring the wine."

"Deal."

"Wait," Davis called. "I thought you needed help with something in the store."

She shrugged. "Nope. I'm all set. You kids have fun!" Grace dropped behind the steering wheel and drove away.

I creaked upright, dusting my clothes and backside, then collected my basket and bags. "Sounds like you got your night back."

"Really?" he asked. "I was just played by a meddling old lady."

I wanted to ask him for clarification but decided it was better I didn't know. "I should head back to the manor."

"Why don't we walk you?" Davis offered. "I hear it's unwise to be out alone after dark."

"You're alone after dark."

He tipped his head over one shoulder, as if weighing my words. "I have a dog."

I cast a pointed look at Violet. "I'm sure she's incredible protection."

Davis shifted her leash into the opposite hand, then tugged the bags from my grip. "Apparently. No one has ever tried to attack me on our evening walks."

I sighed playfully. "Fine. Let's go."

We moved down the lane at a snail's pace. I wasn't sure if I was prolonging our inevitable goodbye or avoiding our arrival, when I would definitely invite him inside. I thought again of our kiss, and my confusion returned. Why had he run away that night? The only reasonable explanation was that he didn't want to become romantically involved. But if that was true, then why volunteer to walk me home?

"How's everything at the manor?" Davis asked. "Are you staying warm? Not still heating bathwater on the stovetop?"

"No. Things are good. The water isn't especially hot, but it's not cold, either, and I can live with that."

"Very patient of you," he said, glancing at me from the corner of his eye. "The offer stands to help you find another place, if you get tired of this one. No hard feelings."

"I'm okay," I said, taking the final steps to my front door. "I appreciate the offer, but I like it here." I inhaled to steady myself, then braced for rejection. "Do you want to come inside for coffee? Or I could probably drum up some tea and brandy."

Davis stuffed his hands into his pockets and looked at me from beneath dark lashes. "Coffee sounds nice."

I nodded, then unlocked the door to let us in.

Violet trotted ahead of us.

I followed her to the kitchen, wondering if Davis would mention our recent kiss or if I should. Maybe that was his reason for accepting my invitation. I winced. What if he planned to apologize again. "I'll get Violet some water."

Davis unfastened her leash, then paused to check the thermostat. "Do you mind if I use the restroom? It's been a very long walk."

"Help yourself."

I put on a pot of coffee and set a bowl of water beside the back door. Violet took a sloppy drink, then collapsed beneath the kitchen table.

Davis returned a few minutes later looking mildly concerned.

"You okay?" I asked.

He nodded. "Just making a mental list of things I need to get done."

I filled two mugs with coffee and ferried them to the table. "You usually go to the UMass games?" I asked, nodding to his shirt and recalling something he'd said when he'd arrived outside the bookstore.

He glanced down at himself, then back to me. "Yeah."

"Ever go with Grace?" I asked, taking the seat across from his.

He frowned. "No. Why?"

I considered his response and the strange sensation I couldn't quite put my finger on, then shrugged.

Davis looked at me, pale-gray eyes flickering over my features.

For a moment, I wondered if he felt the looming awkwardness I did. Or the equally powerful urge to examine the tension further. Preferably with another kiss.

He stood abruptly, chair scraping over the floor.

For a moment I worried I'd said my thoughts aloud. "What's wrong?"

"I should go," he said. "Grace obviously set this up. She somehow knew you'd be there tonight and tricked me into coming."

"I go there every night," I said, bristling at his use of the word *tricked*. I rose and crossed my arms. "What's wrong with running into me?"

He released a humorless laugh. "Nothing, except that this"—he motioned between us—"is Grace's doing. And you're here on a mission. I don't want to take up any more of your time."

"What—"

Davis snapped Violet onto her leash again and headed for the door. A moment later, they were gone.

I locked up behind them, stunned and hating everything about the strange encounter.

At least I had a pot of coffee to keep me awake. I had a feeling my journal entry would be extensive. What sort of person kissed another person, then ran away? Only to walk the other person home a few days later, accept an offer for coffee, then rush off again without taking a single sip of the coffee?

And what did he mean by *You're here on a mission. I don't want to take up any more of your time*?

Did Davis want something romantic from me? Was that the reason for his erratic behavior?

This was why I needed to give up on love. Men were too confusing.

I returned to the kitchen on a groan and caught a glimpse of something white through the window. I peeked into the yard, clearly a glutton for punishment.

Outside, the bunny and three very small versions of itself ate my flowers.

Chapter Thirteen

I managed to lay low for two full days, spending time at the library and around the manor. I'd even perfected a second muffin recipe, though I hadn't dared attempt the black cake again. I'd go broke buying all the necessary fruit, and I could only drink so much cognac and hazelnut liqueur without an intervention. Mostly I'd thought about Davis, our kiss and chemistry. Why did his presence feel so warm and natural to me, and why did I crave his nearness when he kept running away?

The answer arrived in the next heartbeat and kicked me in my shins. *It's because I'm a glutton for punishment, a people pleaser, and terrible with rejection.*

In a burst of restless energy and desperation for a steaming-hot soak, I armed myself with the broom and dared a trip into the ancient basement. The hot-water heater sat as far from the door and stairs as possible, forcing me to cross the entire space with my chicken heart in my throat. Cobwebs were thick in the rafters, and everything was dank and eerie. But my phone's flashlight app solved the problem. As it turned out, the pilot light was lit, but the temperature on the tank had been set to low. I turned the dial to 120 degrees, then enjoyed a deliciously steamy bath. But the furnace refused to heat the home above 66 degrees, so I continued to wear warmer clothing and use more blankets.

I did not call Davis.

He messaged me daily to ask if I wanted him to stop by and look at anything. I received the messages when I left to explore the town and happened into signal range. I politely, but consistently, declined.

Occasionally, Davis texted random facts about Amherst, details about his day or an incredibly corny pun I couldn't resist. Apparently Grace and I weren't the only ones who enjoyed a good dad joke. I found him fun and easy to banter with via text, but tense and hard to read in person. My heart couldn't take the chaos of his hot-and-cold behavior.

Unfortunately, it didn't change the fact I loved everything I learned about him. And I was learning a lot through our messages. For example, he was a history buff, which Cecily would appreciate. And he watched *Relatable Romance*, which I found both unexpected and hilarious for reasons I couldn't quite name. But my favorite thing was how he spent his free time. Volunteering at the local humane society.

I needed to look into volunteering at the Willow Bend Greyhound Rescue when I got home. Emily had adored the Newfoundland her father had gifted her for company on her walks in the woods. Carlo, as the dog was named, lived sixteen years at her side.

Maybe I could foster a retired greyhound and name him Carlo in homage.

I grabbed my journal and the fountain pen while I waited for my apple bread to bake, and I forced my thoughts away from Davis and dogs.

My skills with the pen had improved minimally, but I was learning to take all wins for what they were. I pulled the metal nib downward and began to write.

I wanted a life
With an epic love story
Instead I died alone

I hung my head, then closed the book and stared through the window at my pitiful garden. I would grow old, alone, fighting forest creatures for wilted plants and eating so-so baked goods.

And I'd be happy about it, darn it.

The doorbell rang, and I rose with a sigh of relief, then set my journal on the baker's rack and went to welcome my visitor.

"Hello!" I called, opening the front door with a flourish and smiling brightly.

Olivia stood on the porch, holding a bouquet of white peonies and purple hyacinths. A large basket of small plants sat at her feet. "I heard you're having trouble with your garden."

I grinned. "I am."

"These are for you." She passed me the flowers. "No card."

"They're not from you?" I asked, turning the perfect blooms over in my hands and checking the paper wrapping for an indication of their origin.

"I found them on the doorstep," she said. "Looks as if they came from that place by campus. I recognize the paper."

"Oh." I had no idea which place she meant, or who would send me flowers, but I loved them, and her for coming to my rescue. I made a mental note to ask my mom and Cecily about the bouquet later, then hustled Olivia inside. "I'm so glad you made it."

"I wouldn't miss it. I love bunnies, the little nuisances."

I laughed, understanding completely. Why did a gardener's archnemesis have to be so darn adorable? "I initially thought I was battling one bunny, but as it turns out, that little furball has a family."

Her expression softened. "Well, you know that saying about the mating habits of rabbits. They all have families." She grinned and winked. "It's a good thing I have plenty of vegetables."

I stepped aside for her to pass, then closed the door behind us. "Have you eaten lunch?"

"No, but don't worry about me. I can't stay long."

"I made a charcuterie tray. It's nothing fancy, but please help yourself, if you want to snack," I said.

I'd been experimenting with more light meals lately, especially those that didn't require use of the stovetop, which had recently stopped cooperating.

Olivia set her basket aside, interest clearly piqued. "I love these trays. And you have jam from Edith's condiments."

I smiled. "I do. She was one of the first shop owners I met, and she let me try all of her preserves. The pita chips and garlic crackers are from the gourmet olive-oil-and-vinegar place on Elm. I bought all the fruits and veggies at the farmers' market."

"Mm, mm, mm," she hummed, nesting her hands together as she eyeballed the offerings. "You've been making friends."

I pulled a vase from a cupboard near the sink and added water before arranging the bouquet inside. A smile pulled at my lips as I thought of how much Emily had loved flowers too. Not only had she grown and arranged flowers, but Emily had created an herbarium, or collection of pressed plants and flowers. Over four hundred specimens in total. The concept fascinated me, but I knew I would always prefer people to plants.

"I try to get out and visit the shops every day," I said, responding to Olivia. "I get lunch, pick up coffee, see the sights. I'm becoming a regular at a lot of places."

She smiled and gestured to the bouquet. "Then it's no wonder you've gained an admirer."

"These are more likely from someone back in Willow Bend," I said. Though I couldn't help wondering if someone I'd spoken to regularly since arriving had taken the initiative to welcome me. Maybe the card had fallen out in transport, or a busy clerk forgot to include it.

Or maybe, I thought, *Paul sent them.* He'd written me several letters. Could his affections be more than welcoming friendship?

I wasn't sure how that made me feel, so I pushed the possibility aside.

"How's the manor?" Olivia asked.

Something about her tone made me wonder if Grace had put her on some sort of reconnaissance mission. "It's been good," I said, hoping to sound positive. "I've had a few small issues, but Davis helped with the furnace. And I adjusted the hot-water tank, which was very simple. Other than that, I'm doing well."

Olivia watched me closely for several beats, thin brows knitting. "I'm glad to hear it, but I hate that you've had trouble. It's quite a surprise, because Grace prepared the manor extensively for your arrival."

"It's all under control now," I promised. "As a bonus, I've learned a little about home maintenance." I selected a small plate and added a few of my favorite meats and cheeses.

"This is a fantastic spread," Olivia said. "Thank you for doing all this. You certainly didn't have to."

"I wanted to. My best friend, Cecily, is a charcuterie junkie, and I have fun making the boards. You'd like Cecily. She's hoping to come for the night soon. I've got my fingers crossed it works out." The words sounded calm as they left my mouth, but I was climbing the walls. I missed Cecily more than I thought possible and couldn't wait to introduce her to the town.

"I'd love to meet her. You should bring her to the farm, or the bookstore," Olivia said. "How are you enjoying the letter-writing class? Grace said you've become a regular."

"I adore it," I said. "I've made a bunch of friends, and I'm trading letters with my parents, Cecily, and classmates all the time now. Class is often the highlight of my day, honestly."

She tucked a grape into her mouth. "Too bad the man who sent you flowers didn't include a letter."

I glanced at the arrangement, wondering again who sent them, then concentrated on lunch instead.

By late afternoon, Olivia and I had nearly finished the charcuterie tray and planted more vegetables in the garden. Replacements for everything the bunny family had eaten. She left with a promise to return soon. And we agreed that next time we'd invite Grace and volunteer to share her wine.

~❧~

I dressed for the lower temperatures the next day, then grabbed my basket of muffins and the leftover charcuterie before heading up the lane to Village Books. I'd nearly filled my journals with doodles, poem attempts, and musings, so I needed to buy more. I planned to visit a local park to read and people watch. If I got hungry, I'd finish the meats and cheeses.

Emily's poems circled my mind as I lifted my chin to the sky. She loved nature and found exquisite joy in living.

The weather was perfect as I strode up the lane. I'd been in town less than two weeks, but I could easily imagine living there, and parts of me had already laid claim to my little portion of Amherst.

I smiled at that truth. How had I ever thought I'd spend six weeks here without making at least a few connections? Had I truly believed I might sit alone in the manor for six weeks? If so, Cecily was right—I really hadn't been thinking clearly when I'd made those plans.

An older man in a sharp black suit and burnt-orange necktie stepped out of the bookstore onto the porch, exiting as I reached the stairs. "Hello there," he said, eyes twinkling with delight.

I startled briefly, and he released a good-natured chuckle.

"Sorry. I'm Carter," he said, extending a hand. There was something oddly familiar about him, though we'd never met. "You're Emma, right? I wondered when I'd finally run into you. Grace tells me you're living at Hearthstone."

I accepted his handshake and relaxed at the mention of Grace's name. "I am, and it's beautiful," I said. "Stunning and peaceful."

Carter nodded. He was tall and broad shouldered with salt-and-pepper hair, shiny shoes, and a watch probably worth enough to pay for my entire stay at the manor. "I can certainly appreciate the beauty, but

I think I'd have stayed in one of the new condos with views of town or campus if I were you. I like modern-day amenities and Wi-Fi too much to spend more than a weekend there."

"It's definitely not for everyone," I agreed. "But it's exactly what I need."

He smiled, and his pale-blue eyes crinkled at the edges. "Well, I'm glad you're enjoying your time here." He pressed the door open and moved aside, clearing a path for me to pass.

"Thanks." I strode past him, wondering what else Grace said about me when I wasn't around and how many people she'd told I was renting the manor. "It was lovely meeting you."

I stepped into the bookshop, focused on the corner display of journals, notebooks, and stationery. Davis's voice drew my attention to the counter, and my body changed direction on autopilot. Caught in his tractor beam.

He wore jeans and a plaid button-down shirt, sleeves rolled up again, just like he'd worn them the night we met. His soft brown hair fell across his forehead, and he pushed it back as he noticed my approach. His smile grew immediately.

I set my basket on the counter. "Muffin?"

He reached a big hand into the basket and grasped a plump breakfast treat. "Thanks."

A tingle rushed over me.

"What are you doing here?" I asked, jerking my gaze away from his mouth and redirecting my thoughts.

"I'm ordering a few classics with holiday and winter scenes for a display next month. Any suggestions?"

"Uh, yeah. Of course." I leaned against the counter, my bookish mind diving into action. "Are we talking classics in the literal or emotional sense?"

He cocked his brow and rested impressive forearms on the counter. "Both."

"Then you've already got *A Christmas Carol*," I said, stating the obvious.

He nodded, and I rattled off numerous others that Grace and I always included for the holidays. "Of course."

"C. S. Lewis?"

"Chronicles of Narnia get their own minidisplay around here," he said. "What else?"

"*Murder on the Orient Express*?"

He grinned. "I forgot you like a little mystery with your holidays."

"I do." I paused for a moment, hung up on his words. "How did you know that?" We'd had a lot of conversations since my arrival, a few about books, but I hadn't said anything about mysteries. At least not as far as I could recall.

Davis sobered. "You must've mentioned it."

"I don't think so," I said. Then I thought of another possibility. A very chatty connection between us. "But I have told Historically_Bookish."

The muscle in his jaw ticked. "What do you mean?"

"Grace." I grinned. "I just ran into a stranger who knew my name and where I'm staying, because she told him. I'm guessing she's the one who told you about my winter reading habits."

Davis looked away, probably considering my hypothesis.

"Don't forget *Wuthering Heights*," I said as I tapped a fingernail against the counter to regain his attention. "If you didn't know, I read it every year when the snow begins to fall."

Davis relaxed and turned a clipboard to face me. He'd already listed all the books I'd named. Along with the other titles forming a line in my mind.

"You're good." Or a mind reader.

Hopefully not the latter.

His lips twitched, fighting a mischievous smile. "I know."

I laughed despite myself, and he chuckled in response.

Michael approached with a customer and a smile. "Hey, Ems!"

I waved as he rounded the corner, ducking behind the register to ring up the sale. He set a tablet beside Davis, then got to work.

"Thanks." Davis lifted a hand to Michael.

"Sorry I ran off the other night," Davis said a moment later, voice soft. "I shouldn't have done that."

"Which time?" I asked, still stinging from the way he'd left following our kiss. Still uncertain what had caused him to leave just as suddenly with Violet.

"Both. It's been a strange—complicated—couple of weeks for me."

A woman placed a stack of books on the counter in front of Davis. "Are you open?"

He nodded and moved away to handle the sale.

The tablet Michael had delivered caught my eye. A notification from IBOOM flashed onto the screen.

I stared, momentarily frozen. Was Michael an IBOOM user? I thought I knew everyone in the group.

His customer walked past me, a bag of books in hand, and I jerked my eyes to him.

Michael winked before greeting the next person in line.

Could he have sent me flowers?

I hurried to the notebook display. I chose a navy blue leatherbound book with long narrow ties and a set of new felt-tipped pens, because I was a sucker for colorful writing. And the fountain pen made me nuts.

Grace spoke to a couple near the local history books. I loitered nearby until they stepped away. "Emma!" She marched toward me with open arms. "How are you? How's the manor? Davis fixed all your problems, I trust?"

I glanced at the man in question, unsure how to answer, since he was the cause of a few of my problems too. "Things are good," I said diplomatically. "How are you?"

"Wonderful. You two looked cozy as I was leaving the other night. Did you find something fun to do after I left?"

I bit my lip, recalling the sting of his words. *Grace obviously set this up. She somehow knew you'd be there tonight and tricked me into coming.* "Not really."

Her gaze slid from me to her nephew and back. "He talks about you, you know. He thinks you're smart and interesting."

I gave Davis a curious look, then turned back to his aunt. "You missed the UMass game the other night," I said. Memories of her on the sidewalk, announcing plans to gossip about pickleball and boys, washed back to mind.

Grace wrinkled her brow. "I had other plans. How about you? Big plans today?"

"I actually stopped by to grab this." I wiggled the notebook in my hand. "I'm on my way to check out another local park before tonight's class." Letter-writing was scheduled at a variety of times throughout the week, making it available to everyone. I didn't have anywhere else to be, so I attended them all.

"Which park?" she asked, snapping into motion.

I followed her to the register.

"Puffers."

Davis reached for my book when I stopped at the counter.

Grace turned to face me. "I hear you have a secret admirer."

"Who?" Davis and I asked in unison.

"Whoever sent you flowers," Grace said. "Olivia called on her way home."

I looked to Davis, then Michael, and my cheeks flooded with heat. I forced a tight smile for Grace. "I'm sure they were from someone back home."

Her brows rose. "Are you? Because the way I hear it, you're making quite a splash around town. And I didn't only hear that from Olivia."

I puzzled a moment over her meaning. I had made a lot of new friends. "I'll keep you posted," I said, avoiding all eye contact and busying myself with my purse.

"I expect you will." She chuckled softly as she floated away looking wholly self-satisfied. "Enjoy Puffers park," she called. I returned the signed credit card slip to Davis with haste and grabbed the journal.

"Told you," he said. "She means well, but she's a meddler."

Chapter Fourteen

At Puffers park, I walked the trail until I found a perfect spot to enjoy the pond and people. It was too cold to swim, but I could easily imagine the beachy area packed with families and college students on a summer day. For now, the still water reflected the gorgeous display of early-fall colors, and the view from my elevated location was absolutely breathtaking.

I spread a blanket and took a seat, then unpacked my bottled water and leftover charcuterie, along with my new journal and pens. As an added bonus, my cell phone had two bars of signal, and I planned to use them before heading home. Until then, I had a lot to process.

For starters, I'd realized last night that I hadn't yet allowed myself to think about my parents' big request. They wanted me to take over their shop, their life's work. Their dream. They'd cleared it with Annie before asking me, but they wanted the whole thing to be mine. I swallowed a lump of emotion. It was an enormous honor. But was it my dream? And if they were already old enough to retire, how much longer would Annie and I have them with us? Was that morbid to think?

I couldn't imagine a world where my brilliant, kind, loving parents didn't exist. I didn't want to. A world like that would forever be darker. The thought pressed the air from my lungs.

I pushed the awful idea away, unable to sit with it a moment longer, and I asked myself two tough, but important, questions.

What was I doing with my life? What did I want to do?

Emily once wrote that she found life so startling there wasn't enough time to do anything else. If I truly wanted to emulate her words, I needed to start living. If I wanted to be more like her, I was beginning to realize, it would mean continuing on as I was. Emily had hidden behind her door in the later years. I'd spent my twenties hiding in plain sight, behind my busyness.

The thought was as unexpected as it was jarring. So, I sat with it a moment.

Cecily had known at twenty-one that she was on the wrong path, and though it'd cost her a lot of money and nearly two more years of education, she'd changed directions, gone into nursing, and never looked back.

I'd never been that certain about anything, and I was beginning to wonder if I'd ever been truly happy. Not just complacent.

I stacked a small slice of cheese onto a cracker and pushed it into my mouth. I should've taken inventory of my life sooner. Instead, I'd been running full speed in the same direction since college without questioning why. That wasn't something I could blame on anyone other than myself.

And this, I thought, *is why I'm filling notebooks at breakneck speeds.* There were a lot of things I hadn't given enough thought over the years, and once I'd started, it was as if a dam had broken. I uncapped a lavender-inked pen, opened my new journal, and began to write. The words flowed until my head felt light and my heart unburdened. When I raised my eyes to the beauty around me, I felt as if I were coming up for air.

A kayak glided into view on the water, carving ripples over the smooth surface and distorting the perfect reflections of orange- and amber-leafed trees.

Maybe it was all the time I'd spent thinking lately, or all the poetry I'd been writing. Maybe it was my dramatic side showing. Whatever the reason, as I looked out at my new favorite park view, I realized that my life so far had reflected the world around me, like the water. But at the moment, I was changing like the trees.

My pen hit the paper in a burst of inspiration and emotion.

> Choices are power
> The decisions are all mine
> No more feeling weak

My mission to become Emily Dickinson had failed on several fronts, but the more disturbing truth was that, for a long while, I'd made a terrible Emma Rini too.

Maybe Cecily had been right when she'd said I was looking for an excuse to run away. I'd been sad and unsure what to do about it. I'd blamed all my unhappiness on my lack of romantic love, but I had far bigger problems than that. I just hadn't been willing to examine them. I'd long thought Emily's solitude enhanced her poetry because she had time to see the world clearly and choose the perfect words for each moment. Now, alone on a hill, I felt closer to her than ever before. Thanks to her inspiration, I'd never be an incredible poet, but my world was finally coming into focus.

As for finding my soulmate—if he existed at all—now certainly wasn't the time.

I lay back onto the blanket and stared into the sky. Wanting what I couldn't have made me sad. So, I had to either get over it or manifest what I wanted.

I closed my eyes and smiled. Cecily said I always came up with two extremes. I folded my hands on my torso, then imagined myself twenty years older, surrounded by nieces and nephews, in a home I'd bought with income from my unnamed business, and I was perfectly happy about it all.

What kind of business did I own in this vision? Why hadn't I automatically assumed it was the bookstore? Was I still single? I concentrated on the image of myself, and willed a man to take shape then wrap his arms around me, perhaps ask me how work was today at my . . . office?

The sound of a barking dog made me open my eyes. Violet appeared, carrying a stuffed hot dog, presumably intended for tug-of-war. She happily lunged at me as I rose to a seated position. Her thumping tail wagged her entire body until she began to weave as she walked. Low guttural sounds of sheer doggy joy slid around her mouthful of hot dog stuffie.

"Hello," I cooed, sliding directly into baby talk. "Beautiful lady. I'm so glad you're here. Who is this?" I stroked her fur and tugged gently on the toy.

She pranced in her spot whining and harrumphing, unable to hold still.

Davis strode up the hill behind her, stopping at the edge of my blanket to smile down at me. "We keep running into one another."

"Are you following me?" I asked.

Or was mindful manifestation more fast acting than I'd realized?

He grinned. "I finished up at Village Books and stopped at home to walk Violet before going to the office. She was too wound up to go back in her crate."

"And you came here?"

"She loves this place," he said. "We avoid it this time of day in the summer when it's packed with people, but dogs can be off leash early in the morning, which she likes too."

I raised my brows.

"Find out who sent your flowers yet?"

I blinked at the swift change of subject. Was he jealous? Or just nosy? "No." Though I'd planned to call my family and ask before he'd appeared. I motioned to the empty space at my side. "Want to sit?"

"Woof!" Violet circled the space before me and sat.

I laughed. "Come on. You too. Pop a squat."

Davis lowered himself beside me.

I opened my plastic snack container. "Can she have cheddar?"

"Violet loves all cheese."

"A woman after my own heart," I said, offering her a chunk on my palm.

She dropped her toy.

"That's Frank," Davis said, nodding toward the stuffed hot dog.

I laughed as Violet's big pink tongue swept out, gently scooping the cube away.

"How are things going with the garden?" Davis asked. "Any more bunny problems?"

I frowned. "There are babies, and I think I'm providing the family's main food source. Don't laugh," I complained, attempting to give him the stink eye for his chortle. "They're too cute to chase away, and I can't let them go hungry."

"So you're feeding them."

I rolled my eyes. "Yes. Did you know bunny babies are sometimes called kittens? And a group of rabbits is called a fluffle?" My lips turned down, and I clutched my palms against my chest. "It's too cute. I have to feed them."

Davis snorted and wrapped big palms around bent knees. "My mom kept a garden at the manor."

I stilled, thinking of the place I'd planted my vegetables. "It was where mine is now, wasn't it?"

He nodded slowly. "She fed the local wildlife too."

My heart swelled, and I told it to pipe down. "I'm thinking of starting an herbarium."

"A what?"

"It's a collection of pressed flowers, plants, and leaves. Emily Dickinson was big on it." Considering the amount of time I'd spent outside walking and exploring local parks the last few days, creating an herbarium seemed more achievable and realistic than any of my previous goals.

Davis stretched out his legs and crossed his feet at the ankles. "She was also a big reader and writer. Have you tried that?"

I shot him my most infinitely bland expression.

"Woof."

I gave Violet another piece of cheese and a head scratch.

Davis watched me. "Of course you've already thought of that. So, what do you write about?"

I plucked the journal from the blanket and stuffed it into my bag. "Nothing." *My every thought, feeling, and emotion. My very unhelpful attraction to you.*

He leaned back, planting his elbows on the blanket—unusually fidgety, it seemed. "The other night . . . ," he began, then drifted off. "I overstepped."

I stared, wondering why he felt that way and why he kept bringing it up. I hadn't wanted to kiss anyone in a very long time, and I'd never made the first move. But I did, and he'd reciprocated. While the moment had lasted, I'd been happy.

"I don't normally kiss women I've only seen twice, or tenants of the manor," he said, glancing briefly away as he spoke. "Your presence here has caught me off guard, I think." He gave his head a little shake. "You aren't at all what I expected."

"What did you expect?" I asked, baffled. "Never mind." I exhaled sharply, putting the conversation away and pulling my knees to my chest. "Well, I'm glad we've cleared that up." No need to talk about it again. Ever.

Silence lingered between us, companionable yet charged, until all I could think about was kissing him.

His hand drifted closer to mine on the blanket. For a moment, I thought he might twine our fingers or cover my palm with his. Instead, his attention shifted to the soft fleece. "Is this from the Nifty Knitter on Pleasant Street?"

"Yes." I'd purchased the stadium blanket straight from the shop's window, instantly in love with the checkered pattern and desperate to stop freezing at night.

"For picnics and park days? Or because you're still struggling with the fireplace?"

I considered lying, but sighed and went with the truth. "I can make a decent fire, but it gets incredibly cold upstairs at night, and I don't want to sleep in the sitting room." I'd been thinking about buying a space heater.

For a moment, Davis appeared torn. "I'll come by tonight," he said.

"That's not necessary." Hope sparked in my chest, unbidden. I immediately shut it down.

Davis had sought me out, and he wanted to make plans to see me again later, but he couldn't stop apologizing for our kiss. Couldn't stop reminding me he wasn't interested. Irritation surged as the thoughts registered.

I'd been enjoying a perfectly nice afternoon of reflection, exactly what I'd come to Amherst to find, before he'd arrived with his fluffy dog and charming smile. Hadn't he apologized days ago for disrupting my quest for solitude? I really liked Davis, but his confusion only increased mine, and my time for finding peace was limited.

I rose, spell broken. "Actually, I forgot I have some errands to run, so I should go." I packed my things, wishing I could pull the blanket out from under him like a table magician.

"Now?" he asked. "At least let Vi and me walk you back to your car." He rose, but Violet remained curled contentedly at the edge of the blanket, Frank squashed beneath one of her front legs.

"You should stay," I said. "Enjoy the sunset. I'll get the blanket another time. Maybe leave it at the bookstore," I suggested, already hurrying down the hill.

⁓❧⁓

Daisy climbed out of her car as I finished the walk to Village Books that evening. I raised a hand in greeting, and she hurried to my side. "Emma! How was your day?"

"Long," I said, wrinkling my nose. "How about yours?"

"Same. I feel as if I'm about to drop. I had classes this morning, then worked a few hours afterward. I met friends for a chat and finished some homework. Now my brain is squishy, and I could really use a nap, but it's too late for that and too early for bed." She rolled her head over her shoulders while also rolling her eyes. "I figured this class is a great way to stay awake. Plus it's fun. Who cares about a little fatigue anyway, really?"

"It's a grad student's badge of honor," I said.

She frowned. "So much truth."

I held the door for her to enter the shop, then I slipped inside behind her. "How's your dissertation coming along?"

"Not bad. Our Miss Dickinson was a real mystery. Research keeps me busy. How's your quest? On a scale of one to ten, how Dickinson are you now?"

A laugh burbled from my chest. "I'm getting better at journaling and letter-writing, though I spend far too much time choosing my words, and I can't use a fountain pen for more than chicken scratch and ink blobs."

Daisy wrinkled her nose, then smiled sweetly. "I love Emily, but she isn't someone I'd want to emulate."

"It isn't turning out the way I expected. I definitely like people too much to be a recluse," I admitted. "And I like concepts like faith, fate, and destiny. I'm not sure Emily had any real spiritual faith or where she stood on the other things."

"A mystery," Daisy repeated.

"I hate how little success she had with her work before her death. I wonder if that made her sad. What would she think of the way the whole world knows her now?"

"Excellent questions," Daisy agreed.

"I'm getting better at baking," I said. "I can see why she enjoyed it. There's a bit of art and magic in the process." Much like gardening, I realized.

Daisy perked up. "Emily Dickinson was an incredible baker. She shared her finished products generously with family, friends, and neighbors."

"Something I've been doing as well." Though not yet with my family.

"She even kept a basket and rope in her bedroom," Daisy continued. "She used it to lower gingerbreads and baked goods down to the children who drifted over while her brother and his wife entertained next door."

I thought of standing in Emily's bedroom when I'd visited her home. I'd looked through her window and wondered what she saw as she wrote. Now I imagined the green grass dotted with children in search of fresh sweets.

"Folks found drafts of her poems on the backs of old recipe cards and flour labels after her death." Daisy's expression turned wistful. "As if inspiration had struck in the kitchen and she'd stopped in her tracks to write. I'd kill to be that inspired by anything other than a nap and promise of graduation next spring."

Paul hooked his satchel over a chair at the table and raised a hand to us in greeting.

Daisy grabbed my arm and pulled me toward the refreshments table. "What does he write in all those letters he gives you?" she whispered.

"He tells me about his days. Sometimes he'll recommend a book he's reading or tell me about something he saw that reminded him of me."

Daisy pressed a palm to her collarbone. "That's so romantic."

"It's not like that." I moved aside so she could grab a snack. "I think he's just a nice guy, and I'm new here. He's been trying to make my stay more comfortable since we met."

"Or he's been crushing on you and trying desperately to woo you into feeling the same way."

"There's no wooing," I assured.

"He's a hopeless romantic," she said. "Word around campus is that he married his high school sweetheart."

"What?" I whipped my head around in search of him. "He's married?" I whispered.

"No." Daisy shook her head. "She left him a few years ago."

"That's awful."

"That's life sometimes," Daisy said.

I didn't argue.

Paul joined us at the coffee station, his genuine and easy smile in place. "Hi, Emma, Daisy. What's up?"

I looked away, ashamed by our gossip.

"We were just talking about what goes into a good letter," Daisy said.

"If you figure it out, let me know."

I rocked back on my heels, relieved by his humor. "The process is harder than I expected. There's so much pressure to say the right thing. To not waste space or words." Those were my struggles, anyway.

"It helps not to overthink," Paul said. "Keep it simple and have fun." He lifted his cup in cheers before taking his leave.

My gaze trailed after him, wondering if I'd ever reach that level of letter-writing confidence. I was pretty sure my current level of Dickinson was two out of ten.

Chapter Fifteen

I woke, freezing, at half past two.

My teeth knocked together, and my muscles were locked. "What on earth?" I swung my legs over the bed's edge and gathered the comforter around my shoulders.

The little red light on my new space heater was off.

I stood on quaking legs and thick-fuzzy-socked feet, then went to press the power button. Nothing happened.

I moved to the wall and slapped the light switch.

Again, nothing happened.

All the cuss words I knew spilled from my mouth as I struggled to still my chattering teeth.

The power was out. The furnace was off. My new space heater was useless.

And I was probably getting hypothermia.

I fumbled on the nightstand for my phone and accessed the flashlight app; then I scanned the wider space around me. Unexpected panic welled in my chest. I was alone and cold in a home that wasn't my own. I didn't know how to fix the problem, and the space heater was likely the cause. I'd probably overloaded the outdated electrical system. Davis was going to be pissed. He'd made it clear he planned to overhaul these things when I left, but I'd insisted on staying, even after he'd offered to help me move. And I'd denied him access to look at the furnace before I went to bed tonight, even after he'd offered to stop by and take a look.

I'd tried to fix another problem on my own and failed. Apparently my hot-water-tank victory was a fluke.

Suddenly all the other failures in my life formed a kick line and danced into my mind, each stomping a little harder on my heart until tears began to brew.

I'd moved to Amherst to escape my constant, habitual search for love, but my ridiculous heart had latched on to someone who ran hot and cold and didn't want me. I'd planned to embrace the solitude, but instead, I hated it. I loathed the endless silence. I'd wanted to bake cakes, read, and create poetry, but I'd failed and failed. Now I'd wrecked a historic manor's electrical system. And there wasn't any way to hide or run from that. I had to face Davis and explain what happened or freeze to death in my denial.

My pride spent several long moments debating the options.

Eventually I crept downstairs using my flashlight app and the occasional shaft of moonlight through windows to guide me. I flipped every light switch I came across, not expecting, but hoping, that maybe part of the house still had power.

When I raised my phone to the thermostat, I saw that the temperature had fallen below fifty degrees.

I dropped my head gently against the wall and thunked it lightly a few times. Thankfully I'd dressed warmly before bed, because I had to go outside to get a cell signal.

If this was actually the 1850s, I'd have to walk to a neighbor's home for help and hope I wasn't eaten by whatever lurked in the shadows.

I slid my feet into sneakers and crept into the night. The extraordinarily loud crunch of gravel beneath my feet seemed enough to wake the dead, and the reaching limbs of ancient oaks looked unusually ominous and gnarly. I didn't stop until the streetlights came into view, along with a single bar of service on my cell phone screen.

I dialed Davis from a patch of moonlight on a mosaic of fallen leaves, thankful my cell phone's battery still had a charge.

He answered on the second ring. "Hello?" His voice sounded low and scratchy with sleep.

I pushed images of him in bed from my mind. "It's Emma."

"Emma? Are you okay?" His voice cleared, and I felt instantly horrible for waking him.

"I'm okay," I said. "But the power's out. It's cold, and I hoped you could help."

"Give me ten minutes."

I took a seat on the curb and waited in a cone of light from a streetlamp.

His truck turned onto the lane nine minutes later. Violet rode shotgun at his side.

He powered down his window as I stood. "Get in."

I hurried to the passenger door, a comforter tied around my shoulders like a cape. "Thank you for coming."

Violet licked my face as I settled, and the truck began to roll once more.

"I wanted to do this earlier," he said, voice thick with fatigue. "Not at two a.m. What happened?"

"The power's out."

He frowned in my direction. "You mentioned that. Anything else you can tell me?"

I shook my head, avoiding eye contact.

I gave myself a swift mental kick for not hiding the space heater before I'd felt my way downstairs to call for help.

The truck rocked to a stop outside the manor, and we all piled out.

I unlocked the door, and he led the way inside. Violet stayed with me, while Davis headed to the basement, presumably in search of the fuse box.

I dashed up the steps, desperate to hide my crime. I was nearly at the top when my toe caught on my blanket and pitched me forward. "Shit!"

"Woof!" Violet lunged, steadying me as I made it to the second floor. The tip of my big toe throbbed as I hopped into the bedroom and tucked the space heater behind the open door. And then we went back downstairs to wait.

A few moments later, the manor came to life.

"Fixed for now," Davis called, clomping back up from the basement. "I need to spend some time with the breaker box soon, but this should hold you." He stilled and looked around, eyes squinted against the light. "Do you sleep with all these lights on?"

"I tried all the switches before calling."

He made a small sound I suspected was laughter.

"I didn't want to bother you," I said, crossing my arms and clutching the blanket more tightly around my shoulders. "I hate that you had to rescue me. Again."

"At least you didn't fall down this time."

I looked away, then at Violet, thankful she would keep my secret. "Can I offer you a cup of tea before you go?"

He nodded. "Sure. That sounds nice."

I moved into the kitchen, shutting off extra lights as I went and hoping he'd stay for a while before racing back into the night.

Davis followed. "Any trouble with the stove or hot water? I'm guessing cold baths and takeout are getting pretty old."

"Nope." I filled a kettle and placed it on a freshly cleaned burner, then flicked the gas flame to life.

His eyes widened at the flash.

"I relit the oven's pilot light, then cleaned the stovetop burner tubes and ignitions." *Thank you, North Amherst Library.* "The thing probably works better now than it has in years. I don't know what clogged it up, but whatever it was might as well have been tar. I'm surprised you didn't notice when you prepped the place for me or found the problem after your last guest."

"How'd you know how to do that?" he asked.

I would never tell. His expression was too priceless. "I turned up the temperature on the hot-water heater too. I hope that's okay. No one wants to bathe when the dial is set to low." That also seemed like something Davis should know, but I didn't want to dwell on problems already solved.

Several minutes later, we carried our cups into the sitting room, and Davis started a fire in the fireplace.

Violet curled on the floor near the hearth and began to snore.

I thought of Emily, wondering what she'd say if she could see me now. The words of one of her poems came swiftly to mind. *The soul should always stand ajar, ready to welcome the ecstatic experience.*

Alone in the night with Davis and his dog, quietly enjoying a fire, definitely felt like an ecstatic experience, even if I knew it shouldn't. And though I came to town to break my habit of longing for love, I suddenly felt badly for Emily, who'd never had any known lovers. How awful, for a woman who felt things so deeply, to have missed out on the wonders of romantic love and its incredible chemistry.

"How's the social media coming for Grace's store?" I asked, redirecting my errant thoughts.

Davis frowned. "Slow."

"Does everyone at Village Books use the same IBOOM handle?" I asked as a new thought tickled the back of my mind.

He rubbed a palm against his darkly stubbled cheek, and for one small beat, I let myself imagine what it would feel like to do the same. "Yeah. Why?"

I bit my lip as a dozen little things popped into mind and a swarm of bees took flight in my stomach. "Does Grace have season passes to UMass?"

"Not that I'm aware of. Why?"

I couldn't remember seeing her in anything with the team's logo, or even in the team's colors, but online she'd seemed like a huge fan. And she didn't like hot wings, but online she'd gone as far as to rate several local shops. She'd looked borderline confused when I'd mentioned a wing buffet the first time we'd met.

"What are you thinking?" he asked, one brow arching high.

I weighed my next words carefully in case I was wrong. "She's seemed off every time we've spoken in person. Kind and sweet, but not fun-loving and silly. No dad jokes."

I suppressed a groan as my mind spooled faster.

"Michael carried a tablet with him to the register today when you were working. The IBOOM group was up," I said. "Oh, my goodness. Historically_Bookish is Michael," I said, feeling utterly daft. Of course I hadn't connected so fully with someone more than twice my age. Of course Grace had seemed different in her emails than on IBOOM. She wasn't Historically_Bookish.

"Michael?" Davis asked.

"It has to be, right?" I sifted mentally through our online encounters and compared those to the in-person conversations we'd had in town. "He's taking classes at UMass, attends all the home games, always has a wink or smile for me."

"Michael," Davis repeated, his voice hardening on the word. "Is your online best friend?"

"I wonder if he's the one who sent flowers," I whispered, more to myself than to Davis.

Davis frowned. "Does it matter?" he asked. "What about number ten on your list? Giving up on love?"

"I'm not trying to find love, and I'm not falling for Michael. I'm just trying to make sense of the senseless. Besides, if it's not Michael, then who? Because now I'm convinced it's not Grace I've looked forward to chatting online with every day for the past few years."

A small shiver wiggled through me despite the warmth of the fire, and I rubbed my palms against my arms to erase the goose bumps.

Davis stood, limbs unusually stiff. "I'll start a fire in your upstairs fireplace," he said. "It's going to take a while for the furnace to get the whole place warm."

I listened as he climbed the stairs, imagining Michael as Historically_Bookish, and wondering if the possibility annoyed Davis. Because something certainly seemed to.

And if so, *why?*

Violet's ears perked, and she trotted into the kitchen. I followed, too restless to be left with my thoughts.

She rose onto her hind legs and wedged her big head under the lace curtain, then pressed her nose to the window.

The brown-and-white cat sat on my patio. A collection of bunnies dotted the garden. "Welcome to my menagerie," I said, stroking her soft fur.

Davis reappeared, looking aghast.

"You look like you saw a ghost," I said, unable to hide my humor.

"No, I just—" He looked around the room, then back to me. "Have you ever had a plan that seemed perfect, until you tried to execute it—then everything that could possibly go wrong did?"

"Uhm." I drew out the sound, then laughed. "I came here to become Emily Dickinson. Of the ten things I'd hoped to accomplish, I'm only succeeding at the ones that matter least." And often not very well. "So, yeah. I can relate."

His keen gray eyes were on me again, and the air thrummed between us.

"Why?" I asked, a little too breathlessly. "What was your plan?"

I wasn't sure who moved first, but in the next heartbeat, Davis and I met at the room's center. Toes nearly touching, my back arched, and our gazes locked. One of his hands rose tentatively and skimmed my arm from elbow to shoulder. A small smile tugged his lips as I struggled to breathe.

"Is this part of your plan?" I asked, since he hadn't answered my question. At least not in words.

He shook his head. "I was thinking of an old literature professor who pushed us to dig deep with our papers, in our work, and in our lives. He kept this quote on the board all year and used to hit it with a yardstick when someone volunteered something profound. 'Make the most of your regrets.'"

"Henry David Thoreau," I said. "You had Professor Donohue."

Davis released me, falling back a step, expression lit with interest. "Sophomore year."

I hated the loss of his touch, but curiosity kept me focused.

"He was my first class freshman year. Eight a.m. I was nervous, not even sure I was in the right room, and he opened with a swat of that yardstick. I nearly spilled my coffee."

"I can't believe we had the same professor. I graduated about three years ahead of you, but we might've been at the same parties."

"I doubt that," I said. I hadn't gone to parties. It was hard enough just to make it to all my classes with the long commute back and forth from Willow Bend. "I went to every game I could, though. I always sat right behind the row of topless guys with red letters painted on their torsos."

Davis barked a laugh and raised his hands into the air. "*M.*"

"Shut up."

He pressed his hands to his chest. "Sophomore to senior year. Swear on Sam the Minuteman."

"Imagine if we'd met then," I said, smiling. Instead of here and now.

"I was more fun then," he said. "You would've liked me. I still liked myself a little."

I offered a sad smile. "I kind of like you now."

His features softened into something like remorse, and I hoped I hadn't said the wrong thing. "I should get going."

The words knocked me back a step. Why was he leaving abruptly again, when everything was going so well? Because I said I liked him? *That can't be it,* I told myself. Davis knew I liked him already or I wouldn't have kissed him.

He patted his leg, and Violet jumped to his side.

"You don't have to go," I said.

"It's late, and I've got an early morning," he countered. "The fires should keep you warm if the breaker blows again." He turned and I followed.

It took a moment for his words to settle. Davis had lit a fire in the bedroom fireplace. "What about the bats?" I asked, not in a hurry to become the next Mrs. Dracula.

He stopped beside his truck, brows furrowed. "What?"

"You said bats roosted in the chimney so I shouldn't mess with that fireplace."

Confusion turned to irritation as he unlocked the door. "Well, I made sure the chimney was clear."

Violet hopped inside and waited.

His tortured expression would've broken my heart if I wasn't so befuddled.

"Call me if you have any more trouble," he said.

Then he drove away.

Chapter Sixteen

I dragged myself up the steps to my room, alone and miserable. Davis and I had been students together at UMass. I'd never given thought to us being on campus at the same time, having the same teachers, and walking the same paths.

I couldn't help wondering if we'd have hit it off then, or if there were versions of us in another life who enjoyed the good without all the bad. How long could I endure the mixed signals that kept me confused and on edge? Never mind his hasty departures, yet another form of rejection. Annie and Jeffrey met at UMass; so had Mom and Dad. I'd never begrudged Annie's opportunity to follow in our parents' footsteps, living on campus and meeting her mate there. I was proud of the sacrifice I'd made so she could have the college experience she wanted. But I'd also silently mourned that I hadn't had the chance to do the same.

I supposed, in a way, my experience was similar to Emily's. She'd attended Amherst College for a short time before returning home, where she stayed until she died. I'd simply skipped the part where I left home.

Until now.

Fire crackled in the fireplace as promised, and I sloughed off my blanket cape, overheated by my catastrophic frustration. I needed twelve hours of sleep to clear my head, and a long phone call with Cecily to untangle my thoughts.

Unfortunately, I couldn't use my phone as much more than a flashlight in the manor. So, I'd have to settle on writing another letter.

Cecily would flip when she heard about the possibility Michael, not Grace, was Historically_Bookish. I still didn't know who'd sent my mystery bouquet. And I was pretty sure I'd nearly kissed Davis again tonight. Leave it to Professor Donohue and his yardstick to ruin my fun, even twelve years later.

Emily Dickinson once wrote that she considered her friends her estate.

I couldn't agree more. And I hated being separated from my best friend when I needed her most.

❦

I stayed in bed as long as I could manage the next day, avoiding my life. When my stomach growled and my bladder cried, I forced myself upright and slogged downstairs.

Ten minutes later, I carried a mug of coffee up the lane to the mailbox, eager to send off my latest to Cecily. The morning grew brighter when I saw a letter from her awaiting me. I tore it open immediately.

> Dearest Emma,
> I had no idea you really liked this guy. I think you should call so we can talk about this properly. Writing letters isn't getting the job done for me. Friendly reminder, you don't actually live in the eighteen hundreds.

I could practically hear her huffing, and I smiled.

> I love that Davis and his dog make you happy. I want you to be happy. Are you happy? Please tell me

the answer is yes, because that was literally on your list
of things to do there.

I considered the question, unsure how to answer. I wasn't *un*happy.
I liked the town, the manor, and my new friends, but I wasn't reaching
the goals I'd set for myself, and that frustrated me. I blew out a long
breath and read on.

You say you're a subpar Emily Dickinson, but I
think you're a really great Emma Rini, and isn't that
better?
All my love,
Cecily
P.S. Call me you nut!

I wiped my eyes and nose with a wad of tissues I'd tucked into my
bra. I squeaked when the phone in my pocket rang.

Cecily's name graced the screen, and I nearly broke a finger answering so fast.

"Finally!" she said. "I miss you. How are you? Tell me everything.
I'm trying to respond to all your letters, but work has been intense, so
I'm behind."

"I miss you too," I said, voice cracking as tears welled and began
to fall.

"Are you crying?" She gasped. "Is it the handyman? I can be there in
an hour. If he's done something to hurt you, I can make it in forty-five
minutes."

"No," I said, waving a hand she couldn't see. "It's not him. Not
really. Amherst Emma is just an emotional mess."

"I'm not sure I like you speaking about yourself in third person,"
she said. "I'd say this whole trip has pushed you over the edge, but it's
more likely this is the first time you've let yourself feel anything other

than busy in a really long while. Brace yourself. You might've opened the floodgates."

I thought something similar not so long ago. "Great."

"Hey. Letting yourself feel things is good," she said. "You're not hiding behind checklists and the store anymore. All that time alone probably has you paying attention to yourself, your thoughts, and your needs for a change. That can be hard. You can always come home if this isn't what you wanted. You call the shots."

I tensed but couldn't speak. I didn't love the way things were going in Amherst, but I wasn't ready to return to Willow Bend.

"Just remember," she encouraged. "You're hurting, and you have a huge support system here. Family, friends, the store, the community. No one will care or judge you for coming home early. We'll just be glad you're back."

I took a seat beneath a tree and pulled up a handful of grass. "Thanks for saying that, but I have to see this through."

"Are you sure?"

A couple I recognized from class waved as they crossed the sidewalk at the end of the lane. "Morning, Emma."

I waved and smiled, hoping I was too far away from the street for them to see my puffy, red eyes and tearstained cheeks.

"Who was that?" Cecily asked.

"Pam and Jack. They came to one of the letter-writing classes on a date. They own an alpaca farm outside town."

Before Cecily could comment, a woman jogging by called out as well. "Hi, Emma!"

"Hi, Kate," I called. "Kate works at the café where I have lunch sometimes," I explained to Cecily. "My friend Daisy introduced us."

Cecily hummed, the small thoughtful sound she often made when coming to an internal conclusion. "Sounds like you've found a community there too."

I let the warmth of that truth settle over me. "I have." And for a moment, I imagined what life might be like if I stayed in Amherst long term.

"Well, that changes things," Cecily said. "I didn't like the idea of you in that big house, all alone and sad. But I guess you aren't alone. So—you're staying?"

I nodded absently, still caught in the dream of laying down roots for a fresh start. "Yeah."

If I didn't live in Willow Bend with my family, would our time spent together during visits be more enjoyable? Would the moments mean more? I could still come home on Saturdays for family dinner. Though I'd be tempted to get season tickets to UMass if I lived right down the street.

"I'm still trying to get enough time off work for a proper visit. Until I do, you need to call me sometimes. Hang on, I'm sending you something."

My phone dinged with a text message.

"That's my work schedule. The letters are fine, and texts are, too, but I like to hear your voice and know you're okay."

"I wish I could hug you."

"Soon," she said. "What's on your agenda today? More baking? Gardening? Journaling?"

"I don't know. The bunny has babies, so I'm mostly raising the produce to support its family now."

Cecily snorted.

"I've started pressing flowers, though, and that's kind of nice."

Cecily was silent, probably waiting for me to crack.

"Okay, it's a little boring, but it's pretty."

"That sounds more realistic. How's the baking?"

"I don't hate it, but I'm not a huge fan. I'd rather be anywhere than trapped in the kitchen."

"Hard to bake from somewhere else," she said.

Accurate. Not to mention I'd accumulated a stockpile of muffins and breads. Probably enough to survive an apocalypse.

A small hatchback turned down the lane, and I watched as it rolled to a stop in front of me.

"Someone's here," I said, pushing onto my feet and wiping the hollows beneath my eyes.

A girl with black hair and goth makeup rose from the driver's seat. "Emma Rini?"

"Yeah."

"Who is it?" Cecily asked.

"Not sure."

The woman fished in her back seat and came up with a bundle of flowers wrapped in familiar paper. "For you." She passed the bouquet to me, then returned to her ride and reversed away.

"Emma," Cecily said. "What's going on? I knew we should've done a video chat."

"Flowers," I said, admiring the white peonies and purple hyacinths. "They're just like the ones I got before, but this bunch is way bigger." I peered into the paper, searching through the stems and buds for a card.

"Still no idea who they're from?"

My fingers connected with the corner of a small card-stock rectangle, and I pulled it into view. "This one has a card."

"Oh, tell me, tell me, tell me," she sang. "Are they from Davis? Apology flowers? Maybe from the guy who writes you all those letters? Paul?"

Or Michael, I thought. I needed to fill her in on that revelation too. I'd written it in the letter, but she was right—talking was faster.

"What does the card say?"

I stared at the inky curves. "It's just a heart."

"Is that romantic or creepy?" she asked. "I'm confused by your dual timeline. In the twenty-first century, I'm leaning toward creepy. In the late eighteen hundreds, I'm guessing sweet?"

"You and my family are the only ones who know what I'm doing here," I said. "So, if it's from one of them, definitely sweet." Though Davis had seen my original list of goals. Becoming Emily had been one of those. Could he have sent me flowers?

I wrapped up the chat with Cecily, eager to ask my parents if the flowers were from them. But first I texted Annie.

I sent a set of quick messages letting her know I loved her and looked forward to becoming an aunt. I probably didn't tell her either thing often enough, and that was on me. I also let her know she could visit me in Amherst anytime, if she wanted to get away before the baby arrived. The invitation was a long shot, but also an olive branch. I hoped she'd take it. I didn't bother asking if she'd sent the flowers. She was still unhappy with me when I'd left.

A call to my parents quickly confirmed they hadn't sent the bouquets.

And the mystery continued.

I walked back to the manor, interest piqued, and filled my mug with fresh coffee.

I was in the market for a new hobby, so I headed to the study. I'd incorporated journaling, reading, writing poetry, baking, and gardening into my days. It seemed like the right time to further embrace the era, especially since I couldn't manage to embrace the solitude.

A set of books outlining life in the late 1800s, specifically for women of Emily's social status, caught my eye. So I pulled one from the shelf then settled onto the window seat. I nearly laughed at the first few suggestions for female hobbies. I couldn't sing, paint, or draw, so I immediately dismissed those possibilities and also skipped the sections on playing the piano or violin. Croquet had grown in popularity during Emily's lifetime, but I couldn't exactly invite a bunch of modern-day women over for croquet without seeming mad.

I skimmed onward several chapters, then paused to read aloud.

"Women frequently held salons, or small gatherings of friends and acquaintances of particular note in society. Participants traded stories and gossip while enjoying tea or hors d'oeuvres." A salon sounded nice, but I wasn't sure I wanted to host anything. Emily wouldn't have, especially by the time she reached my age. In fact, she sometimes spoke to people through a crack in the door. And she'd only attended her father's funeral by leaving her bedroom door open and listening to callers and the pastor from the second floor.

I sighed and made a note to circle back to salons if necessary.

The pages on embroidery seemed promising. I was sure I could buy everything I needed at a craft store in town. I made a list for reference and moved on.

When I made it to the chapter on crafting with human hair, I closed the book. "Embroidery for the win, then."

❧

The next day, I met Daisy and Kate at the coffee shop on Elm and Vine. Kate told us about a new set of condos going in a few blocks from downtown. The land developer planned to raze a pair of historic farmhouses and their respective barns to clear the way.

"Those buildings have been standing there longer than the colleges," Kate said. "Why not make the land into parks or living museums? Why not designate the homes as historic and use federal grant money to restore them?"

Daisy patted her mouth with a paper napkin. "Davis Sommers tried."

My ears perked. "What did Davis do?" I asked.

"Everything he could," Daisy said. "That's what I heard, anyway. My roommate's boyfriend works in the history department at the college, and I guess Davis was there all last month, working with a professor to apply for grants. When that wasn't going to happen fast enough, and without guarantees, he talked to someone in the law school about possible legal actions he could take to slow the land developer long enough to acquire the grants."

"The land developer is his dad," Kate said.

My jaw dropped. "No." I thought of Michael and Grace saying the Sommers men were a big deal in town and how different their goals were. I couldn't help wondering what that meant to their relationship. My parents and I didn't always see eye to eye, but I'd never have to consult legal counsel to settle a disagreement.

"Mr. Sommers has saved a lot of small businesses, but I think he'd trade every historic property in town for something with ten floors and fifty potential rental units," Kate said. "I don't know how many people realize his kindness has a price. He offers help that leaves folks feeling indebted to him. Like making big donations to little league teams, dance schools, and community projects. Then no one wants to step on his toes because he helped them. That's how he ends up getting his way on the big things like this."

I frowned. "That sounds incredibly manipulative."

Daisy gave me a pointed stare, and Kate nodded.

My phone began to buzz in my pocket, drawing my attention to a series of notifications from IBOOM. A quick peek revealed a GIF and snark war happening in real time between Historically_Bookish and a part-time clerk in Salem we often teased for being too uptight.

I gave my friends a polite lift of one finger to let them know I needed a second; then I scrolled through the comments to see what all the commotion was about.

Witch_Please_1692 worked a couple of days a week at a mystic-themed shop, and only responded to posts when they wanted to complain. This time they'd taken issue with the *Outlander* display post made days prior.

Witch_Please_1692: Not sure what's worse, that joke or the display itself. No one's reading that series anymore. I suppose being stuck in the past is typical for anyone in Amherst.

Historically_Bookish: You realize you have 1692 right in your handle, yeah? Who's obsessed with the past?

Historically_Bookish: Also, Outlander books are literally timeless

Historically_Bookish: 😄

Witch_Please_1692: 🙄

Historically_Bookish: You just don't understand time travel. I made a similar joke tomorrow, but you didn't get it then either

Witch_Please_1692: (GIF of a child wearing a painfully bland expression)

Witch_Please_1692: Defending yourself today? No @ED_Fan to rescue you? Surprised the two of you aren't attached at the hip with them in your town

Historically_Bookish: Most things probably do surprise you

I snorted an indelicate laugh, then quickly pressed the Like option on that comment, because it was hilarious. And because I couldn't resist, I began to type.

ED_Fan: I think @Historically_Bookish is holding their own

Witch_Please_1692: Me too. Likely every night

My jaw dropped, and a rumble of laughter burst from my lips. I pressed a palm to my mouth. A few heads turned my way in the café, including Daisy's and Kate's. I pretended not to notice, too rapt in the online battle.

Other members of IBOOM began to jump on board, with images of things going up in flames or otherwise being burned.

"Everything okay?" Daisy asked. "I can't tell if you're amused or ready to throttle someone."

"Amused," I admitted, tucking my phone away.

How had I ever thought Historically_Bookish was Grace?

Was Michael really the one behind the handle? I recalled him smiling and winking from his spot at the register. He'd been exceptionally warm and welcoming from the day we met in person. I remembered him asking me about the manor and sticking up for Davis when I'd called him a grouch. In fact, it was Michael who told me Davis was an architect like his dad. Not Grace. Almost as if Michael and I weren't meeting for the first time that day, but old friends.

I sat with the possibility for a moment, comparing my interactions with Michael in person against my relationship with Historically_Bookish online. There were definite similarities. Both were playful and funny. Both loved the Minutemen. My gut said the energy wasn't a perfect match—but I'd once thought Historically_Bookish was a seventyish woman, so what did I know?

❧

The threat of thundershowers in the forecast kept me inside most of the next day. This time I was prepared for hours alone indoors. I'd purchased everything needed for the art of embroidery. And I tried. But I was bored and restless before sunset. Not to mention injured. Loose threads piled on the floor at my feet. My thumbs, and multiple cotton canvases, were dotted with my blood.

"Masochists," I whispered to the ghosts of women past.

I'd accidentally stabbed myself with a needle at least one hundred times in two hours, and I couldn't take it anymore. The nearly finished scrap in my hands wasn't worth the pain. A series of small black Xs formed a rough circle where a garland of delicate flowers should've gone. Jagged, chicken-scratch letters leaned against one another inside.

If I squinted, I could make out the words *Salty Bitch*. Which I absolutely was.

I dropped my masterpiece onto the arm of the couch, then tipped over sideways, dragging my feet up beside me. I was exhausted and starving. I wanted comfort food. Something warm and savory, like mashed potatoes or baked macaroni and cheese. I'd attempted a recipe for something called scalloped eggs several hours prior, but it had involved slicing hard-boiled eggs, then dipping the slices into a mixture of butter and beaten eggs before baking them over fat-moistened breadcrumbs and covering them with minced meat. I'd barely avoided getting sick before shoving the casserole into the oven. By the time it'd finished baking, I'd lost my appetite, but I better understood why women were so much thinner in those days.

Regardless, I refused to miss dinner too. Which meant I had to order out.

I grabbed my keys, phone, and purse, then headed into the night. Too much time alone with my thoughts was making me batty. While embroidering, I'd silently rehashed every awkward or unpleasant conversation I'd had in a decade, and I needed fresh air.

My thoughts moved immediately to Davis, still wondering about the historic barns and farmhouses he'd been trying to save. Had it worked? Did he have a new plan? Or would his father win in the end? Didn't he see the value in protecting history? Wasn't that half the draw of this town?

A crooked smile worked its way across my face as I thought about Davis reaching out to the law professors for help. Probably a good idea, considering he hadn't been able to properly fix my water heater, and that kind of work was supposed to be his forte. Maybe he wasn't always the quickest student in class.

It felt good knowing I'd handled things myself. I supposed I usually did manage to reach my goals, whatever they were. I'd just never taken any time to appreciate that. There was always something else in need of my immediate attention.

Honing my embroidery skills, however, might break my success streak. Hours spent alone stabbing a cheesecloth and my fingers had made me edgy. The hunger didn't help.

It was probably a good thing I hadn't had cell service or internet access all day. I might've picked a long-overdue fight with Annie, or demanded Davis explain his erratic behavior toward me. I had plenty of male friends, and I'd experienced my share of chemistry, but never both at once. And I'd never met a stranger whose presence consistently made me feel as if I'd finally come home. Until he ran away.

Apparently life in the 1850s made me extra dramatic. Perhaps I'd soon swoon.

The air felt cool and refreshing as I strode along the sidewalk toward town. Thankfully, my oversize hoodie and yoga pants kept me cozy and warm. I placed an online order with the local pub as I walked.

The wind picked up quickly, pushing gray clouds over a black velvet sky, moving my feet a little faster as well.

Several minutes later, I arrived, entering through heavy wooden doors and leaving the blustery wind behind. The pub's interior was dimly lit and decorated in a vaguely nautical theme. Warm, buttery scents hung in the air, drawing me in further.

I approached the bar with a smile, curly hair piled haphazardly on my head and dark-rimmed glasses perched on my nose.

The bartender raised her brows to me, then delivered a tray of drinks to a group of women on red vinyl barstools. "What can I get you?"

"Pickup for Emma."

She nodded. "Just a sec."

I stepped aside to wait.

A familiar figure came into view. Davis's broad shoulders curled over a tall glass of amber liquid as he spoke with a man I didn't recognize. The man appeared amused, but Davis looked grim.

Then I remembered his friend Clayton owned a local bar.

And apparently that was where I'd chosen to order my dinner.

Chapter Seventeen

I huddled deep into my oversize sweatshirt and flipped up the hood, rethinking my need for macaroni and cheese. Was I supposed to approach him? Ignore him? He was with a friend, and frankly, I looked like a person who'd spent all day alone and then walked six blocks in the wind.

Once again, Emily's words came to me, reminding me how important it is to encourage others. *Others might not need me; but they might.* Maybe Davis could use another friendly face. I couldn't help thinking of the rift between him and his father that Kate and Daisy mentioned at the café. Imagining tension of that magnitude with my parents twisted my heart.

"Emma?" The woman behind the counter lifted a bag of takeout overhead, snapping me back from my internal angst.

I inched forward, moving closer to the bar and Davis with each step.

His voice rose above the noise of the crowd to my ears. "It's complicated. I don't know where to go from here."

I turned to watch him, wondering what, if anything, I could say.

"Have you tried the truth?" The man leaning across the bar asked. He wore a name tag with *Clayton* on it, confirming my suspicion. "She already knows about the magazine."

I froze. They weren't talking about Davis's father. So, who was the "she" in question? Grace? Had he lied to his aunt about something? Did he have a girlfriend? A vise tightened in my chest. Having a girlfriend would explain why Davis kissed me one minute, as if it meant everything, then ran away the next.

I hated the possibility more than I should. Much more. And I hated myself a little for feeling that way.

But what did the magazine have to do with anything? Did he mean the opportunity for Davis and his work on the manor to be featured in *Architectural Digest*?

"I offered to help her move," Davis said. "Things weren't supposed to get this complicated."

I blinked. Stunned. Davis had offered to help me move.

Behind Clayton, the swinging kitchen doors opened and closed with continual traffic, allowing brief glimpses inside. Line cooks worked over steaming grills and stovetops. The appliances held my attention.

The manor's nearly debilitated stove and problematic water heater came to mind. Not to mention the furnace and allegedly bat-filled fireplace.

Only one of the stove's burners had worked reliably before I'd fixed the others. It'd baffled me that a previous renter hadn't complained. Also, Grace had emailed shortly before my arrival to confirm she'd personally given the place an inspection and everything was in working order.

What reason did she have to lie?

Then it dawned on me. I knew Davis's reason to want me gone. *Architectural Digest*.

"Order for Emma!"

I snapped back to the moment, taking the final steps to the bar.

Clayton straightened, and his eyes traveled to me as I reached for the bag.

Davis got to his feet in the same heartbeat, eyes wide and lips parted.

I curled my fingers around the takeout. "Thank you."

"Emma." Davis barely breathed the word, but I heard it along with everything else I'd missed before now.

My spine stiffened, and I suddenly needed confirmation. "Have you been trying to make me leave the manor?"

His jaw tensed and his expression hardened. He didn't speak.

I rocked back on my heels, knocked momentarily off balance by the truth in his eyes. "You have?"

He moved forward, hands parted before him, and my world tilted. "I can explain."

My chin swung left, then right. This was impossible. Wasn't it? I'd concocted a theory that couldn't possibly be true. Why was he confirming it?

"I have to go." I took a play from his book and nearly raced out the door.

I hustled down the sidewalk, clutching the takeout to my chest and waffling between horror and red-hot anger at his audacity.

The night wind blew down my hood and stung my eyes and ears. For the first time in my life, tears didn't accompany the shock.

I felt unprecedentedly numb.

The first frigid drops of rain fell like bullets from the sky, pelting my hands and stinging my cheeks.

In the distance, thunder rolled.

I swallowed an exhausted moan. What kind of person embarked on a quest for happiness, only to wind up less happy than they'd ever been in their life?

Oh, yeah. *Me.*

"Emma!" Davis's voice cracked through the chilly air. "Wait!"

My steps faltered, and I spun wearily to face him.

"I'm sorry," he said, flipping his palms up in surrender. "I just need you to listen."

I bit my tongue and waited.

A wicked flash of lightning split the sky, and rain began to fall in earnest. A million tiny drops pinged mercilessly against the darkened street and sidewalk; others caught in halos of light around streetlamps. All combined to chill me to the core.

When Davis didn't speak, I walked away once more.

He jogged past me and stopped, blocking my path. Rivulets of rain swiveled jagged patterns over his forehead, nose, and cheekbones. His guilty, shame-filled eyes pleaded with me while my heart continued to break. "Five minutes," he begged. "That's all I need. At least let me drive you home?"

A gust of wind beat the oversize sweatshirt against my torso, and I wrapped both arms around my middle to hold myself together. "No." The offer and his stalling drove daggers through my heart. He shouldn't need more time or the right conditions to speak his truth.

"It's not what you think."

I tried to step around him, but he opened his arms like a gate. "Wait! Okay. You're right. It is what you think, but not for whatever reason you're imagining. Things weren't supposed to turn out this way."

"How can you know what I'm thinking?" I asked, hurt and anger ripping through me. "You can read my mind now? Then go on. Take a guess."

Davis made a low, growling sound of frustration, and I sidestepped him once more. "I never meant to hurt you. It wasn't supposed to be like this."

"What then?" I challenged, stopping after only two steps. "Explain it to me, because I cannot understand."

Again, he fell silent.

This time I moved into his personal space and tipped up my chin to glare. "Were you trying to make my stay miserable? Did you want me to leave? All those times you offered to help me find somewhere else to stay, was it just to get me out of your way?"

He offered a single stiff nod, and the familiar burn of frustration tears stung my eyes.

"All so you could be in a magazine." I silently thanked the wind and rain for masking the traitorous quake in my voice.

"It's a huge opportunity." He raised his palms again. "I was a coward, and I'm sorry. I thought I could make it your choice to leave. It was a shitty thing to do. I know that, but—"

"But?" I choked on a laugh. "There's a *but* to that statement?" I shook my head, falling back enough to catch my breath.

"Being featured in that magazine would change everything. It would change my future. Allow me to break away from my dad's company and finally form my own. A company that saves and restores historic properties instead of leveling them to make room for more condominiums."

"You could've been straight with me," I said, admiring his plan, hating his execution.

"Grace and I agreed on all the changes. Then you showed up."

The take-out bag in my hand swung and spun in the wind. I imagined hitting him with it.

"I didn't want to be the bad guy, but I needed you out of the house if I wanted to get started. I never expected this connection." He motioned between us, eyes pleading. "I wish you could understand—" He stopped himself again, and my hackles rose impossibly further.

"The only reason I don't understand is because you've never tried to tell me," I snapped. "Instead, you lied and schemed."

"I panicked!"

"You pretended to fix things and care about my comfort while intentionally making me miserable. You made sure the stove would give me problems, knowing I had to use it if I planned to stay so long. You probably blew out the pilot light on the hot-water tank. Then you set it to low after claiming to fix it."

His sheepish look confirmed my accusations.

"Were there ever really bats in the bedroom fireplace, or was that a lie too?"

"There might've been a bat," he said. "At some point."

I scoffed and tried to get around him.

"Don't go! Emma, please."

I stopped. "What about the other night when I nearly froze to death?"

"The system's old, and you've been here full time for two weeks. No one ever stays that long. Running lights, a blow-dryer, the stove—and I saw the space heater hiding behind the door in your room. The fuse box was bound to have a problem eventually."

I shoved past him. "I wouldn't have bought the damn space heater if you didn't keep messing with the furnace! And I left my big blanket with you and Violet in the park that day."

He turned and kept pace at my side. "I know. I have the blanket in my truck. Also, I didn't blame your space heater. I understand why you needed it."

I glared but kept walking.

He raised his palms again in peace. "I'd planned to tell you everything that night. I wanted to confess and sort it all out before things got worse. Then we nearly kissed again, and I freaked out."

Breath whooshed from my mouth in a cloud of steam against the falling temperature. My steps faltered, and I plowed to a sudden stop. "You keep running away because you know you're being an ass and lying to me. You keep coming back and playing with my emotions when you know what I came here to do."

Davis ran a hand through his sopping hair, then over his rain-slicked face. "I'm so sorry. I hate the way things are, but you're right. You came here to stop looking for love, and I knew we couldn't come back from this. I had to tell you what I'd done, and I didn't deserve your forgiveness. We were over before we ever began."

I bit my trembling lip, gut wrenched from the loss of what might've been. "The worst part," I croaked, no longer caring to hide my emotional overload, "is that none of this had to happen. If you would've just told me the whole truth on the night we met, I would've moved out instead of settling in, and we'd both be happy right now."

The weight of a dozen failed relationships settled on my shoulders, and an ugly truth appeared. I'd always blamed my family or my job for ruining my prospects at love. But here, in Amherst with Davis, the only common denominator was me. Things had fallen apart before getting off the ground because I'd wanted a man who lied to my face every day for the sake of his job. The irony was not lost.

"What?" Davis asked, stepping bravely into my personal space. "What are you thinking right now, Emma?"

Spears of icy rain stung my cheeks as I raised my tear-filled eyes to his.

"You want us to be honest," he said. "Take your own advice and let me have it."

I think I'm cursed in love, I declared silently. *I'll never have the one thing I've always wanted, and this catastrophe of a would-be romance is one more way the universe is telling me to let that dream go.* Hot tears rolled over my frozen cheeks. "I was wrong to kiss you that night. You knew it, but I didn't want it to be true. I came here because I needed the time and space to find happiness on my own. I made a big deal out of that." And I'd blown it immediately upon arrival. "I caused ripples in my family. Had a huge fight with my pregnant sister. Forced my parents, who want to retire, to work full time again. All so I could forge a new path for myself—and I turned my back on all of it the moment I saw you."

Something darkened in his gaze. "What are you saying? You really think what we have is a mistake?"

"What do we have?" I asked. It surely wasn't romance. Not the kind I wanted. Were we friends? My friends didn't lie, then keep up the ruse.

My heart ached so deeply I pressed a hand against my chest, hoping not to collapse. I'd caused this mess—unintentionally, maybe—but I was the one on a mission. If I'd stuck to my goal, everything would be completely different.

Davis lifted a hand in my direction but stopped short of touching me. He glanced away, then back, as he let his arm drop. A measure of hope lifted his brow. "Maybe we can start over. Forget this happened and do things the way we should've from the beginning."

I swallowed a sob at his offer. "You didn't answer my question."

Thunder boomed, and lightning struck. The fine hairs on my arm stood at attention.

I didn't blame him for avoiding the ugly truth. The foundation we'd built upon was quicksand. One part his willful deceit and one part the abandonment of my goal. A recipe for disaster.

"Emma," Davis pleaded, but no words followed.

We'd already said them all.

I squared my shoulders as the pain gave way to numbness. "Goodbye, Davis."

I turned away, allowing the sobs to come and moving at double time back to the manor. "Do not follow me."

This time he obeyed.

Chapter Eighteen

I received another bouquet of flowers the next morning and considered tossing them into the trash can. The card contained only a heart as before, and a call to the florist ended in frustration. Apparently it was a breach of confidentiality to tell me the name on the credit card that paid for them.

Since I couldn't confirm Davis had sent them, and I loved flowers, I added them to the vase on the kitchen counter and removed the blooms that had already faded.

I decided to fully concentrate on my goal to understand and emulate Emily for the next few days, and I chose to embrace only the positive. Words from the poem that helped me get out of my shell during college came back to inspire me.

> Not knowing when the dawn will come, I open
> every door.

I had only a few weeks to pursue this major life quest, and I couldn't stop seeking opportunities to embrace the journey and all it entailed.

During my letter-writing classes, and walks in town, I mentally evaluated every interaction I'd had with men since arriving in Amherst. And a few women as well. Someone was sending me flowers. But who?

The mystery was driving me bonkers and taking up more mental bandwidth than I wanted.

Back at the manor, I finished two more embroidery projects. Neither was any better than the first.

When it rained again on Friday, I holed up in the study with another book on Emily Dickinson. I set the tome aside when my eyes grew tired and my lids began to droop. Stretching onto my feet, I waffled between taking an afternoon nap or making a pot of tea. Something on a nearby shelf caught my eye, stalling the decision. An image of a golden peony, embossed on dark-green cloth binding, drew me to the bookcase. I plucked the book from the shelf. *Floriography: The Secret Language of Flowers.*

Curiosity soared as I thought of the bouquets of white peonies and purple hyacinths. Hardly the typical floral combination. I took the book with me to the kitchen, put on a kettle, then began to read.

It seemed unlikely that my bouquets held a secret message, but the possibility made me smile. I knew flowers were used to send silent messages in the Victorian era. I'd heard, for example, that certain kinds and combinations had special meanings. The petal colors and stages of the bloom did as well. And that the art became very nuanced in an era when eligible women were closely monitored.

I flipped to the glossary where the flowers were grouped by common meanings. My traitorous eyes and hopeful heart ran straight to the romance-related categories. None of those contained peonies or hyacinths.

It couldn't be a coincidence that I'd received the same set of blooms on repeat. But who would send them?

Mom, Dad, and Cecily had already confirmed the flowers weren't from them.

Grace didn't have any reason to send a bouquet. She'd already provided a lovely vase of wildflowers upon my arrival.

I skimmed the names of flowers in every list until I found what I was looking for. Purple hyacinths signified sorrow and regret. White peonies, shame over one's behavior. Both meanings were tied to

Greek mythology, specifically to the god Apollo. Both were meant as apologies.

Davis.

I closed the book, shoved all thoughts of him aside, and doubled down on my embroidery.

⁓❧⁓

I was elbow deep in dough when the doorbell rang two days later. Davis stood outside with my blanket from the park in one hand, a bag of takeout from Clayton's pub in the other.

I stared coldly, despite parts of Old Emma clapping internally at his arrival. "Yes?"

He perused my flour-covered face, arms, and apron with a cool, blank stare. "I washed your blanket and picked up a repeat of your order from the other night." He lifted the bag between us. "I thought it might've been cold by the time you got home in the storm."

My stomach gurgled on cue, delighted by the delicious scents wafting upward.

"Am I too late?" he asked.

For a moment, I hoped his words held a double meaning.

His blue-gray V-neck sweater highlighted his eyes. His jeans and loafers implied he'd come from the office rather than a jobsite. And he'd brought me dinner. "It looks as if you already have plans."

"I'm making homemade noodles." From a two-hundred-year-old recipe designed to torture me. "They won't be ready tonight." In fact, all I'd managed to do so far was to create a giant wad of unruly dough, which I still needed to cut into strips and hang to dry.

"So, no plans?" he asked, looking slightly confused.

"No." In fact, until the doorbell rang, I'd considered pairing day-old muffins with wine and calling it a night.

His eyes crinkled at the corners. "Peace offering?"

I felt my will weakening as I met his gaze.

"I messed up," he said. "It won't happen again."

I rolled my eyes and leaned against the jamb. "Fine."

I'd already spent hours imagining this exact scenario and all the ways I could respond when he came back asking for forgiveness. Initially, I'd fantasized about shutting the door in his face, but as the days passed, I remembered how limited my time was in Amherst, and I'd started to think of our falling-out as a blessing. Davis was officially an obstacle removed from my path by fate.

I took the blanket and bag from his hands.

"Really?" he asked.

"Yeah, but I'm not ready to trust you again," I clarified. "And I've been thinking we might as well figure this out." I waved a hand around, indicating the house.

He narrowed his eyes. "What do you mean?"

"I mean there's no reason you can't get started on your renovations while I'm still here. A lot of the things you want to do won't affect my stay. So, for the next three weeks, I think we should split the manor. You can work in the areas I'm not using or don't have access to anyway, and I'll stay out of your way. We both get what we want."

"But—"

"You can start tomorrow morning. Thank you for the food." I stepped backward into the foyer; then I shut the door in his face.

❦

Davis arrived early the next day and set up shop in the locked supply room, where he intended to create a first-floor primary bedroom and en suite bath. As promised, I stayed out of his way.

He returned the following day with a tool belt fastened around his hips, worked for several hours, then left before dinner.

On day three, I passed him in the driveway on my way to letter-writing class at the bookstore.

"Morning." He leaned over the tailgate of his truck, digging through a toolbox.

"Hello."

He'd pinned his wavy hair away from his forehead with the help of a backward ball cap, unleashing the full power of his ethereal eyes. "Emma—"

I raised a palm. "Have you been sending me flowers?" I'd received another bouquet of hyacinths and peonies after dinner the previous night, identical to the other deliveries and again with no indication of the sender. I'd gone through half a bottle of wine trying to make sense of the little heart drawn on the card. Was it supposed to mean something to me? Was it a clue?

His brows arched. "Someone is still sending you flowers?"

I stared, waiting for something in his expression to suggest he was behind the deliveries and playing dumb to cover it up. I found nothing of the sort. "Never mind."

If the flowers weren't from Davis, then who?

"I'm late for class. I'll catch you later?" I asked.

"Sounds good."

The morning sun shone warm and bright as I hustled up the lane. Determined dregs of summer still warring with fall. The previous cold snap had passed, and according to the local meteorologist, we were in for a few days of relatively warm temperatures. I certainly wouldn't complain.

I was making progress on my mission to find happiness.

"Hey, Emma," Daisy, said, joining me as I entered the bookstore. Her golden waves spilled over the shoulders of a maroon UMass sweatshirt.

I appreciated her contagious enthusiasm.

"Did you finish your letter?" she asked, eyes sparkling with mischief.

During our last class, Grace had read us a short but direct letter written by Benjamin Franklin, to his friend William Strahan, British printer to the king. Strahan voted for use of force against America, inciting Franklin to write:

> Mr. Strahan,
> You are a Member of Parliament, and one of that Majority which has doomed my Country to Destruction. You have begun to burn our Towns and murder our People.—Look upon your hands! They are stained with the Blood of your Relations!—You and I were long Friends:—You are now my Enemy,—and
> > I am,
> > Yours,
> > B. Franklin.

Our assignment was to think of someone who needed a piece of our minds and to write to them. Whether we sent the letters or not was up to us. Completing the exercise was all that mattered.

I'd written Annie.

I didn't deserve the strange cold shoulder she'd given me lately, or her overreaction to my taking time for myself. Something had been broken between us for too long, and the feelings had crested the surface like an iceberg when she hit her third trimester. I wanted to know why. I deserved an explanation at the very least. An apology at most.

"Yes," I said, answering Daisy's question. "You?"

"Boy, did I. At least seven to ex-boyfriends as far back as middle school and several professors who shall not be named." She grinned. "Definitely never sending any of those, but it was cathartic."

Her mention of professors reminded me of the one I'd had in common with Davis, and his face popped into my mind's eye. Thankfully, I had better things to think about.

We waved at Grace, arranging snacks on the refreshments table, then headed her way. She smiled warmly as we approached.

"What happened to your fingers?" Daisy asked, as I set my basket of exceptionally good muffins beside Grace's bowl of apples.

"These are my embroidery wounds." I frowned at the numerous tiny bandages.

She laughed. "Haven't given that up yet, huh?"

"Never."

Grace studied me. "You ladies look lovely, as always."

"Thank you. So do you," I said, admiring her soft green pashmina and simple drop earrings.

She'd secured her white hair in a nice chignon and looked utterly at ease in her skin. "I hope my nephew isn't ruining your peace, working at the manor every day now."

Daisy's eyes widened at the information. "Davis Sommers is at your place, and you're here?"

I shrugged. "He's busy making a name for himself in the world of historic properties, and I love this class."

"Davis has a way of getting what he wants," Grace said. "Just ask his father." The cat-that-ate-the-canary look on her face told me she was referring to something specific.

"The barns and farmhouses?" Daisy asked.

Grace nodded and winked.

Daisy pumped a fist. "Yes! Take that, Big Commerce."

Grace's smart blue eyes slid to me. "I saw him talking to you not long ago." She pointed a finger to the door at the front of the store. "Carter stopped by to rattle Davis, but he wasn't biting, so he left. I've been meaning to ask you what he said."

It took a long moment to recall meeting anyone named Carter. Then the handsome man in the black suit and orange tie came to mind. "That was Davis's father?" He'd seemed so young. Far younger than my parents. Also strikingly handsome and confident. On second thought, I should've realized the connection immediately. "He said you told him I was staying at the manor." I wrinkled my nose. "And that he would've stayed at a condo with a view."

Daisy stuck out her tongue in disgust.

Grace sighed. "That's Carter."

Paul appeared, and Daisy and Grace greeted him before breaking away from the refreshments table. Daisy chose a seat and took out some paper. Grace greeted other classmates.

"Apple cinnamon?" Paul asked, tilting his head toward my muffins.

"Pumpkin spice," I corrected.

His smile widened. "My favorite."

"Try one," I encouraged, pride filling my sails.

As it turned out, once I'd unfucked my oven, I was a pretty good baker. I'd moved on to using more modern recipes, which also helped. And everything I'd made in the last few days had been delicious. The noodles were a work in progress, but I had a list of other Victorian-era meals I also intended to try.

He peeled the paper back and raised the little pastry. "Sorry I missed you at the last class," he said. "My TA was out with the flu, which left me with about two hundred papers I hadn't planned to grade."

"Yikes. How'd it go?"

"I have new appreciation for my TA and residual nightmares." He took a bite of muffin and hummed pleasantly.

Grace frowned from afar, and I wondered if she was eavesdropping. I blamed Davis, yet again, for putting the unflattering thought in my mind.

I left Paul to finish his treat and headed for the chair beside Daisy.

"Ems," Michael said before I reached my destination.

I turned toward the checkout, where he raised a hand in greeting. I wondered again about Michael. I didn't know much about him. I knew he worked part time and went to school full time, pursuing his master's degree in business administration. He was handsome and fit. Kind and funny. But was he the one behind the Historically_Bookish handle? *Was he* my longtime online friend?

I pointed to my basket on the table. "Get a muffin when you have a minute. They turned out great."

He bobbed his head, then started ringing up the next customer in line.

I had to find a way to ask him about IBOOM without sounding like a nut if I was wrong.

"Look at you," Daisy said, as I lowered onto the chair beside hers. "Your muffins bring all the boys to the class." She pumped her shoulders as she sang.

"Stop."

Her grin widened. "Okay, *boys* is a stretch of the word here, but you get it."

I rolled my eyes. "Paul is here because he wants a creative escape. Just like us."

She leaned closer. "If you say so."

"Welcome, class," Grace said sweetly, moving to the head of the table and saving me from an uncomfortable conversation. She gave her usual explanation of purpose for any newcomers and encouragement to those of us still trying to get the hang of things. "Letter-writing is truly a lost artform," she said. "But that doesn't mean we can't bring it back."

She donned her glasses and smiled slyly as she lifted a page before her. "Today I want to read a passage from *Moby-Dick* author Herman Melville to Amherst's own Nathaniel Hawthorne. The men were friends for a time, sharing a mutual respect and admiration of talent and calling. Until Melville, more than fifteen years Hawthorne's junior and at least as many times more audacious of personality, scared him away with sheer, unbridled infatuation.

"Melville writes

> "*No man can read a fine author, and relish him to his very bones, while he reads, without subsequently fancying to himself some ideal image of the man and his mind . . . There is no man in whom humor and love are developed in that high form called genius; no such man can exist without also possessing, as*

the indispensable complement of these, a great, deep intellect,
which drops down into the universe like a plummet.

"Melville couldn't contain his enthusiasm, and it eventually pushed the more subtle Hawthorne away. Melville was still writing about the loss decades later. It begs several points of thought. How well do we really know others? How easy is it to overstep when we are full of energy and words like Melville, but the object of our affection is guarded and quiet like Hawthorne? Today, let's think of someone opposite of ourselves and send them a letter of appreciation." She removed her glasses and tucked the paper into a folder on the table, signaling it was time to begin.

Daisy guffawed. "I had no idea those two men were even friends."

"Melville dedicated *Moby-Dick* to Hawthorne," I said.

She shook her head and lifted her shoulders. "I knew that, but it never occurred to me that they knew one another outside of reading one another's work."

I pressed my lips. I'd heard somewhere that the men had only lived about six miles apart, but I supposed that was a much greater distance then than it was today.

Grace patted Daisy's shoulder. "How's it going over here?"

"We're just getting started," she said.

"Who will you write to?" Grace asked, eyes sweeping to meet mine.

"Yeah, Emma," Daisy said, picking up on Grace's pointed tone and faux innocent expression. "Who are you writing to?"

"I'm not sure," I admitted cautiously, unnerved by Grace's quiet intensity and wondering where she was headed.

The older woman smiled sweetly. "Davis gives me the impression the two of you are becoming quite close."

Daisy's eyes bulged.

I briefly considered unloading every sordid detail, just to get it all off my chest. Instead, I went with the simpler version. "Yes, we've become friends."

Grace's smart blue eyes widened by a fraction. "He seems awfully affected by the other men in your life, for someone who's just a friend."

"I don't have other men in my life," I said. What had she said to him?

"You receive letters every day, and I hear you're still getting flowers. You certainly are the belle of the ball at class time." She tipped her head slightly, and I followed her gaze to Paul, then Michael.

"Also friends," I said.

"What about the flowers?" Daisy asked.

"I have no idea."

"You have a secret admirer," Daisy said. "It's so romantic. Especially since you're swearing off men. What if the sender is your soulmate?"

I fought the urge to drop my head against the desk.

Another classmate called to Grace, and she moved on. Daisy got to work, apparently inspired.

I turned my attention to the stark white paper before me, and I knew exactly who needed a letter from me today.

Dear Emma,

I paused, allowing myself a moment to enjoy the endearment. I needed to be nicer to myself more often. And I should expect others to be nicer too.

I want to remind you that you're resilient. You thought you were defeated more than once in your search for peace and joy, especially during your early days in Amherst, but you understand yourself better now, and you've begun to heal. That took guts. And I'm proud of you.

I hope you never stop writing letters to yourself and the other people you love. What a wonderful way to make them feel special.

The words flowed freely; then I wrote a half dozen more letters before leaving Village Books. I stuffed three into envelopes headed for Willow Bend. One to my folks, another to Cecily, and the last to Annie. I discreetly tucked a letter into Daisy's cubby and left one with Grace's name on it at the counter. I added the letter to myself to a collection of kind words I planned to take out and read whenever I was down.

Whatever else had happened during my time in Amherst, I was grateful for the progress I was finally making on me.

Chapter Nineteen

Cecily arrived two days later, an apple pie in hand. "I stopped at a roadside stand. I couldn't help myself. I had cider. It was amazing."

"Bless you," I said, drawing her into a tight hug. "I'm so glad you're here."

She released me with a grin. "Back at ya."

Her thick brown hair hung over her shoulders in carefully constructed waves, and she wore a fuzzy red wrap sweater and jeans in place of her usual scrubs.

She passed me the pie, then turned in circles as she moved through the foyer. "This place is incredible. It looks exactly like the online photos. If your SUV hadn't been parked outside, I would've thought I landed back in time."

"It's pretty great," I agreed, unsure if I ever wanted to leave.

"Show me around!" Cecily rocked onto her heels. "I want to see everything." She dropped her overnight pack on the table beside my vase of fresh flowers. "Wait. Are these—"

"Yep."

"Still no idea who sent them?"

"Nope."

I glanced through the nearby window, where the sun had yet to set. If I hurried, I'd have time to show her around the manor and the town while it was still light. She was sure to go bonkers over downtown at sunset. I thought of Emily and her appreciation for nature and all its wonder. She'd written that nature never knocks, but also never intrudes. And I thought of it often in the fall.

"Let's get started." I set the pie on the table and clasped my hands. "The home was built in 1812," I said, affecting an overly formal tour guide tone and leading the way through the foyer.

Cecily fell into step at my side.

We embarked on what I'd mistakenly thought would be a quick spin around the property, but Cecily was an obsessive history buff. Specifically where fashion and interior design were involved.

Cecily ran her fingertips over the wallpaper and wooden trim. We stared reverently at the ornately plastered ceilings and admired the study's crown moldings until my neck hurt and my eyes dried out.

"Look at this fabulous handrail and spindles," she said as we ascended the main staircase. "And this carpet runner is marvelous. I can picture us in nineteenth-century ball gowns, making our entrance to a party with men in tails and caterers carrying silver trays with champagne flutes."

I paused on the landing to admire the stained glass. The stunning piece caught my eye on every trip up or down the stairs. "This might be my favorite detail," I said. "In the morning, sunlight streams through and casts everything in a soft golden glow. It gives me goose bumps."

Cecily stopped beside me, her attention sliding across the glass without interest. "Pretty."

"Pretty?" I gaped. "You don't have a lengthy and thorough description of the work? Or a story about its origins and relevance when compared to the overall design scheme?"

"Sadly, no. It doesn't belong here."

I frowned at her, then at the stained glass. "What?"

"It's probably from this decade. Odd, because it's the only thing I've noticed so far that doesn't fit the era."

When I didn't move on, she added, "It looks high quality, and stained glass is certainly appropriate for the time, just not this particular piece. The placement is nice, though, overlooking everything and creating that heavenly glow you mentioned. I can see why you enjoy it."

Her words rattled around my head for a long moment. Then I suddenly saw the stained glass with new eyes. "Iris was Davis's mother's name." Something told me the window represented her and her influence over him and this place.

"Davis lost his mother?" Cecily asked.

"To cancer," I said, hooking my arm with hers and towing her onward. I had so much more to tell her. "Let's talk about that after the tour."

Three hours later, Cecily and I moseyed along Pleasant Street, feeling the warm buzz of local wine in our systems and the satisfaction of our very full stomachs. We'd created a personalized tasting tour of Amherst, stopping at each café to order small plates and generous pours. We finished every sip and bite between bouts of gossip and laughter.

In no hurry to go home, we'd decided to wander. Eventually we parked ourselves on a bench, the perfect seats to watch the unobstructed sky.

Cecily noshed on fudge she'd pretended to buy for a coworker, eyes fixed on the heavens. "You're thriving here," she said. "Doing all the things you said you'd do. I didn't understand why you needed to leave Willow Bend, but I'm glad you did. It's like you've come alive again. And it's amazing."

"What are you talking about?" I asked, side-eyeing her as I reached into her bag for a bit of fudge.

"You," she said, as if that explained everything. "You're a go-getter. A doer. A busy person who makes the rest of us look like slackers. I don't think you've ever set a goal you didn't meet. Or surpass!" She sighed, obviously deeply content. "You said you needed to come here to change your path, and look." She stretched one arm out like a game show host. "You did it. I'm always so cautious. You give me hope by making things look easy. Like anything is possible."

I snorted. "Well, you're drunk, because nothing is easy for me. Ever. Except maybe our friendship." I rested my head on her shoulder. "As for the rest of it, I just want to make people happy. Accomplishing things does that. So, I keep going."

Cecily pulled back an inch, turned my way, and frowned. "You do all the things you do to make other people happy," she said, paraphrasing my statement.

I raised my brows. "Yeah." Duh. I wouldn't run myself ragged just for me.

Her frown deepened. "You don't have to earn people's love. Tell me that's not what you think."

"Of course not." I huffed a small laugh. That wasn't what I'd said. Or meant.

Was it?

I inhaled a deep, shuddering breath, unsure.

"Emma." Cecily's tone sobered. "People love you because you're you. You've got this great big heart, and you share it with everyone you meet. Your love of books, music, laughter, and terrible jokes is contagious and inspiring. You give great hugs, and you always know what to say to lighten someone else's load. You're a wonderful and kind human who makes people feel seen and appreciated, even if all they did was pass you on the street. And you'd still be all those things, even if you never completed another task, or checked another thing off a list."

My mouth opened, and the pressure in my chest increased. I wanted to believe her, but I wasn't sure I did. And I knew that was a problem.

Cecily squeezed my hand. "I know we never talk about this, because it was a dark time for your family, but it's been on my mind since you left town. So far, this conversation is supporting a theory."

I dared a glance at her, terrified by what she might say next and still recovering from what she'd said last.

"Is it possible your ten-year-old heart and mind misinterpreted the praise you received for all your efforts while your mom was sick? Maybe you got it twisted, way back then, and started thinking you needed to trade works for love."

I blinked. "No. I don't think that's it." But again, I wasn't so sure.

Had I equated service with worthiness and created my own misery in the process?

I sucked in an audible breath as so many things began to grow clearer. For the first time, I could imagine what my choices might look like from my parents' perspective. They'd seen me hustling for so long, it probably seemed as if I wanted to stay busy. But I didn't put all this pressure on myself because it brought me joy. I was trying to make their lives easier, the way I had when Annie and I were small. When Mom was sick and Dad was spread too thin.

At ten, I'd been too young to verbalize the pressure I'd felt or to ask for the hugs and attention I needed. So I'd clung to what I was given. And praise soon took the place of affection. "Wow," I whispered. "It's so fucked up."

Cecily wrapped an arm around my shoulders and pulled me against her side. She rested her head to mine as we watched twilight swallow the sun. "You are worthy, Emma Rini. You are loved. And you are worthy of love. Just. As. You. Are. Somewhere along the line, I think your family started to believe being busy made you happy, so they let you do more and more until you'd traded your life for their happiness. I'm sure it hasn't occurred to them that you think you have to do all this to maintain their love." Her arm tightened on my shoulder. "I can't believe I didn't realize it sooner. Now that I know, I'm going to be more conscientious of what I ask of you. And I'm going to insist you take breaks when you can. I think you should do the same for yourself."

I wiped a budding tear from the corner of my eye. Maybe living like Emily wasn't my only reason for wanting to leave Willow Bend, I realized. Maybe part of me hoped my family would miss me. The thought was so unexpected I didn't know what to do with it. "I'll try."

Something told me that attempting to slow down in Willow Bend would be much more difficult than anything I'd hoped to accomplish in Amherst, and that was saying a lot.

"That's all anyone can do," she said. "Now, not to pile on the big stuff, but I think we need to talk about that handyman."

I let my eyelids close for one beat, then reopened them and straightened. "I've got bigger things to think about now. I'd rather not talk about Davis."

She released me to fish another bit of fudge from her bag. "Okay, but remember how much I love you, and be gentle with my best friend while you work on her. She's incredibly important to me."

My phone rang, and Annie's name centered the screen.

Cecily squeezed my hand, then rose. "I'm going to try to get a good photo of the shops with their little twinkle lights," she said, stepping away to allow me some privacy.

I took a deep breath and answered. "Hi, Annie."

"Hey." Her tone sounded cautious, but light.

"Everything okay?" I asked.

"No."

My muscles tensed as I waited for the bad news, or a verbal thrashing. When Annie remained silent, I nudged. "What's up?" When she didn't respond right away, I tried again. "Talk to me." The words were an overdue plea.

Annie huffed. "Some pain in the ass keeps sending me handwritten letters like she thinks it's the nineteenth century. One of them was pretty mean."

I stiffened, thinking immediately of the letter I'd sent inspired by Benjamin Franklin. "She sounds terrible."

"She's not," Annie said, with a sigh, and my heavy heart grew instantly lighter. "Why are you sending me letters, Emma?"

"I miss you," I said. "And there are things I want you to know. Like the fact that I love you, even when you've been mad at me for years."

"I'm not mad." Annie paused, and silence gonged. For a moment I wondered if I'd somehow dropped the call. "I'm—I don't know. Frustrated. Dissatisfied."

"With?"

"You." She groaned. "Us. Ugh!"

I tracked Cecily with my eyes as she snapped photos of the cafés and shops, backlit by the rising moon. "For what it's worth, I'm sorry for letting things between us get this bad or go on this long. I've recently come to realize some things need said so other people don't draw the wrong conclusions."

"Are you sorry you called me a brat?"

A laugh broke on my lips, and I covered my mouth with one hand. "I don't think I used that word, but I'm sorry if I made you feel bad. I'm taking a class, and we were assigned to write letters that put our negative feelings front and center, so I tried."

"Well, you get an A," she said. "I have been a brat."

Tears welled in my eyes, and my hands dropped to my lap. "Can we please talk this out?"

"I think you're ridiculous for taking this dumb sabbatical right now," she said. "But I like getting your letters."

My heart filled with hope as the first threads of repair wound through our rift. "Will you write me back?"

"I'd rather text," she said. "I don't want the things we say to take two days to arrive. I like the twenty-first century. I belong here, and so do you."

"Then I'll text," I said.

I wasn't as much like Emily as I'd hoped to be at this point, but I was sure she'd approve of anything that could heal my relationship with my sister.

There was a long beat of silence before Annie spoke again. "You haven't mentioned my flowers."

The words hung between us for several seconds before I understood what she meant. "You sent the bouquets?"

"I wanted to say I'm sorry for being distant and grumpy lately. And for being a brat before you left." She exhaled long and slow. "I'm not good at writing how I feel, so I tried saying it with flowers. You're living in the past, and I remembered people used to send messages in bouquets. I figured there was a fifty-fifty chance you'd know what they meant, and even if you didn't, they're still flowers, and you love those."

"I do," I whispered.

"At least tell me they're pretty."

"They're perfect." A wedge formed in my throat, and my eyes welled with unshed tears. Annie missed me, and not my busyness. She'd made an effort to reach me where I was, in Amherst, being overly dramatic while searching for my inner nineteenth-century poet. Even though she thought it was silly. "Thank you."

Annie made a throaty and disgruntled noise. "Mom's calling on the other line. She's so far up my ass lately, she'll probably meet the baby before I do."

"Oh, sweetie," I said. "That's not where your baby is."

"Gross. I have to go. Love you." Annie disconnected before I could respond, but the overall conversation was an incredible win.

◦✦◦

Cecily and I woke to the sounds of Davis working outside the next day. We'd slept until nearly lunch, so we made coffee and raided the fridge, then ferried it all onto the patio. The sun was warm, a minor resurgence of the extended summer, soon to be snuffed by fall.

We wore yoga pants and sweatshirts, our hair tied into matching messy knots.

We'd gotten in late after enjoying a UMass game from nosebleed seats. Then she and I had talked in front of the fireplace until nearly dawn, making short work of the apple pie. The perfect end to a very good night. UMass had won.

I'd even impressed her with my fire-building skills and pantry full of baked goods.

"This is the life," Cecily said, digging into our robust spread of fresh veggies, chunked cheeses, and fruits. "No wonder you aren't in a hurry to come back to Willow Bend. I love it here."

I bit my lip, contemplating my next words. The idea of staying in Amherst had taken up space in my head, and I wanted her opinion on the possibility. Was moving here permanently a legitimate option? Or was the coward in me simply plotting a longer escape? Cecily had a way of seeing things I missed, and I needed her insight. "I really do like it here," I hedged, not sure I was ready for the hard truth.

"Who could blame you. This place is rife with history. The people are fun. The town is quaint. The house is gorgeous. And the views are—"

Davis appeared at the corner of the manor, as if on cue, already sweaty from hauling baseboards and wooden trim, and heading in our direction.

It seemed out of his way to pass by the patio, but I didn't comment. And I refused to acknowledge the way his T-shirt clung to his torso and biceps.

Cecily was sure to do that for me.

"Ladies," he said, nodding as he passed.

Cecily gaped, and he fought a grin.

"Stop that," I hissed when he was gone.

"Tell me that was Handsome Handyman."

"No. That was Davis."

She whistled softly, attention fixed in the direction he'd disappeared. "Nice."

I rolled my eyes and shoved her shoulder. "Stop. We're friends, and I'm here to work on myself."

She watched me closely, probably fighting the urge to make a joke about working on him instead. "It's no wonder you fell for him," she said, more contemplatively. "He's unfairly attractive. If he's half as kind and bookish as you claimed, you never stood a chance."

"He's also focused on his career, and I'm working on me."

Davis reappeared, carrying a pair of folded sawhorses. "Emma," he said, a little too gravelly. "Would it bother you if I worked out here? It's a beautiful day. I'd hate to spend it indoors if I don't have to."

"Knock yourself out," I said, feigning cool and making a little cheese-and-cracker sandwich. I considered introducing him to Cecily but didn't want to start a conversation that might derail my efforts to let him go.

He nodded, then carried on.

Cecily crunched a carrot. "Do you think he'll take off his shirt?"

I pointed at her in warning.

The clatter of wood jerked my eyes back to Davis. He'd set up the sawhorses and arranged several lengths of baseboard over the supports. He pulled a set of leather gloves from his back pocket, slid his hands inside, and widened his stance.

Cecily hummed.

He palmed a block of sandpaper and began making slow strokes over the wood.

"Holy f—"

I spun to glare at Cecily. "Do not."

She shoved a chunk of cheese between her lips and chewed. "Fine. What's the scoop on this Paul guy?" she asked. "When do I get to meet him?"

The rhythmic scratch of sandpaper on wood stuttered, then stalled for a moment before beginning again.

Cecily grinned.

I narrowed my eyes.

"Everything you've told me so far makes me think he's into you, and he's the kind of guy you always saw yourself with," she pointed out. "Smart, sweet, into books and history. And he writes you all those letters. Pretty romantic, no?"

A shadow stretched across the grass, drawing my attention and pulling Davis along behind it. He paused to run a forearm over his brow as he approached. The opposite hand pressed to his hip. Sweat-dampened hair clung to his temples and forehead. "Care if I grab a glass of water?"

"Not at all," I said brightly. "Since you're not working at the moment, I'd love to introduce you to my best friend, Cecily."

He flashed his most charming smile in her direction. "Davis. Nice to meet you."

"You as well," she said. "I've heard so many things." Being Cecily, she dragged the smallest word in her statement as long as she could.

Davis's brows knitted, unsure how to take the implication. "Can I get either of you anything while I'm inside?"

"No, thank you," I said, as Cecily announced, "You should join us. Have you eaten?"

I kicked her under the table, which would've been stealthier if our table had a cloth.

Davis gave me a terse look. "No, but thank you. I have a lot of work to do, and I know how much Emma's missed you. I don't want to interrupt."

She shot me a stinky look.

"Maybe the next time you're in town, you can swing by my buddy Clayton's pub," he suggested. "Food's great, and so's he."

"I'd love that."

Davis went inside and closed the door.

I fought a smile. "Do not try to encourage anything. It's not going to happen."

"At least tell me his friend is that good looking," she said. "Then point me in the direction of that pub."

I shook my head slowly. "You're a nut."

"I'm on vacation, and all the doctors I work with are married or obsessed with themselves."

A pang of guilt hit my chest, and I cracked. "Fine. Clayton is nice looking, but I'm definitely not going back to his pub."

"Never say never." She shrugged. "Besides, maybe he delivers."

Chapter Twenty

Cecily left the next morning, and my heart sank at the loss. But her visit had revived me. She'd helped me uncover some uncomfortable truths about my faulty thought processes and made me question things I'd blindly accepted about myself and others for too long. Most importantly, I'd realized that, in some ways, my family was still recovering from Mom's cancer. That revelation alone was profound enough to change everything. Healing and nurturing those relationships would be the first thing I worked on when I got home.

I'd been making myself miserable, working around the clock in search of love via earning praise, instead of opening myself up to share time and receive affection. Which meant I'd essentially created a lifestyle that had kept me away from the things I wanted most. I'd never even adopted a dog because I was too busy to take on a new responsibility. More irony. Because the dog would've cheerfully given me its time and affection, if I'd made room for it.

I was willing to bet my family would have as well.

Round and round I'd spun, working to earn compliments and thanks. Believing that would make me happy, and knowing it was never enough.

*Attagirl*s were not love.

I'd had it twisted from the start.

And busy or not, surrounded by people or not, I'd been a recluse in my own way in Willow Bend. But unlike Emily, my aloneness had been unintentional.

Another line from Emily's poetry circled in my mind as I began a new journal entry.

> A word is dead when it is said, some say. I say it
> just begins to live that day.

As usual, I agreed. Cecily's words had spoken straight to my heart, and in turn, she'd opened my eyes.

I made a trip to the mailbox, then to Village Books, delivering letters and picking up a small stack addressed to me. Afterward I took my sweet time walking home. I knew how few trips like this one I'd have before I returned to my life in progress in Willow Bend.

I planned to make big changes in the way I treated myself and interacted with my family, but I wasn't sure six weeks would be enough time to cure all my problems. Something wiggled and itched in my mind, telling me I had more work to do.

I made my way to the study, eager to begin another routine I'd come to cherish. I tucked both feet beneath me on the velvet armchair and watched leaves fall from trees outside the study's window. A new favorite indulgence. Time to be still and enjoy the beauty. For once, the silence didn't feel stifling or oppressive. I felt swaddled and safe. I had a full evening of soaking and self-pampering ahead that would keep me busy until bedtime, and an entire day of visits, phone calls, and other things planned for tomorrow. The only question was how soon to run the bath and pour the wine.

I dragged my attention to the stack of letters in my hand. Paul wrote to me faithfully, and I'd begun receiving messages from Mom, Cecily, Daisy, and other classmates as well.

Headlights flashed over the drive, and the shape of a large pickup truck came into view a moment later.

Davis was back.

I watched, rapt, as he climbed down from his truck, no signs of Violet or his work gear, as he headed for my front door. Had he forgotten something when he left for the day? I rose to get closer to the window when he moved into the light cast from my porch. He wore fresh jeans and a button-down shirt, unbuttoned at the top to reveal the neckline of a white tee beneath. His hair, no longer damp with sweat, lifted on the breeze.

Maybe he'd come to visit me.

Why would he do that? And why did my heart skip recklessly at the prospect?

I glanced down at myself, still neatly dressed from a morning out with Cecily before she'd gone. I looked comfortable but cute, and shockingly not covered in ashes or dirt.

The doorbell rang, and I hooked curly hair behind my ears, straightened my glasses on my nose, and headed for the foyer.

I opened the door as casually as possible with my heart pounding erratically in my ears. "Hey."

"Hi." Davis smiled, appraising me slowly. "I was placing orders for materials and realized I need to get a measurement on something for the new en suite bath." His eyes lifted over my head, indicating the rear portion of the manor where he'd been working. "I didn't want to let myself in the back without letting you know I was here."

"Well, come on in," I said, slightly deflated.

He stepped into the foyer while I closed the door. "More letters from Paul?"

I glanced at the envelopes in my hand, suddenly—unreasonably—self-conscious, and set the stack on the table. "Among others," I said.

"I was never great at writing. Much to the dismay of my aunt." He grinned. "Luckily my taste in books seems to please her."

A smile formed on my lips as I imagined Davis bantering with Grace about reading and writing.

Davis moved past me, slowing slightly as he passed the stairway. He gave the stained glass above the landing a long, silent look before continuing to the jobsite.

I softened as I watched and decided to wait in the kitchen for his return.

"Accomplish what you came for?" I asked when he reappeared a few minutes later.

"Almost. Need to grab a better measuring tape from the truck. Be right back."

I lit the flame beneath a freshly filled kettle as he breezed to and from the front door. "Would you like to stay for hot chocolate?" I asked when he rounded the corner once more.

"I'd love to. Give me five minutes."

"Perfect." Cecily and I had bought a ton of toppings, and I hated when things went to waste.

Davis washed up at the sink a few minutes later, then took a seat at the table. He watched as I moved to the pantry.

"Water's almost ready," I said. "I'm grabbing the toppings."

"Whipped cream and sprinkles?" he guessed.

As if this were amateur hour.

I retrieved my hot chocolate charcuterie tray and set it on the table before him. "Yes. And more." It was heavily laden with mini marshmallows, peppermint sticks, chocolate, caramel, mint, and peanut butter chips, plus a variety of brightly colored sprinkles, jimmies, and sugars.

His eyes widened.

"Whipped cream and chocolate syrup are in the fridge."

Slowly, he turned his awestruck expression to me. "Were you Martha Stewart in a former life?"

"No, but I did have a local chocolatier speak at Rini Reads last fall. She brought a similar tray with accoutrements from her shop. I just ripped it off."

He stole a chocolate chip and tossed it into his mouth. "Grace's speakers always seem to talk about birds and history. Nothing as delicious as hot chocolate."

"Sounds like Grace needs to up her speaker game," I said, joining him at the table to wait for the water to boil. "Also, Martha Stewart is very much alive."

The familiar zing of energy coiled in the air between us, and I smiled.

"Tell me more about your friend Paul," he said, dropping another chocolate chip into his mouth.

I selected a small piece of peppermint from the tray, unsure how to answer his question. "Paul's a nice local professor."

Davis munched, nosy but unbothered. "Ever find out who sent you flowers?"

"Why?" I asked, adding a bit of challenge to my tone.

"Is there a reason it's the same bouquet every time? Are those your favorites or something?"

"They are now," I said. "They're a message sent in the language of flowers."

Davis's expression turned painfully bland. "Adorable," he said, not sounding as if he thought it was adorable at all.

I beamed just to watch his frown deepen, a little trick I'd learned recently.

"Does that smile mean you're removing *Give up on love* from your list?"

The kettle whistled, and he stretched upright. "Never mind. I'll get that."

We remained silent a long while as we stirred our drinks, then perfected our topping selections. I admired the care Davis took in building a perfect hot cocoa, as if he might receive a grade at the end. Then I forcefully peeled my eyes away before he noticed me staring.

"You never answered my question," he said.

"You told me to never mind."

He pursed his lips, the old grumpy expression falling back into place. "Have you changed your mind about giving up on love?"

A lump formed instantly in my throat and chest, forcing me to look briefly away. I took a steadying breath then shook my head, wishing I could answer differently. "No."

I wasn't in the market for romance, but I was learning to love myself and this town more with each passing day. I hadn't anticipated wanting to stay, but I did. I wasn't sure where that left me.

Dammit, Emily. What am I supposed to do now?

Chapter
Twenty-One

The following day, I sat beneath an oak tree on the gravel lane with my journal and cell phone, scribbling plans for my perfect version of Rini Reads and hoping my parents wouldn't take offense at the changes I wanted to make. I hadn't been able to sleep after Davis left the night before. I'd toiled with existential questions and dug deep into my heart. What did I want from my life? Where did I want to live? What did I want to do?

I'd discovered that I wanted to run a bookstore, but not Rini Reads. At least not as it currently existed. And I'd filled a notebook with ideas on how I could make it my perfect bookstore. I walked the lane with Emily's words in my ears as lunch drew near. She thought the truth was rare, and therefore a delight to tell. I couldn't disagree. Then I took a deep breath and made a very important phone call.

"Emma?" Mom answered on the first ring. "Are you okay? You don't usually call until evening. Your father and I can be there in ninety minutes."

I laughed. "I'm fine. I was just thinking of you and wanted to talk." Because Cecily had been right. Some things were too important to wait for days to say. This wasn't the 1850s, and I liked hearing my loved ones' voices anytime I wanted. Like now.

"Oh, thank heavens. We're doing well. Missing you and recalling vividly why we stopped spending so much time at the store. This is a lot of tough work. And I'm not going to lie, we think it's kind of a drag."

"Mom!" I gasped, then laughed. "What?"

"It's true. Entrepreneurship is a young person's game. These days we only like the parts where we get to talk to customers. It's hard to believe how much we used to love it. Back when our lives were still ahead of us. Now our lives are right here. All around us. You and Annie, Jeffrey and the baby. Our book club and neighbors. It's just not for us anymore."

I let her words settle in, and I knew they were true. My parents were just as social and excitable as I was. They hated to miss out on anything, and while Rini Reads had once been their dream, dreams could change. Mine had. "That sounds perfectly reasonable." And another weight lifted from my heart because it was clear to me now that my parents hadn't been avoiding me or abandoning me. They'd been living their lives, believing the busyness of the store fulfilled me.

"I've been thinking a lot about things," she said. "I realized that we haven't asked you if you still love working here. You're certainly incredible at it, but your dad and I have been talking, and we've made a lot of assumptions. I think we might've gotten a few things wrong."

I sighed, leaning my back against the broad tree trunk and letting it bear my weight. "I do enjoy working there."

"But?" Mom asked.

I bit my lip, warring internally with the truth and a lifelong desire to please her. If I said I wanted to change everything about the store, would she care? If I admitted how left out I've felt, would she understand? Would she feel responsible? I feared that more than anything, because I could finally see my life was the result of choices I'd made, not choices she'd made. I should've spoken up about all these things long ago.

"Emma?"

"I haven't been happy," I admitted. "Not for a long time." My voice wobbled on the simple words.

"Oh, sweetie." The concern in her tone ripped through me, and for a moment I wanted to take it back. "Why? What's wrong? Has something happened?"

Emotion clogged my throat, and I forced it back, knowing this was the moment. I could speak the truth as Emily recommended, or I could continue allowing my bitterness to fester.

Fresh instinct kicked inside me, and I knew it wouldn't be the latter. Not anymore, and hopefully never again, because I wasn't the same woman who'd left Willow Bend. I had a clearer view of myself, my family, and my future now. I couldn't go back to peering at life through a dirty window. I wouldn't.

I started speaking and didn't stop. The words rushed from my lips like water through a broken dam. "I love the store, but it became a burden when Annie got married and you and Dad stopped coming in as often. I felt intense, unfair pressure to work harder and make you proud, but I made myself miserable in the process."

"Honey. I had no idea. You seemed so content, always busy. Why didn't you ask for help?"

"I did." I cleared my throat, needing to say something else I knew would hurt her. "I just didn't know how to make you hear me." I'd said the words a dozen times, even created graphics and spreadsheets to justify my need for help. I tracked the store's sales volume and ever-rising demand, but when I directly requested a part-time employee or two, all my parents saw was how smoothly everything already ran.

I hadn't pushed the matter. That was on me. But they hadn't listened, and that was on them.

"I didn't realize," she said. "We didn't know."

"You knew," I corrected softly. "You didn't take the time to help me find a solution."

"We knew you—" She stopped short of finishing her thought. "Oh, no."

"Yeah." I could hear the realization settle in. I swiped a tear from my cheek and kept going before I lost momentum. "Another thing that's been killing me is how close you and Dad are to Annie and Jeffrey. I want that for you, but I want to be a part of our family, too, not just the one who runs the bookstore. I know I'm single. You're two happy couples. I'm a fifth wheel, and maybe I won't say yes to every invitation, but I want to be invited."

Mom made a soft strangled sound, and my heart broke a little more. "I didn't want to hurt you," she said. "I know how much you want to find love, and I worried you'd be bored or sad listening to us talk about our trips and little dates. I'm so sorry. I should've known leaving you out wasn't the answer."

"You didn't know because I never told you."

"I'm your mother," she said. "It's my responsibility to make sure both of my daughters are valued and prioritized."

I snorted an ugly little laugh. We really were the closest, most loving, but most dysfunctional family in all the land.

"I've been so clueless," she said. "Your father and I are your parents. And your friends. There's no reason you wouldn't be just as interested in what we're up to as Annie. You don't need a spouse to want to hear what we're doing. You're on an Amherst adventure, which I can't relate to at all, but I'm hooked on your evening calls. I carry my phone around every day at dinnertime, waiting for updates. I want to know everything you're willing to tell me because I love you."

Tears blurred my eyes as I absorbed her apology.

"I swear we've never meant to leave you out," she said, more fervently. "And we spoke to Annie first about giving you the shop, because we wanted to let her down easy. Not that we thought she'd have an interest in owning it, but because she'd grown up there too. We didn't want her to think we were playing favorites by choosing you over her to inherit something so essential to our family. For the record, she had no objections. More than that, I hate that we didn't ask you if taking over was what you wanted. If it's not, we can sell it, no hard feelings. We can use the proceeds to take a family cruise!"

I laughed. "No! Please don't sell it. I've been thinking a lot about being a bookstore owner, and I've got an idea I'm excited about. I've even considered staying in Amherst to make it happen," I admitted, "but only if that makes the most sense in the end. Not because I'm running away or upset with anyone back home."

Mom was silent, probably stunned, possibly hurt, so I hurried to fill in the blanks.

"I want the store, but it was your first baby, and I don't want to diminish that by making too many changes. If reimagining things makes either of you sad or uncomfortable, I'll look for another space to lease, and we can totally take that cruise."

"You want our store?" Mom asked, her voice soft and thick with emotion.

My throat tightened, and I knew it was true. I could set up shop anywhere and succeed, but deep down, I wanted to succeed with the store I'd grown up in. "Yes."

"Ed, she wants the store."

"Well, hot damn!" Dad bellowed in the background.

"Honey, we don't care what you do with this place. We know whatever you do will be great. We're just thrilled to see it stay in the family. It's our legacy now."

I wiped my eyes and smiled widely. "I think you'll love what I have planned, but I want to work on the details before I share."

"Of course."

"Mom," I said, a thousand emotions lightening my heart and head. "Thank you so much for supporting me so I could take this trip. I needed it more than I knew."

She sighed, and I imagined her pressing a palm to her chest. "I love you so much, sweet girl."

We spoke for a few more minutes before saying our goodbyes, and I slowly released ten years of tension.

I pulled my knees up to my chest and rested my notebook there. The more I thought about owning Rini Reads, and the changes I'd make, the more excited I became. Taking over for my parents no longer felt as if they were dumping their responsibilities on me. It felt like a gift I'd earned by proving I was the right person for the job. Their trust and faith were priceless, and I planned to make them proud.

A week ago—even twenty-four hours ago—I never would've imagined looking forward to returning to my life in Willow Bend. What a difference a day could make.

The phone rang as I scrolled through images of adorable dogs in reading glasses, and I stilled when Davis's number appeared on the screen.

"Hey," he said. "I wasn't sure you'd answer."

"Why not?" I looked toward the stone manor down the lane. No sounds of power tools or falling drywall met my ears.

"You've been hard at work for a while. I thought you'd have your ringer off."

I dragged my gaze from window to window, wondering if he could see me from wherever he was now. "I just talked to my mom, so this is a good time. What's up?"

"What were you working on?"

I turned back to my notebook, pleased with the progress. "I'm making plans for the bookstore."

"Want to talk about them?" he asked. "I was just about to break for lunch, so I have some time," he said.

I raised my eyes to the sound of his voice, now in stereo, both through the phone's speaker and in the space to my left. I disconnected the call to watch him approach.

His navy T-shirt was untucked over his blue jeans, and he'd pinned his hair away from his face with a backward ball cap once more. He'd traded his tool belt for a thermal lunch tote, and I smiled at the perfect combination of my new favorite things.

"May I?" He motioned to the space beside me on the blanket he'd recently returned.

I scooted over to make more room.

Davis sat and placed the bag between us. "Not quite as cool as your hot chocolate charcuterie, but I've got soup and sandwiches." He unpacked two croissants wrapped in parchment. Two small thermoses, presumably filled with soup. Utensils, bottled water, and napkins.

I set my books and phone aside and tried not to overthink the fact he'd gotten up this morning and packed a lunch clearly meant for two.

"Chicken salad," he said, pointing to the sandwiches.

I selected a croissant and peeled away the wrapping.

Davis opened his thermos. "And potato soup."

I smiled. "I love potato soup."

He slid his eyes briefly in my direction. Whatever he was thinking, he kept it to himself.

"Do you always pack a lunch for two?" I asked, with hope plucking at my chest.

He wobbled his head a little as he wiped his mouth on a napkin. "I try to eat with Grace a couple of times a week, but she made other plans today."

"Lucky me." Grace was either my favorite person or a thorn in my side. I couldn't decide which. I sank my teeth into the flaky croissant to redirect my thoughts and moaned in satisfaction.

"Good, right?"

"Amazing. Where'd you get all this?" I asked. The packaging gave nothing away.

"I bought the soup and croissants from a café in my neighborhood. The chicken salad is mine."

I paused midchew. "What do you mean it's yours? You already had it at home?"

Davis frowned. "No. I made it."

"No. You didn't."

His grumpy face returned, and I fought the urge to laugh. "Are you suggesting men can't cook, or are you only doubting my abilities?"

"I'm suggesting this sandwich came straight from heaven."

His irritation eased, and a glint of pride shone in his eyes. "It's one of my mom's recipes, so you aren't completely wrong."

I reached for his hand, prepared to offer an understanding squeeze, then thought better of it and pulled away.

His gaze tracked my retreating hand, then moved to his thermos. He dunked a spoon into his soup without comment.

"I heard about your fight to save some historic properties near downtown," I said, still dying to get the details. "Farmhouses and their barns."

He nodded, a small smile pulling at his lips. "I won, and I've already gotten interest from *Architectural Digest* about this project." He nodded toward Hearthstone Manor.

"You're kidding!"

Davis shook his head, a slight blush on his cheeks. "I sent some in-progress photos with details about the home's history and future. An editor called to ask about including this project with a few others in an issue leading up to the big winner's announcement."

I let my mouth and eyes open wide.

"I planned to woo you with a bottle of wine later. The magazine's team wants to tour the place and take some professional shots. I told them I'd get back to them because I needed to check with the home's tenant."

"You name the time," I said. "I'll make myself scarce."

He opened his lips, as if to say something, then went for the soup instead. A moment later, he caught my eye. "Thank you."

"Don't mention it."

"Tell me about the new plans for your store," he said, turning the spotlight onto me.

For a moment, I considered dodging the question. My idea was still so new, it felt fragile. But this was Davis, and he'd grown up in a bookstore, just like me. He was the perfect person to brainstorm with. And I could use the input. So I let myself dive in.

"I think I need to pull everything out and start over," I said, taking a little inspiration from his renovation of the manor.

His brows rose. "A total remodel."

"Total," I agreed. "I want to make the shop pet friendly. A place where people can bring their pets and hang out with a good book. And I'm going to get a dog. It can be the store's mascot. Preferably an older dog who needs a home. Something docile and loving, like a retired greyhound. We have a rescue in town where I can volunteer when I get home. And there's a dog park about a block away from the shop, so we're in the perfect location. We already get lots of pet traffic on the street."

I passed my notebook to Davis. "Here. I wrote a lot of the little details as they came to mind."

He scanned my words while I kept going.

"I can offer a light beverages service for people and whipped-cream cups for pups. I'll need to replace the floors to handle doggy toenails and inevitable messes. I'll buy more comfortable seating and maybe a half dozen pet beds in various sizes. Water bowls for the entrance and a cookie jar of pet treats at checkout. Transitioning our stock will take a while longer, to diminish losses. But I think I can do it in under a year. I'll strategically replace romance books as they sell with new releases in other genres. I want a good mix. There should also be sections dedicated to other categories like poetry, pet books, and local authors. Maybe even a tribute to Emily Dickinson somehow."

Davis nodded thoughtfully, still turning the pages of my notes. He shared opinions and ideas, and asked insightful questions, like how I'd advertise, and if I'd considered hosting monthly visits with therapy dogs.

I pulled the notebook from his grip and added those questions along with a dozen other ideas as we finished our meal.

A familiar car turned onto the drive as Davis gathered his gear and our trash.

I stood to greet the now familiar delivery car as the driver shifted into park and climbed out with another bouquet. I accepted the flowers, then poked my nose into the buds for a deep inhale.

Davis stood, squinting against the afternoon sun as the car drove away.

"Thanks for sharing your lunch," I said.

"Thanks for hanging out."

We parted ways, and I searched the flowers for a card. Once again, Annie had skipped that part. This time, however, the blooms weren't an apology. This bouquet held honeysuckle and daisies.

Davis's gaze traveled from my wide smile to the bouquet in my arms, and he raised a questioning brow.

I pulled my blanket from the ground, not bothering to stop or explain.

Then I rushed back toward the manor, excited to decipher the new message.

Chapter Twenty-Two

A little searching in *Floriography: The Secret Language of Flowers* revealed honeysuckle and daisies to represent admiration and affection, two concepts that melted my heart when coming from my little sister. I felt the same way about her, and I made a mental note to order a similar bouquet for her the next time I went to town.

I tucked the flowers into a vase and set them on the kitchen counter, then checked on my homemade noodles. The dough was finally dry: some of the long strands were bendy, others easily broken. I bagged them all and hoped I wouldn't regret it. Then I started dinner, knowing it would take hours to prepare. I'd chosen a recipe from Emily's era and inspired by Davis: asparagus soup. Still not a fan of cooking, I poured a glass of wine from one of many bottles I'd procured during Cecily's visit and got to work.

"Beef, bacon, ale, spinach, cabbage," I read, setting the ingredients on my countertop and acknowledging their presence. "Asparagus, salt and pepper, flour, mint, sorrel, beet leaves, and marjoram." I paused to wrinkle my nose. Hopefully the soup would survive without beet leaves because I had no idea where to procure those, and I didn't have any marjoram. I tossed an extra mint leaf onto the pile of veggies for good measure. "Why did everything require so many ingredients two hundred years ago?" It wasn't as if they could hustle to the local Whole Foods for all these things.

As I worked, I reflected on my time in Amherst. For the ten goals I'd set, my progress so far was mixed. I journaled, read, and wrote a lot of haiku. I'd found new perspectives on my troubles and made amends with my mom. But I hadn't become more like Emily, as planned.

In truth, the woman I'd longed to emulate didn't live a life I wanted. She'd been riddled with anxiety and probably as unhappy as I'd been in Willow Bend, if for different reasons. I'd put her on a pedestal all my life because her poems spoke to me and helped me through hard times. But I'd confused the things Emily did—like writing poetry, baking, and gardening—with who she was, and I'd done something similar to myself as well.

I, Emma Rini, ran my parents' bookstore, but that didn't define me, and I controlled my destiny.

I found happiness in Amherst, just not in the solitude as expected. I'd found happiness in getting to know myself and making strides to heal the unacknowledged wounds in my family. I found hope in a future of my making. Becoming Emily wasn't the goal anymore. And giving up on love was something that would take more than a handful of weeks to do, no matter where I was.

Methodically, I cubed the beef and rolled the pieces in flour, then dropped them into a pan with bacon on the bottom. Step by step, I followed all the numerous and boring instructions until I finally added a lid to my stockpot and refilled my glass with chardonnay.

While I waited for the soup to boil, I relocated to the study to look through the plans for my revised shop and brainstorm more. Emily's words came to me as I scribbled, my mind moving faster than my pen could capture the thoughts. She believed beauty wasn't made. It simply *was*.

I agreed. Amherst was beautiful, as was my life here. I felt alive for the first time in too long, and I closed my eyes to soak in the joy.

The bell rang a while later, startling me awake. I blinked, confused by the darkness and wholly unsure if the wall clock indicated it was six in the morning or six at night.

"My soup!" I'd accidentally fallen asleep. A wild trip down the hallway to the kitchen revealed a lot of smoke and a truly horrendous smell.

The bell rang again as I unlidded the stockpot, whose contents had boiled down to sludge, then extinguished the flame.

"Coming!" I called, sending up prayers that Davis hadn't come to visit right when I'd set the house on fire again. I sagged in relief at the sight of Grace at my door.

"Hello, sorry to disturb," she said pertly. "I found these in your cubby when I closed up tonight and thought you might like to have them."

I accepted the little pile of envelopes with a grin. "Thank you." I'd missed my usual evening trip to the store thanks to the chardonnay and impromptu nap.

"Everything okay?" she asked, giving a delicate, but audible, sniff.

I dared a look over my shoulder, thankful the smoke alarms were playing nice. "Failed recipe," I said. "I'm getting used to it."

Her smile was strained as she nodded, and the idea she had something more she wanted to say crossed my mind.

"Would you like a cup of tea?" I offered. "The patio is nice this time of day. We can sit outside and watch the bunnies enjoy my garden."

"I would love that."

Several minutes later, we sat in the cool air, a tray with cups and teapot between us. I'd snacked with Cecily at this table not long ago, and it occurred to me that having guests and playing hostess was nice. I made mental plans to continue the practice in Willow Bend. Maybe I'd invite my family to my place for a change.

Grace sipped her tea, ankles crossed beneath her chair as she scanned the rear yard. "So many memories here," she said.

I wondered if anything particular came to mind. Tea with her sister? A toddling Davis playing in the grass? "I'm really sorry about your

216

sister." The words came out before I thought better of them. I couldn't imagine her loss.

Her eyes flickered to mine, misted with emotion. "Thank you. Iris was an incredible woman. Much younger than me, but fiercely independent. I never dreamed anyone or anything could get the best of her."

A lump formed in my throat, and I nodded, honored by her willingness to discuss someone so dear to her. "Davis said she gardened too."

Grace set her cup aside and blinked back her unshed tears. "She was amazing at everything she tried. The best mother I've ever known."

I smiled. "How fortunate for Davis to have two strong and loving women in his life."

A tear fell over Grace's fair, wrinkled cheek. She laughed softly as she swept it away. "Raising him was an honor. He's turned out quite well," she said. "I think Iris would be pleased."

I was certain of it.

"I wasn't perfect," she continued. "I did the best I could, having never raised a child of my own. Davis still had his father, after all. I was only a stand-in. There was a tricky balance involved." Her expression softened. "From what Davis told me, it's much like your situation with Annie."

"No." I felt my eyes widen. "I didn't raise her." Suddenly the idea of taking any credit from a sick mother and worried father seemed callous and selfish. "I helped where I could. That's all."

"Ah." She nodded, and her lips pursed into a small grin. "Mr. Rogers's mother said when there is tragedy, look for the helpers. They're always there."

Now it was my eyes that blurred with unshed tears. "I'm not a hero," I croaked.

"To her, and to your parents, you were."

Her words hit like torpedoes, spoken with such assurance I sucked in a ragged breath. The possibility my family saw me as a hero gutted me in multiple ways. I wanted so badly for them to see my sacrifices and acknowledge them, but I didn't want credit for credit's sake. I wanted them to know I did it all from love. I'd do it again, a thousand times.

And I knew with certainty any one of them would do the same for me.

The thought made me so homesick I could puke.

"I know I come off as meddlesome at times where Davis is concerned," Grace said, interrupting my internal meltdown. "It's only because I love him so dearly. I want him to be happy. He's worked all these years to be different from his father and to make a difference he can be proud of. Not that Carter is all bad," she added quickly. "Few people are all one thing. Iris wouldn't have loved him if he was truly awful, but her loss changed us. Carter turned to business instead of fatherhood to fill the void. Sometimes I worry Davis has forgotten to prioritize himself. He rarely spends his free time with anyone but Clayton."

"And Violet," I said, thinking of how the sweet doggo looked at him as if he were her whole world.

"He thinks he saved that dog's life," Grace said. "I think she saved his. Maybe not literally, but if not for her, he'd work more and get out less. She needs him, so he goes home. They take walks. Get fresh air and sunshine. Socialize. He's not the sort to leave her alone more than absolutely necessary."

"He's her hero," I said.

Grace raised her cup again, looking pleased at my assertion. "Yes, and all heroes need a break. It's nice when they find one another, don't you think? Seems like that sort of relationship might be a love story for the books."

My cheeks heated at her implication, having called me a hero moments before. Then I thought of all the ways a potential romance with Davis had tanked, and my cynical side reared its head. "Yeah. Fairy tales."

I cast my gaze over the garden, embarrassed by my response.

"How about you?" she asked.

"Me?" I dared a look in her direction. Were we still talking about relationships?

"How's your mission to connect with Emily Dickinson coming along? Davis told me all about it."

I wondered what else Davis had told her about me but kept that question to myself. "I'm revising the plan as I go."

She grinned. "Smart girl. The tree that bends grows strong." She checked her watch, then stood. "I hate to rush off after one cup of tea, but pickleballers wait for no one."

I smiled. "Of course." I walked her back to her car and waved as she reversed away.

I hurried back to the kitchen and fanned the remaining smoke through open windows before it permeated the walls. I thought about my conversation with Grace and the way she made it seem as if Davis's life was the only one she meddled with.

She'd told Davis about the letters I received from classmates. Did she think my potential suitors affected Davis somehow? Why would they? And why hadn't I asked her to clarify?

A sudden bout of coughing changed the direction of my thoughts. I cursed my ruined soup and ability to fall asleep in a heartbeat these days. Darn peace and tranquility.

The doorbell rang again, and I abandoned my fruitless efforts to clear the smoke to find Davis on my porch.

He wore his usual jeans, with a gray boatneck sweater over a white T-shirt, and he'd traded his work boots for deck shoes. His hair was damp from a shower, and the moment I opened the door, I wanted to drown in the fresh, clean scent of him.

His brows furrowed before I said hello. "Is that more smoke? Seriously?"

I grimaced. "It's under control. A minor mishap. No big deal."

He stared at the space behind me. The pointed downturn of his lips suggested he could smell the burned beef, bacon, and veggies.

"I was making asparagus soup, but I fell asleep."

He shook his head, apparently equal parts amused and flabbergasted.

"Can I help you with something? Or did you sense the smoke and rush over to complain?" I asked.

Slowly, his attention returned to me. "I got a call from the magazine," he said, a spark of happiness lighting his eyes. "They want to send a photographer this week. I invited Grace out for dinner to celebrate, but she suggested I ask you instead."

I nearly laughed at the timing of his request. She was tenacious. "Honored to be your second choice again today," I said, only partially teasing.

"Would you like to join me for dinner at Clayton's pub?"

I dithered.

"Come on," he said, with the wave of a hand. "We can talk about my nosy aunt. And you can get away from that horrid smell."

The burned-soup scent registered again, and I frowned. "Give me ten minutes to change."

On the way out, I grabbed my purse, phone, and key from the entryway table and gave the butterflies in my stomach a stern, but silent, warning. This was not a date.

"More letters?" he asked, nodding toward the pile of envelopes I'd left on the table.

"Grace delivered them."

Davis raised his eyes to me and stiffened.

"What's wrong?" I glanced down at myself, turning one way then the other. My ice-blue sweaterdress and suede booties were both seasonally appropriate and fantastically comfortable.

"You're overdressed."

"I like this outfit," I said defensively. Something in the clench of his jaw suggested he was deflecting, and I nearly asked if it was my dress or the fresh stack of letters that bothered him.

I pushed the idea away, afraid of reading too deeply into my conversation with Grace.

For a long moment, neither of us spoke or moved.

"Is there a problem?" I asked.

"Nope." Davis opened the front door and motioned me through it.

I snatched the letters from the table on my way outside.

We climbed into the cab of his truck a moment later.

The interior smelled like Davis, with underlying tones of leather and the outdoors. I focused on the letters in my hand as a necessary distraction.

"Grace said you get a lot of love notes," he said flatly, shifting into reverse.

He'd pushed up his sleeves, revealing thick ropes of muscle that flexed beneath his skin when he turned the wheel.

Instinct tickled my spine.

"Why would she say that?" I asked.

He slung one arm over the back of the seat and twisted at the waist to look behind us. He used the opportunity to give me extensive side-eye. "That's not a denial."

I returned my attention to the envelopes, wondering what Davis would think if they were love notes. "Just letters from classmates, family, and friends," I said, flipping through the stack. "Cecily, Mom, Daisy, Paul, and—" I stared at the unfamiliar script on the final envelope. "Huh."

"What?"

"I'm not sure." Curious, I opened the last envelope and tugged the paper from the sheath. Perfect calligraphy filled the page, with a signature at the bottom that read, "Forever yours."

"Who's it from?"

I turned the paper over, then looked at the envelope more thoroughly. "I don't know," I said. My eyes returned to the short message.

> Emma,
> I was reading a classic today and thought of you. Having never been a fan of Mr. Darcy, I can see his dilemma now firsthand. He was a man previously

in command of his own being who quickly became powerless in love. The shift is immeasurably frustrating. The results, unsettling. Yet I remain a glutton for more.

Why is it that authors a century gone can so easily know our modern hearts? Were some of us born in the wrong era? Or do some things simply transcend time?

Forever Yours

"That's how it's signed," I said, feeling a little breathless.

Davis turned curious eyes my way.

I cleared my throat, unexpectedly touched by the anonymous letter. I read the page again, pausing at the final line. Had the author forgotten their signature? Or was Forever Yours meant to be a pseudonym?

"So you do get love letters."

I folded the letter and tucked it away, unsure what else to do. "This is a first."

I turned my attention to the world outside my window, watching the small town and its happy pedestrians pass by.

"Did you get any further with your store plans?" Davis asked, changing the subject when silence dragged between us.

"A little," I said. "I didn't come up with a lot of new ideas, but I broke everything down that I already had in the notebook. I made sensible lists, charts, a budget, and timeline. Then I looked more carefully at my predicted costs to decide if I'll need a small business loan."

Davis grunted as he made our final turn. He piloted his big truck onto the edge of a slim lot outside Clayton's pub and turned off the engine. "You'll need a business plan to get the loan. Have you written one before?"

"I have an MBA," I said. "Business plans are directly in my wheelhouse. So, if I need to get a loan, I'm confident I can. But I have savings too. I used a little of it to stay here, but it's still enough to make a significant dent in how much it will cost for some of the necessary changes." I looked around more carefully. "Is this a parking space?"

"It is now," he said, climbing out.

I gathered my things, then turned to find him opening my door.

Davis offered me his hand, and electricity sizzled through me like always, curling my toes at his touch. He helped me down, then pulled me close to his side. "Mud," he said, pointing to the dark ground.

"Thanks."

Music spilled from the pub as we approached the door, and it didn't sound like the jukebox. "Is that a band?"

Davis steered me through the crowd by my shoulders until we reached a booth near the kitchen with a **Reserved** sign on it. "This is us."

We took seats on either side of the table, and a woman in a logoed T-shirt appeared.

"Hey, Davis." Her smile was warm, and her expression curious. She was petite with lots of makeup, but I guessed her at around fifty. Her name badge said *Tina*.

"Hey, Tina. This is my friend Emma. I told Clayton we were coming."

"You want your usual to drink?"

He nodded, and Tina looked at me. "What about you, doll?"

"I don't know," I said. "What do you recommend?"

"Our hard ciders are good."

"Sold."

She winked, then swung her gaze to Davis and pumped her brows before heading toward the bar.

"That's Clayton's aunt," he said with a chuckle. "She might not look like she'd be one of Grace's friends, but she is. They're thick as thieves. Tina and my mom grew up together."

"Ah." I smiled. "This really is a small community."

"You have no idea."

The kitchen door swung open, and Clayton appeared. I recognized him from the night I'd publicly confronted Davis on his dirty deeds. He was better looking than I'd originally thought. His eyes were bluer. His beard tidier. His smile mischievous and bright.

Davis rose to clap his friend on the back. "Clayton, this is Emma Rini. Emma, Clayton Darning."

"Hi," I said, offering him my hand.

He accepted the shake, then rocked back on his heels. "It's nice to finally meet you."

Davis scanned the room, appraising the crowd. "Looks like the band's a hit."

"That is no joke." Clayton clasped his hands together and bounced his attention from his friend to me, then back. "Why don't you two have a spin on the dance floor. I'll get dinner started."

The opening notes to "Brown Eyed Girl" rose from the guitar, and Davis tented his brows. "Should we?"

I only debated for a moment, knowing full well what my heart would think of this later. The absolute last thing I should do was spend time in Davis's arms.

So why was my hand already in his? And why were we moving toward the dance floor?

Davis stopped where tables and chairs had been moved back to accommodate the band and crush of bodies. He caught my waist and pulled me close as another couple spun past. Heat from his nearness singed my skin and sank deep into my bones. I would absolutely regret this in the morning.

Then we began to sway, our bodies falling into step as if we'd danced together a thousand times.

"A photographer is coming to see your progress on the manor?" I asked, circling back to his incredible news. How had we gotten sidetracked from something so incredible?

He nodded, a glint of pride in his heated gaze.

I tried desperately not to think about his big hand splayed across my back, or my chest only inches from his.

"I know exactly what I want to show them. If you aren't opposed to wearing a hard hat, I could take you into the work area later and see what you think."

"I'd like that."

We drifted around the floor with the other couples, a familiar tune weaving the moment into a memory.

"Everything okay?" he asked after a few moments.

"I was thinking about the house," I lied, then something true came into mind. "I gave Cecily a tour. She's an enormous history buff. She scrutinized every detail."

"Did she approve?" he asked.

I nearly smiled at the quiet confidence in his tone. "Mostly."

"Mostly?"

"She thought the stained glass on the landing was out of place."

Instead of the frown I'd anticipated, a soft smile curved his lips. "I almost forgot about that," he said. "It's for my mom."

"Iris."

He dipped his chin. "You remembered her name."

"Of course."

The song ended, and a slower melody began, but Davis didn't release me. So I stayed, telling myself this was just another conversation between friends. We were simply in one another's arms instead of seated on a couch or across a table. I had to believe this moment meant nothing, because if I let myself hope for more, it would be my undoing. Losing him briefly after learning he'd lied had crushed me, but it had set me back on the path I started. I'd grown and healed in the days since, and I'd resolved old family wounds. I had a solid plan for the bookstore and my future. And my time in Amherst was dwindling. I couldn't bear to spend another minute nursing a broken heart. So if holding me meant nothing to Davis, it couldn't mean anything to me.

"Emma," he said cautiously, his voice so low I might've missed it had my ear not been pressed against his chest.

A round of applause crashed through the moment, and I sprang away.

The song had ended, and the band announced a break.

I had a feeling I'd dodged an unnecessary and night-ruining let-down. Davis probably sensed how completely I'd relaxed in his arms and wanted to remind me this wasn't a date. We were here to celebrate his accomplishment with the magazine.

Tina waved from our table, where a number of dishes had appeared.

"I guess that's our cue," I said, moving woodenly in her direction.

She greeted us with a broad smile as we reclaimed our seats. "Welcome back. I've got your spinach-and-artichoke dip with pita chips," she said, pointing at a bowl-and-plate combo. "Tomato-and-basil bruschetta." She pointed to a long wooden board at the table's center. "And blueberry goat cheese salad with house vinaigrette."

I set a hand on my stomach, willing the butterflies away. "This looks delicious. Thank you." Maybe if I ate enough, the food would settle my nerves.

"I can't claim any glory here," she said, flashing a smile at Davis before taking her leave.

Davis served a little from each dish onto two plates, then passed one to me. "What kind of soup did you say you were making?"

"Asparagus."

Davis wrinkled his nose before tucking a bit of bruschetta into his mouth. Then he sucked a drip of oil from his thumb.

I looked away, hating the ideas that move had given me.

"How's the progress on your goals list going?" he asked, pulling my eyes to meet his.

"So-so." I sipped my water to ease my dry mouth. "I'm satisfied overall, I think."

"How do the flowers and all your suitors work with your need to give up on love?" Davis asked.

"The bouquets are from Annie," I said, enjoying the surprise on his face at my reveal. "And the suitors are a figment of your aunt's imagination."

"Not all of them, I'm sure." Davis's lips quirked as he dug into his salad with new gusto.

It was possible he wasn't wrong, so I bravely showed him my mysterious letter.

Davis wiped his mouth on a napkin, eyebrows high. "You're letting me read it?"

"Why not," I said, smiling again. "You claim to know everyone in town. Maybe you can help me figure out who sent this."

Something like satisfaction flashed in his eyes, and he reached for the letter. "Challenge accepted."

We divided the next two hours between the table and the dance floor, enjoying a multitude of amazing foods and speculating on the identity of Forever Yours.

By the time we left, I was a little tipsy.

"I'm not sure you should drive," I said. "You've had a lot to drink."

"I had two beers in almost three hours and plenty of food. You had four ciders, and I'm at least twice your size."

I folded my arms and leaned my head back to frown at him. "Are not."

I lost my balance, and he caught me with a shake of his head. "I'm not sure if you're arguing your size or the number of ciders, but either way, you're wrong."

"I think I should walk it off," I said, gripping his wrist with both of my hands while I regained my bearings. The air felt crisp and cool, guaranteed to shape me up before I got home.

Davis wiggled his hand free from my grip and set it on my back, silently nudging me forward. "All right. I guess we'll walk."

"Yay!"

He chuckled.

We walked in companionable silence for several moments before a sleek black car pulled up to the curb at our side.

Davis stiffened, and he tucked me behind him as the dark window powered down.

I peeked carefully around his arm, clinging to the back of his sweater for balance.

"Hey, kiddo," a man said, a strangely plastic smile on his face. "Kind of late to be out for a walk, isn't it?"

A pretty blonde leaned across from the passenger seat. Her tight red dress rode high on her thighs as she waved.

Davis didn't acknowledge her.

"What do you want, Dad?" he asked, sounding immediately exhausted. It was Carter. The man I'd met on the porch of Village Books. Davis's father.

He sucked his teeth, apparently irritated by Davis's response. "You haven't responded to my messages."

"I've been busy."

"Clearly." Carter's gaze flicked to me.

Davis's hand, still bent behind him, tightened on my hip. "I started the reno at Hearthstone Manor. *Architectural Digest* is coming to photograph it this week."

We stood there in silence before his dad made a low, disappointed sound. "Avery Lindor made an incredible offer on that property, and I've already accepted."

I gasped, the buzz of the cider burning away.

"You had no right," Davis replied, his tone cold and flat.

"You sure about that?"

My stomach tightened, and my heart rate rose. Had Carter sold Hearthstone Manor? To an investor? Why?

As if on cue, Davis's father spoke again. "One old house and a bookstore isn't enough reason to tie up all that land. Not with a multimillion-dollar deal at stake. Another set of condominiums will bring more money into this community than you can imagine, and it will continue to do so for decades to come. Don't be childish and sentimental. Be reasonable and realistic."

"The property is in a trust," Davis said. "It's intended for me."

Carter's brows rose. "Is it?"

My mind ping-ponged with the conversation. How could this be true? And why hadn't Davis mentioned the possibility of his father selling the property before?

His dad wanted to turn his childhood home, where all his memories of his mother still lived, into condos.

"I'll call you tomorrow, Dad." Davis turned and urged me forward. "Now's not the time."

He dropped his hand from my hip, and the inches between us felt like a chasm.

Chapter
Twenty-Three

I set a lidded container of muffins inside the manor's official work zone the next morning, before starting my day. Davis had removed a portion of the wall separating the previously locked section of the home and the larger downstairs, where I rattled around. He'd built new frames with two-by-fours, the drywall only beginning to go up. He'd hung heavy plastic sheeting for the meanwhile, meant to prevent dust and debris from slipping into the main areas. The sheeting made it easy to stretch an arm inside and leave the treats. I'd found recipes for pet-friendly baked goods online while looking for ideas I could implement at a pet-friendly bookstore, and I knew just the doggo to taste test them. I left a letter on top explaining as much. I also thanked Davis for a fun night, hoping to defuse any awkwardness he felt following his father's roadside ambush.

After his father drove away, Davis had dutifully walked me to my door, but we'd barely spoken all the way home. I'd pressed a kiss to his cheek, certain he needed it, and he'd nodded thoughtfully in return, saying goodbye only with his eyes.

Hopefully the letter and muffins would remind him nothing had changed between us. If he needed a friend, I was available, even if that meant more time spent in companionable silence.

I paired a fuzzy peach-colored sweater and socks with jeans and sneakers for the gorgeous autumn day, then opted for glasses over contacts and used a headband to keep my hair away from my face. I stepped into the sun and spotted Davis, still in his truck, halfway up the lane.

He slowed and lowered his window.

I smiled and waved.

"Sorry about last night," he began, looking ashamed for nothing that was his fault.

"What do you mean?" I asked pleasantly. "I had a great time." I had, but I'd never look at his father the same again.

I recalled the strange familiarity I'd felt the day I'd met Carter at Village Books. I didn't understand it then, but I could see the similarities in his eyes and Davis's now. Not in the color but the shape. The set of their jaws. The broad build of their shoulders. But Carter was a wolf in sheep's clothing—or in his case, designer clothing and a Mercedes. I wondered how many people in this town had seen him smile while he took advantage of them. I couldn't imagine how it would feel if one of my parents tore me down for my passion or sold my childhood home for money no one needed. The idea of this town without Hearthstone Manor and Village Books hurt me deeply.

Now that I'd seen behind the Carter Sommers veil, I wouldn't be fooled again.

Davis scraped a hand through his hair, then nodded, presumably understanding what I was doing. We didn't have to talk about his dad's poor behavior, or his own response, unless he truly wanted to. If he did, this wasn't the best time. I had letters to write, and he had work to do.

"I should've stuck around a little when I brought you home," he said.

I tipped a hand to my forehead, shielding my eyes from the sun. "Rain check," I said. "You name the day. Right now I'm off to letter-writing class."

"All right. Still interested in seeing the progress I've made?"

"Of course!"

"I can stop back with Violet this afternoon," he said. "I'm cleaning up today in preparation for the photographer. I'll bring Violet over. I know she'd love to see you."

My heart lightened at the mention of that fluffy girl. "When?"

"Four?"

I raised a hand in goodbye. "See you then."

When I hit the sidewalk outside Village Books, Daisy called out. "Hey, Emma!" She wore jeans and a white peacoat, unbuttoned to reveal an emerald-green blouse with miniature white polka dots. Her blond hair lifted on the breeze. "How's the transition to eighteen-fifties spinster coming along?"

I held the door for her to pass, and we made our way through the shop to the class area in back. "Not great."

She laughed. "How's everything else?"

My thoughts drifted to the conversation between Davis and Carter, then to my letter from Forever Yours and the small gift I'd left for Davis and Violet. "Complicated."

Was Forever Yours in this class? Would Davis think my little surprise was too much? Was I trying too hard? Could he save the manor and bookstore?

Daisy nudged me with her elbow a few moments later. "Emma?"

"Hmm?"

"I asked who your letters were for," she said, casting a look at the envelopes in my hand. "But I can see you're not quite awake. Relatable."

I smiled, as if she'd guessed my problem correctly, then motioned to the refreshments table. "Can I get you a coffee?"

Daisy lifted the giant hot-pink travel cup in her hand and wiggled it gently. "You'd better pour yourself two."

I set my things on the table, then went to grab a drink.

"Hey, Emma," Michael said, refilling the water pitcher. "Good game the other night."

"It was," I said. "Do you happen to have season passes?"

He stilled, brows uncharacteristically furrowed. "I do. Why?"

I bit my lip, unsure how to ask if he was my online friend, Historically_Bookish, without sounding ridiculous if I was wrong. "Do you like wings?"

Michael made a goofy face. "Of course." He set a hand on one hip and cocked his head like a cop in a crime show, homing in on evidence. "Are you trying to ask me out? Because I'd love to, but only if my girlfriend can come along. She hates to be left out." He cracked up and relaxed his stance. "I'm kidding. What's up? Really? Need a recipe? I hear you're delivering baked goods all over town. I'm actually a little jealous about that."

I had no idea how to respond. Was he only joking about the date, or was he also joking about having a girlfriend? "Do you ever post on IBOOM?" I blurted, throwing the question into the air. There were too many mysteries in my life at the moment, including who wrote the letter signed as Forever Yours. At least I could get an answer on the person behind Historically_Bookish, even if I sounded a little silly asking.

Michael stilled. "Sometimes. Why?"

A customer set a pile of books on the counter beside his register, and he turned in her direction.

I marched dutifully to class. What was I supposed to do with his answer? The handle was available to all employees, but who used it most?

Paul's cheerful voice turned my head. He shook hands and exchanged waves with a number of classmates, then greeted Grace with a kiss on her cheek.

"Good morning," Paul said brightly. "Hi, Emma. How's Cecily doing? She made it home safely?"

"She did," I said. "She had a really nice visit. I think she'll come again as soon as she can."

"Glad to hear it," he said. I smiled. Paul was kind and easy to be around. His letters brightened my days.

My cheeks heated as he watched me, and I wondered if I had a little crush on him.

I spent so much time thinking about Emily and Davis, my family and the bookstore, plus a myriad of other things. Did I somehow overlook the guy standing in front of me?

"Careful, Rini," he said. "You appear to be blushing."

Daisy's face jerked in my direction, lips parted with interest.

I bit my lip as the anonymous letter came to mind. Was Paul Forever Yours?

Did I want Paul to be my secret admirer?

"I'm going to get settled," I said, leaving him with a small shake of my head.

Daisy leaned her shoulder against mine and grinned the moment I took the seat beside hers. "What was that about?"

I shook my head, baffled at the direction my thoughts had taken, and a little embarrassed she'd caught me. "Nothing."

"Oh, yeah? Then why are you blushing?"

I bit my lip and laughed. "You caught me lost in thought, that's all. Hey, do you know if Michael has a girlfriend?"

She looked over her shoulder, then back to me. "How many men do you need?" she teased. "There must be something in the water at Hearthstone. How soon can I visit?"

Grace took her place at the head of the table, a warm expression on her pretty face.

I wondered if she knew what her brother-in-law was up to, and that she might lose the store. I also wondered, hopelessly, if I could do anything to help Davis make sure that didn't happen.

"Hey," Daisy whispered. "I don't know about the girlfriend, but I can find out if you want. I was only teasing earlier."

I shook my head. "It's okay. I'll figure it out."

"Welcome, class," Grace began. "Today's letter for inspiration was written by a local favorite, Emily Dickinson. Our classmate, Daisy Macnamara, kindly suggested it. She's become quite an expert on Ms. Dickinson's life and is finishing her MFA at UMass this semester. She'll defend her dissertation next month at the Emily Dickinson Museum, and I'd love to see many of you there. Thank you, Daisy."

Beside me, Daisy beamed.

She turned her cheery expression on me. "I thought you'd like hearing something from her vast collection. Maybe it will even inspire you in your quest here."

"In 1862," Grace began, "Emily responded to an article in *The Atlantic*, written by Thomas Wentworth Higginson. He was calling for young writers to submit work for publication in the paper. Emily responded to that call. She was eager to know if her verse was alive. An interesting and powerful choice of words, I think. Also quite right. Any fan of her work would say her words were very much alive.

"Emily sent several poems for his review, and he responded with his advice. Together, they shared correspondence over many years and became rather good friends. Many historians and Emily enthusiasts believe this particular letter changed her life. She was brave, and she put herself out there by sending this query and her work. She gained the advice she sought and a longtime friend for her efforts. As you think about who to write today and what to say, consider writing to someone who might not expect it, and see if this is the letter that changes your life."

I put my pen to paper before Grace finished her commentary.

I had a new friend to write as well.

> Forever Yours,
> I've read your lovely letter at least a dozen times. Your words touched my heart, and I want to thank you for them, but I don't know who you are. Am I meant to refer to you as Forever Yours? Please allow me to return your kindness. Tell me something about yourself. Maybe your name?
> Emma

When class ended, I carried my letters to the cubbies for distribution. I paused at the spot with my name, the letter for Forever Yours in one hand. I planned to leave it there, hoping he'd find it if he tried to leave another message for me. But he'd already been there. A single envelope with my name in perfect calligraphy waited inside.

I exchanged my letter to him with the new letter for me, then turned to find Grace and Daisy waiting.

"Emma," Grace said sweetly. "I wanted to thank you for having lunch with Davis when I had to bow out. I hear the two of you had a lovely time, as always. And a few friends noticed you out dancing last night as well." She hung her folded hands before her. "I guess things just work out sometimes."

Daisy's jaw nearly unhinged.

"We were celebrating Davis's win with the historic properties you told me about," I said, directing my words to Daisy.

She closed her mouth and pumped a silent fist.

"And," I added, moving my eyes back to Grace, "*Architectural Digest* is sending a photographer to Hearthstone for an upcoming article about the restoration process."

Grace slid a knowing look to Daisy, and the younger woman's mouth fell open again. "Well, I'll leave you to it," she said, having planted all her seeds.

Paul strode in our direction before Daisy could hit me with her questions. "Cool calligraphy." He pointed at the envelope in my hand, then passed a letter to Daisy and then me. He held onto her envelope an extra moment when she tried to take it. "I know you're about to get your MFA, but it wouldn't hurt you to work on your handwriting. I practically need a decoder to read these."

She pretended to kick him. "I'm working on it. Those fountain pens are the worst, and I don't have the necessary time or patience. I'm doing my best. Emma doesn't even use the pen Grace gave us."

They turned momentarily accusing looks at me, then laughed.

"Stop," I said. "My pen's clearly broken."

The familiarity between them was endearing and something I hadn't noticed before. "Do you two know one another?" I asked. "Outside class, I mean?"

Paul shot her a mischievous grin. "I had Daisy's older sister in my first English Lit class as a professor. I was a train wreck. I'm only slightly better now, but I keep trying," he joked.

"He's still her favorite teacher," Daisy said.

"Speaking of class," Paul peeked at his watch. "I'm teaching in an hour, so I'd better get going."

We said our goodbyes; then Daisy hooked her arm with mine. "I hope you have time for coffee, because you have so much to tell me," she said. "Starting with who wrote that letter. I saw your expression the moment you picked it up. It's the reason I ran over to your cubby."

I tried to fight my smile but failed.

⁓✤⁓

Back at Hearthstone, I spent two more hours reviewing and improving my plans for a Rini Reads remodel; then I switched gears to give my brain a break. Caffeine coursed through my body. Coffee with Daisy followed by a pot of tea had helped me do a weekend's worth of work in a few hours. The crash coming later would be totally worth it.

I curled onto the window seat in the study, pushing aside some of the craft supplies I'd used to make my extensive bookstore plans. I'd done my work, and now it was time to embrace my inner nineteenth-century socialite and swoon for the fun of swooning.

I opened the letter from Forever Yours, giddy and eager to lose myself in the words.

> Emma,
> Did you know the love between poets Robert Browning and Elizabeth Barrett Browning began with an extended exchange of letters? According to

237

their heir, those letters were the only ones they ever exchanged, because once they married, they were never apart again. Can you imagine that kind of love?

I can.

Forever Yours

I pressed the page to my chest and suppressed a squeal as I scanned the additional page included with his letter. A copy of one of the Brownings' correspondences, and the transcript.

I had no idea who Forever Yours truly was, but somehow he knew me well.

How could I give up on love when there was at least one man in the world who wrote things like that? A man who saw straight to my heart.

I let my head fall back and my arms go limp on a bone-deep sigh. If I could fall in love via letters, then spend the rest of my days exploring the life with that man, I'd die happy. There wasn't any point in denial. The possibility was too romantic to resist.

The distant crunch of gravel drew my eyes to the study window, and I straightened to get a better look. A familiar pickup truck rolled to a stop, and panic shrieked through my bones. Davis and I had afternoon plans, and I'd lost track of time again.

I nearly hit the ceiling when my doorbell rang. "Shit. Shit. Shit." I raced through the manor on fuzzy-socked feet and slid to a stop in the foyer. Then I opened the front door with an apologetic frown.

Davis and Violet waited outside.

"I'm so incredibly sorry, but I'm not ready. I got busy and didn't realize so much time had passed."

Davis wrinkled his nose and forehead as he scanned me. "What are you wearing?"

I dropped into a squat before my fluffiest friend and covered Violet with kisses and hugs. Then I rose to face her human. "This is my brainstorming outfit. Come in and close the door."

"Wow. You're all jazzed up," he said, stepping into the foyer.

"It's called happiness," I corrected. "I'm excited. I've made a ton of progress on my bookstore plans, and I've also consumed a lot of caffeine."

"Ah."

"Come with me." I beckoned him with one hand as I crossed the foyer.

"You have a sticky note on your bum," he said.

My hands flew behind me on instinct, searching for the little runaway. "What does it say?" I pulled the note free before he could answer. "Sweet treats," I read. "I wondered where that went."

Violet trotted into the study at my side.

I'd leaned a giant whiteboard against the bookshelves and covered it in brightly colored notes, pictures, and text. "Ta-da!"

Davis rubbed his chin with one hand and crossed the opposite arm over his chest. "You made a murder board. Nice."

"It's not a murder board." I guffawed. "This is a miraculous thing of beauty."

He approached slowly. "All you're missing is the red yarn that ties it all together."

The board clearly outlined my vision for big change at Rini Reads. Potential names for the revised shop. To-do lists. Fun images of pets reading books. Shelters, rescues, and other related businesses in Willow Bend, as well as a carefully detailed timeline for all the steps necessary. "I stopped at the craft store after coffee with Daisy. I couldn't wait to get started. I guess I should've set an alarm."

"There's a marker in your hair."

I pulled the hot-pink highlighter from my messy bun and tossed it onto the desk with the two dozen other writing utensils, sticky notes, and construction paper remnants. "Give me five minutes to change."

"You sure you don't want to go in those big-ass boxer shorts and your 'Get Lit' shirt?"

I hustled up the steps to my room. "Brainstorming outfit," I called as I ran.

"Do you care if we take Violet on her walk first?" he asked, projecting his deep tenor through the ancient home.

"Nope!" Honestly, I probably needed to burn off some of the excess energy.

Did Emily Dickinson enjoy caffeine?

What would she think of me soaring around the manor in men's underwear?

I probably didn't want that answer.

Several minutes later, I returned to Davis in yoga pants and a long-sleeved T-shirt. I pulled the tie from my hair and gave my curls a quick finger comb. "Ready!"

He dragged his gaze over me and sighed. "Shoes."

I grabbed a stack of letters from the table and stuffed my feet into my sneakers. A moment later, we were out the door.

Chapter
Twenty-Four

Davis beeped his truck doors unlocked and motioned for me to climb aboard.

"I thought we were going for a walk?"

"We are." He opened the passenger door, and Violet jumped inside. "She wants to visit another park."

I looked to the pretty tail-wagging blonde. Her wide pink tongue lolled cheerfully from her open mouth. "How can I say no?"

Violet licked my arm as I buckled up.

"Can we stop at the bookstore?" I asked. "I want to put a few letters into the cubbies."

Davis shifted into drive, looking unimpressed. "Weren't you just there?"

"Yes, and I received a bunch of letters. Now I want to drop off my responses."

"Can't you drop the letters off at your next class?"

I shrugged.

"How'd you have time to write all those letters and create your murder board?" he asked, slowing to a stop at the end of the lane.

"Caffeine." I hopped out with a smile. "Be right back!"

Davis and Violet waited while I hurried into Village Books, heart hammering in my chest. I waved to Michael, then dropped my letters into their respective boxes before slowing as I approached the cubby marked with my name.

An envelope leaned neatly against one wall. My name, not Forever Yours, was scripted neatly on the front.

I pounced forward on a burst of dopamine. The anonymous letter exchange was addictive, and I already wanted more. Something about the writer, and the direct path of his words to my heart, made opening each letter feel like Christmas morning. I swiped the treasure with greedy fingers, then made a beeline for the front door.

"Where's the fire?" Michael called.

I waved an arm overhead and smiled but didn't slow down. I wasn't sure what I'd do if Michael was Historically_Bookish and Forever Yours. He'd been at the store earlier when I found the letter after class, and he was still there now. Unlikely coincidence? Or just a guy working his shift?

Davis heaved a labored sigh when I climbed in. "Any other errands you need to run, or can we walk my dog?"

I rolled my eyes and tore into the envelope as we merged into traffic.

> Emma,
> It's too soon. I know. But I found another letter I had to share. I hope you liked the last. I'm already shamelessly hooked on these correspondences, both the historical ones and our own.
>
> This is a note to Virginia Woolf from Vita Sackville-West. You might know Vita and her husband weren't monogamous, and Virginia's spouse only cared that she found joy. Vita's words speak to me. Their urgency. The sincerity. Their truth. If I could write half as well as Vita, I'd write a similar letter to you.
>
> Forever Yours

I flipped to the second sheet of paper and absorbed the first few words.

> I am reduced to a thing that wants Virginia. I composed a beautiful letter to you in the sleepless nightmare hours of the night, and it has all gone: I just miss you, in a quite simple desperate human way. You, with all your un-dumb letters, would never write so elementary a phrase as that; perhaps you wouldn't even feel it. And yet I believe you'll be sensible of a little gap. But you'd clothe it in so exquisite a phrase that it would lose a little of its reality. Whereas with me it is quite stark: I miss you even more than I could have believed; and I was prepared to miss you a good deal. So this letter is just really a squeal of pain. It is incredible how essential to me you have become.

I pressed my lips together in delight, familiar with the letter Forever Yours mentioned and enclosed. I'd only ever dreamed of a longing like hers, and never dreamed of being on the other side.

"Another admirer?" Davis asked.

I peered over Violet's luscious fur. "No."

He dared a glance in my direction as he drove. "Then who?"

"It's from Forever Yours."

Whatever Davis thought of that, he kept it to himself.

I wanted to keep speculating about the secret author, but it didn't seem right to talk about it with Davis. A man I'd kissed once in reality and a thousand times in my memory.

I folded and tucked the letter into its envelope, then snuggled with Violet as we motored away from downtown.

We followed a winding, tree-lined road into the forest. Shade blocked the sun, and the truck grew momentarily dark. When the canopy receded and the light returned, Davis parked near a building marked as **Visitor's Center**.

"Woof!" Violet stood, eager to get outside.

Davis gave her a soothing pet, unfastened his seat belt, and caught my eye. "I like this place because the trails and views are amazing. More serenity. Less people."

"Your favorite," I teased.

"You should be able to find a lot of specimens for your herbarium here."

I opened my door and climbed out, stretching my back and shoulders. "You remembered my herbarium."

"Of course." Davis set a hand on one hip. "And Violet loved your muffins, by the way. I enjoyed the surprise of finding them and your note."

My cheeks heated at his approval, and I looked away.

"What else are you working on now?" he asked. "Besides plans for a revamp of your store."

"Embroidery," I said with a severe eye roll. "Noodles. Soup."

He laughed quietly, and the sound warmed my chest. "Hope the noodles turned out better than the soup."

"I think half will disintegrate in broth, and the rest will be the consistency of leather," I admitted.

"Sounds delicious."

Violet jumped down from the cab, and Davis locked the truck.

"I think my next hobby will be uncovering the identity of Forever Yours," I said, only partially joking. "I saw a novel at the Emily Dickinson Museum featuring her as an amateur sleuth alongside her housemaid."

"A real Sherlock and Watson story," he said.

"Exactly."

We followed Violet past a wooden marker etched with the words Robert Frost Trail, and I immediately thought of the opening line to one of his most well-known poems, "The Road Not Taken."

Two roads diverged in a yellow wood.

I took a moment to appreciate the narrow trail before us. "This is beautiful." A well-trodden path wound through the forest ahead, a dark ribbon among brightly colored leaves.

Many think the poem, about a fork in a road, means that we should take chances and do brave things—take the paths not taken. In reality, Frost suggested that it's the smaller choices that make up our lives.

I supposed I could've chosen to cut Davis out of my life for the rotten things he'd done. If I had, though, I wouldn't have had this hike, or any of the other memories we'd made together.

"You doing okay?" he asked.

"Just feeling inspired."

I would be more conscientious about how I spent my time. And the memories I chose to make with it.

He passed me a fallen leaf, mostly green with yellowed edges. "White oak."

"Thanks." I collected an array of leaves as we meandered and let Violet smell every patch of moss, exposed root, and fallen acorn along the way.

"Thinking about the calligraphy guy?" Davis guessed when the silence between us stretched too long.

I bit my lip as a spark of excitement burst through me. Maybe I could talk to him about this after all. "I'm wondering if he was in one of the letter-writing classes. That would make sense, right? Since we're encouraged to leave letters for one another."

"Maybe. I've never taken the class," he said.

"Do you think it could be Michael?" I asked. "He's not in the class, but he's at the shop a lot. And he said he uses the Historically_Bookish handle on IBOOM."

"Michael?" Davis's frown returned. "The clerk? He's like twenty-three."

"He's twenty-five. He took a gap year after high school, then another after undergrad."

"Right." Davis adjusted Violet's leash in his hand. "I forgot who I was talking to for a minute."

"What's that supposed to mean?"

Davis stopped and stared. "You talk to more people in a single day, while trying to become a recluse, than I do in a month."

"I've given up on becoming a recluse," I said. "I'm too people oriented, and I like doing things. Anything. All the things. Which means I'm a miserable failure on this particular quest."

He slowed to turn curious eyes on me. "What about the list?"

I shrugged. "I do a lot of those things every day, and the real point of it all was for me to be happy again. I'm making solid progress on that."

Davis nodded. "Good."

"Do you know if Michael has a girlfriend?" I asked, still wondering if he'd been joking earlier, and if he was my admirer.

Davis looked over his shoulder in my direction, pushing the leafy branch of a sapling out of our way. "That's a question for my aunt for sure."

I bit my lip, unwilling to ask Grace about Michael. Daisy would get the clarification for me if I couldn't bring myself to simply ask him. *Are you my longtime online friend?*

Are you sending me love letters?

In person, he was kind and pleasant, but the chemistry was different. Not like in the banter on IBOOM or in the letters from Forever Yours.

The narrow trail opened ahead, and Davis hung back to let me pass.

My limbs were warm from the hike, my cheeks cool from a hearty fall breeze. I sucked in a surprised breath at the view as I emerged from the trees.

"Welcome to Mount Norwottuck," Davis said reverently. "The highest peak in the Holyoke Range."

I stepped onto an outcropping of rocks near the edge, awestruck by the endless beauty. Tingles spilled down my arms and my spine. "Amazing."

"You can see the entire Pioneer Valley from here," he explained.

A blanket of treetops in every shade from green to scarlet stretched across the expanse below us, reaching all the way to the horizon. A perfect cloudless blue sky arched above. It was like looking at the ocean. The vast world beyond, the encompassing peace, and sounds of nature made me feel small, but not insignificant.

I stood, unmoving for long moments while Davis and Violet rustled behind me.

"You like it?" he asked, finally joining me on the rocks.

I nodded, unable to pull my eyes away from the view. "I never take the time to do things like this. I've missed so much."

"You're here now." The warmth of Davis's words reached into my chest and turned me to face him. He passed me a bottle of water and an apple, then cracked open a bottle of his own.

I returned my eyes to the scenic view, transfixed by the first radiant shades of sunset and thinking of a similar moment I'd spent on a park bench with Cecily not so long ago. I thought of how many things had changed in a short period of time and how many others never would. Like the fact I wanted moments like this in bulk. A lifetime subscription of memories with my life partner and our dog. Climbing mountains, having picnics, and whatever else the future had in store.

I'd been kidding myself to think that leaving Willow Bend for any amount of time would erase this from me. I wanted a big, epic love, and a loud, full life. But for the first time in years, I was ready to wait for it, however long that took. Because finding the right person would be worth it.

Chapter
Twenty-Five

Davis's headlights flashed across Hearthstone as dusk settled over the day. A bouquet of wrapped flowers awaited outside the door. More beautiful, fragrant honeysuckle and daisies.

I climbed out and swept the blooms into my arms, thankful the darn bunny hadn't beaten me to them. "Do I still get a tour of your work in progress?"

Davis pulled a hard hat from behind his seat and met me at the door with Violet.

We kicked off our shoes in the foyer, then moved into the kitchen. I set a bowl of water out for Violet and arranged my flowers in a new vase beside the others.

"From your sister again?" he asked.

"Yep. I used to say I didn't see the point in giving or receiving flowers, because they're expensive and they just die. But now I get it. I look forward to this. I love them." I leaned forward to give each bouquet a sniff. "Ahhh."

He shook his head, then grabbed the kettle for tea.

I hadn't stopped smiling since we'd reached the summit during our hike. Not even when we'd raced the final rays of daylight out of the forest. I was sure I'd left something behind today. Emotional or mental, whatever it was, I didn't want it back.

We relocated to the sitting room when the water boiled. I carried a tray with two cups and a teapot. Davis went to the fireplace to start a fire.

I filled each cup with tea, then curled on the couch with one. "Are you ready for the photographer?" I asked. "Feeling nervous? Excited?"

"Both," he said. "And maybe a little hopeful." His cheeks darkened, the way they sometimes did when he seemed to say more than he'd intended.

He wasn't just hopeful that things would go well, or even that he'd win the contest. I knew now that those things were only the icing. He hoped to save his childhood home and the bookstore. A property that had meant the world to his mother. One where he kept her memory alive.

Davis took a seat on the floor before the hearth and turned to face me. He pulled his knees to his chest and rested strong arms across his knees. Something in his expression was resolute, and I braced for what would come. "I've been in competition with my father all my life." He exhaled long and slow. "First for my mom's attention and affection. Later for accolades and awards of any kind. He set the academic bar high, which kept me scrambling in high school and college. I was athletic, so he did his best to never attend a game or practice and to make belittling meathead jokes about anyone who played sports. He pressured me to join his firm when I followed him into architecture. And since then I've been seeking approval from a man who will never give it. Somewhere around age thirty, I saw my life more clearly, and I stopped trying to please him. I started asking myself what I wanted, and what would please me. I moved into historical renovations full time, and the rift between us grows bigger with every job. I resent him for making me like this. I hate the universe for taking her and leaving him. Then I get so damn mad at myself for feeling any of this." He released his knees and another long breath. "I'm not real pleased with myself right now for dumping all of that on you, but I hope it helps you understand why I'm kind of a mess."

"I don't think you're a mess." I felt honored that he'd shared such personal parts of himself with me. And I was doing my best not to fall in love with him for it—and all the other reasons he gave me every time we were together. "I love that you're fighting for this place, even if I'm not sure why there's a fight." I offered a small smile. "I heard you say it was left to you. Can he really change that?"

Davis quieted for a long beat. "My mother put the property in a trust for me. When I marry. My father is the trustee. The property was meant to be a wedding present. She knew she wouldn't be here for that day."

I set my teacup aside and crawled onto the floor with him. "She's with you every day," I whispered, and I put my arms around his waist, leaning my head on his shoulder.

His arm slid around my back, and we sat in the quiet for long moments. "I've been married to my job for so long, I've barely dated. Getting married was something I thought I had forever to do. Now I'm thirty-four, single, and fighting with my father over a property I adore, and he wants to throw it away. How did I get here?"

"We get busier until there's no room for anything else, even ourselves."

"It's kind of ironic, isn't it," he said. "Two extreme workaholics sitting together after a long day of hiking and picnicking."

"Maybe there's hope for us yet," I said.

Davis tipped his head against mine. "I'm glad you're here, Emma Rini."

"Back at ya, Davis Sommers."

He shifted beside me, forcing me to sit straighter. He rose and offered me a hand. "Ready to check out the progress before I get famous tomorrow?"

I accepted with a smile, then stretched up at his side. "What if you never marry? Do you have to marry to get the property?" I asked.

"No. It's mine on my birthday. Married or age thirty-five was the deal, but dear old Dad can go pretty low in the name of getting his way.

I've hired a lawyer to check for loopholes. Meanwhile, laying a public claim in *Architectural Digest* tomorrow by telling my story, Mom's story, will help. Because the only thing Dad values more than money is being adored. He'd risk his reputation if he sold this place out from under me and the whole town found out."

I hoped he was right.

Something else came to mind then. "I wonder what your dad's date thought of your exchange the other night?" Did he not care what the younger woman thought?

Davis's featured bunched in an embarrassed cringe. "That was my new stepmom, Heidi."

I clamped a hand over my mouth, embarrassed by my mistake and wholly stunned by the reality. "Stop."

"She's thirty-five. We were in the same high school graduating class. Different schools, thank God."

I squeaked, then tightened my hand.

He expelled a long breath. "Yeah. He's basically the worst. I didn't realize how much it bothered me until recently." Davis sighed, looking more vulnerable and younger than I'd seen him. "All these years, I've let myself believe he didn't affect me. I thought my ability to ignore him was proof of that." He raised tired gray eyes to mine, taking time to choose his words. "His hostility does more than just make me mad. It sometimes brings out my worst. Like when I was so determined to get into this magazine that I lied and schemed just like him." His jaw locked and he rolled his eyes upward. "I am truly sorry, Emma."

I stepped forward, chin up, and my eyes locked with his. "I understand. You love this place, and I hear love can make a person do things they normally wouldn't."

Davis nodded, expression painfully serious. "I wasn't myself when I did those stupid things to try to get you to leave. It doesn't make what I did any better, but I need you to know that's not who I am."

"I think I know who you are," I whispered. "And I forgive you."

Chapter
Twenty-Six

Davis arrived the next morning in black dress pants and a pale-blue button-down that emphasized the cool gray of his eyes. His face was smooth shaven, and his hair slightly damp from a morning shower.

Something had shifted between us the night before. His confession, and my easy acceptance, seemed to smooth the cracks between us. We'd lingered in the driveway later, watching stars and prolonging the good-bye. Even several feet apart, I'd never felt more connected to someone.

Seeing him back on my doorstep in the sunlight, I whistled. "Wow. You look nice. Someone should come and take your picture. Oh, wait." I grinned and swung the door wide, inviting him inside.

"I haven't been this nervous since prom," he said. "Maybe not even then."

I had plans to make myself scarce when the photographer from *Architectural Digest* arrived.

"What if I trip over something and fall on my head?" Davis asked flatly. "What if I accidentally left something on the floor and the photographer falls on *their* head?"

I laughed and motioned him forward. "Nothing's going wrong today. It's your time to shine. Can I get you a cup of tea or coffee?"

"No. I've had more than my share already. Dear lord. What is that smell?" he asked.

"Vinegar." I ignored the disgust in his tone. Mostly because I didn't disagree. I closed the door and went back to the kitchen.

"I should probably be glad the place isn't on fire again," he said, following. "Are you cleaning?"

I sent him eye daggers over one shoulder. "I'm cooking, thank you. And for the record, I've never set the place on fire."

"Not for lack of trying."

I washed my hands and returned to my work with a shake of my head.

Davis nervously paced the floor. His gaze traveled over the collection of vases scattered throughout the space. "That's a lot of flowers."

"And I love them all," I said, casting a smile to the multitude of honeysuckle and daisies in question.

I'd found a recipe in a book about colonial life and decided to give it a try. Hopefully it was still good after one hundred and fifty years. The canning jars I'd discovered in a cupboard were washed and waiting near the sink, as were a pile of cucumbers I'd picked up at the farmers' market. I sliced the vegetables into spears and set them in a bowl, then added dill and garlic. In a pot on the stovetop, I heated water, cider vinegar, sugar, salt, and some pickling spices to a boil. So far this was my favorite recipe, mostly because it didn't require ninety ingredients, so it was unlikely I'd mess it up. I had a Cornish hen in the fridge I planned to prep for dinner.

"No breakfast pastries today?" Davis asked.

"In the pantry. Help yourself." I pointed over my shoulder, then hefted the pot with an oven mitt.

Next, I slowly poured some of the mixture into each jar.

A sudden crashing sound rent the room as the jar before me splintered. Hot water splashed off the broken glass and countertop, stinging my cheek. I released the pan in a scream, and the rest of the steaming concoction dashed over my bare feet and ankles.

"Fuck!"

"Whoa." Davis's calm tenor seemed to echo through the cacophony of terrible sounds.

He caught me by my waist as I backpedaled away from the water, then set me on a chair. He threw towels over the mess on the floor, tossed the pot into the sink and turned on the water. He came to my side while I examined the red splotches on my arms and legs. "Here."

Davis passed me a washrag doused in cold water, then pressed a second cloth to my stinging feet. "You okay? Are you cut anywhere?"

"No, but damn." I pressed the back of one hand to my eyes, always ready to spill a few tears.

"Good. You take this, and I'll handle that." He gave me the second cold compress, then turned back to the disaster in my kitchen.

The urge to scream again nearly overcame me. I wanted to flip my chair and stomp the broken glass. Pickles? Really? I couldn't manage the simplest recipe on earth without nearly needing a paramedic?

"Emma?" Davis said, brows arched in concern. He tossed a wad of sopping paper towels and a dustpan of glass shards into the trash. "You're moaning."

I slumped in my seat. "I just want to make one decent recipe before I leave here, and I thought this was something I couldn't possibly ruin."

"This had nothing to do with you," he said. "It happens. Like when a bartender fills a clean glass, then lifts it and the bottom falls out? It's science."

"Yeah, well, I used to be good at science."

"Maybe you should extend your stay," he suggested. "Give yourself more time to do the things you want to do. Or, since you've already made a nice little niche for yourself"—he stood with another full dustpan—"why leave at all?"

My gaze snapped to his, and the world stilled. I'd considered staying in Amherst not long ago. I could be happy here, could easily build a life. For Davis to suggest the same was almost too much to bear. Why would he say it? Did he want me to stay? For him?

Again I wondered if Davis was my secret admirer, the anonymous letter writer slowly stealing my heart. Why couldn't he be?

Then I remembered my track record for love and the fact Davis had his hands full. He was at odds with his father, concentrating on his career, trying to protect Hearthstone and Village Books. How could he possibly have time to think of anything else? Never mind enough time to write love letters?

I quickly returned to reality.

Davis was simply being kind and reminding me I had friends here.

"I've given that more thought than you know," I admitted.

Emily's perfect attitude on the matter came to mind. Wherever we are, that is home. Here in Amherst, the sentiment seemed exactly true. But once I was back in Willow Bend again, I'd be home there too. My trajectory had changed these last few days. My path of perceived obstacles had cleared. "I have a store to run back home. I have to go." I set the rags on the table and crossed my legs.

He dumped the pan with a dip of his chin.

Something about the small movement made me hollow with regret. Why couldn't things be different?

"Are you still working on ideas for the revised bookstore?" he asked, kindly breaking the tension.

"I finished the business plan last night, and it looks good." Inspiration had hit before bed, and I'd wrapped most of the details with a bow. "It's going to be hard to say goodbye to Amherst, but I'm looking forward to getting a start on revamping the store. Maybe if I'm wildly successful, I can open a satellite shop here one day. At a good distance from Grace's shop, of course. I wouldn't step on any toes."

"Paws," he corrected, and I grinned.

I'd miss my new friends, but we had the internet to connect us. And I hoped to continue with the letter-writing classes, at least a couple of times a month.

"The changes at Rini Reads are going to be great," he said. "I'll try to come up and see them when you finish."

I blinked, completely thrown by his offer. "Really?"

"Sure," he said. "And you should come back to check out the renovations here when they're complete."

I nodded, and Davis checked the now cleaned space around him. "If you're okay, I'd better give the renovation space another look."

"I'm good." I rose and forced a smile, frustrated by the pickles, but heart-warmed by his offer. "Break a leg," I said. "I'll bet the camera loves you."

A few hours later, I dialed Davis on a whim and burst of excitement. Seated in the bookstore after letter-writing class, I clutched a gently crumpled page in my sweaty grip.

"Emma," he said. "I was going to stop by the manor tonight after work. I wanted to tell you first. They interviewed me today! A reporter freed up in time to ride with the photographer, and we did the whole piece this afternoon. It was amazing. And no one fell on their head." He laughed, and the sound reached my heart through the line.

"Really? That's amazing!" And he'd wanted to tell me first? Not Grace or Clayton? Or anyone else? I'd surely lose sleep over this, which was fine, because I'd already be up thinking about his suggestion I stay in Amherst.

All these small things meant something, right?

"I know!" Davis exclaimed. "Thank you so much for encouraging me and for putting up with me the last few weeks. I really do appreciate you."

"I feel the same," I said.

There was a beat of silence. "What made you call?" he asked. "You never call. Not even when you're freezing to death, or the house is on fire."

"Stop." I laughed. "It's about my secret letter writer, Forever Yours."

"Yeah," he said cautiously.

"I wrote him and asked for his name. He wrote me back, and he wants to meet. Maybe you're the wrong person to call, but . . ." I'd wanted to tell him first. Wanted to know what he would say. Should I go? Was it weird? Was it safe?

Did he already know about the letter because he wrote it? I shook away the thought and silently chastised myself for projecting my desires onto him.

"When?" Davis asked.

"The letter was in my cubby when I got to class."

A bout of laughter drew my attention to Michael behind the counter.

He raised a hand and winked.

I hoped it wasn't him. Michael was great, but he wasn't the one I wanted. Not by a long shot.

"When does he want to meet?" Davis asked.

"Tomorrow night. For coffee." I took a moment to breathe, but it didn't calm me. "What should I do?"

"What do you want to do?"

"I don't know." Until I met the man behind the letters, I was free to hope for what I wanted. Once I knew the truth, I'd have to deal with it, even if I didn't get the answer I wanted.

"Can I come by tonight?" Davis asked. "We can hash this out over pizza and wings? Maybe I can even get that relic of a television at the manor to play the UMass away game for us."

"Deal!"

We said goodbye, and I hurried outside.

A cool autumn breeze ruffled my hair as perfectly calligraphed words raced through my mind.

> Emma,
> Of course I will tell you my name. I doubt I could deny you much of anything. Meet me at the café on

First Street tomorrow night at seven, and I'll tell you whatever you want to know.

Forever Yours

❧

I spent the afternoon under a gorgeous autumn-leafed tree outside the manor, making preliminary notes on a proper business plan. When the wind grew chilly, I took the opportunity to journal inside Village Books. I left a short note for Forever Yours in my cubby, agreeing to meet the next night.

I passed Grace and Michael stocking a fresh display on my way back out.

"Hey," I said. "Looking good!"

Grace beamed. "Thank you."

We made small talk for a moment before she switched gears. "Have you spoken with Davis?" she asked. "I'm dying to know how it went at the manor this morning. I'm sure it was great, but I wish he'd have stopped by on his way out."

"I hear it went well," I said. "He's coming by to watch the game tonight." I glanced at Michael to catch his reaction. "Pizza, beer, and the game. What else could I ask for?"

He smiled but made no comment.

I tried another approach, nodding toward the *Outlander* display. "The IBOOMers were worked up about that one this month."

"Why?" Grace asked, confirming once again she wasn't Historically_ Bookish. Not that I needed confirmation. "Oh, can you ring them up?" she asked Michael, motioning to a family headed for the checkout.

He hurried to the register.

A customer pulled Grace aside, inquiring about Nathaniel Hawthorne.

I sagged, no closer to knowing who was behind the Historically_ Bookish handle than I was when I'd arrived. Honestly, Emily Dickinson could probably conduct a better investigation from her grave.

I buttoned my wool coat to the top before stepping outside. Then, in the spirit of new routines, I dialed my mom.

She answered on the first ring. "Hey, hon! How's it going? Did you find your secret admirer? Made any more bookstore plans? What's going on with the bunnies?"

I dashed the toe of my sneaker against the porch and laughed. "You really are hooked on my shenanigans."

"We are," she agreed. "Your dad wants answers, too, but he asks me to relay the information. So, start with the bunnies. We worry about those little guys."

"Well, don't. Because the bunnies are living their best lives," I said. "I've been working with Grace's friend, Olivia, to make a little veggie town for the family, and they love it."

"She's the farmer, right?" Mom said. "The one who owns Seeds of Love?"

"That's the one."

I told her about Olivia's recent delivery of items for a small-scale flower bed display. "A wheelbarrow, a picnic table, a statue of a gnome in a pointy hat. It's all so cute. We set it up outside a hutch, also hers, where the fuzzy bunny family can get out of the elements this winter and stay warm. She filled the hutch with hay, and I removed the string and pie plates from the garden's perimeter. Grace plans to feed the bunnies when my plants die. Until then, there's plenty of produce to keep them busy and full."

Mom groaned. "So stinking adorable. I can't stand it. What else?"

Then I filled her in on the status of my admirer.

"You can't go alone," she said. "He could be deranged."

"I'm sure it'll be fine."

"Ask someone to go with you," she said. "Just in case."

I ran through a mental list of people in Amherst I knew well enough to request as a personal protection detail. "I'll see."

"Do you think this could be your guy?" she asked, implication of happily ever after thick in her tone.

I sighed. "I'm trying not to." I was here to break that habit. So why was it so hard?

"What if it's your soulmate?" she asked.

I kicked a mound of stones. "I don't know. I guess if that's true, things will have to take shape on their own, because I can't keep trying to force an outcome that isn't meant to be. Maybe I'm just not meant to have what you and Dad have, and I need to get okay with it."

Mom made a small sad sound. "Oh, hon. You're meant to have your heart's desires, so be careful with your thoughts. Sometimes the lies we tell ourselves are the most dangerous ones."

"Mom." A lump rose in my throat, and I glanced toward the manor at the end of the lane. "I've made some more plans for the bookstore. Do you want to hear?"

"Please!"

I opened my mouth with the intention to outline the barest of concepts for her, mostly to direct the conversation away from my love life. But once I started talking, the words kept coming. My enthusiasm snowballed as I spoke, and I had to force myself to stop. She'd previously assured me that I could make any alterations I wanted once the store was in my name. But hearing my detailed plan to dismantle the shop as she and Dad had made it might be hard for her to hear.

"I love all of this!" she cheered, drawing a shocked smile over my face.

"You do?"

Something tightened in my gut as I thought of Davis. This was the kind of support he should receive from his father.

"Of course! I can't wait to tell your father. Will you really get a retired greyhound?"

"I think so," I said. "I'll know more once I spend some time at the rescue."

A small noise cracked over the line, and I stilled, listening closely. It took a long moment for me to understand what I'd heard. "Are you crying?"

"No." Mom sniffed. "I'm just so happy." She laughed through a loud sob then, no longer trying to hide her outburst. "It's just that you've been unhappy for so long, and when you left I was afraid you wouldn't want to come home. But instead, you call now, and we talk about the important things, and you're making brilliant plans for your future. I'm just so proud of you, and so happy to be included."

"Mom," I croaked, wiping at each of my leaking eyes. "Jeez. Now I'm crying."

We spoke for several more minutes before saying heartfelt goodbyes. I dialed Cecily next.

"Should I call 911?" she asked at ten times a normal conversational speed. "You never call me, so this must be an emergency."

"Funny," I said, smiling against the phone. "I'm letting go of the eighteen fifties, and I miss you, so I had to call immediately. Tell me everything. Then I have news for you too."

"Hallelujah. Okay. Let's see. I worked a triple; then I slept like the dead until I hit snooze too many times, woke up late, and ran out the door again. My body is on autopilot. My brain is operating on sheer fatigue and madness. I'm not even sure this conversation is really happening."

"You sound like an audiobook I pumped up to times four. Is it okay for you to be in the ER like this? Not as a patient?"

She snorted. "Adrenaline will take over when it's time. Meanwhile, I'm talking fast because there's so much to say and not enough time. What's your news?"

"Forever Yours, the anonymous letter writer, wants to meet. Should I go?"

"One hundred percent," she said confidently. "But don't go alone in case he's deranged."

I rolled my eyes. "Okay. Your turn. What else is going on?"

"I googled your boy Davis last night while looking for his friend Clayton, who is also hot, by the way. Shame on you for gatekeeping."

I laughed. "Okay."

"Turns out Davis is a big freaking deal, Emma. Did you know? He lives in a restored home that was featured on the local news last year. He made *Architectural Digest*'s top thirty under thirty a few years ago, won up-and-coming talent of the year while he was still getting his degree, and he was on his college swim team. You have to look that up, because the photographs . . . ," she said, slowing her speech to emphasize each syllable of her final word.

"I'll be sure to ask him about it. Meanwhile, what should I wear to the café tomorrow?"

"Something hot."

"Helpful. Any chance you're coming back to Amherst this week? Got time for one more girls' day out?"

"I might be able to swing that if I trade a shift with someone," she said. "Let me see what I can do. But if I manage it, we need to visit that pub."

"Deal."

"Now listen to this," she said. "I set an alert to let me know if Davis's name popped up again, and I got a notification as I was rushing out the door. He's in *Architectural Digest* magazine again! I think it's that interview you wrote me about. The photos were taken at the manor!"

"What?" I gasped. "They were just here this morning." She had to be mistaken. The article was surely from some other time. "What was he wearing?"

"Blue shirt, black pants, a whole lot of sexy all over. Shoot. I'm at the hospital now. Read that article! Immediately. Gotta go."

I leaned against the tree trunk to catch my breath, thumbs dashing across the screen in search of the *Architectural Digest* website. I stilled when a text notification arrived. Annie had sent a message.

Stunned. I hurried to see if she'd gone into labor early.

Annie: I'm half in love with Forever Yours on your behalf

I typed a response at high speed, thrilled she'd gotten my letter on the subject already.

Me: Meeting him tomorrow night

Annie: 😶

Annie: Be careful

I grinned. This was the kind of relationship I'd missed having with my sister. I couldn't wait to get home and finish mending ours.

Me: How's my niece or nephew doing?

Annie: So far so good

The sense something wasn't quite right overcame me again, and I forced my fingers to type.

Me: Are you and your baby okay?

Long minutes passed before Annie responded. I spent each with bated breath. Finally, the little bouncing dots appeared. My sister was typing.

Annie: I'm just done being pregnant

Annie: Baby is ready to meet you

I wasn't sure she'd answered my question, but I knew better than to ask again.

Me: I'm going to be a stellar auntie

Annie: It'll involve long hours

Me: Yep

Annie replied with a single question mark, so I sent one back.

Annie: Won't you be at the store?

I grimaced, hating that I'd missed so much of her pregnancy and a million other things, assuming she didn't want me around. In reality she'd been mad at me for not being around.

Yet another vicious cycle.

Me: Nope. I will be playing with my new niece or nephew

Annie: I hope you mean that

Me: I do

I meant it more than she would likely understand until I showed her.

I was returning home an improved, happier woman, who would always make time for my family, my friends, and myself.

Annie responded once more, this time with a single red heart.

I thought of the heart drawn on a card for my second bouquet of flowers, then sent a final text too.

Me: Thank you for the flowers. They mean more than you know

I pocketed my phone, feeling as if my life was finally coming together in the ways it was meant to all along.

Chapter
Twenty-Seven

Davis arrived after work with Violet, a pizza, hot wings, and a six-pack of locally brewed and bottled hard cider, and a small leatherbound copy of *Jane Eyre*.

We sat on the floor in socked feet, eating off paper plates and talking like two kids in a college dorm room while watching the UMass away game on the ancient television in the sitting room. The coffee table was littered with napkins and empty cider bottles. *Jane Eyre* sat on the carpet between us.

"This is my favorite," I said during a commercial, tapping one finger against the book's beautifully floral cover. "How'd you know?"

He wiped his mouth on a napkin and shrugged. "I'm glad you like it. It's part of a Cranford Collection. I thought of you immediately when I saw it. You and all the flowers you've been planting."

"I absolutely love it." In fact, the gesture warmed my heart a little too much, so I went for another wing. "Tell me all about the interview today." He'd hit the highlights while attempting to find the game but quieted quickly at kickoff. I'd read the article twice after I finished texting with Annie and marveled each time.

In the piece, Davis spoke about the preservation of history and his love for Hearthstone Manor with sheer joy and reverence. He was clearly doing exactly what he'd been called to do.

"Everyone at the office was talking about it," Davis said. "So, Dad was seething, but couldn't say any of the things he wanted. Instead, he clapped me on the back and smiled."

I laughed. "I would've paid to see that."

"It was pretty incredible. Now that everyone in our world associates me with this place, it'll be impossible for Dad to try to steal it or otherwise ruin things for me without tarnishing his reputation."

I reached for my cider and took a long, satisfied swig.

"Today was a good day. Tomorrow will be even better." Davis worked his brows. "How are you feeling about your big date?"

"Thankful that you agreed to go with me," I said. "Everyone back home is worried I'm walking into the next episode of *Unsolved Mysteries*."

He snorted and stretched his long legs out before the fire. "You're safe with me, Rini. Any guesses about who you're meeting?"

I took another wing from the pile. The hot and spicy sauce burned my tongue and throat in a gloriously savory way. "Assuming he doesn't stuff me into an unmarked van and drive away, I'm sure whoever it is will be fine."

Davis arched his brows. "*Fine* doesn't sound like you're very excited to meet this mystery man. Are the letters creepy? Does he give stalker vibes?"

"No." I bristled, ready to defend my admirer, even to my clueless crush. "He's sweet," I said. "Kind and genuine. He's compassionate and bookish. He sees me, and it's been a long time since I've felt seen by anyone other than Cecily."

"I see you," Davis said, setting his bottle aside and fixing me with the full weight of his smoldering gaze.

My breath caught, and I swallowed hard. Suddenly the silly thought I'd had in class about dating Paul seemed downright absurd, and the possibility my longtime friend and current admirer might be Michael made me want to cry. The only man I wanted sat right in front of me, close enough to hold and beg to see things my way.

The flicker of hope diminished as a new thought came to mind. Davis was right here. He'd confessed all sorts of personal things to me. We'd regained a strong footing after an earlier fallout. If he had feelings for me, why not say so? I'd kissed him once, so he knew I wouldn't reject him, if that were his fear. But I couldn't imagine Davis fearing anything. Look at all he'd overcome.

I wet my lips as the silence grew suffocating. What I'd told Mom was true. I couldn't force what I wanted into reality. "You claim to know everyone," I said, refreshing my smile. "Help me figure out who he is."

He relaxed by a fraction, lips twitching on one side.

"We can make it a game," I suggested. "I'll guess too."

Davis twisted the cap off a new bottle. "Pretty sure you have the advantage here, because I have no idea who you talk to every day."

I fought the urge to ask "Is it you?" How ridiculous would I feel if I were wrong? How awkward would I make things for Davis? *Wait!* I scolded internally. *Stop forcing.* "You have hometown advantage. You start."

He heaved a laborious sigh, attention jumping to the television as refs argued a penalty on UMass. "He writes in calligraphy, right?"

I nodded, thrilled by his willingness to play along.

"So, he's clearly a giant nerd."

"What?" I wrinkled my nose in faux offense. "Be real."

The slow slide of his eyes in my direction made it clear he was being very real.

"There's nothing wrong with perfect penmanship," I argued. "I think it's nice."

"It's calligraphy," he said. "You be real."

"You're trying to make it sound dumb."

"Didn't have to try," he said, taking another pull from his bottle.

I watched him, trying to puzzle out a solid comeback to defend my admirer's honor. "I think uncommon interests are cool. It probably means he's deep."

"Agreed. Right now, for example, he's probably deep in his mom's basement, watching documentaries."

"No." I laughed, and it doubled me over. The silly, rumbling laughter kept coming until I wasn't sure why I couldn't stop and my lungs cried for air.

Davis's lips twitched, but he refused to smile. "Your turn to guess."

I wiped tears from my eyes and set my plate aside. "Fine. I think there's a small chance it's Michael, but I'm not sure." I held my breath as I waited for his response.

Davis stared at the screen. "Do you want it to be him?"

I looked away. "No. But I would like to know if he's the one using the Historically_Bookish handle. That mystery is killing me."

"Why?"

My eyes met his again, and I willed him to confess he was my friend and admirer. "Because Historically_Bookish is important to me. I hate that I don't know who they are. Plus, whoever wrote those letters didn't take the task lightly. Maybe they're the kind of person who'd spend just as much time and effort on all the things that matter."

A deadpan expression crossed his handsome face, and a shadow of doubt shaded my little flame of hope. "I bet the dexterity and small motor skills used in calligraphy are important in tying complicated knots—around your wrists—so he can keep you in his mother's basement."

I wadded a paper napkin and threw it at his face. "I'll bet he's incredibly smart."

"That only means the cops will never find you."

I hopped onto my feet and carried our plates and napkins to the kitchen, laughing and wiping tears onto my sleeve. "You're ridiculous."

Davis collected an armload of our bottles and followed.

I tossed the trash and washed my hands while he lined the empties on the counter for recycling. When I turned back, he was watching me intently. "Seriously, I like the way his letters make me feel," I admitted softly. "I know I came here to swear off love, but that's not who I am. I want to believe romance is alive and anything is possible."

Davis leaned in my direction, and his soft gray gaze lowered to my lips. He raised a hand gently to my face, and I gripped the counter beside us in case I swooned. "Your hair is—"

I let my eyes fall shut as he swept his thumb against the corner of my mouth, dislodging a piece of hair that had adhered to my skin on dried hot sauce. "Ugh." My lids jerked open. "Oh, gross." I cringed and reeled back. "I've been sitting in there with food on my face?"

Why was my life like this?

Davis caught me by one wrist, his lips parted in amusement. "It's just hot sauce."

I stilled, and our breath mingled. The familiar electric charge of his nearness swept through me, along with memories of his kiss.

"Emma," he whispered. "I think—"

Violet barked and broke the spell. Her nails danced merrily across the kitchen floor, and a low, desperate howl raised the rafters.

Davis released me, turning swiftly to quiet his sweet dog.

Violet stood on hind legs at the back door, whimpering and whining as I gathered my marbles and flipped the light switch, bathing the yard in a burst of light.

A pack of little fuzzy shadows bounced into the cover of trees beyond.

From the sitting room, a sports announcer called, "Touchdown, Huskies!"

Davis's disappointed sigh matched mine.

Our Minutemen weren't the only ones having a complicated night.

On my front porch, just after midnight, I couldn't stop myself from hugging Davis goodbye. To my delight, he set his chin atop my head and held me gently for one precious moment. Then he whispered, "I hope your secret admirer is exactly who you want him to be," and I felt my eyes sting with tears.

Because wasn't that the same as saying he had no idea who it was?

～❦～

I arrived early at Village Books the next day, eager to take a slow, contemplative look at all the men in my class—and one, specifically, who wasn't a fellow student but worked the cash register. I sat at the long table, facing the store and front door.

"You're lost in thought," Daisy said, sliding onto the seat beside mine. She set a disposable cup on the table, a curl of sweet-scented steam rising from the top.

I forced a smile, tuning into the moment at hand. "Just thinking about what to write," I fibbed. "How about you? Do you have a plan for today?"

"I'm writing to my professor to beg for a second chance on my last written assignment," she said. "I really blew it, and my academic scholarships turn to dust if my grades drop."

"I'm sorry." I set a hand on her shoulder, and she tipped her head to lean on it briefly.

"Thanks. Are you really thinking about writing letters?"

I wrinkled my nose. Busted. "Do you ever get any letters that aren't signed?"

"Like, intentionally?" She slumped in her seat and rested her chin on her hands. "No. Why? Have you?"

I pressed my lips into a tight line and scanned the room for prying eyes or ears. Then I matched her posture and lowered my voice. "Have you ever gotten any letters written in perfect calligraphy?"

Daisy's brows rose.

"No," Daisy answered. "Why?"

Paul came into view before I could respond. "Hey, Emma, Daisy," he said, strolling over with a wide smile.

I bit the insides of my cheeks, wondering again if it could be Paul.

Daisy rose and meandered toward the refreshments table, where Paul unloaded a box of pastries from a logoed bag. "Aww. You brought breakfast."

"Danishes," he said.

"Ever take any calligraphy classes?" Daisy asked.

I imagined thunking my head onto the desk but stayed strong.

He cast her a goofy look. "I have. About twenty years ago, the middle school art instructor insisted on teaching calligraphy. Every Amherst native between thirty and forty-five can probably still manage some pretty decent basics." He tipped his head curiously. "Are you looking to learn?"

"Just curious," she said, resuming her seat. "I have a heavy enough course load already."

"Let me know if you ever want a crash course," he said. And for the first time, I noticed the fountain pen Grace gave classmates tucked into the spiral of his notebook. He hadn't used it on the letters he'd left for me with his signature, but that didn't mean he couldn't have written others.

Chapter
Twenty-Eight

I changed clothes seven times before deciding on a velour wrap dress in the perfect shade of apricot and taupe ankle boots that matched my purse. How was I supposed to choose an outfit that said I cared enough to skip the jeans and sneakers but also understood this meeting was extremely casual? The unkillable romantic in me insisted on something pretty because there was always a chance this would be the story we told our grandkids.

So, I had to be prepared.

I made a special trip up the driveway to text Cecily a selfie.

Me: Outfit check

She responded with three little flame-shaped emoji. Then a trio of dots began to bounce, letting me know she wasn't finished.

Cecily: Hottie with a body

Cecily: Go meet your soul mate, then tell me everything

Cecily: Send pics! Take pepper spray

"Okay, weirdo," I said while responding with a thumbs-up emoji.

I debated my next move for an extended moment, then sent the same image to Annie.

Me: Blind date. Thoughts on the look?

Annie consistently had opinions on everything, especially fashion.

I was disappointed when she didn't respond. After a few minutes of waiting, I made my way back to the manor and awaited Davis's arrival.

I hurried to the foyer when the doorbell rang. I checked my face in the mirror near the door and touched a hand to my upswept curls. I'd added a stroke of eye shimmer on my lids in a shade close to my skin tone and glossed my lips to a shine. Mascara darkened and lengthened my lashes, and a touch of powder finished the natural but elevated look. It was the best I could do without it looking like I'd tried too hard. And it was the most I could do with the tremor of nerves buzzing through my hands.

"Here we go," I told myself, before pulling open the door.

Davis waited outside in a black suit with shiny leather shoes and a belt. His button-down shirt nearly matched the color of his eyes. He looked impossibly taller in his fancy business wear, and my skin thrummed with the need to touch him.

"I'm meeting with my dad and an investor for dinner later," he said. "They ambushed me, and I can't get out of it, but I won't need to leave you for about an hour. You should know by then if you're feeling safe. If not, give me a sign, and I'll bring you straight home."

Appreciation welled in me, and I was torn once again between my feelings for the man before me, and a man whose identity I didn't even know. Forever Yours had left one more letter today, giving me a free pass to not show tonight. No hard feelings. Complete understanding. Then he'd included snippets of letters he'd found and loved. Pieces he hoped might make me smile.

From Napoleon to Joséphine:

> When, free from every worry, from all business, shall I spend all my moments by your side, to have nothing to do but to love you, and to prove it to you?

And my favorite of all . . .

> That I did always love
> I bring thee Proof
> That till I loved
> I never lived—Enough—
>
> That I shall love alway—
> I argue thee
> That love is life—
> And life hath Immortality—
>
>
> This—dost thou doubt—Sweet—
> Then have I
> Nothing to show
> But Calvary—
>
> —Emily Dickinson

If Forever Yours was half as sincere and genuine in person as he was on the page, I'd be out of my head not to pursue something with him. *It would be ridiculous,* I assured myself, to avoid a real connection with a man who cared for me, in favor of pining for a relationship with someone that was never meant to be.

I lifted my chin and squared my shoulders. "Let's go."

✦

We arrived at our destination a few minutes later, and Davis parked at the end of the block. I nearly shook with adrenaline.

"I love downtown at night," Davis said, peering through the windshield at the street outside.

Strings of bistro lights crisscrossed the sky above the street, hung from lamppost to lamppost all down the block. Twinkle lights illuminated the awnings and windows of shops and cafés. People walked hand in hand, pushing strollers, or leaning against one another in shared laughter, everywhere I looked.

My door opened, and Davis stood outside, offering his arm. I curved my fingers gently around his bicep, and we moved toward the café.

"Don't be nervous," he said, setting a warm hand over mine where it rested on his sleeve. "I think you're going to have an incredible night."

I tried to absorb his enthusiasm but couldn't quite manage. I swallowed my pride and met his eyes. "Question."

"Shoot."

I inhaled slowly, steeling my nerve to say something I really shouldn't. "What if the man who shows up tonight isn't the one I want?"

Davis's jaw locked, and his frown deepened. "What does that mean?"

I shrugged.

"Who do you want it to be, Emma?"

The raw timbre of his voice sent gooseflesh over my skin, and I willed myself to speak the name on my tongue. To clear the air. To be brave when it counted. Even if it meant ruining my quest, our friendship. Everything.

The gentle purr of an expensive car drew our eyes to the road, breaking the intensity of our connection. Davis's dad climbed out of his Mercedes and raised an arm. "There you are, Junior. I thought we'd find you at that pub for sure." He buttoned his suit jacket and turned to smile at a gentleman emerging from the passenger side. "Davis, this is Avery Lindor, the investor I told you about. We had to move the meeting up by an hour. You don't mind, do you? Avery, this is my son."

I looked to Davis, who seemed equally shocked by the turn of events.

And I felt the last thread of hope I didn't realize I'd been holding on to slip away.

He straightened, and a wall fell between us. His baffled and somewhat murderous expression schooled into something fake and cold. "Excuse me," he whispered, tipping his head toward the door to indicate I should go inside. Then he moved quickly down the walkway to meet the men.

I willed my legs to move and pushed thoughts of my confession from my mind. Tonight, I would meet my letter-writing friend, and we'd have a cup of coffee. Then, I'd head home to kick my own ass for trying to confess my feelings to Davis without any sort of plan.

The bell above the door jingled as I entered the café, drawing a few sets of eyes. I didn't recognize any of the faces, and no one seemed particularly interested in me. I chose a table near the window, where I could watch Davis speak to his father and the other man. I also had a good view of everyone entering the café.

I set my phone on the table to watch the time, then gave the shop's interior an appreciative exam. The space was warmly lit with exposed brick walls and patterned tile flooring. A white service counter protruded from the back wall, where it disappeared into the kitchen, and a series of large chalkboards detailed the menu options.

A young woman with a pink apron and logoed shirt approached a moment later. Her white-blond ponytail bounced behind her in a corkscrew. "Hi," she said brightly. "What can I get you?"

I returned her smile. "I think I'll have—"

The café door opened, and Davis moved inside, followed by his dad and the other man. Davis's eyes found mine immediately, and the apologetic expression on his face said it all. He couldn't sit with me while I waited, but he also wouldn't leave.

I offered him a thumbs-up and my most believable grin.

The men chose a table next to the wall with exposed brick. Davis took a seat facing me and dipped his chin stiffly in acknowledgment when he noticed me staring.

"Do you need a minute?" the young woman asked.

"Sorry. No." I flipped my attention back to her. "I saw a friend and got distracted. I'll take a chai-tea latte and a pumpkin spice scone, please."

"Sounds good." She turned and hustled away on white sneakers. "Be right back!"

I admired her confident enthusiasm. I, on the other hand, was struggling to feel anything other than anxiety about who would show up and what I would say. About how the conversation would go, and if this moment might actually end a friendship instead of solidifying one.

I fretted over the way I'd wondered if this could be a story to tell our grandkids. Why were some desires so difficult to let go, or even modify? And why was the first man to hold my heart in a real and wonderful way someone unwilling to tell me if he felt the same? The chemistry between us was undeniable, and the comfort I felt in our small silent moments was divine. He'd hinted at his feelings and gone out of his way repeatedly to spend time with me, go on adventures with me, and listen. And I'd told him my mission to give up on love was over. Even that hadn't motivated him to make a move or speak his heart. So if he truly cared for me, I guessed it just wasn't enough.

I checked the time on my phone when my drink and scone arrived, and I told myself it was easy for anyone to be a few minutes late. I checked again when I finished my tea and the scone was nothing but crumbs on my little plate. After forty minutes had passed, I walked to the bathroom, fighting the sting of rejection.

I'd been stood up.

Long-buried memories of being skipped over and left out crept through me as I washed my hands. And the fear of being unwanted attacked brutally as I checked my hair in the mirror.

I tried a few silent affirmations in combat, but the negative thoughts were far too strong.

Tears welled in my eyes, unbidden. Then Cecily's sweet words returned to mind, and I replayed them on a loop until I felt strong again. *You are worthy, Emma Rini. You are loved. And you are worthy of love. Just. As. You. Are.*

Whatever happened to my admirer tonight had nothing to do with me. I'd put myself out there, and it hadn't gone as planned. That was all. I was just fine. And this feeling of abandonment had nothing to do with Davis. Nothing at all.

I lifted my chin, squared my shoulders, and left my old, unwanted thoughts in the restroom behind me.

I was calling an Uber and going home.

I found Davis leaning against the wall outside the restroom, hands deep in his pockets, sympathy on his brow.

Emotion stung my eyes and nose once more. "What are you doing?"

"Checking on you."

"Well, I'm heading out," I said. "I'll give you a call tomorrow."

He levered himself away from the wall before I could pass. "I'll drive you."

"What about your meeting?"

Davis waited for me to meet his eyes. "My dad and his cohorts are determined to trade every ounce of history in this town for the almighty dollar. I've said everything I can possibly say to stop them, but they weren't swayed. The whole meeting was a ridiculous waste of time." He shoved a hand through his hair. "I never should've left you. I told them goodbye the minute I saw your face when you walked past. I should've told them goodbye the moment they showed up."

Emotions returned in full force, and I nodded so he wouldn't hear my voice crack.

Then I left the café on his arm.

Chapter
Twenty-Nine

We rode in silence for several long moments as Davis drove us back through town. I felt his heated gaze on my cheek when he stole frequent looks in my direction, but I trained my attention outside the windows, willing my heart rate to settle. My thoughts were tangled and overwhelming. I didn't even know why it mattered that I was stood up.

Or why I was still aggravated that Annie couldn't take ten seconds to give me input on my outfit? I thought we'd made progress.

All the little irritations seemed to pile up and compound. I suspected the fact my time in Amherst was coming to a close had something to do with it. Specifically, my unprecedented feelings of dread and general upset. That, and the tension of preparing to meet my admirer, coupled with him not showing, had thrown me into some kind of spiral.

Whatever it was, I didn't like it. I wanted my pajamas, a muffin, and a fire. Maybe also my journal and some wine.

"I'm sorry about tonight," Davis said, breaking the awful silence.

"Not your fault." I forced an easy-breezy expression. "Blind dates probably have a high no-show rate. If I dated more often, I'd likely be used to it."

"That's not something you should ever get used to," he said gently. "This wasn't the way I wanted this to go—"

My phone buzzed, and Davis's device did as well. He paused midsentence, focus sliding to the cup holder, where his phone held the same notification as mine. A message from IBOOM.

He pressed the power button to darken the screen, but it was too late.

My avalanche of emotions clutched onto something new. "Are you Historically_Bookish?" I asked flatly, unsure why I hadn't asked days before. Asking Michael had felt awkward, because I didn't know him well. But I knew Davis, and I was too wound up to let it go. I deserved an answer to something tonight. If not the identity of my admirer, then this would have to do.

Davis clenched his jaw and fixed his gaze on the road.

"You have season tickets to UMass football," I said, ticking off the facts as they came to mind. "You love hot wings. Your best friend owns a bar. We have a similar sense of humor. You knew I loved *Jane Eyre*!" I thought about the book he brought me. I'd never mentioned it was my favorite. Not in person.

And he'd been so confused the day we'd met at the manor. That could only mean—

"You were so confused by my appearance on the night I arrived, because you were expecting my dad. You thought he was ED_Fan."

Davis grimaced. The truck slowed, and he turned onto the gravel lane. "Emma." He inhaled deeply, slowly, as tears of frustration pricked my eyes.

"Are you Historically_Bookish?" I asked again, voice cracking from too many emotions in too short a time. Of course he was. No one else made any sense. "Why didn't you just tell me?" I asked. "You knew how much I wanted to meet the person behind the handle. I confided in you."

Why was he lying to me again?

"I wasn't sure at first," he said. "I put it together in a few days, but by then we'd fallen into something I really liked and didn't want to ruin. Things were going well. Then we kissed, and I knew I had to come clean about the manor. Telling you I used the bookstore account on IBOOM seemed insignificant in the face of our bigger problems. I wanted to fix those, then go back and fix the rest. I had a plan. It just—"

The truck's headlights landed on a familiar white SUV, and all thoughts of disappointment disappeared.

"You have company?" Davis asked, disappointment thick in his tone.

"That's Annie!" I unfastened my safety belt and reached for the door handle as he slowed.

"Wait," he said, shifting into park. "We need to talk about this."

My sister opened her driver's side door and stepped out. Her bump looked twice the size it had a month before.

"I have to go," I said.

"Wait!" He leaned across the seat as I jumped out. "Emma, we have to talk—"

I shook my head, exhausted from the list of letdowns tonight and looking forward to something much better. "Another time. Goodbye, Davis." I wiped the pads of my fingers under my eyes to check for smeared makeup, then made a run for Annie.

This was the highlight my trip needed.

"You're here!" I wrapped my sister in a hug, elated to see her face. "I missed you," I said, meaning it to my core. Then another thought emerged. "What are you doing here?"

I pulled back, and the tears on her cheeks became clear in Davis's headlights as he reversed away. Her makeup was wrecked and her cheeks bright red.

"I left Jeffrey," she said on a sob. "And I have to pee."

"Oh, hon, no." I turned her toward the manor. "Let's go inside."

"Wait." She sniffed loudly, then pushed a button on her SUV's key fob, and the trunk opened. "I need to get my things."

She wiggled away from me and headed to the open hatch.

The SUV's interior light illuminated a piece of luggage, a massive makeup-and-toiletries case, and a canvas tote with unfolded clothing spilling out.

Annie looped the shoulder strap for her canvas tote over one shoulder, then hefted the toiletries case in one hand. She reached for the luggage with the other.

"Whoa." I stopped her. "I'll get this. You get the hatch."

"I can do it," she said. "I put it in here, and I can carry it twenty more feet to your door."

I leaned my weight onto the suitcase when she tried to pull again. "Will you please stop? You're like twelve months pregnant. You're obviously upset. You've been crying. You drove forty miles in this condition, and you came to me. You knew I'd help, no matter the problem. So, you should also know I'll stand here and face off with you over this luggage until the baby's born if I have to. I won't, however, stand by and watch you strap another bag to your body like some kind of tiny sobbing pack mule."

Annie tried to glare, but her tear-filled eyes ruined her attempt.

"You can be mad at me," I said. "But give your kid a break. Don't stress your body any more than it already is."

She cast her gaze aside. "Okay. Thank you."

I let us in the door and deposited the suitcase in the foyer. I pointed her to the bathroom and headed for the kitchen, refusing to think of Davis or all the conversations we'd had online. How I'd thought of Historically_Bookish as one of my closest friends, and he hadn't been honest with me about who he was.

Annie returned a few minutes later and sat at the table while I put on a kettle and set out a tray of baked goods and charcuterie.

We didn't speak as I prepared two cups of tea and ferried them to the table.

Annie nibbled on fruit slices while she waited. Her splotchy skin and desperate mood had cleared by the time I sat down.

I felt Emily's presence with me as I placed a bottle of water beside Annie's tea. In a letter to her cousin, Emily had written the perfect words for this moment. *Affection is like bread, unnoticed until we starve.* Before my trip, I'd been at odds with my little sister for too long, and I was starving. Seated across from her now, I wanted nothing more than to hug her tightly. To tell her how much I loved her. And to fix every broken bit of us immediately.

"How was the drive?" I asked instead.

"Dark and lonely." She sniffled. Her puffy brown eyes snapped to mine. "I'm leaving Jeffrey."

I forced myself not to respond, because Annie leaving Jeffrey was ludicrous. He adored her and vice versa. But my opinion on the topic didn't matter unless she asked for it, maybe not even then. So, I kept my thoughts to myself. "You want to talk about it?"

She slumped. "No."

"Okay."

"He told me I should be nicer to people."

"Oh?" I bit my tongue. *Bold move, Jeffrey.*

"He thinks it's nice you started sending me letters, and that I should call you and answer your texts more often. For the record, I didn't answer tonight because I was driving. You look very nice, but you were gone when I got here, so I didn't get to tell you. I told him to butt out, then I burst into tears, because my hormones are a mess, and he apologized. Then he went to get my favorite ice cream from the parlor on Main Street. I packed some things and left while he was gone."

Ironic, given the catalyst for their fight, that she would come here, but I kept that to myself too.

"I just started driving," she said. "I wound up here. Hopefully your invitation to visit still stands."

"Always."

She narrowed her eyes, seeming to see me for the first time since her arrival. "Did you have a nice night?"

"Nope." I lifted my cup, running my thumbs along the warm sides. "But it's improving now."

Annie's lips formed a small, hesitant smile. "I'm sorry I've been so awful. I don't want to fight with you anymore. We never should've been like this."

"Why were we?" I asked, still unsure what exactly had gone wrong along the way.

"You stopped making time for me a long time ago, and it pissed me off." Her expression turned self-deprecating. "I'm not completely over it."

I rolled her words around in my head, trying to make sense of them. She was angry I didn't spend more time with her? She could've tried being a little nicer once in a while. Maybe not taken every opportunity to either snap at me or avoid me. "I've been busy."

"Busy," she said in chorus with me. "Yeah. I know."

I bristled. "I've been working more so you could work less. I've been exhausted all the time." *And growing bitter,* I realized. "I barely do anything other than work and attend Saturday-night family dinners."

"Hire help," she said. "No one asked you to do everything."

"You don't think I've brought that up? Mom and Dad always say they'll come in more often so we don't have to hire help. Then they just don't show up. I've been stuck in this cycle for years."

She rolled her eyes.

"What is your problem?" I blurted the words that I'd held back for years.

"You're my problem!" she said. "And Mom, Dad, and Jeffrey. You all treat me like a fragile little infant, and that was way before I got pregnant. You push me out of the serious conversations and only ask me about petty things that don't matter. It's as if none of you see me as a full-grown woman who has actual thoughts. I have a degree," she said. "I have a brain. No one wants me to use it. And for the record, I am not fragile. I was a gymnast and cheerleader for twelve years. I could bench-press my weight since I was eleven. I'm not some meek little thing you all have to protect and look out for."

I blinked as confusion clouded my brain. "No one thinks you're weak. We're all half afraid of you."

"Because I'm mean," she said. "Just like Jeffrey told me."

"Well, kinda."

She laughed and crossed her arms over her bump. "Has anyone considered I've just been pissed off my whole life?"

I smiled. "What?"

She sighed. "I'm not blaming anyone for it, but Mom got cancer when I was small, and I don't remember her being carefree or fun. I remember being smothered, micromanaged, and pushed. When you reminisce about your childhood with her, I feel left out, because all those happy days were before I knew her. My earliest memories are of her puking in a bucket after chemo and you rushing me away to get ready for school. The mom I had was dying, and the sister I wanted was becoming my mom. None of that changed when she got better. I just wound up with two moms. She clung to Dad, and you kept taking care of me. Everyone still treats me like that preschooler who needs rushed out of the room when something tough or uncomfortable comes up. And I resent never having a sister to talk with about boys and my period."

I sat back in my chair, imagining our childhoods from Annie's perspective for the first time.

"Sometimes I think I married Jeffrey just to have a partner. A lifelong confidant because fate had taken the one I was meant to have. Or maybe I was just in a hurry for the world to see I was an adult."

"I know you're an adult, Annie. And I've always been here for you. I tried to be whatever you needed me to be."

"You tried to be my mother."

"That may be the way you see it," I said firmly. "But not once, for even a second, have I ever wanted to be your mother. I want to be your sister."

She seemed to mull that over, so I pressed on.

"You married Jeffrey because you love him," I said. "You're a good match, and you challenge one another in ways that have made you both better people. You got a lifelong best friend and confidant in the process. And that's just the icing."

"He used to challenge me," she said, more softly. "These days he just agrees to everything I say and acts as if he's on my payroll instead of being my husband."

I watched her as she watched me, daring me to prove her wrong. "He told you to be nicer today."

"He asked how I was feeling, and I bit his head off because I'm stressed out. My response pressed his buttons because he's also stressed out, and he unleashed years of complaints about how I push people away. But I could tell he specifically meant you."

I made a mental note to hug Jeffrey until he gasped for air the next time I saw him. He was always trying to mend the bridge between Annie and me. Always encouraging her to find joy.

"Ever since I fell, he acts as if I'm dying, and I don't need that right now. I'm upset enough. Even if I don't show it like he does."

My senses went on alert and my muscles tensed. "You fell?"

Did she need a doctor? A hospital? I scanned every visible inch of her across the table, heart rate rising.

"Did you fall today? Before you left home?" A B-reel of terrifying images churned in my head.

"Last month," she said. "I was carrying a basket of laundry down the steps. I couldn't see over it and my belly, so I missed a step and slid. Jeffrey wasn't home. He'd been telling me for months to stop carrying the baskets. But I was on my way down, the basket needed to go, so I took it. I didn't see the harm because it wasn't heavy."

Heat climbed the back of my neck as tears filled her eyes once more. "What happened?"

"My feet slid on the carpet, and I kind of bounced down a few steps on my backside. I bruised my tailbone a little, but it wasn't broken."

"The baby?"

"We had an early-morning ultrasound at the hospital the next day. The baby's okay."

That must have been the appointment they'd mentioned before I left Willow Bend. I'd known something was wrong. I should've pushed for answers.

"I've had a little spotting in the weeks since then," she said, voice cracking slightly. "Nothing too serious, but the doctor is keeping a closer eye on me. I made it past the point of concern as far as gestational age."

I ran the mental math and frowned. "But you're not due yet."

"No, but the baby is big enough to survive on its own now. Premature delivery was the biggest fear." She released a shaky breath, not sounding at all as if the time for worry had passed. "My blood pressure is elevated, and Jeffrey is supposed to keep me calm, comfortable, and content. Then he picked a fight with me today." Annie swiped a tear from her cheek and looked away.

My heart broke wide open, and I moved around the table to embrace her. "It's going to be okay. You and Jeffrey will be great parents. And you and I are going to talk through all our misunderstandings before you go home."

"I'd like that," she said, pulling me more tightly against her and leaning her head onto my shoulder.

I'd never been so thankful for Hearthstone Manor and its quiet solitude.

Chapter Thirty

Annie and I talked for hours. I showed her around the manor and stayed close when we walked up the stairs. We changed for bed eventually, but neither of us were ready to say good night.

We settled in the sitting room, faces washed, with eyes swollen from so many shed tears.

I built a fire and brought her a blanket for her legs, then propped her feet on a stack of pillows. "I'm doing this for the baby," I said, when she tried to push my hands away. "This isn't for you, because you are a strong, independent woman."

She laughed. "I'm sorry I've blamed you for mothering me and being busy. I was horrible for so long. I don't know why you still talk to me."

I sat on the floor and leaned against the couch. "You're my sister." I reached for her hand and gave it a gentle squeeze. "I mean, there were days I wanted to buzz your hair off while you slept, and I definitely complained to Mom more than I should've. But mostly, I just wanted us to be okay again."

She released my hand to run her palms over her bump, looking exhausted, emotionally and otherwise.

"Have you called Jeffrey to let him know you're okay?" I asked, wishing I'd thought of it the moment I saw her, instead of hours later.

"I tried when I got here, but there's no cell service."

I stretched my legs in front of me on the carpet, pointing my toes toward the fire. "We should walk up the lane and make the call. He's probably worried sick. Cell service clears up about halfway to the sidewalk."

"You've really been living here alone like this for a month?" she asked. "No cell service. No internet. No one to talk to. Aren't you going nuts? I practically jump on Jeffrey every time he walks through the door after work, desperate for conversation. I want to stay home when the baby comes, because we can afford it. But I think being alone with a baby will make me feel even lonelier than I do now, if that makes any sense."

I twisted on the carpet to face her. "Come back to work at the bookstore," I said. "You can choose your hours, and we can hang out. Bring the baby with you. Then we'll have time to catch up every week. Just us, no Jeffrey or Mom and Dad."

Her eyes lit for the briefest of moments, then dimmed to the disgruntled expression she too often wore. "Babies are loud and demanding. People don't want that when they shop for books."

I smiled. "What if the bookstore wasn't quiet anymore?" I asked. "What if it was bright and lively. With pets."

Annie's brows rose. Lover of all furry things, she sat upright, interest piqued. "Go on."

"Ever wish you could put your degree in design to use?" I asked. "Your house is basically finished. Every room looks like a magazine spread. What if you took your talents commercial?"

She grinned. "Tell me more."

"Be right back." I hopped to my feet and headed for the hallway. "I made a murder board!"

Annie's laughter followed me to the study, where I collected my whiteboard and stack of notebooks filled with research and ideas.

I returned a moment later and placed the notebooks on the couch at her side. I propped the whiteboard against the coffee table and opened my arms. "Voilà!"

She examined the materials for several moments before returning to me. "Oh my goodness, yes!"

I pumped one fist in the air.

Suddenly Olivia's words echoed in my mind. When I first met her, she'd said, *We share what we love with the people we love.*

And I wanted to share my new bookstore adventure with Annie.

She scooted to the edge of the couch, examining the board more closely. "It's brilliant." She glanced quickly at me, then to the notebooks at her side. She set one on her lap and freed the pen stuck in the spiral binding. "Can I write in this?"

"Absolutely." I took a seat beside her, where I could watch as she made notes and sketched. Everything about her energy screamed enthusiasm and joy. This was the youthful, happy Annie I'd left when I went to college. The one I'd been missing for years.

"Do you have any plain paper and other color pencils?" She asked without looking up from her sketch.

"Yep!" I hustled away with a smile. When I returned, Annie was on the floor with the whiteboard, moving my magnets and writing on the attached sticky notes.

"What if we partnered quarterly with rescues for pet adoptions?" she asked. "We could keep information at the counter for potential foster families, then throw themed events that would bring in business and get animals adopted. A day for homing black cats near Halloween, or a home-for-the-holidays weekend between Thanksgiving and Christmas. Maybe fundraisers in the summer?" She turned to face me, a pen caught between her teeth.

I hiked one eyebrow. "Did you say *we?*"

Her cheeks flushed. "I'm not trying to take over, I swear. But I could help with event planning and logistics. Not just design."

"You could be my partner," I offered. "If you want. Even if you need lots of time off for the next eighteen or so years. I don't have to own the store alone."

She grinned. "I might get bored after the transition is complete and your event calendar is set. But I can definitely help you make these changes and get ready to promote the daylights out of it. You'll probably want rid of me after that anyway."

"Probably," I agreed.

Annie laughed.

My heart swelled as I watched her work. "Hey. You know what we need?"

"Whiskey?"

"No. A hot chocolate bar."

"That sounds amazing."

I made another trip to the study for art supplies, then stopped in the kitchen to see what I still had on hand for the chocolate bar.

Not much. Davis and I had made short work of the leftovers from my sweets charcuterie with Cecily.

I delivered the paper, markers, and colored pencils to Annie. "Will you be okay if I run to the market? I'm low on all the good toppings. Or do you want to do this later? I guess it's gotten kind of late."

Annie furrowed her brow. "You can't offer a pregnant lady hot chocolate, then take it back. Plus, I'm all worked up now. I need to get my thoughts on paper before I forget."

"In that case, I won't be long. Benefits of a college town? Lots of things that literally never close. Do you want me to call Jeffrey while I'm out? Or do you want to walk up the road together later? Because I think he needs to know you're okay."

She pursed her lips, shamefaced. "Will you let him know I'm here and safe? And sleeping?"

I nodded. "Got it. All is well, and you'll be in touch tomorrow."

"Thanks."

I grabbed my purse, keys, and phone, then stopped again. "You parked behind me."

"Keys are on the table. And we need to talk about the hottie who dropped you off tonight when you came home," she called. "No wonder you wanted feedback on your outfit for that date."

"He wasn't my date," I said. And I didn't have the emotional energy to unpack my Davis Sommers drama tonight.

All that mattered until morning was Annie. My love life, or continued lack thereof, could wait.

I smiled at my bouquets as I turned for the door. "Thank you again for all these incredible flowers."

"No problem," she said. "I would've sent more than those three, but the extra medical appointments are eating into my pocket money."

I stared at the fat arrangements of honeysuckle and daisies for an extended beat, then swung my head and shoulders through the archway to the sitting room. "You sent the bouquets of hyacinth and peonies."

Annie didn't bother looking up from her work. "Mm-hmm."

Apology bouquets.

The last few deliveries had been different. Honeysuckle and daisies. Flowers denoting affection.

"Are you leaving tonight?" she asked, spearing me with a tarty glance. "Or are you waiting to make those drinks after the baby arrives?"

I grinned and ducked back into the foyer. "Already out the door."

A few moments later, my phone popped and dinged with a dozen missed calls, texts, and messages from Cecily, Mom, Jeffrey, and Davis. I scanned the most recent first.

Davis: Can we talk? Please?

Davis: I can bring breakfast tomorrow for you and your sister

I responded quickly to put the mess behind me, at least for now.

Me: No thank you. I need this time with her

I sent one more message before swiping the app away, not quite ready to revisit my romantic failure.

Me: I'll reach out when I'm ready to talk

Perhaps via IBOOM, I thought dryly. Since that was where our relationship had begun.

I returned Jeffrey's call first as I motored down the driveway in Annie's car on my way to the all-night grocer.

The mysterious flowers on my foyer table also had to get in line for my attention, but I knew I'd lie awake at night thinking about them.

The call connected, and I worked up a bright smile I hoped he could hear across the line. "Hey, Jeffrey," I said. "Annie's with me. She's okay, and she's already in bed for the night, but she'll call you first thing in the morning."

"Oh, thank God." The rush of air from his lungs brought tears to my eyes.

"I should've called sooner. I'm sorry."

A soft sob crossed the line.

"She's okay," I repeated, infusing my voice with promise. "And for the first time in a long time, she and I are okay too."

"Really? You talked."

"And cried. And talked some more," I said. "It's part of the reason I didn't think to call sooner. I'm on a hot chocolate run now."

He made another sobbing sound. "I shouldn't have argued with her. I'm supposed to keep her calm and happy."

"Yeah, but she can be a pill," I said teasingly. "And you're only human, though I've wanted to have you knighted for sainthood a hundred times over the years."

"I really love her, Emma," he said. "She's everything I aspire to be, and I don't want a world I can't share with her and our baby."

"You're all going to be fine," I assured him. "Why don't you surprise her by driving up for a visit in the morning?"

"You don't think that would be too much? I want to give her time, if that's what she wants."

"Call me a romantic," I said, finally accepting that was exactly who I was. "You can never go wrong with a grand gesture."

"Then I'll be there," he said.

The line grew quiet as I parked outside the all-night grocer.

"Did she tell you about the fall?" Jeffrey asked.

I turned off the car and sat in the darkness, save for the light from streetlamps along the nearby road. "Yeah."

"I should have brought the basket down before I left for work."

"Not your fault," I said. "Things happen."

"She could've broken her neck or lost the baby. Or both. I wasn't there. She was alone, and I wouldn't have known what happened until I got home that night."

A shuddered breath leaked out of me at the scene he painted. "You can't think like that. It's not what happened. And you would've left work to check on her if you didn't hear from her all day. You've probably been looking for her all evening, and you know she was fine when she left."

He moaned. "You know me well."

"I know you love her," I said. "I would've done the same thing."

"Keep her comfortable and insist she sees a doctor if anything seems wrong. She's stubborn, but she loves that baby, so it won't be hard to convince her. We only have six days to go."

Gooseflesh rose over my skin as his words hit like arrows to my heart. "What are you talking about? Six days until what?" Annie wasn't due for weeks. She'd just said as much tonight. "What might seem wrong? What specifically am I watching for?"

Jeffrey heaved a bone-weary sigh. "She's been struggling with pre-eclampsia for a couple of weeks. She's had some early contractions and bleeding. The doctors recommended a C-section, and it's scheduled for next week."

My ears rang, and my vision blurred. Annie was sick. The baby was in danger. And no one had told me. Not even Annie, after all the other confessions we'd just made.

Why would she keep that from me?

"Watch her closely for me," he said. "She barely talks about any of this. It's as if she's so scared her only way to deal with it is to pretend it's not happening. She gets mad every time I mention it. She's supposed to stay calm, so I let her do what she needs to do."

I whispered a few top-tier swears.

"She asked me not to tell you," he said. "But you're there now, and I'm not. Promise me you'll take care of her tonight."

A wave of nausea swept through me, strong and hot. I thought I'd be sick in my car. "Okay."

"I'll be there in time for breakfast," he said.

I disconnected and went shopping. I dialed Mom while I filled a basket with hot chocolate toppings. She and Dad were equally relieved to know Annie was okay.

Jeffrey had gone to them in search of Annie as soon as he'd realized she left home. Dad had patrolled the parking lots of her favorite stores, salon, and spa, looking for signs of her car. Mom had kept a pot of soup warm in case Annie appeared on the doorstep.

They'd all sleep better tonight knowing she was okay.

I called Cecily on my way back to the manor and filled her in on the night's Rini-family commotion. Then I asked her to share everything she knew about preeclampsia.

"It's not rare, especially in a first pregnancy," Cecily said. "It sounds like her doctors are monitoring her condition, which is good. She's probably struggling with swelling and headaches. She'll need to rest and to go home with Jeffrey tomorrow so she's close to her hospital and medical team. Delivery of the baby is the only cure for preeclampsia."

I turned onto the main road toward the manor, making good time without traffic and suddenly in a major hurry to be back. "Jeffrey said she has a C-section scheduled for next week." Six days from now, and I was scheduled to leave Amherst in five. "The day after I get home."

Had she planned it that way? Waiting for my return?

I pulled onto the gravel lane and breathed a little easier to be home.

"Cesarean births sound scary, and they are a major surgery, don't get me wrong. But in Annie's situation, it's for the best. She's in good hands, and delivering this way will put her doctors in control while reducing stress on mom and baby."

I'd come to Amherst because I'd wanted to quit searching for a big, epic love. But I already had all that in front of me. And it was growing. One little niece or nephew at a time.

Chapter
Thirty-One

Jeffrey arrived early as promised, a large bouquet of dahlias, Annie's favorite, in one arm and a bagged spread of breakfast foods in the other. I sent him to her room with the flowers while I set up breakfast on the patio.

They made up instantly, both too desperately in love to imagine another night apart.

After our meal, we spent the day together, laughing and exploring the town where they'd met and fallen in love. Eventually, Jeffrey suggested they get a room at an inn downtown for some much-needed alone time and for Annie to stay off her feet and rest.

I hugged Annie tightly and vowed to be present in her life and her baby's. She wouldn't lose me to books or busyness ever again.

It was hard to believe that five short days from now, Annie and Jeffrey would be parents.

I would be an aunt.

I slept soundly that night, in the knowledge my little sister was in good hands and an addition to the family was on the way. I dreamed of the kick-ass shop for book-loving people and their pets my sister and I planned.

All in all, my future was shaping up beautifully.

❧

Thoughts of Davis followed me the next few days as I puttered around the manor, soaking in the last of my stay. I wrote letters to Forever Yours that I didn't send, and a few to myself, reminding me of all the new things I'd experienced in Amherst. The hikes and friends. Embroidery and baking. Bunnies and pilot lights. Every day delivered something new here. I resolved to keep the magic going long after I returned home.

I deleted half-finished texts to Davis before bed each night, always overthinking the content. My heart splintered between forgiveness and frustration. Why had I made such a big deal of things? Why hadn't I texted the moment Jeffrey took Annie to the inn?

Then I recalled the pain of wanting a man who couldn't tell me how he felt. Or that he was my longtime online bestie.

Then again, maybe his feelings weren't what I thought.

The more time passed, the harder it became to reach out, and before I knew it, my bags were packed for the trip home.

On my final evening in Amherst, I went to letter-writing class.

Daisy and Grace stood close together, whispering excitedly when I arrived.

"There she is," Daisy said, breaking away to meet me and grab my arm. She rushed me back to Grace, then released me with a wide grin. "I can't believe it," she said, faux irritation on her brow.

"What?" I asked, glancing from her to Grace, then back.

"He's in Chicago for an interview on national news, and you didn't tell me!"

"Who? Davis?" I asked, wholly stunned.

Grace nodded, her pink lips pursed into the proudest of smiles. "Now maybe Carter can stop feeling superior to his son and gloating about it."

"No kidding," Daisy said. "This is next level."

I blinked, blindsided by the news and rush of emotions. "Davis is in Chicago?"

"Yes!" Daisy said. "He left this morning. Wait. You mean you didn't know?"

Grace looked equally confused. "The contest thrown by *Architectural Digest* scheduled a local-interest segment that will air on stations across the US. They invited Davis to speak with the anchor because his interview in the article did so well. It was all very last minute, but not exactly something he could pass up, especially given the pressure Carter and his investors are putting on him."

"They say he's become the face for the contest," Daisy said. "And for saving historical homes."

My gut ached selfishly with remorse. I was thrilled for Davis but brokenhearted for me. Not long ago, I was Davis's first call when sharing news.

"Emma?" Daisy asked. "Are you okay?"

I nodded, numb to my toes. What was real anymore? If not the bond I'd formed with Davis this month, then what about the years we'd spent becoming friends online?

The content of Grace's letter-writing lesson was lost on me as I doodled more than I listened or wrote. It had only taken a moment for me to realize something worse than knowing Davis hadn't mentioned his enormous victory to me.

With Davis in Chicago, I couldn't even say goodbye.

⤶⋇⤷

I packed my car the next day, ready to go home and start living.

I took pictures of the manor, my garden, and my murder board, for memories' sake. Then I filled a basket with fresh-baked muffins for Grace. I left the nineteenth-century soup recipes for another visitor to try.

As it turned out, I wasn't a recluse, a poet, a gardener, or a baker. I was a bookstore owner with a complicated but incredible family and so much life still ahead.

I ran a hand along the stained glass at the top of the stairs, mentally thanking a woman I'd never meet for the wonderful human she'd brought into this world.

I left my key on the foyer table and saw myself out.

My phone rang as I waved goodbye to Michael and Grace at the bookstore a few minutes later.

"What's up, sis?" I asked, smiling as I climbed into my car.

"I need your thoughts on a name," she said. "I'm two days from having this baby, and we haven't decided."

"Edward," I said.

"We're having a girl."

"Bella."

"Stop." She laughed. "Be serious."

My chest tightened with an unexpected burst of emotion. "You didn't tell me you were having a girl."

Images of Annie as an infant popped into mind. She'd had tufts of thick dark hair on her head, along the rims of her ears, arms and shoulders. The visual was hilarious in hindsight, but seven-year-old-me had been greatly concerned.

"We haven't told anyone else the gender, so keep it to yourself," she warned. "I need help. I'm desperate."

Glee replaced nostalgia as her words sank in. She'd come to me for help. Not our parents or even her friends. "What about Mom and Dad?"

"Nope. They're going to be surprised, and you're going to pretend you are too."

"Absolutely," I vowed, and a few pesky tears stung my eyes.

"We like Virginia," she said. "I want something that's a little old-fashioned without trying too hard. Something less common but beautiful. There are too many Michaels and Kaitlyns. Jeffrey says I'm overthinking and I should pick the name I like best. This is really hard."

"I think Virginia is perfect. Like Virginia Woolf." I smiled as a famous line of hers presented itself in my mind. *It is a thousand pities never to say what one feels.* I planned to start telling my family how much they meant to me as often as it crossed my mind.

"Okay," Annie said. "She's not the reason, but yes. Like Virginia Woolf. Thank you. When are you coming home?"

"Now, actually. I'm in my car, at the end of the lane."

"Good. Come see me. If not today, then tomorrow. Don't wait until I'm at the hospital. I'll be freaking out then."

Jeffrey's laughter boomed in the background. "You're freaking out now."

"Am not!" she yelled. "No, he's right, I am," she added softly.

"I'll be there in an hour," I promised. "Don't go into labor without me."

"Bite your tongue."

"See you soon!" I buckled up and shifted into drive. "I'll swing by my apartment and grab a few of your baby pictures to bring over."

"Great."

I laughed. "Love you too." I gave the manor one last look in my rearview mirror, then headed home.

Chapter
Thirty-Two

The next few days in Willow Bend were my busiest ever.

I hung a sign in the bookstore window announcing **HELP WANTED**, right beside a sign announcing **IT'S A GIRL!** The response to both was wonderful. I reviewed applications between phone calls to contractors and local pet-related companies. I'd even contacted a real estate agent, because my new rescue dog, aptly named Emily, would appreciate a little more room to run and stretch her legs on the regular. The moment I'd looked into her eyes, it was love at first sight. When I read the name on her kennel, I knew she was destined for me.

Cecily zipped through the door, sending the bell overhead into a frenzy. She wore her usual scrubs and toted two steamy lattes. "I did it! Applications opened for *Relatable Romance: Regency Era*, and I applied to be a liaison!"

I met her with a hug, then took my latte. "You're going to kill it."

"I know!" She sipped her drink in pure delight. "I just have to brush up on local history facts during the era and be ready to talk about nuances of dress, speech, and culture here at that time."

"No problem," I said, unable to hide my indulgent smile.

"I love this stuff!"

A familiar hatchback pulled against the curb outside, interrupting our chat. I blinked to confirm I wasn't imagining it.

"What?" Cecily turned to follow my line of sight. "Who's that?"

"The flower delivery person from Amherst," I said, jaw falling open as the young woman got out. She collected a massive vase of honeysuckle and daisies from the back, then marched to the bookshop door, barely able to see around the blooms.

"Goodness!" Cecily gasped, hurrying to help her inside.

"Emma Rini?" she asked, craning her neck until she spotted me. "Delivery." She had a huge smile as she set them on the counter. "One more thing." She pulled an envelope from her hoodie pocket and passed it to me. "Have a great day," she said, then turned on her toes and walked away.

My eyes trailed to Cecily's.

"Apology flowers," she said. "Like the others?"

I shook my head. Annie had sent the apologies. These were from someone else.

"Do you think they're from him?" she asked, deftly avoiding the D-word, or mentioning Forever Yours.

Cecily and I had an unspoken agreement never to mention Davis's name. I'd cried my eyes out over what might have been, on the night Virginia was born. My emotions ran high after leaving the hospital, and Cecily helped me sort the good from the bad. Good: Annie and her baby were both healthy and happy. Bad: I texted Davis the night I left Amherst, wishing him well on his television debut, but he hadn't responded.

I'd done my best not to think of him, but it wasn't easy. Thankfully, I stayed so busy visiting with Annie and my new niece, plus making changes at the store, that I fell asleep quickly most nights. I'd also accepted the true identity of Forever Yours would remain a mystery. My best guess was that Paul wrote the letters, then chickened out before our meeting. If I was right, it was for the best, because I didn't care for him in that way.

Besides, I found the big love I'd gone in search of, right where I started. I had incredible friends, a great job, and a devoted, growing family all around me. Not to mention the dog I'd always wanted in my very near future. I stood with an open mind and heart, ready for whatever came next.

But I never imagined receiving this particular bouquet again.

"Open that envelope, or I will," Cecily said, moving in close, fingers spread wide between us.

I released a shaky breath, suddenly overcome with adrenaline and anticipation. I unearthed the letter, typed this time instead of hand-written, and read aloud.

> Dearest Emma,
> Please accept these flowers as an unending apology for all the times I've fallen short. You deserve better, and you make me want to be better. I want to spend a lifetime thanking you properly. I should've been braver and revealed myself to you as planned at the café, because I'm madly, epically, in love with you.

I gasped as I read the signature. "Forever Yours." Cecily grabbed my arm, vibrating with energy as she read over my shoulder. "Oh my goodness. It's not over. The flowers. The letter." She made a small squeaky noise as I struggled to breathe.

Was this real? The letters and flowers from Amherst reached me all the way in Willow Bend?

"What are you going to do?" Cecily asked.

"I don't know." The paper rattled in my hand as I turned to pace. I wasn't sure what I could do.

Behind me, the bell above the door jangled, and I took the moment to compose myself.

"Emma." Davis's voice scattered goose bumps across my flesh.

I spun to find him in jeans and a wrinkled T-shirt, an expression of hope on his handsome brow.

Beside him, Cecily covered her mouth with both hands, eyes wide, looking exactly the way I felt.

"I'm sorry I missed you on the day you left town. I was in Chicago."

My hands fell to my sides, and air rushed from my lungs. Davis was in Willow Bend.

"I got your text," he said when I didn't speak. "You didn't respond to me the night your sister arrived. I thought you'd never speak to me again. I slept with my phone almost every night after that." His smile turned self-deprecating. "Then you wrote to me when I was on set for the interview, but I didn't know. I didn't have my phone all day, and when it was time to go back to the hotel, no one on set could find my phone. They finally found it. I just got it back yesterday." He scraped a hand through his messy hair. "I tried to get a flight, but I couldn't, so I panicked and rented a car. I started driving. In hindsight, I'm not sure I saved any time. Waiting on a morning flight might've gotten me here sooner, actually." He barked a laugh. "I wasn't thinking. I just needed to act. I ordered flowers when the shop opened today, and I dictated a letter." His gaze darted to the giant bouquet on the counter. "You got them."

"You drove from Chicago?" I croaked. Tears pricked and stung my eyes. "That's like fourteen hours."

"Thirteen and change," he said. "I took liberties with the speed limit through the night."

Joy filled my heart to the point of pain as I let the truth of the moment settle in. "The letters? The flowers? Those were from you?"

He nodded, a heady mix of emotion on his handsome face. "I think I started falling in love with you the moment we met," he said. "Your goofy jokes online gave me reasons to smile long after the moments had passed. Your advice when I struggled with one thing or another gave me strength. Your compassion, your love of history, your family, and books left me in awe." He dared a small smile, taking one step closer. "Granted, I thought you were your dad for a while."

I laughed. "I guess I'm lucky he's taken."

Davis brushed the backs of his fingers across my cheek. "You were one of my favorite people long before I ever set eyes on you. Getting to know you has changed everything for me." Sincerity burned in his gorgeous gray eyes. "You inspire me to be brave."

I wet my lips, willing my body not to move. I wanted to hear every word he had to say and more. "How?"

"I'm selling my house," he said. "And my portion of the family architectural firm. I'm moving back to Hearthstone Manor, and I'm opening a historic restoration company."

My jaw dropped. "That's incredible."

"You taught me it wasn't selfish to chase my dreams."

I smiled as I wiped a falling tear from my cheek. "It's not."

"I'd love to help you renovate your bookstore," he said, taking another baby step in my direction. "You're not too far away, you know."

A small laugh burbled from my lips. "A very reasonable commute," I agreed.

"Far better than Chicago."

My smile widened impossibly farther. He'd driven all night to get to me. Careful, thoughtful Davis had needed to see me that badly. "And an incredibly generous offer."

Emotion twisted his features as he moved closer. "Anything for you. I am Forever Yours, after all."

"Davis." A lump formed in my throat, stopping my words. So I rose onto my toes, and I kissed him. "I really wanted it to be you," I said, pressing my forehead to his.

"Is that a yes on the help?" he asked, a wicked gleam in his eyes. "It'll mean spending lots of time together for the next fifty years or so."

"That's an extensive renovation you're planning."

"You have no idea." Davis kissed me again, taking his time and holding me close.

I wobbled slightly when our lips parted. "You should bring Violet to meet my new rescue dog, Emily. I'm picking her up soon."

"Emily, huh?" He laughed. "Aptly named."

"I thought so. We're house hunting too. I think my apartment will make an excellent office space for the new store."

"Sounds like a lot of change ahead for both of us," he said. "I want to experience it all with you."

"Me too." I set my cheek against his chest as I thought of my new rescue dog and the woman whose poetry had brought me to this point. I wasn't sure what would happen between Davis and me in the future, but I knew something with sudden clarity. "I'm going to call the shop 'Emma and Emily,'" I said. "For lovers of pets, books, and poetry."

"'Emma and Emily,'" he repeated, smiling, then pressed his lips to mine. "Perfection."

I couldn't have agreed more.

Went searching for love
And found it everywhere
Just opened my eyes
—Emma Rini

Acknowledgments

Thank you, dear reader, for joining Emma on her Amherst adventure! My gratitude absolutely overflows for you and each of the brilliant, beautiful humans who made this book possible. From my critique partners, Danielle and Jennifer, who read every one of my words and make them better, to the daring team at Lake Union Publishing who took a chance on a mystery writer with a penchant for hope and happiness. Melissa Valentine, Carissa Bluestone, and Jodi Warshaw, you probably thought you were just doing your jobs, but you were actually making my dream come true. Thank you. Finally, to my remarkable literary ninja of an agent, Erin Niumata, thank you for believing in me and my craft. If I could fly to London and hug you, I'd be there by dinner.

About the Author

Julie Hatcher is an award-winning and bestselling author of mystery and romantic suspense. She has published more than fifty novels under multiple pen names since her debut in 2013.

Writing as Julie Anne Lindsey, Hatcher has earned many accolades for her work, including the 2020 National Readers' Choice Award for Romance Adventure and the 2019 Daphne du Maurier Award for Mystery/Suspense, among others.

When she's not creating new worlds or fostering the epic love of fictional characters, Julie can be found in Kent, Ohio, enjoying her blessed Midwestern life—and probably plotting murder with her shamelessly enabling friends. Today she hopes to make someone smile. But one day she plans to change the world.